The Lilean Chronicles: Book One

Redemption

by

Merita King

Published by Merita King

Eastleigh

Hampshire

United Kingdom

© Merita King 2011

Cover art © JL Stratton 2012

The Lilean Chronicles: Book One ~ Redemption

ISBN 978-0-9570520-1-7

ABOUT THE AUTHOR

Merita King has loved the science fiction and fantasy genre in both books and movies since she was a young child. She was greatly inspired by years of watching movies and reading books and wanted to make a contribution to this genre for many years. Her stories all contain a strong spiritual thread as she believes that spirituality is universal and crosses all boundaries. She believes the creative process is largely intuitive and can be very effectively blocked by too much pre-planning. "Plot lines, characters and events all come to me intuitively," she says, "and this makes the act of writing a constant pleasure." She is a psychic medium and lives alone in Hampshire, UK.

DEDICATION

For RBR my friend, my soul mate. You are everything. The one who understands. The one who doesn't judge.

Also for MSV who brought him to me and reminded me that if you can dream it, you can do it. You made this possible.

Live the journey, for every destination is but a doorway to another!

CHAPTER ONE

Farra awoke with the now familiar searing pain in her chest. She clutched at herself and waited for the pain to subside. These episodes were coming every night now and always after the dreams. These dreams that began so suddenly and without warning. They occurred only occasionally at first but gradually increased until two weeks ago when they started coming every night. She would wake in a hot sweat, troubled with the swiftly retreating knowledge that she must hurry, but before she could remember where or why, the dream would fade into the morning mist. Every time it was the same. A voice calling to her, urging her to listen, to hurry. She spent hours researching dreams and their symbolism in an effort to understand why this might be happening to her. She even went to a therapist who told her she must be sexually repressed and should consider the prospect that she may be homosexual. It wasn't until she bumped into an old friend from college that she found a possible explanation that felt comfortable for her.

Erin McClusky was once the campus tramp but despite that fact, Farra Duncan and she got along like a house on fire. They forged a friendship that endured all the way through college and only ended when Erin went to rehab due to her Duomol addiction. Farra never realised that her friend was hooked on that stuff. Oh she knew that the occasional joint came their way but Duomol? Never in a hundred years would she think that stuff would come between them. Erin was lucky; she lived through her addiction and the therapy they dished out in rehab and came out the other end with her sanity intact; many addicts on Duomol didn't. It was invented as an ingredient in a new super fuel. It was environmentally clean, was cheap to produce and wasn't flammable like so many other fuels. What the inventors didn't realise until too late though was that the Duomol ingredient of this new fuel was highly addictive. It smelled wonderful, like summer flowers in the morning and that was the problem. Once you smelled that smell you wanted to smell it again and again. Before too long the people producing it were addicted and started filching a little here and there for their own private use. The most popular way of using it was as perfume. A little dab behind the ears and they got a high that lasted them almost a whole day and anyone who came into close enough contact to smell it was hooked very quickly. They passed it around their friends and the addiction spread like a forest fire. It killed quickly; most addicts were dead within six months of their initial exposure.

The odour molecules of Duomol work like any other smell until they reach the olfactory epithelium at the top of the nasal passage. Once there though, they work very differently from all other smells. As soon as the host's brain registers how beautiful it smells, the brain cells start to die at an alarming rate. Symptoms usually start with mild headaches, dizziness and that sort of thing. Within weeks most addicts are experiencing memory loss and impaired motor functions and need help to walk and dress themselves. At three or four months most are catatonic, doubly incontinent and need to be fed intravenously. At five months, coma followed by death at around six months. Farra's friend Erin was very lucky; her parents found out by sheer accident two weeks after her first exposure and got her in hospital within twenty four hours. She received the only known cure – complete removal of the olfactory cpithclium. Shc wasn't quite the same as before. She walked with a stick and obviously no longer had any sense of smell and her long term memory was scratchy in places, but she was alive.

Farra was delighted to bump into her in Joe's coffee shop and they spent a happy hour and a half catching up. It was during this chatter that she told Erin about her dreams and how she wanted to know what they meant, if anything. She told her about the therapist she saw and they laughed about Freudian psychology and how everything has its roots in sex. It was Erin who said that it might not be a dream at all but a spirit haunting her and trying to get her help.

"Oh Erin please, that's crazy," she laughed out loud at the thought.

"Just think about it Farra. You remember that old place we used to hang out in during the summer vacation and how stuff would get moved around all on it's own?" she leaned forward, wide eyed as if to emphasise the point.

"Yeah I remember." She was sceptical at first, accusing Erin or one of the other girls of moving stuff to scare everyone but then she remembered the night they all saw a chair move across the room all by itself and how they all heard a woman crying in an upstairs room that they knew was empty.

"You know you've always been open to this stuff, susceptible," Erin continued.

"So how do I find out? If it is a ghost, how do I find out what it wants?" Farra asked.

"When you go to bed, write it a letter asking it what it wants. Read it aloud a couple of times and then go to sleep as normal. If it is a ghost, you should find its answer in the dream and then once it knows you're listening and want to know, it'll step it up a bit. And you have to let me know how it goes, okay?" She made Farra promise.

She decided that Erin was nuts, that the damage done by the Duomol was more than she realised but when she went to bed that night, she thought, oh what the hell, it can't do any harm so she tried it. Nothing amazing happened but after that night the dreams came more often. There was still that voice urging her to hurry.

"Hurry Farra please, he needs you. Please help, find the truth. Farra. Farra please."

As the dreams increased she would wake with the now familiar pain in her chest that always seemed to accompany them. One morning as she showered she noticed what looked like a small bruise on her chest. She touched it but felt no pain. She didn't know it then but that bruise was to become a symbol of the rarest of honours, given to very few that proved themselves worthy.

She had the dreams every night for three weeks before she saw him for the first time. As the familiar voice rang in her ears with the same urgent plea, she found herself looking into the handsome face of a man who possessed the most tangible presence she had ever encountered before. This ghostly shade stood before her in the hinterland between sleeping and waking and she felt no fear. She felt as though she had known him all of her life and she knew that this was one of those defining moments in her life. A moment that meant the choice you made would decide the path of your life forever. A moment where you know things will never be the same again. She didn't hesitate.

"What must I do?" she asked the shade.

"Help him Farra, find the truth. Moxal 3."

"How?"

"I will be with you always, fear nothing," he smiled and she trusted him immediately.

"I don't even know who you are," she said with a half smile.

"My name is Leon. I am the memory of a nation almost lost. There is one who can save us from extinction but he needs your help. Wake up child."

She awoke and clutched at her chest until the pain subsided. As she showered she noticed the little bruise was now twice its previous size.

She signed up for deep space military service after she finished college. Her parents both served and so it seemed the most natural thing for her to do the same. She worked hard and excelled at sports and all the physical fitness pursuits and disciplines. She was an expert in unarmed combat, stealth combat techniques, survival skills and several martial arts. The discipline that gave her most pleasure and satisfaction though, was Advanced Weapons Handling – Combat & Survival with Blades. She gained top honours in that class and got a medal for it. She loved blades of all types and designs and had quite a private collection of her own. She beat all the men in her class, many of whom carried the scars to prove it. After she did her statutory three years she signed up for the Deep

Space Tactical Unit, or DSTU's as they are known. This organisation is a sort of deep space SAS who specialise in covert operations across the galaxy. She saw action in a covert operation in the Nebugord system and earned herself the bronze arrow. This is an award for bravery under fire in a hostile environment where the chances of survival are slim. Even though her effort only got her the bronze, she was proud of her little pin and wore it always. She thought her life was all mapped out and she was happy about it. Until the dreams started and everything changed. Now here she was, unemployed and packing for a journey to a shit pile of a place out in the butt hole of nowhere because a ghost told her to do it. She wondered if she was nuts! She correctly anticipated the reaction of her superior officer when she gave him the news.

"You're what"? yelled Major Whelan as his bushy grey eyebrows shot to the top of his head.

"I'm resigning the corps and going to Moxal 3," she stated calmly.

"What the heck do you want to go to that hell hole for?" The Major couldn't believe what he was hearing.

"I might become a Cleaner Sir and maybe a Ranger in time, cleaning the mines. Be an interesting job I reckon. A bit different, y'know?" she offered.

"You're mad." Major Whelan was incredulous. "Mad as a fuckin hatter, get out!"

Major Whelan was old school. One of those men who always looked like an off duty wing commander even when he was on the golf course, at the supermarket or taking a piss on a train on his way to a Billy Kool concert with his grand kids. He rose at six am sharp even on Sundays, ran five miles every morning in all weathers with a fifty pound pack on his back and pressed the creases into his pants so sharp you could slice an apple with them. He called every man under forty five boy and he always doffed his cap to every woman he passed. Oh, and he always signed his title as well as his name, even on birthday cards. Major Whelan was the butt of many a private joke around the corps but he was generally well liked by the students. He took Farra under his wing when she first signed up and gave her a pep talk about being proud to serve, being a hero and doing one's duty.

A month later she allowed herself to be strapped into a cryo cell for the journey to Moxal 3. She experienced cryo sleep a couple of times during her time in the Corps but she was never under for longer than a few hours. She felt a momentary rush of claustrophobia as the cell lid was locked down and for a fraction of a second, she almost cried out but her self discipline kicked in automatically and she willed her body to relax. She noticed a subtle change in the air that she was breathing. It tasted different, sort of sharp and bitter at the same time. There was just time to think, oh yuck, before darkness descended. Leon was waiting for her in the hinterland and she felt no fear.

"Register for cleaning duties when you get to Corporation HQ and allow yourself to be cheated by the Rangers into duty in the deeper level tunnels. There you will meet a man who will become a lifelong friend. He will help save your life more than once, but first you must save his. You will recognise him immediately; you won't have met anyone like him before. His kind are like shadows of legends told and retold around the firesides of drunken men. He is kept prisoner in the deep tunnels and the fate of countless planets depends upon you freeing him and returning him to his people."

"Who is he, why is he so important?" So many questions she needed answers to but so few of those answers came.

"He is the first step towards fulfilling your destiny and in helping others fulfil theirs. They call him The Animal and treat him as such. He is a pawn in a totally misguided political plot to control a large sector of the galaxy. It is a plot doomed to failure but they do not have the intelligence to realise the error of their greedy ways. If you cannot free him, many planetary systems will enter into a war that will last for centuries. Countless numbers will die in retribution for his death and nothing good will be achieved."

"So he is an important person then?" she asked, still not sure that she'd know him when she met him. "How will I know him?"

"He is Prince Toma of the Drycenian Nation," he said without preamble.

She was shocked. A Drycenian? Everyone talked about them but she knew no one who had actually met them. They are indeed legends. No one knows much about them except that they keep themselves and their lives very private, they don't invite outsiders into their community and they are supposed to possess the most amazing technology, far in advance of anything anyone else has. The prospect of meeting them herself excited her.

"Wow, a Drycenian, my god." For the first time she saw Leon smile at her reaction. She couldn't wait!

The sun on Moxal 3 was more intense than anywhere from her previous experience. It was tortuous and unrelenting and although she felt some trepidation at entering the mine complex, she found herself eager to do so, just to get out of the furnace. The Moxal 3 Mining Corporation complex enjoys something of a reputation but the buildings she found herself in were so ordinary in appearance that she was almost disappointed. It looked positively prehistoric, like something out of an archaeological excavation. She was ushered into what appeared to her to be a kind of waiting area with several other new employees and told to wait. She made a quick examination of her surroundings and fellow volunteers. They were a mixed bunch; probably equal numbers of ex cons and those who failed to get into the military or security forces, along with a couple of wide eyed youngsters wanting to make their mark and be tough. Amazingly almost half were females. As a woman she expected to be in a minority in this place but she found the company employed many females and even a couple of other female cleaners. For the most part these women looked more like men than most of the men did and she knew right away that she'd find no like minded companions amongst those of her gender here.

She wanted desperately to take off her over shirt but she was conscious of the blue bruise on her chest and didn't like the way people stared at it, so she tended to keep covered up. She still didn't know what it was or why it was there, but it didn't trouble her and Leon told her not to worry, that it was a gift afforded to few others and that all would become clear in the fullness of time.

During her cryo sleep journey to Moxal 3 she learned that Leon was a spirit of a man who died during some kind of war, that he and others like him journeyed from what he called the land of the dead to help those of their kind still living as a sort of spiritual guide. She learned that this was a gift seldom given to someone from another planet, a different race from that to which Leon and his people belonged, that it was known as a choosing and that the little bruise was the mark of the chosen. She learned that to be chosen was a privilege that entailed a life of hardship, risk and self sacrifice. She was proud!

Training for the job of cleaner was remarkably short and before long Farra found herself down in the depths of hell, acting as living bait for the terrors that lurk down there. No matter how many are dealt with, there are always more and she never lacked for work. The mines of Moxal 3 are rich in deposits of Cornium Ore, a valuable mineral. But the tunnel complex is also home to a terrible predatory creature known as Uvees because they are only visible in UV light. Ordinary light renders them invisible so the cleaners are all issued with special goggles to help them see the UV end of the light spectrum. These goggles are counted out at the start of the shift and counted back in again at the end. No one is allowed to keep hold of their goggles; the company don't want anyone going into the tunnel complex unless they are officially supposed to be there. The cleaners work in groups of at least three and each team is the responsibility of a Ranger who gives them their work rotations and acts as a sort of bridge between the team and the management levels, sorting out any problems they might have.

The Uvees are pack creatures and the tunnel complex is crawling with them. They look a bit like a crocodile with much longer hind legs than normal. The two front limbs are shortened and stubby and fitted with six inch claws that could take a man's head off with ease. Their jaws are fitted with razor edged teeth that grow continuously so they have to bite and gnaw to keep them from becoming too large for their jaws. They make short work of bones but also use their teeth to gnaw at the tunnel walls to get to the Cornium Ore they need for its mineral content. The Cornium

Ore is a necessary part of their diet and wherever it is mined, the Uvees are found. The Cleaners' basic strategy when working the tunnels is simple. One acts as bait, luring the creature out into the open so that the other two can kill it with their SB17's, a weapon made especially for the purpose. The SB17 uses laser light pulses of a certain wavelength that only react with flesh instead of explosive bullets that might cause damage to the tunnels and cause rock falls. Even so, the turnover of cleaners is high and the average lifespan hovers around the twelve to eighteen month mark. Consequently the pay is high and the time off is good. Eight hours on then eight off continuously for three days, after which you get three days off. The system works well enough although there is a bit of a black market for anyone wanting extra hours. It is not strictly allowed for cleaners to deal with each other to do extra duties. As the rotation system gives them only eight hours off at any one time, double duties mean going for sixteen hours straight with only eight off and tired cleaners get themselves killed. The management knows it goes on of course and they turn a blind eye on the understanding that the death of anyone killed during an illicit double duty would not incur compensation for their families left behind.

Farra got along with her co workers well enough and managed to avoid the lewd propositions one or two of them put to her on a monotonously regular basis. They were a dirty, greasy bunch and the thought of doing the wild thing with any one of them sickened her. She remembered her therapist who said she should consider the prospect that she might be homosexual and laughed to herself. The men here were disgusting enough but the thought of doing it with any of the women here was worse. She determined never to allow herself to end up looking like any of the women here so she paid attention to her hygiene. Although she is tough, she is a beautiful woman and she was going to make sure she stayed that way. She hated the way the dust and greasy atmosphere made her hair look and feel. A natural brunette, she has long, thick hair that she kept tied up on top. Moxal 3 is peppered with thermal vents, so hot water is plentiful and she washed herself and her hair twice every day but still she remained sweaty and always felt greasy. Her survival technique skills came in very handy and she soon made herself a plentiful supply of skin exfolliant from the salt tablets they issued everyone with, mixed with a little cooking oil she managed to get from the kitchen staff by trading a pack of cigarettes. Although she doesn't smoke, she always has packs on her for trading purposes.

She survived her first three day tour of duty and earned herself seventy two hours off. She slept the first fourteen hours straight and only awoke when she heard her name being called softly. The pain in her chest was now just a dull throb and as she opened her eyes she saw Leon standing beside her bed. She only saw him in her dreams before and she was struck by the presence of the man. She was shocked to see him so solidly for the first time. No longer just a shade, he now towered over her, a magnificent specimen of his race with a steely gaze and a no nonsense energy. Without even needing to ask she knew he could read her mind. His eyes shifted from holding her gaze down to her chest.

"Look," he smiled. She went to the piece of broken mirror nailed to the stud wall of her cabin and looked. The bruise on her chest was now gone and replaced with what looked like a small scar in the shape of a star.

"What the?" she exclaimed as she turned and looked at Leon, the question left hanging in the air.

"You are one of us now; we give you this gift as a symbol of our belief and trust, of our unyielding faith and of our love. Find him Farra, the time has come. Find the Animal. Find Prince Toma. Free him and you'll be ready for the most important task of your life."

There are basic recreational facilities in the complex for use by off duty personnel and she wasted no time in making full use of them. It was a surprisingly easy task to find out about the existence of The Animal. All it took was the offer of a drinking contest and once her unwitting opponent was out of his mind drunk he was only too eager to talk. He sang like the proverbial canary. Prince

Toma was something of a celebrity prisoner in the tunnel complex and although not a prison, he was kept there because the nature of the place helped ensure no one would risk a rescue attempt for fear of the Uvees that lurked in the dark. All she needed to do was befriend the appropriate Rangers and with payment of a modest fee, she could get to see him. Five packs of cigarettes later she was being escorted through the tunnels by Ranger Mason.

She was surprised to find that the prisoner was not locked up but just held within a small room. The fear of the Uvees was enough to ensure he dare not try to run. She didn't know quite what to expect as she entered his room but whatever it was, it wasn't the sight that greeted her. The first thing that struck her were his eyes. Such kind eyes she had never seen before. They were a sort of yellow colour and were slightly larger than one would think normal. Those eyes were mesmerising, they held her. She didn't quite know what to say so she just stared at him. A small throb in the middle of her chest reminded her of the task in hand.

"Hello Toma," she said softly. The prisoner looked at her in surprise. He obviously expected to be abused and she realised that these visits were probably a fairly regular occurrence. She wondered what he suffered at the hands of her work colleagues and she suddenly felt angry for him. "I am a friend. I'm here to help but I don't have time to explain now. When I come next time, be ready to leave with me."

He started to speak, to question her and as he did so she suddenly realised why everyone called him The Animal. His kind yellow eyes, dark curly hair and muscular body all worked together to form what looked like a very finely formed human. It was those fangs that gave him away. A sharp intake of breath gave away her surprise; she hadn't expected this.

"Sorry," he said and turned away embarrassed.

She was immediately shamed. "No, I'm sorry, I didn't know. I've never met anyone like you before, please forgive me." She hoped she hadn't ruined things before they'd begun. If he wouldn't trust her they were sunk.

"Don't be afraid, I won't hurt you. I'm not an animal," he said.

She went to him and put a hand on his shoulder. "Be ready." She gave his shoulder a quick squeeze and left the room.

A week later she awoke in the middle of the night, the dull throb in her chest now an automatic signal for her to listen for Leon's telepathic instructions. When she was safely alone he would appear solidly, otherwise he spoke inside her mind and she learned to listen and trust.

"It's time Farra, gather your things. Take only what will fit into your back pack and do as I say. Don't be afraid, I'm with you every step of the way. I will guide you through the darkness but you must obey me without question. You know what lurks in the shadows. Without the goggles you will be completely blind and a moment's hesitation will cost too high a price. Alone, the two of you cannot survive if the creatures target you."

"Ok, you're the boss." She tried to sound light hearted but both knew she was a little apprehensive. That was okay; a little apprehension would give her just enough adrenaline to keep her sharp.

It seemed to take forever to make her way along the tunnels and it was very disconcerting not being able to see and needing to follow Leon's instructions as to where to put her feet. After an hour she was beginning to understand why she never enjoyed playing blind man's buff as a kid. She groped her way along a half mile of dusty tunnels, down creaking stairwells and rusty mezzanines but finally Leon made her stop and wait. She could see a doorway framed in a dull light up ahead. At Leon's command her training in stealth combat came in handy and she crept up behind the single guard and with a quick movement he dropped to the floor. She silently put him out without killing him and entered Toma's room. She was out of breath and put her hand up to her eyes to shield them from the sudden light.

"It's time, come on," she said and Toma was at her side in an instant.

Together they began the painfully slow business of making their way down into the deepest levels of the tunnel complex. The two of them carried no weapons on them save for her blades which were useless against the Uvees. In order to use a blade on them she'd need to get so close that she'd be toast before she could unsheathe them so stealth was the order of the day. Four hours it took them to make their way half a mile through the tunnels. Many times they needed to hide and wait while creatures crept past sometimes so close they could smell their acrid breath. Just when Farra was beginning to wonder if they'd ever get out of this place, a swift blow on an aged rusty padlock brought them both stumbling out under a clear star filled night sky. So wonderful to be able to see again and the air, so fresh and clean! She decided that if she ever went blind she would commit suicide.

The clean air revived them both and after some much needed water, they ran directly westward for three hours until all at once Toma stopped and hunkered down by some rocks.

"What's up?" she asked, concerned that something was wrong.

"Nothing. May I borrow one of your blades?" he asked her.

"Yes err sure, why?" She took the blade from its sheath and handed it to him.

"Watch," he smiled and quickly made a clean incision into his forearm and she saw that his blood was as red as hers. She didn't know what she expected it to look like but she hadn't expected it to look quite so much like hers. He handed back her knife and gently pressed open the wound to reveal a tiny glinting metallic object the size of a peanut just under the skin. Using a fingernail, he gently removed it, then reached inside his jacket and took out a small phial that contained something blue. He spread this blue gunk over the wound and held it up for her to see. "Watch this," he smiled. She watched in amazement, her eyes widening as she saw the wound he just made with her own blade, heal itself right up until there wasn't a mark to be seen.

"Shit, what is that stuff? Can I have some of that?"

"It's a common salve, nothing special," he laughed at her incredulity and handed her the phial. "A small token of my gratitude and the first of many."

"Thanks." She took the phial and examined it more closely. The blue stuff looked just like some kind of petroleum jelly. She put it safely into her backpack and watched as Toma held up the object he removed from his arm. It was the size of a peanut and a similar shape but it had a flat side and a curved side. It looked like polished metal. "What on earth is that?"

"Our ride out of here," he said as he gently pressed his thumb to the curved side of this little object which immediately began to beep quietly and pulse with a tiny light.

Four hours later a wind picked up around them and blew the dusty earth into their eyes. "Here they are," Toma said as he stood up and looked out into the middle of the dust storm. A small craft appeared out of the swirling dusty turmoil and landed hastily a hundred yards away, its engines as silent as the grave. Farra was in awe. Three men came running towards them, their joy at seeing Toma alive and well, obvious. They embraced each other and spoke together in a language she didn't understand. She suddenly felt self conscious. Toma took her hand and urged her towards the craft. "Come on, there'll be time for the formalities later."

The small rescue ship docked safely with the battle cruiser at a safe distance from the planet and she was introduced properly to Toma and his people. He was indeed a Drycenian Prince, the only heir of the current Drycenian King Lomas VII. He was captured whilst acting as envoy on a preliminary mission of goodwill to a nearby planetary system that was aimed at creating a system of mutually convenient and peaceful friendship and trade. She learned that a revolution of sorts had risen up with the intention of gaining control of the four local planetary systems, at the helm of which was a man no one knew the name of. He was both evil and mad, she heard and his delusional ravings inspired a band of desperate ne'er do wells into obeying his every whim on the promise of power and riches to come.

King Lomas looked into her face and suddenly went pale. Tears streamed down his cheeks. "What you have done for me, for the Drycenian Nation and for countless races across this sector of the galaxy will never be forgotten. We are and forever will be, in your debt. You have only to call and you will have my sword and my life." He put a hand on the hilt of the magnificent dagger that hung from his belt, stepped backwards a pace and bowed his head to her.

"Well I err, that is ermm, I err." She found herself lost for words and became aware that she suddenly didn't feel at all well. She stumbled and passed out.

CHAPTER TWO

As Farra began the long climb back to consciousness she became aware that something felt wrong somehow with her body. At first she couldn't work out what it was, just something that wasn't quite normal. Sounds came, muffled and far away. She strained to hear but couldn't catch the words. Then she heard her name called. Her mind fixed onto that familiar word and drove her upward. Her instincts told her this word was her salvation. As the feeling came back into her body she realised she felt wet all over. Even her face felt wet. It felt warm though; comforting in a strange way, womblike. She felt like she was floating. That sound again, louder now. Her name being called by a man. She didn't recognise it as Leon's voice though. Who could be calling her and why? She opened her eyes and for a moment couldn't see anything but twinkling silver light. As her eyes focussed she realised why she felt like she was floating.

"Farra, Farra, can you hear me? Blink if you can hear me." A soft voice that made her feel more at ease. She tried to answer but no sound came although she could feel her mouth moving. Then at once it hit her, the realisation of what it was that wasn't quite right – she wasn't breathing. Her instincts took over and she panicked and thrashed, fighting for the air she knew she must have but wasn't aware that she didn't need. "Relax Farra, don't fight it. Your body knows what to do, relax please. It hurts less if you relax into it." That voice again, so soft and reassuring. "Don't try to breathe Farra, you don't need to breathe right now. Relax please." More urgency in that voice now.

She willed herself to obey, eyes wide with fear. It took all of her mental resources to resist such instinctive survival needs like breathing but resist it she did and she found to her amazement that although very strange, it didn't hurt. She allowed her mind to relax and come to full wakefulness and found herself floating in a silvery thick liquid. It looked like water but Farra realised it probably wasn't. It didn't act like water for a start. It didn't slop around when she thrashed or moved her arms and legs. It just sort of, wobbled like thick cream and it twinkled like crystal. It was beautiful. She noticed there were tubes and wires connected to various parts of her body that snaked up through her liquid filled environment and out to, she didn't know where.

"Good girl, that's it. Hello there Farra, I'm Doctor Jam. It's a pleasure to meet you." Another pair of kind yellow eyes to go with the soft voice, another warm smile, another set of fangs. She remembered now. She was in the Drycenian ship. She fainted or something when being introduced to the King. God how embarrassing. "You can't answer me, so don't try, just blink once if you can hear me and understand me okay?" She blinked and managed a smile. She had little choice but to run with it, whatever this situation was that she was in, but she had to admit it was beginning to feel okay. "You are being taken care of so don't worry. You are in what we call the tank. The fluid that surrounds you now is doing the job that your breathing would do and is acting as anaesthetic and healing elixir to help your body heal itself. Okay? With me so far?" She smiled and blinked. "Good. I've fixed up your cuts and bruises and enhanced some of your senses and physical abilities and if I may be so bold, you're now as near perfect a specimen of Earth female as it's possible to find." She smiled as she listened to the doctor tell her of the changes made to her body.

"Your bones have been strengthened with a bio-metallic filament that grows within and around the cells of the bone, giving them a vastly increased loading capacity and strength. Be careful if you lose your temper now my friend, if you punch someone, you'll destroy their face! I've also altered the structure of your inner ears so that your hearing should be somewhere between five and seven times as acute as it was before. I've enhanced the rods and cones of your retinas and added an ultra sensitive layer beneath the lens. You now have the ability to see in extremely low light conditions but because of the sensitivity of this layer to light, I've added a sort of extra eyelid inside to protect your sight when in normal light conditions. You can now see the UV end of the spectrum without needing those clumsy goggles." She was amazed at what she was hearing.

"I've also added a telephoto function nanochip to the lenses inside your eyes which will give you the ability to see things much further away than you ever could before. It works in a similar way to a camera lens and will bring things closer to you. The musculature around the orbits of your eyes will operate this new addition without you having to think about it. As soon as you naturally strain to see something far away, the chip in your lenses will enable you to effectively bring whatever you're looking at, much closer so that you can see it more clearly. When going from light to dark, it will take just a second or two for your eyes to change from the normal daylight system you have naturally, to the low light or UV system. Your eyes will look different when using this low light system though, so be prepared for anyone who sees it, to comment. Don't worry, it looks cool." She had been listening with rising astonishment at the list of changes made to her body. She didn't feel any different, or at least she didn't think she did. She wondered if she looked any different. The soft voice of the doctor continued.

"You gave us quite a scare at first. We naturally assumed you are a Lilean but as soon as we got you hooked up, your blood and bone structure proved otherwise. Not to worry, all is fine now." That reassuring smile again. She hadn't a clue what he meant by 'Lilean' but she couldn't ask him without a voice of her own. She tried to convey her feelings by frowning and looking bemused and shaking her head but to no avail. The doctor just told her not to worry, to relax and that she'd be out in the fresh air before too long. She drifted off to sleep and it seemed like just moments later when she was awakened by a click. She started awake at once and looked around. Everything she could see was slightly distorted by the refraction of light through the fluid she floated in but she noticed someone was opening the door and entering the room. Then footsteps tapped across the floor, the swish as fabric clothed legs walked and then a small thud as a hand laid itself on top of her liquid crystal tomb.

Wow she thought to herself, my hearing is incredible, I could hear a mouse fart a mile away, this is so cool. She couldn't help herself, she grinned from ear to ear. She saw the familiar smile of the doctor looking down at her.

"I see you're feeling on top of things again. That's wonderful because it's time to bring you back out into the fresh air. This will probably be a little uncomfortable for you going from the liquid environment to air breathing again but just remember to try to relax while your body adjusts okay?" She nodded. "Don't worry and don't fight it, your body knows what to do." He called for his assistants to aid him and together the three of them pushed buttons, switched switches and watched digital read outs. "Now Farra listen to me carefully. As the fluid that now surrounds you drains away your body will instinctively react and try to breathe in the usual way again. Because your lungs have fluid in them which your body needs to expel, you will cough and splutter and find it hard to breath for a few seconds much like a coughing fit if you swallow something the wrong way. The main thing is not to panic and struggle with it. Just allow your body to expel the fluid and fill your lungs with air again and the process will be over quickly. The more you panic and struggle, the more your airway will constrict and the longer it will all take. Okay?" She nodded. With a great rush the fluid suddenly drained through the floor of the tank and she found herself unable to breathe. Despite all of her good intentions, she panicked. Instincts like breathing are hard to control and as she thrashed, vomited and coughed, the doctor's pleas went unheeded. Immensely strong arms held her firm, preventing her from harming herself or anyone else. That soft voice now had an authoritative edge. "Farra you must try to relax and stop fighting it. Let your body do what it knows how to do." Then softer, the soothing returned. "Just relax, let it all come up, that's a good girl." Oh God how her lungs hurt. She thought they would explode any second now. Gradually the pain subsided as she coughed up the last of the fluid and her lungs filled with the most glorious fresh tasting air she ever tasted.

"Welcome back my friend, welcome back," Doctor Jam beamed. She looked down at herself, soaking wet, hair bedraggled and covered in watery puke.

"Ugh."

"Hello Farra," a female voice beside her said. She turned and looked into the brightest yellow eyes she ever saw. "My name is Elka, let's get you cleaned up." The nurse helped her to stand up and slipped a strong arm around her waist while she got used to being upright again. "Come with me. Let's get you washed off and freshened up." She allowed herself to be steered into an adjoining room where there was a raised dais in the middle of the floor surrounded by several upright metal posts. A large showerhead hung down from the ceiling. She looked at the garment she was clothed in. It was made of the thinnest veil like material she ever saw and it felt like gossamer. She ran a hand over it. "The material helps the liquid in the tank to penetrate the body," Elka explained. "Its fibres react with skin cells to create a membrane like structure through which the fluid can pass to the cells and blood stream within. It's a far more effective way than simply injecting the fluid into the veins."

"It's amazing," was all Farra could think of to say. As she stood there she became aware that the garment was beginning to feel different. Small threads began to untangle themselves from the fabric; curling up and falling away. "What's happening?" She looked at Elka who smiled at her patiently.

"On contact with air for more than a couple of minutes the garment disintegrates prompting the skin cells beneath to readjust themselves back to normal. You wouldn't survive long if your skin remained as a porous membrane in the same way it does with this garment on in the tank. Now step up here." She was indicating for Farra to stand underneath the showerhead. Once she was in place, Elka spoke strange words and the upright posts emitted a fine misty spray. It was warm but there was a sharp quality to it, as if the water droplets were charged with an electric current. "The mist completes the process of readjustment for the skin and makes sure that all of the fibres from the garment are removed. Any that remained on the skin could still maintain that area as a vulnerably porous membrane."

"What would happen to me if that happened?" Farra asked.

"All the fluids in your body could leech out and harmful foreign particles could enter unhindered," Elka replied flatly.

Two hours later Farra was showered, dried and dressed and feeling fitter than she could remember. It was amazing, she felt as if she was invincible. She was enjoying the most wonderful meal in ages when Doctor Jam entered.

"My word you look wonderful, how do you feel?" he asked as he examined her eyes, turned her head this way and that, put a probe into her ears that beeped, then stood back and smiled as if examining his handiwork.

"I feel fantastic, better than ever, amazing actually. Thank you." She felt suddenly aware of the inadequacy of those two words but they were all she had.

"It's nothing really; normal routine stuff actually but you Earth people haven't experienced this kind of medical advancement yet. It was the very least we could do after what you have done for us and you must also be aware that anything you want done or changed, we can do for you. If there are any small changes you want cosmetically, you have only to ask."

"You and I are gonna be good friends Doc," she smiled at him, mentally drawing up a list. Hair removal to being with, then a nip here, a tuck there. Then she suddenly remembered something. "What did you mean when you said something about me being a Lilean?" The doctor looked blank for a moment.

"Oh, yes. When we removed your clothing to get you ready for the tank we naturally assumed that you are a Lilean, we almost delayed tanking you while we recalibrated everything. It wasn't until we got you hooked up to the DMS that we could see by your blood and bone structure that you're from Earth. It makes a difference to how we treat you. There are some treatment techniques that have to be done differently to a Lilean than to someone from Earth. Their bodies are different in a few ways, their blood and bone structure are different. As it turned out in your case there was no need to worry though."

"I'm from Earth, a small island in the Northern hemisphere to be exact. What's a Lilean?"

"That mark on your chest. It's the sign of a Lilean." The penny suddenly dropped and she realised what he was on about.

"Oh I see. This mark just appeared with the dreams," she tailed off, suddenly unsure of whether she should continue to tell him about the dreams, her spirit friend and her special task that was so important.

The doctor looked awestruck. "So you're chosen? Wow," he exclaimed.

She looked at him surprised. Why the hell did everyone else know more about it than she did? "Yeah, I guess so."

"Is this a recent development?" he asked kindly, suddenly aware of her lack of knowledge and understanding.

"Just over six months or so." She found she was relieved to be able to speak with someone who knew about it without having to fish for information as she did with Leon.

The Doctor nodded reassuringly. "You have someone who speaks to you yet?" She nodded. "Hmm good. Do you see them?" Another nod. "You know who they are?"

"His name is Leon, that's all I know; apart from he's dead of course."

"And you're okay with that part of it?"

"Sure, why shouldn't I be?"

"Well some people have a bit of a problem with the concept of life continuing after the physical body ceases to function," he explained.

"Well not me, I've always believed," she said with pride, remembering her conversation with Erin.

"No wonder it's advanced so quickly then. How much do you know about this Leon and the reasons for you being a chosen one?" he asked her.

"Very little actually," she replied. "He says I have an important job to do, part of which involved Toma. The rest of it has something to do with helping someone. Someone who is to save a nation that was once almost lost and who now needs my help. It has something to do with finding the truth about something or other. That's about all I know."

"Ok not to worry, I'm sure this Leon with tell you what you need to know at the appropriate time. One thing I can tell you for sure though, is that he is Lilean. Only Lilean spirits do the kind of thing he's doing with you."

"So Lileans are from a planet called Lilea I presume?" she asked. She hated all this not knowing; it irritated her no end.

The doctor smiled. "Yes that's correct. Have you ever heard stories about an army that roamed from planet to planet killing everyone who wouldn't let themselves be brainwashed into submission?"

"You mean the Transmortals? Yeah we learned about them in the military but I've never come across them personally."

"Yes that's them. If true evil ever existed, they personify it perfectly. In a nutshell, they are ruled over by a being who says that everyone must allow themselves to be brainwashed. Transformation they call it. They believe that only when the whole universe has been transformed can their heaven, a place they call, The Veil, come into being and that all who resist this transformation must die."

"Jeez I know they brainwash people and kill others but I've never known exactly why." She couldn't believe what she was hearing but wanted to know more.

The doctor continued. "This ruler was told by some kind of prophet that he would be killed by a man from the planet Lilea, so he took his army there and killed everyone he could, especially all the children. In his madness and desperation to fulfil what he saw as his ultimate destiny, he tried to ensure that the prophecy of his demise could not come to pass, so he had all children murdered, some of them torn from their mothers' wombs and killed by his own hands." Farra was disgusted by the imagery the kind doctor's words were bringing to her mind. As a woman, this last image was almost more than she could bear. She was moved to tears and could almost hear the screams of those violated mothers and the cries of those newborns who never got to take more than one breath. The doctor saw her distress and tried to console her.

"Lilea and its people just about survived the apocalypse and are still rebuilding their civilisation today. Lileans are the stuff of legends Farra. A race brought to the very edge of extinction who clawed their way back by sheer will, strength and courage. They can be very single minded when needs be, they never give up. Some call them defiant but that defiance helped them survive. They can be hard to get to know on a personal level but when you've been through what they went through a little hesitation is understandable. If your mission has something to do with Lilea or its people, which is likely as you'd never be a chosen one unless it had something to do with Lilea, then you're in for an exciting ride." She was pleased that she was learning more about it.

"How come you know so much?" she couldn't help herself, she had to ask.

"We make it our business to know what goes on around the galaxy," he smiled. She realised that he wasn't going to give away any more state secrets just yet so she let it lie. At least she knew more now, which made her feel better. It also made her feel incredibly humble and proud too. "Now come with me," the doctor said brightly. "The King wants to know how you are." It wasn't until they entered into the large chamber that Farra suddenly realised she hadn't a clue how to behave around a King. She'd never met royalty before, should she bow or something? Before she could think anything else, the King appeared before her, smiling. She bowed her head reverently, hoping that she wasn't being insulting or anything.

"My dear friend no," the King said suddenly, taking her by the hand. "You bow to no one. Now tell me, how are you feeling? Better I assume."

"Wonderfully better yes. I feel incredible. Thank you so much," she said but the King waved away her thanks.

"Always a pleasure my dear. Now, do you yet know what is the next step on your journey? The doctor tells me you are a chosen one of the Lilean spirit people. Have they given you further details yet? Can we help in any way?"

"Not yet, no. As soon as he tells me anything, I will let you know," she promised.

"Good, good. Now walk with me, tell me all about yourself." King Lomas slipped an arm through hers and together, like old friends, they walked and talked for hours. Farra confided her whole life story to him and afterwards she felt like a weight was lifted from her shoulders. It was so long since she was able to be so completely honest with someone and she didn't realise until now, how good it felt to have a confidante. She asked the King about Drycenians and he gave her a brief history of his race. He told her about the very earliest beginnings of the Drycenians; how archaeological excavations revealed their earliest ancestors to be a savage and barbaric race of cannibals. She thought about those teeth!

"Those early Drycenians were little more than grunting savages, hunting each other down, killing and eating their victims. They roamed Drycenia 4 for thirty thousand years until they just vanished, seemingly overnight," he explained.

"What killed them?" she asked, genuinely interested.

"No one knows. Our excavations reveal a period of approximately five thousand years without any trace of Drycenians at all. Nothing. The earth is bare during that period and then just as suddenly as they disappeared, they return changed."

"How changed?"

"Their basic physiology is the same but there is no sign of the savagery evident in the older Drycenian excavations; no cannibalism and in fact there are very obvious signs of massive social integration and co-operation. Technology suddenly appears too. It's very strange and interesting; we find site after site displaying artefacts and bones showing the older ones to be savages, cannibals. Then they disappear totally for five thousand years and when they reappear, they are suddenly socially integrated, peaceful, co-operative and have technology they didn't have before. We can find plenty of evidence for the before, and plenty for the after, but there is nothing to show of any sort of transitional period between the two."

"How intriguing," she exclaimed.

"Yes indeed," Lomas agreed. He went on to tell her how, after the Drycenians reappeared, their technological advances happened at an amazing rate with the consequence that they got into space before any other race in that sector of the galaxy and were able to learn about other planets and their inhabitants without having to interfere with their advancement. They took on the role of observers and kept a close eye on all that happened around their part of the galaxy. Because they were so advanced, they were usually the first race that other civilisations met when they themselves first explored space. Their knowledge and their wisdom found fertile soil in the minds of these new explorers and they became legendary across the galaxy for their technology and their habit of silent observation.

"You see Farra, we have always been very aware of the need to not interfere with the natural order of things. Planets that are not as advanced as our own might not be able to cope with the wider ramifications of great technological advancements. It wouldn't help at all if we waded in and gave them the secret to, say, Ultra Wave Pulse or a cure for all their diseases. The universe is a living organism you see, and everything within it happens at exactly the right moment. Interfere in one part and the effects will be felt in all other parts. One has to be holistic when dealing with such things. Everything is connected, everything has a spiritual energy and the universe knows best how to keep itself balanced and in order. We simply observe, advise and help where it is appropriate and right for the balance of all things."

"So that's why you know so much about everyone," she suddenly caught on. "You've been observing everyone for all this time so you're bound to know everyone's business."

"Quite," he smiled and patted her hand.

Doctor Jam hummed as he worked. He enjoyed fixing Farra up. It was a while since his more advanced skills were required and he was feeling quite fulfilled and happy at the job he'd done on her.

"Hi Doc," a familiar voice entered the medical bay.

"Farra, hello my dear. What can I do for you?"

"Well, you umm; you remember what you said about umm," she was losing her nerve.

"Yeeeeessssss"

"You remember you said if there's anything I'd like done. Err changed, y'know, cosmetically I mean?" She bit her lip, amazed at her own forwardness.

"Oh that, yes I remember. What would you like me to do for you?" He was now all ears; he loved his work and regarded himself as an artist of the highest order.

"Well, can you do hair removal?" she asked hopefully.

The Doctor gaped at her. "You want your hair removed? Are you sure?" He reached out and touched her brunette hair.

"Oh no, I mean body hair." She laughed at the thought of waking up to find herself bald.

"Ahh, I see. Yes that's easy. Do you want it all removed? I mean, all of it?" The question hung in the air between them and Farra went as red as a poppy.

"Not quite all of it no. Just the underarms and legs will do for a start," she coughed nervously.

"Oh yes that's no problem at all. Remove your clothes and sit up here." No more than fifteen minutes later she was redressed and delighted that she wouldn't have to bother with hair removal ever again. During the short and painless procedure she gave Doctor Jam a list of what she wanted done and he assured her it would all be simple and painless. He advised her against making her breasts bigger and was able to show her what she would look like, with the aid of his Medi-H machine.

"Step up here, that's it. Now stand completely still. Hold your breath." A beep and a flash of red light later and she was now standing gazing in awe at a life size 3D holographic version of herself with huge breasts.

"I see what you mean Doc, they don't look right at all." She burst out laughing and it was the doctor's turn to blush. "Let's stick with what we've agreed on," she decided.

"Good idea," he agreed. "When do you want to start?"

"Whenever you're available."

"Okay no time like the present. Roll up your sleeve for me."

Farra looked at herself in the mirror in her quarters. She liked what she saw. She would soon have a light golden tan that would never fade and which would act as an active sun block. Wherever she went, once the sun's rays touched her skin, the new compound in her skin cells would adjust itself automatically; allowing just enough sunlight through to ensure she got enough vitamin D. She would never burn, never peel, never get skin cancer and wouldn't have to worry about covering up her skin to keep it safe. She examined her eyes and was pleased that there would soon be no sign of the fine lines at the corners that she was all too aware of recently. She isn't old but she isn't a kid either. In her early thirties she was becoming aware of lines and loss of structure in her skin and although she was an action girl, she wanted to look good. Now, with the Hypercoll serum injection, her skin would soon look as smooth as a baby's bottom and would age at a third the rate of normal. These two changes were achieved by a simple injection. She was fine with needles but she was worried about something.

"How long will it last?" she asked

"It's permanent, no need to worry; you won't wake up one morning and find you've aged forty years."

"But I thought injections were temporary. Doesn't the body eventually expel anything put into it?"

"Yes but what I'm injecting into you isn't simply a serum. This fluid contains your own DNA with the relevant changes made to it. Once inside the body your bone marrow will start making this changed DNA, thus making these changes a permanent part of your body make up. Within a couple of weeks the changes will be complete." He explained it all so patiently for her.

"Wow, that's amazing Doc." She was deeply impressed and the doctor beamed with pride.

"Oh it's nothing really, very simple procedures," he said modestly. "Now, come with me, we have to get you used to working with your new abilities." He beckoned for her to follow him out of the room. They entered a large empty room that looked like some sort of storage area. As if reading her mind he told her that it was used for many purposes, including combat training for the troopers, entertaining and assemblies as well as storage.

"Now let's test your hearing first of all. You stay here while I walk up to the other end of the hall. I want you to signal me when you can hear this noise." He showed her a small device he held which beeped when he pressed a finger to it. "I want you to hold up fingers to match the number of beeps you can here, okay?"

"Sure Doc, no problem," she replied and watched as he walked two hundred yards to the other end of the room. She saw him hold up his hand. She strained her ears and heard four beeps. She held up four fingers. Two beeps, three beeps, one beep very quietly. She held up the correct number of fingers each time. The doctor indicated again and she strained her ears, waiting for a beep but none came. She strained harder but didn't hear a beep. She looked up at the doctor and shrugged her shoulders, shaking her head. To her amazement she heard his answer.

"Well done my dear, no beep that time. Can you hear me now?" It was if he was standing right beside her, she was amazed. She gave a thumbs up and nodded and saw him smile broadly. "Good girl, now can you see what's written on this card I'm holding?" She looked and could see that he was holding a piece of white card a couple of inches square. She couldn't see what was written on it though despite straining her eyes. "Just relax," he said, "don't try to force it." She tried to relax and just stared at the card, willing herself to see. Suddenly the whole image leapt closer and she instinctively moved back away from it, as if it was going to hit her. She heard the doctor laugh.

"Jesus," she exclaimed, "that was surreal. Let's try that again Doc." The doctor held up the card again and this time she just relaxed and gently squeezed the muscles around her eyes in as natural a way as she could. The image leapt forward again and the card was now a foot square with two words emblazoned across it.

THANK YOU.

"You're welcome," she said and laughed as the doctor walked back over to join her.

"Everything seems to be functioning very well but it will take a little while for you to become totally natural with its use. Just remember if it doesn't work, then you're probably straining too hard. Just relax and try again without straining."

"Sure Doc, no problem. This is so amazing."

"Now, I'm going to bring in a couple of troopers to help with the next part," he said. He pressed a call button on the wall. Someone answered and he spoke in Drycenian. Within a couple of minutes three troopers entered the room and joined them. They were padded up for combat training and she realised that she was going to have to spar with them. She remembered that she now has stronger bones and greater strength and would need to know her new capabilities. She hoped she wasn't going to hurt anyone.

"Now," said the doctor. "The first thing I want you to do is just to push and shove a bit, no punching okay? Let's start gently." She and the troopers moved in to the centre of the room and spread themselves out. One of the troopers came at her and she gave him a hard shove backwards. He went flying back twenty to thirty feet, arms circling trying to keep his balance, which he lost and sat down hard on his backside.

"Shit," she shouted, "are you okay? I'm so sorry."

"Yeah I'm fine," he said rubbing his rear. "Nothing broken."

CHAPTER THREE

Leon looked down at Farra as she slept and felt a mixture of emotions. She looked so fragile, as though one blow would break her. Knowing what she'd already been through proved how tough she really is and how much endurance she can muster when the need arises. He felt so proud of her; so proud and so sorry to involve her in all of this. Ever since he journeyed to the land of the dead during that terrible time so long ago, the spirits of the Lilean race resolved to right the wrongs that were done to them and their kind. Lileans have a warrior mentality and an endurance to see a thing through no matter what the odds. Honour and integrity demanded that justice be done. When the odds seemed overwhelming, the fury of the lost Lileans kept them focussed. Leon let his thoughts drift as he did so more often lately to that terrible day and night when his life ended. He fought bravely to defend his family; his beautiful wife so near to giving life to his son. The weapon that took him damaged his physical body so severely that there would be no going back to the land of the living.

He was forced to watch his young wife; her cries ringing out as the life inside her fought to be born. His own blood stained her garments as she lay in the ruins of their home struggling with the pains of the imminent birth. It was as if the new life inside her was aware of the danger as the pains took hold many days too early. For two days and nights she struggled with the ever increasing pains before she could contain her anguish no more and cried out in agony. Her cries alerted one of the invaders who stood nearby surveying what remained of the once magnificent Lilean Landscape. This one was different from the others; he seemed to dominate over them. They were afraid of him and obeyed him without question. As Leon blended with the energies in the land of the dead he gained the ability to see in a totally different way than ever before. This invader; the one the others looked to as their leader, who dominated them so easily was himself afraid. Leon could see the man's fear clearly; his aura was saturated with it.

The cries of the young woman giving birth alerted him and he turned quickly and walked towards the sound. The woman, Leon's beautiful young wife cried out once more before her cry was suddenly joined by that of the new life now freed from the safe confines of her perfect body. His lusty cries rang out into the night, strong and healthy. Leon looked at his son with such love the feelings overwhelmed him. The invader found them lying there; the exhausted woman covered in her husband's blood, the gore from the birth soaking the ground beneath her and the newborn boy between her thighs still connected to her body by the pulsating cord. The screams of the child rang in the invader's ears and fear turned to loathing. He stooped down and picked up the child by the feet; roughly slicing through his life giving connection with his now dying mother and held him aloft.

"You will not be the one foretold to me Lilean child," the invader screamed into the night sky. "You cannot kill me, you will not bring me down. You will not see me out. No prophecy of yours will end my days. You and your people will be forgotten before I am replaced." The man was filled with the madness of hate and fear; Leon could see it and smell it pouring from him. He was terrified for his son but was incapable of doing anything to help the vulnerable newborn who still screamed into the night, held roughly aloft by this madman.

"Oh my fine strong son, how strong your spirit is. I am so proud of you but I cannot help you now in your hour of need. I love you so." Leon watched in horror as the invader pressed one massive hand over the boy's face, suffocating the life from him. He then flung him into a midden amongst the filth.

"You will not be the one, Lilean child, you will not be the one," he snarled. The invader removed the cowl from his head and Leon saw the madness and hate in his eyes as he looked down at the lifeless body of his newborn son. He turned and walked away little realising who that child was to become and how both of their destinies were to be entwined. Leon knew he must act quickly before the child's spirit had time to depart from the physical vessel. He rushed to the midden and in his anguish he cried out for help from those of his kinfolk who also dwelt in the land of the dead. The group of spirits gathered around the tiny body and as he looked on a young female stepped forward and whispered into the child's ear. He couldn't hear her words and he knew they were not for his ears anyway, so he did the only thing he could do, he prayed that they were in time. With hands extended the spirit group began to chant ancient words. Ethereal blue light surrounded the child's still body as it lay there amongst the filth. All of a sudden a lusty cry rang out once more into the Lilean night and the spirit group vanished, all but the young female who remained by the child's side. She looked at Leon and smiled.

"I am Syra and I will be with him always. I will guide him and help him discover his destiny. He will have a life of many trials and sacrifices and often will have no one on whom to depend or lean for support. But fear not, I will be with him, he will not be alone and he will grow into a fine man; a warrior who will right this great wrong. The fury of the Lilean race will be his rock and his stay. Now give him his name."

"I name him Vincent Richard," he told her proudly as tears poured down his cheeks. He was totally overwhelmed with emotion, so much that he didn't know which to feel first. He was grief stricken at having to make his journey to the land of the dead with his wife as his son began his journey in the land of the living without their love and guidance. At the same time he was relieved that the ancient ones saved the boy. So many Lileans journeyed to the land of the dead that night, were they all to be extinguished? The whole race? Not while his son lived. Whilst Vincent lived, the Lilean race lived. He hung around as Vincent lay there in his filthy prison. When his hunger and despair became too great, Syra would appear and soothe him and he slept. His spirit was so strong and Leon was filled with pride at the boy who was the result of the love bond between himself and his wife. After three days and nights more Lilean survivors appeared and banded together. He was happy that Lilea would continue and he watched as Syra encouraged the tiny starving and exhausted boy to scream his lungs out once more. His cries were heard by a band of survivors, three of whom he recognised. Good people, they were neighbours and Leon knew his son would be cared for well. He watched as they lifted him from the midden that was his home for the past three days and brushed the filth and decay from his body. One of the survivors, a woman was still nursing her own young child so she took Vincent to her own breast and he suckled greedily. He was moved at the selflessness of the people he was so proud to call his own. As his son was nourished for the first time, a soft voice caught his attention.

He turned towards the sound and saw his wife calling to him. "Come now husband. Our son lives. He will grow into a man and right the great wrong. Come now, it is time for us to make our journey and allow our son to make his. When the time is right, you can return." She held out her hand and Leon, taking a last look at the tiny boy he loved so much, finally journeyed to the land of the dead with his wife.

He shook the memories away as he gazed down at Farra as she slept soundly. It was time for her to take the next step on this important journey. It would involve many dangers and would test her trust of him to the limit. He didn't doubt her, he couldn't doubt her, too much depended upon it. He knew she would do what was necessary. Great care was taken by the ancestors when they decided who should be the chosen one for this task. It was not a choice that was ever taken lightly. When the ancestors decide a choosing is necessary many eons of time may pass before the subject is chosen. Being outside of the physical land of the living means that time has no jurisdiction over them and they can move forward and backward through time as necessary. There was never before a chosen one from the planet called Earth and some were against the decision. Earth people are still comparatively primitive and possess unpredictable emotions and the capacity for great deceit. They also possess the greatest capacity for love of any race the Lileans knew of. So the choice was made and the young female became the chosen one at the moment her heart stuttered into life within her mother's womb. It would take over thirty Earth years before the time came to awaken her and during that time there was much to learn. How well she learned, Leon thought. He was pleased that she was the one, he liked her. He would be proud to have a daughter such as her. He bent down and reached for the little star on her chest, which glowed brightly at his touch.

"Farra. Farra wake up now. Wake up. It's time."

"What's up?" Farra woke with a start and saw Leon standing by her bedside.

"The time has come. Get dressed, there is limited time," he urged. She yawned, stretched herself and obeyed. An hour later she was showered, dressed and had joined the small group at the despatch port, having told them of the mission Leon had given her. King Lomas, Toma, Doctor Jam and a couple of Drycenian Troopers were discussing last minute tactics. The doctor was fitting her with a minute tracking device.

"This won't hurt a bit. It goes under the skin on the inside of the wrist, just hold still." He applied the applicator device and pulled the trigger. A small prick of pain made her jump. She looked at her wrist and found there was no trace of the tiny device. He went on to explain how it worked. "This is a temporary tracking device, a minute version of the one you saw Toma using to call the rescue vessel. It will give out a constant signal that only Drycenian technology can pick up so no need to worry about the enemy picking up the signal. The device will continue working for eight hours without solar energy to recharge it, so if you're not out of the tunnels within those eight hours we'll be down there to get you. Be aware though that if we have to do that your cover will be blown and the mission will fail. Stealth will not be our first concern."

"Ok, don't worry, we'll be in and out before you know we've gone," she lied.

The doctor asked once again. "Are you sure of what you have to do?"

"Yes." she replied. "Leon will guide us through to the deepest layer of the tunnel complex, right down to the bottom. Once down there I'm to retrieve a package hidden in a crack in the tunnel wall. Get in, avoid the guards, keep away from the Uvees, get the package and get out. Piece of cake."

"Remember that the Rangers will be aware of Toma's disappearance and will be on high alert. Patrols will be doubled, if not more. You don't have to do this, you could wait until the furore dies down a bit," the doctor offered, knowing he was wasting his time.

"No way," she replied. "Leon said that once they regroup themselves after Toma's escape they will take pains to get rid of the package I'm going in there to find. They will know that something big is up and won't want that package falling into the wrong hands. I have to get it now or it will be gone forever."

The doctor smiled sadly. "Yes I know, I know. What is the package anyway, do you know?"

"Just a data chip and a notebook, according to Leon. It's a small package roughly the size of a pack of cigarettes. It'll fit in a pocket easily. It has to be retrieved now, it just cannot wait. It's now or never, and never ain't an option Doc."

"Now remember," he reminded her. "It'll take a second or two for your night sight to kick in. Just relax your eyes to the dark and wait, okay? If you panic and rub your eyes you'll get the bio mechanical signals mixed up and the system won't know what to do and you'll be in the dark for longer. Just blink a couple of times and widen your eyes, that'll give the sensors the nudge to kick in."

"Ok, will do," she assured him. She liked Doctor Jam, he fussed over her like a father.

She took the King's proffered hand. "Remember also that you will be able to see the Uvees clearly now too," he reminded her. "So no need to worry about them creeping up on you unannounced like the last time you were there."

"We'll be fine," she assured him. "Leon will guide me every step of the way. So long as the Troopers do as I say without question, we'll be okay."

"They are at your command," he assured her. Turning to the two volunteer Troopers he said, "she is in charge, do as she says."

"Yes sir," the two voices replied in unison and with a final nod they boarded the rescue vessel once again for the journey back into the depths of hell.

The three made their way silently to the same entrance door they used for their escape and found to Farra's complete surprise that the very same rusty padlock still lay broken in the dust. The door was still standing open a couple of inches as she and Toma left it in their haste to escape and for a moment she wondered if this was a trap to lure them in. Leon put her mind at rest quickly and assured her it was safe to enter. Once inside the darkness enveloped them like a blanket and Farra forced herself to relax, widen her eyes and blink so that her night sight could kick in. Once it did she was amazed at the clarity of her vision. Although the colours weren't normal, she could see perfectly well and had to remind herself that despite her being able to see, others couldn't see her at all without aid.

Following Leon's precise instructions, the three made their way along corridors and down through several more layers of tunnels until they reached the very deepest levels that were never used now. These deepest depths were abandoned to the creatures and it was small comfort to know that they wouldn't have to worry too much about running into Rangers here. Time and again they pressed themselves against the tunnel walls and waited for a creature to pass by close enough for the Troopers to despatch them with a dart. The Dart Gun the Troopers used is an artistic weapon. Tiny darts; clear cells filled with a highly toxic compound found only on the Drycenian home world, are fired from a small gun powered by a black laser power unit. This means it is totally silent in use and it can be small in size, enabling it to be carried, stored and hidden with ease. This silent weapon ensures no noise to alert the other creatures to their presence. It takes seconds for the deadly poison to speed its way to the creature's brain and stop it dead. It was the most effective silent killing device Farra ever saw used and she was in awe of its capabilities.

"Stop," Leon urged her. With a signal to the Troopers, all three froze on the spot. "There are 2 Rangers coming," he said. Farra signalled her companions to ready their darts. Voices ahead in the tunnel, one of which she thought she recognised as her Supervising Ranger Thomas Leary. She heard a snatch of conversation before the Troopers did their job.

"Where is it?" said Leary.

"A hundred yards or so down here in a crack in the wall. High up near the roof on the right hand side. It's small so look carefully, we don't wanna be around here too long. I wanna live to screw the captains wife again," the strange voice laughed then a thud as they both hit the floor, the darts doing their job with unyielding accuracy.

"Look up to the left now," Leon urged. She looked and after a bit of fumbling around with her hands, she felt a crack in the smooth tunnel wall. She delved her fingers inside, controlling the urge to withdraw her hands as images of creepy crawlies running down her arms invaded her mind uninvited. For a cold moment she felt nothing but damp stone but then something soft. She grabbed it and pulled. "Good girl, you have it, now let's get out of here," he said. They turned and began the long trek back. Farra should have known things were going too well. As they rounded yet another corner, they found their way blocked by a thick metal wall that wasn't there on their way down.

"What the fuck?" she said aloud.

Leon hushed her immediately. "The rangers are beginning to lock the place down. This wall is part of their automated system in the event of gas leaks. You'll have to go another way around," he told her. "It's longer but you can still get out. Trust me child. We must be quick before all our escape routes are cut off. Come on now, go left here."

"Of course, sorry," she sent him her apology telepathically. They made their way around and along a long tunnel but before they had gone fifty yards, Leon stopped them.

"Three Rangers are coming this way." Farra gave the word to the Troopers who readied their darts. They heard voices up ahead and pressed themselves against the wall of the tunnel but there was no way they could avoid being seen and conflict seemed inevitable. She took a deep breath and waited. The voices got nearer. Suddenly one of them gave a grunt and the three heard a thud. Her night sight allowed her to notice one of the Troopers lowering his weapon. Unfortunately the second trooper missed his target, who was now on high alert and yelling his head off for back up as the third started backing up the way they came.

"Quick, shut him up" Farra hissed. The trooper didn't miss a second time and both remaining Rangers were dealt with. They waited in silence for a few seconds to hear if anyone else was coming this way alerted by the shouts of the Ranger. No sounds of boot steps came to her ears but what she did hear chilled her. She knew that sound only too well now. "Oh no, oh shit, no," she hissed.

"Get ready; you have no more than ten seconds," Leon ordered. She passed on this information to the Troopers. The three of them formed a tight formation facing the direction of the sounds and waited. The ground began to vibrate.

"Here they come," she said. "You know what to do." As the creatures rounded the corner and came into view the Troopers both opened fire with laser bullets. These weapons use pulses of laser light rather than metal bullets. They annihilate everything they touch but make a hell of a noise. Not the automatic weapon of choice where stealth is required. This current situation however, demanded firepower that could be relied upon first hit. All three creatures were dead within ten seconds but both Farra and her companions knew that probably every Ranger in the complex would hear the commotion and be on their way down to investigate.

"Run," Leon ordered firmly. "Straight ahead and down the first set of steps you come to, on the left about thirty yards along."

"Come on," yelled Farra as she took the lead and they ran. All the while Leon giving them instructions like a sergeant major, which she followed without question.

"Stop," Leon ordered. "Hide behind those crates." They hid and after a few minutes a group of seven Rangers appeared.

"I'm sure the sound came from this end of the tunnel boss."

"Nah I reckon it's the next level up."

"Whatever, I need a piss anyhow." Farra and the Troopers heard boot steps coming towards them.

"Get ready and be silent about it," Leon told her. She readied herself. When the Ranger came around the block of crates, already unzipping his pants, she took him from behind and with a skilfully clean movement of her now far more powerful arms, twisted his neck so far around that he could play the owl in the pea green boat in his kid's next school play. She took his guns from him and found a blade in his right boot, which she pocketed. The gun was a standard issue Kopek 7 with twenty round clips. She fished on his body for extra clips and found three. One of the Troopers got an idea. He indicated to his companion and together they stripped the body of the Ranger down to his underwear. Clothed in his uniform, one Trooper rejoined the group. Once he managed to manoeuvre himself behind two of the other Rangers, he gave the nod to the two he knew were watching from behind the crates. As he took care of these two with the two guns taken from the body of the Ranger, his companion trooper used both dart guns on another two. Farra flung the Rangers blade with practiced skill and watched as it sank effortlessly into the heart of another. All of this took place at the same moment, meaning that five of the Rangers all bought it together, leaving the last one wondering what the hell had hit them. The element of surprise was on Farra and the trooper's side, and this last one was despatched with ease by the Troopers.

"Now run," Leon urged. "Keep straight ahead and when the tunnel forks into three, take the centre hole." They could hear footsteps and voices from all around. It was as though they were surrounded by Rangers. "Don't worry," Leon assured her. "The acoustics of the tunnel system makes it difficult to know which direction a sound is coming from. Your enhanced hearing just makes them all seem louder and more confusing. Just keep going and trust me." They finally reached another heavy door with a padlock that showed no signs of rust, unlike the previous one. One of the Troopers pushed to the front and reached inside the pocket of his jacket. The small device was the size of a poker chip with a tiny button on one side and a magnetised surface on the other. Once attached to the padlock, the trooper touched the button, which blinked with a red light three times. A couple of seconds later, with a click, the padlock fell open and they were outside.

"I have to get one of those," Farra exclaimed to the amusement of her companions. "Let's get away from here." They ran for two hours without slowing, before she indicated to her companions that it was safe to call the rescue craft to get them. The craft landed in silence a hundred yards away. Once the dust cleared, the three rose to make their way to it and away from Moxal 3 forever. They were halfway there when shots rang out in the dark. They had been discovered.

"Quickly, inside," Leon ordered and Farra shouted to her companions.

"Hurry." A bullet whizzed past her left ear so close she heard the whistle as it flew past and ricocheted off the hull of the rescue craft. Any closer and a part of her ear would be missing! "Shit, that was close," she swore as she strapped herself into the seat alongside her two companions, both of whom nodded in agreement.

"Hold on tight, no time to see the scenery," the pilot said. The engines roared and Farra, with her newly enhanced hearing, thought her head would explode.

"Oh shit," she screamed and clapped both hands over her ears.

Back on the Drycenian Battle Cruiser, the doctor took a look at her ear.

"There you are that should do the trick," he said as he gently removed the probe from her right ear. "One of the cells had come loose from its anchor point deep within your inner ear which meant it was unable to obey your brain signals telling it to shut the noise down to a more manageable level. I've injected some Bioknit directly into the surrounding muscle tissue. It'll take dynamite to remove it now."

"Thanks Doc," she smiled. "I appreciate it, I really do."

"Are you ok?" he asked her quietly.

"huh? yeah I'm fine. You're the doctor, you tell me," she smiled.

"I didn't mean physically." He gave her his most intense gaze and she got the point.

"Oh, yeah I'm okay I guess." Despite being an expert in various combat and weapons techniques, she actually doesn't like killing anyone unless it is totally unavoidable. "I don't like killing if I don't have to Doc but I had to, there was no choice down there."

"I know, you carried out your task perfectly and if it helps at all, remember what your friend Leon told you. Many lives will be saved now."

"Yeah, I'm holding onto that Doc, thanks." She left him in the medical bay and thought she would stop at the obs room and watch the stars before turning in. She found Toma was already there.

"Hey Toma, are you okay?"

"Yes thanks, I'm fine. You were very brave today, you did a good job, well done."

"Thank you," she smiled. She looked out at the stars and sighed. "It's amazing isn't it?"

"What?" he asked.

"Look at all those stars. I wonder how many of them have planets with people on them and how many of those people are looking up at these same stars and asking the same question."

"A lot," he replied, "but no matter how many times you meet them nor how many planets you visit, it never stops being amazing."

"I'm glad about that," she sighed.

The door opened behind them and King Lomas, Doctor Jam and another officer who introduced himself as Commander Byron entered. The doctor carried a large tray on which were drinks and food. Lomas spoke first.

"It's no good we can't wait until the morning. We want to see what was in the package now. You said Leon said it was a book?

Well I won't sleep a wink until we look at it." He was clasping his hands and almost shaking with excitement. Farra laughed at the sight.

"Ok then come on let's get comfortable and what have you got there to drink?"

Down in the tunnel complex all hell had broken loose. Alarms sounded as Rangers thundered along companionways and down staircases. Voices bellowed commands which were hastily obeyed by frightened subordinates. In a small office on level one of the tunnel complex, McGreedle calmly packed his backpack with money from the company safe, took his gun from the desk drawer and headed out by way of the secret staircase only he and few others knew about. He was so angry his face was purple with rage. How dare this happen when everything was going so well? The Boss wasn't going to be pleased at all, no siree not one little bit and who'd get to take the fall out? Him of course. The Moxal 3 end of the operation was his responsibility and now it was all fucked up good and proper. There was only one thing to do, quit this shit hole and get out and as far away as he could. He could use some of the fake ID's he managed to grab as he packed and change his name and start afresh somewhere else. This place was done for, he could see that now. Nope, there was nothing for it but to cut and run while he still had his life. He reached the hangar where the company top brass kept their personal flight craft. He didn't possess one of his own but he had the use of a shitty little under cutter with no legs that belonged to the company and it was this he headed for now. He knew it was always kept fuelled and ready so all he had to do was hop in and go. As he rounded the corner and entered the hangar bay a voice rang out over the tannoy.

"Going someplace McGreedle?" the voice asked.

"Oh shit," he whispered to himself as he recognised that voice. "Oh shit, no."

A single shot rang out. A single shot that no one took any notice of in the melee and chaos that was now the Moxal 3 Mining Corporation complex. The shot could be heard from as deep as level three but no one down there paid any attention. The Rangers and staff who got themselves down that far were too busy dying to notice a shot from high above somewhere. The noise and chaos reached the Uvees who were now taking full advantage of the situation to fill their empty bellies. Pickings were scarce down here usually but tonight they feasted.

CHAPTER FOUR

"Well come on Farra, open it up." Lomas was skipping around like an excited child. "I want to see it, come on, open it up." Farra couldn't help but laugh at the sight of the King skipping around like a schoolboy with a new toy.

"Okay okay, hold your horses. Give me time to draw breath. I've spent the past six hours trying to avoid being eating alive by the Uvees or captured and murdered by Rangers for this little package. Its opening should be done with reverence." She tried to give Lomas a serious look but she couldn't control herself. She burst out laughing and he pretended to scold her.

"Now young lady, just you do as you're told. I'm the King around here and you have to do as I want."

"Ha ha ha yes Your Majesty, anything you say Your Majesty, your wish is my command Your Majesty." Farra was laughing so much she could hardly speak.

"Right then, get on with it!" Lomas said, exasperated.

She took the small package from inside her jacket where she stowed it as soon as she retrieved it down in the tunnel. It was indeed small as Leon told her; a little larger than a pack of cigarettes, wrapped in soft leather of some kind and covered in dust. She brushed off the accumulated dust and dirt. The leather wrapping was the softest she could imagine and it glowed like polished walnut.

"What beautiful leather this is, I wonder where it came from," she remarked.

Doctor Jam was very interested in this too and he brushed his fingers over it. "I could find out where the leather came from, I mean which creature it came from," he said.

"You could?" she replied.

"Yes quite easily, if you would let me take it for an hour or two. It won't be damaged and you'll get it back of course."

"Okay, yes, I'd really like to know." She was genuinely interested. She unwrapped the leather gently and handed it to the Doctor who took it and smiled. Inside was a small cube of what looked like glass but wasn't.

"So this must be the data cube Leon was talking about?" she said as she held it up to the light and turned it around and around in her fingers.

"Wow I haven't seen one of those for ages," Commander Byron exclaimed. "It's a data cube from quite a few years ago. Very old fashioned nowadays but a very reliable piece of hardware these were." The group looked at him wide eyed.

"Really?" asked Lomas.

"Yes sir, indeed" he replied.

"So how do we get the information off it?" Farra asked him.

"Oh that's easy, even I know that," said Doctor Jam looking up from the leather he was still running his hands over. "We put it into the streamer and wait." There were nods of agreement from the other Drycenians present.

Farra looked bemused. "What's a streamer?"

"Well," began Doctor Jam, "it's a sort of super computer that can read anything from any piece of hardware from any technology in the known galaxy. It doesn't matter where the hardware comes from or how old or new it is. If it's technology and data based, we can decipher it."

"My god, is there anything you can't do?" Farra asked, genuinely impressed. The Drycenians laughed amongst themselves and Lomas looked thoughtful for a moment.

"Well, we can't swim," he replied.

"Can't you?" she asked. "Why ever not?"

"Our bone density is all wrong and water cannot support our bodies. We sink like stones in water and to us it feels like falling through air would feel to you. Most unpleasant so we avoid it. Now, the data cube problem is solved easily. What's in the book, anything?"

Farra looked down at the little book she held in her hands. "It's got something printed on the front cover," she said as she leaned over to get more light. "Oh it's three initials, must be who it belonged to originally."

"Well what are they then?" Lomas asked as he tried not to sound impatient.

"Oh, sorry err let's see. It says V.R.D."

"I wonder who or what VRD was?" said Lomas

"Maybe we'll find out inside," Farra said and began to open the little book. They got their answer on the very first page. "This looks like someone's work record," she said as she read from the first page.

'Moxal 3 Mining Corporation Work Record for Vincent R Domenico.'

"That's VRD, that's who this belongs to," she said as she looked up at her friends and smiled. "Vincent R Domenico. Sounds kinda nice don't you think?"

Doctor Jam nodded. "Continue, please. What else does it say about him?"

'Assigned - Cleaner grade 1 – Level 5.'

"Level five?" Farra exclaimed in surprise. "There are five levels of tunnels down there. We found this in level five so that means he was down there in the deepest levels when he first joined the company. Talk about jumping in at the deep end!"

'Assigned - Cleaner grade 2 – level 4'

'Assigned – Cleaner grade 3 – level 3'

'Assigned – Cleaner grade 4 – level 2'

"It seems that as he got promoted, he got to work higher and higher up in the tunnel complex," she said. "Obviously as he ingratiated himself with the company, his workload got easier." She was about to continue when Byron cut in.

"It's typical of this type of company. A sort of institutionalised bullying tactic used to sort out who is with them and who isn't. You'd think they'd start new recruits off gently and gradually increase their workload and responsibilities and danger levels as their experience increased. This company does things the other way around. They send them straight into the heaviest danger and they either get killed off or they learn to work with the system. Obviously this, err what's his name?"

"Vincent R Domenico," Farra reminded him.

He nodded and continued. "Obviously this Domenico learned to go with it and was rewarded with promotion."

"Must've been horrendous working down there all the time," she remarked. "I only worked there for two weeks and I never got down below level two and that was bad enough." She continued reading.

'Promoted to Tactical Combat Centre – Assigned Moxal 3 Moon.'

'Graduated Tactical Combat Centre – grade – honours.'

'Assigned Moxal 3 Mining Corporation – grade – Security Enforcement, Head of Dept.'

"Wow he really made his way up didn't he?" she said and everyone nodded.

"He must've been one hell of a soldier," Lomas remarked and decided he was beginning to like this Domenico character. "What's next?" he asked as she turned over to page two.

"My god," she looked up at him wide eyed with astonishment. "I don't believe this," she said.

"What?" everyone spoke in unison.

"It says here; *relieved of duties, employment terminated.*"

"What?" Lomas couldn't believe it either. "Does it say why?"

"Nope. It just says this, under the heading, Reasons for Dismissal, *incarceration in Cryo Stasis.*"

"My god," exclaimed Byron. "What the heck did he do to deserve that I wonder?"

"Well that's all there is as far as his work record goes," she remarked as she turned another page. "Oh look here, there are handwritten notes." She quickly leafed through the rest of the little book. "The whole thing is filled with handwritten notes. It must be Vincent's writing, his own notes. Don't you think?"

"One can assume so," Lomas agreed. "Read it for us."

Farra read from Vincent's notebook and throughout everything her Drycenian companions listened, nodding from time to time; the occasional "my god" or "wow" the only interruptions. There were dates and names, details of conversations overheard, observations, security code numbers, together with Vincent's own deductions and thought processes. It became clear to Farra and the Drycenians that the Moxal 3 Corporation was, at least at that time, very corrupt in the way they operated. One entry read;

New recruit named Lazer arrived and asked to work higher levels first due to danger. Request was denied. Lazer assigned to level five tunnel complex and given triple shift working alone as punishment. Body parts discovered three days later.

"Jesus," Farra exclaimed, "he must've been terrified down there all alone. I don't know what the rules were then but now you have to work in groups of three, no one is ever allowed to work alone."

There were precise detailed notes about what seemed to be some kind of company politics going on at the time. Vincent didn't seem to understand what it was all about, but he knew something wasn't quite right so he listed names, dates and times of secret meetings held, snatches of conversations he overheard and one name kept coming up time and time again. James McGreedle, Facility Warden.

"What do you suppose these numbers are?" she said as she pointed to short strings of numbers in the margins that accompanied all his entries that applied to conversations, meetings and money.

Byron smiled. "Oh that's easy," he said. "They apply to the data cube. They tell us where on the data string there is something that illustrates this entry in the book. See here, where he talks about hearing a snatch of conversation?" Farra nodded. "That number in the margin tells us where on the data cube we can find something that will back up this entry; further evidence if you like."

"Oh I see," she said. "Mr Domenico, I think I like you." Lomas and the doctor laughed. Further along in the notebook Vincent entered details of money going missing from the company accounts. Some of the amounts were small but as time went along the sums got bigger and bigger. Again these entries were accompanied by a code number string. Throughout everything the name of the facility warden kept coming up time after time.

"I wonder what part in all this James McGreedle had to play," she said. "I never met him personally. I only ever saw him once when he passed by me in the rec room."

Byron offered her a way to find out something more about him. "It should be easy enough to find out about him," he said. "We can access data banks from many planetary systems. As well as looking for Moxal 3 records, if he ever lived, worked or spent a night on any of the planets in this whole sector, we'll be able to find details about it." She and her companions were very pleased to hear that.

"Good, I think it would be a very good idea to follow that name up," Lomas replied and told Byron to go and work on it right away.

"Yes Sir," he said as he turned and left the room.

"Oh look here," Farra said. "He's written something personal."

Why won't Donaldson do something? Thought he was a friend. How wrong, no such word as friend.

"He must've tried to confide in someone; this Donaldson," she remarked. Lomas looked thoughtful and exchanged a knowing glance with the doctor. Farra saw something pass between them, a moment of understanding and her curiosity was piqued. "What?" she looked from one to the other and back. "You know something don't you? Well what is it?" A moment of silence ensued during which Lomas and Doctor Jam exchanged another of those looks.

"We may know who Donaldson is," Doctor Jam replied. "If we're correct then the ramifications of this little book extend further than we could have anticipated. It seems that your friend Leon has given us the opportunity to really put the cat amongst the pigeons."

"How? In what way?" she asked.

"You remember Toma telling you that he was kidnapped while acting as my envoy on a mission of goodwill nearby here?" Lomas asked.

"Yeah I remember," she nodded.

"And you remember us telling you about a ridiculous plot to take over control of this sector of the galaxy and of a madman at the helm of a group of revolutionaries?"

"Yes."

"Well, there's one man who has dedicated years to trying to undo the many convoluted threads of this plot and this group. A man who once had dealings with the Moxal System and who would've undoubtedly also had dealings with this mining company."

"So?" she asked.

"So his name is Michael Donaldson," Lomas replied flatly.

"Oh my."

"Yes. The very same Michael Donaldson who is now the very well respected head of the ANA."

"Oh, that Donaldson," she said.

"Yes," replied Lomas. "As you know they are a body of elected people from many planets who together form a totally neutral arbitration body. They oversee trials and sentencing and act as hosts at meetings where the need for neutrality is paramount. That way they can help ensure fairness and stamp out corruption. At the time Vincent was on Moxal 3, Donaldson was just a newly employed junior officer."

"So why are they interested in what's happening on Moxal 3 and Toma's kidnapping?" she asked.

Doctor Jam looked up. "Because Donaldson wants one thing more than anything else in life; to end this take over plot and bring those responsible to justice. It was obviously the reason Toma was taken; to have a Drycenian Prince in your charge would ensure people from all over did whatever you asked them to. No one would dare make a stand against a group who control the Drycenians, even if that control is exercised by blackmail. The fact that Toma was held on Moxal 3 identifies it as having been part of the plot."

"So the conversations Vincent talks about, the meetings, even probably the lost sums of money, were probably to do with this revolutionary group?" she was beginning to understand the wider implications now. Everything began to fall into place.

"Yes," he replied. "He didn't understand but he knew something wasn't right. The murders he witnessed and heard about, the loss of money and secret meetings, it all fits." He looked thoughtful for a moment before adding, "Mr Domenico had great insight. He tried to do the right thing and must've suffered greatly for his trouble. I wonder what happened to him?"

"He obviously went to Donaldson with his observations but the man wouldn't listen," she offered. "Somehow this book and the data cube got into the hands of the wrong people, McGreedle and his lot who hid it away and got rid of Vincent and sent him to Cryo Stasis, whatever that is."

"Yes," Doctor Jam replied. "Cryo Stasis doesn't exist anymore but it was a prison; a legendary prison that no one really knew much about. No one who went there ever came out until the day it ceased operation. It's probable that Vincent died there. There should be records of his stay though, I'll get Byron onto it," he said as he turned and left the room. Lomas looked at Farra's sad face. She looked worn out both physically and mentally.

"You should get some sleep, you look all in."

She looked up at him and smiled. "Yes I am. I feel sort of, redundant now though."

"Why?" he asked as he took her hand in his.

"Well now that I've done what Leon asked me to do, what next? Where do I go and what do I do with my life?" she asked.

"It's far from over yet my dear," he replied. "We have to get to Donaldson and give him the cube and the book so that he can use it to bring McGreedle and the revolutionaries to justice. There will be plenty for you to do before this is over and done with. You mark my words, you're anything but redundant. Now go and sleep, that's an order."

"Yes Your Majesty."

As she lay in her bed safe in the belly of the Drycenian battle cruiser, she skimmed through Vincent's notes again, this time concentrating her focus on the more personal of his entries. She didn't know why but she felt she wanted to know more about him.

I've landed in hell, was the first entry he made after joining the company. *Gotta learn to cheat at dice,* was another and there were quite a few entries concerning playing dice and more to the point, cheating at dice. She surmised from what she read that duties were handed out by the throw of dice. If you lost, you got the shit stick. So Vincent learned to cheat at dice.

"Yep, I think I like you Vincent R Domenico," she said as she continued reading. There were several entries about murders committed by the Rangers.

I told Henry to shut the fuck up.

She found out what happened to Henry in the very next entry.

Ranger Cribbens shut Henry up for good today with his SB 17. Blew his head right off his body.

Then just as she was about to put the little book down and sleep something caught her eye and made her sit bolt upright. She couldn't believe what she was reading. She read it several times over to make sure she hadn't misread it. One short sentence that shocked her rigid.

Voices. Voices in dreams. Am I going mad?

She looked up to find Leon sitting on the end of her bed. "Yes child, Vincent is Lilean. He battled with the voices too, for the whole of his life."

She didn't know what to say next. "Oh" was all she could manage. She looked up at him and waited for him to continue.

"He didn't die in Cryo Stasis, he survived. He still survives today. I know you're wondering," he smiled kindly, reminding her that he could read her thoughts.

"I'm pleased, is he okay?"

"Physically? Of course, he's Lilean," he replied and she noticed a note of pride in his voice and she smiled.

"So what are you not telling me?" She looked at him with raised eyebrows as if to let him know that she could also read his thoughts.

"Do you remember the good doctor telling you about the legend of the Transmortals and how they went to Lilea to kill them all because of a prophecy that a Lilean would kill their leader?"

"Yes I remember, a horrible story. Is it all true?"

"Yes it all happened."

"And?" she urged.

"Well, Vincent was the one who was prophesied to kill him and he is my son."

Her mouth fell open. "Oh my god. Your son? Really? Shit, I mean wow. Really?"

"Yes my child, really. My name is Leon Domenico. The night they invaded our planet was the night I went to the land of the dead. My wife died giving him life as the invaders tore across our lands. I stood by in my new condition as a spirit shade and had to watch as the madman; the leader of the invaders took up my newborn son and smothered him with his own hands before throwing his body into a midden." He passed the details to her without preamble. She was stunned and moved to tears as he relayed the story to her detail by detail.

"Luckily for him, I was there and called to the older spirits for aid who came and repaired his connection with his physical body so he didn't have to join me in the land of the dead. A young Lilean shade spirit named Syra pledged to walk with him as his guide as I'm doing with you. He grew into a fine man but was much troubled in his mind by being able to remember the day of his birth. Syra tried to cover the memories but he thought her words of comfort and presence were signs of madness. He still struggles with it today but is making progress through the painful process of embracing his past in order to move into his future. Syra is beginning to awaken him; really awaken I mean. He is alone and struggling both physically and emotionally and I am powerless to help him. Syra assures me that all is well and that he is beginning to open the door to the past. It's causing him much suffering." The images filled Farra's mind as clearly as if she'd been there herself. She felt such compassion for this man she'd never met.

"So this book and the data cube will prove him right, give him some vindication?"

"Yes but it's more than that. Don't think your job is finished Farra, there is much more work for you to do yet. Your task was not confined to bringing the political plot out into the light."

"It wasn't?"

"No. That was just an added bonus. One that will help millions across this sector of the galaxy. The main thing for you to focus on is Vincent himself. The reason he was sent to Cryo Stasis was because he knew of many murders within the Moxal 3 Corporation and their corruption because of the newly hatched revolution plot. When he tried to expose the murders the Corporation couldn't risk the plot being found out so they framed him for the killings and hid the evidence he'd accumulated; this book and the data cube."

"So not only will it end the plot but it will clear his name too?" she asked.

"Yes. You see, we Lileans are known as a defiant race. We don't like to feel held down by anyone. Honour and integrity are very important to us. Free will to make our own choices is something we hold very dear. For my son to be accused of such crimes and imprisoned for them was very damaging to him, to his very sense of who he is. It was completely natural that a Lilean would never submit to being jailed for a crime he didn't commit. He was bound to escape, and he did. The years of incarceration, the solitude, of running and hiding have taken their toll on him and his sense of self. I worry for him. If those original crimes are revisited and my son found to be innocent of them, then any stain upon him will automatically be wiped free. It is also necessary for him to fulfil the prophecy and end the evil that is the Transmortal Army. It was decided that there should be a choosing and right this wrong for him, for the great thing he will do for us, for Lilea and everyone whom the Transmortal evil has touched. You Farra are that choosing and that is why you're here." She took a deep breath and let all that she heard sink in.

"Okay so what do I do next?"

"Next, you sleep. You've earned it today," he smiled.

"Okay," she sighed.

He gave her a brief run down of what should happen next and what she must do. "The next thing is to find Donaldson and give him the cube and the book. He will be easy to find now that he's an important man. He won't be easy to get to though; due to the nature of his position he is always at risk of being a target and he is well guarded. You must put this book and cube into his hands personally. Don't give it to anyone else not even his most trusted aides. He must receive it into his own hands."

"Right, I understand," she replied and was already formulating strategies in her mind as he continued.

"Then Vincent must be found and brought to where Donaldson is. He must be there in person before any judgements can be made about his supposed crimes. If he's not in attendance, the stain upon his record cannot be removed by any judge in the galaxy."

"Okay." She thought that might be more than a little difficult to achieve given Vincent's habit of disappearing into thin air and not trusting anyone.

Leon was reading her mind. "Yes it will be quite a task getting him there. Your friends the Drycenians will achieve this part of the task whilst you get to Donaldson."

"How will they find him?" she asked without realising she already knew the answer.

"I will tell them where he is of course," he laughed.

"Oh jeez yeah sorry I keep forgetting you can see far and wide." She felt like a stupid kid all of a sudden.

"Once Donaldson does his job the other security bodies will deal with the McGreedle plot and the Moxal 3 Corporation side of things. You don't have to worry about that side of things any more."

"So what do I do then?" she asked, suddenly sad at the thought of her new Drycenian friends leaving her alone on some strange planet she's probably never heard of, jobless, homeless and lonely.

"Then you go to Lilea and do another couple of more personal tasks for me and my son."

"Go to Lilea? Really? Oh wow I'd love to see it." This pleased her and she relaxed. She gave a big yawn and Leon bade her goodnight. She lay down and was fast asleep within five minutes.

In her dreams she was watching the sunrise over the Lilean landscape. White trees gently swayed in the light morning air as giant birds swooped and called overhead. She was at peace with everything and felt as though she were in paradise when all of a sudden something changed. Everything looked the same but she felt a chill deep inside and fingers of fear crept up her spine to the nape of her neck. She didn't know what it was but something was different and it made her frightened. The birds called overhead and as she looked up at them they changed from the benign peaceful creatures of grace that she was admiring just seconds before, into enormous sinister monsters. Their gentle calls became screams and they swooped down at her repeatedly, trying to unsteady her from the cliff edge where she was sitting and make her fall. Furiously she batted at them flailing her arms as they swooped and pecked at her. She tried to scream but no sound came, just a strangled gurgle was all she could produce. Just as she was about to fall from her lofty perch she awoke from her slumber and cried out. She was drenched in sweat and her breath came in deep heaves as if she had been running all day. She looked about her and was comforted by the familiar sights that greeted her in her quarters deep inside the Drycenian battle cruiser.

"Shit, shit," she sighed as she wrapped her arms around her knees and hugged herself.

Leon watched her dreaming and became concerned when the imagery began to turn frightening. He was debating with himself whether to wake her but an ancient knowledge deep inside somewhere prevented him from doing so. He knew what was happening to her and he was all at once both immensely proud and terribly sorry. Her new connection with Lilea, via himself of course, and the great gift that was bestowed upon her and which was now a permanent mark upon her chest was the cause of these new nightmarish images. He understood the symbology of the images she saw of course but he knew he mustn't yet interfere. He must let things take their natural course for a while longer and she would come to understand them herself before too long. He looked upon her like a father and he hated to see her troubled and frightened, especially as he was the cause, even if it was indirectly and very necessary. He stayed in the background and didn't announce his presence to her, even though he knew she was looking for him with her mind as well as her eyes.

She got herself a drink of water and settled back down to sleep, hopeful that now the nightmare was over, she could sleep until it was time to wake up again. Her breathing slowed and deepened and sleep overcame her. When her eyes began to move again under her closed eyelids Leon stepped forward and connected with her mind in order to see what she was seeing. This time she again found herself in the Lilean landscape but this time she was walking down a lane lined with white trees that swayed gently in the afternoon breeze. She could see buildings on either side and she knew instinctively that she was on the outskirts of a village. A man came from one of the buildings and started walking a little in front of her. As they both walked, more and more people came out of the buildings and started walking towards the village. Then all at once everyone stopped dead in their tracks and she was forced to do the same to avoid bumping in to the people in front of her. She couldn't see why they all stopped so she decided to ask someone.

"Excuse me, I'm new here, why has everyone stopped?" she asked but her question was ignored. She went over to a young woman just ahead and asked again. "Excuse me, I'm new here, why has everyone stopped?" but again it was as if she didn't exist. She started to get annoyed and went over to the first man and shook his shoulder in an effort to get his attention but to no avail. Everyone stood rock still like statues while the white trees swayed.

The white blossoms hung down and swayed in the slightest breeze. They were beautiful and she was captivated by them all of a sudden. It was as though they were calling to her to look at them as they swayed, back and forth, back and forth, back and forth. The breeze began to pick up and the white trees swayed even more. Soon the breeze had become a ferocious wind and the trees now flailed their limbs menacingly at her. For a horrible moment she thought they were trying to grab her, but they are just trees, beautiful trees. As she fought to calm herself, still transfixed by the sight of the wildly flailing trees, she felt a sharp pain in her neck. One of the branches hit her and drew blood which now trickled down her shoulder. She reached up and touched a finger to the blood and looked at it and as she did so the trees changed. The flailing branches were now arms; men's arms that reached to grab at her. She turned to run but as she did so, the arms grabbed her and she awoke fighting madly to get away from the foe who now faded into dreamland.

An hour passed since the first of the dreams woke her and once again she sat bolt upright in her bed, hugging her knees and sobbing quietly; frightened but angry at herself for being frightened. She hadn't experienced nightmares since she was a kid and she was ashamed that she could once again be so frightened by them. What were they all about and why was she having them? She could remember them vividly and she suspected that they were caused by having listened to Leon telling her about the day the Transmortals attacked Lilea. This made her feel better and although she guessed that they may continue for a while at least, she was pleased that she was obviously making a real connection with Lilea, a spiritual connection.

Forty five minutes later she allowed herself to succumb to sleep once again and fell into a peaceful and dreamless sleep. Leon looked at her and felt such pride at her courage and understanding that he was almost moved to tears. He never doubted the wisdom of the choice of this woman as the chosen one but now that conviction was even stronger.

CHAPTER FIVE

Farra awoke after having gained four hours of peaceful sleep. She felt a little heavy headed due to the nightmares and the lack of good sleep but she could remember feeling worse many times before during her deep space military career. She has always been one of those people who thrive under stress and performs better during high stress encounters. The fall out is that after the stress is gone, she tends to fall a bit flat for a day or two. She was under stress since the day she was born thirty two years ago. She was given up for adoption at three days old; her mother having been raped during the reconstruction back on earth. By the time she was old enough to notice such things, the reconstruction was over and a tense peace was in place. Her mother was one of those many demonstrators against the amalgamation. England just happened to be in the prime spot on the borders between the American United Western Hemisphere and the Holy Islamic State in the East. Both sides were vying for the last pieces of land, made up of England, France, Spain and the Northern part of the African Continent and England found itself right in the middle of the conflict. Invaders from both sides poured in from all corners and those who demonstrated against amalgamation were treated harshly. Farra's mother was one such victim and feeling no love for a child conceived in anger and hatred put her up for adoption three days after the birth. She tried to get her pregnancy terminated but the clinics and hospitals were overflowing with victims of the conflict and no one was interested in a young woman who couldn't keep her legs closed.

As Farra was adopted by a lovely American couple, the Duncans and grew up in what was now part of the American United West she was lucky to enjoy many opportunities to fulfil a life of military service. Both of her adopted parents served; her mother as a medic on an emergency aid outpost situated on the fourth moon of Algeron Prime and her father rose up through the ranks of the Deep Space Military Service Corps. They met when he was taken to the Algeron Medical outpost after being wounded in action against a band of renegades on Algeron 6. Once they found they couldn't have children naturally, they decided to return to Earth and adopt and so Farra found a loving family with the Duncans and the foundations for her ultimate destiny.

She excelled in the military, especially in combat skills of various kinds and her father was very proud to practice with her in the garden of their home. She gave him many bruises and he soon became aware that there was really no need for him to be soft with her. She carried a few of her own bruises from these sessions and even a permanent scar from a knife wound he gave her. She pleaded with him to get real with her during these practice sessions and he eventually relented, confident of her abilities. He started easy, playing safe with her until she easily sliced through the seam of his pants from front to back, leaving him standing there with his underwear showing. From that moment on he got a bit tougher with her and one day she got sloppy and he gave her a one centimetre scar on her left earlobe.

"That could've easily been your throat, you got sloppy kiddo. If you're too tired, step back and let a colleague shield you till you get your wind back."

"Okay Pops, yeah I know. You want some lemonade?"

He was proud to be there for her the day she got her bronze arrow for bravery. She was in the DSTU's for just 5 months when they were sent to Nebugord Prime for a very covert operation and she found herself alone and stranded, surrounded by hostile alien forces. Her commanding officer was captured and was being tortured so badly she could hear his screams from a mile across the valley floor where she was hiding out. Alone and single handed, she went in, dealt with the hostiles, rescued the officer and got them both out and back to safety. As she stepped forward to have the little bronze arrow pinned to her lapel, her father thought he would burst with pride. She wore that little pin everywhere; it was her most prized possession.

She loved her career in the DSTU's. Every place she visited and every people she encountered taught her something she was grateful for. She had insight and was always aware of the interconnectedness of everything. Even when encountering a very hostile situation she would always look for what she thought of as the gift; that small wisdom so subtle that it is easily missed and would sometimes make a note of the more profound of these moments in a personal journal. Her journal was much like Vincent's own; a small book in which she would write her observations, thoughts and the more memorable moments of her life. She would sometimes leaf back through it and relive some her experiences. There was one she re read more often than any other.

January 15th (earth calendar). location – Sigma Prime, duty – retrieval of escapee from Parkazy Penitentiary. 0715 – Received transmission via secure channel – Dad passed away 4 days before Christmas. Jesus no! Can't go home until escapee secured. Damn his hide, he's so gonna pay when I find him! Now I'm all alone.

She took a month compassionate leave to return home to Earth to bury her father, who was being kept in cryo storage until her return. Her mother passed the year previous after a brief illness and although she mourned her, she was never as close with her mother as she was with her father. She was daddy's girl and she gave him a wonderful send off with full military honours as befitting a veteran of his standing. She kept her composure all the way through the long service until the moment came for her to receive his medals from the Unit Commanding Officer. That's when she lost it. Often when she was on foreign soil on a planet far from home she thought of her dad and those medals and they helped her be strong. She remembered him saying to her, "keep sharp kiddo, keep sharp," and she kept sharp.

She retrieved the little book that once belonged to Vincent R Domenico and read some more. She wanted to get a real feeling of the man; his thoughts and feelings and what made him tick. He was an enigma and she had to admit it, she was intrigued by him. She wondered what he looked like, how he sounded, was he good looking, sexy even? She smiled to herself and said aloud, "shut the fuck up you idiot."

Vincent's entries in the first few months of his employment on Moxal 3 showed her how quickly he was able to get a handle on people and the way they operated, their motivations and aims. He seemed to find it easier to know what people tried to hide, than what they showed willingly. One entry made during his third week on the job showed this clearly.

Hunter asked me if I wanted to spend my first leave with him on Grinmore 4 for some big game hunting. He said he asked me cos I've no family. What the fuck does he want?

It was obvious to Farra that the guy was being friendly, but Vincent couldn't see it that way and automatically assumed Hunter had an ulterior motive for asking him. That told her a lot about the way his mind worked and she made a mental note: suspicious of everyone and everything. At the same time though, she felt sad for him. His life, what she knew of it anyway, was so full of trauma in various guises that it's little wonder the guy's a bit suspicious of people. His parents were murdered at the moment he was born. Hell, he was murdered himself minutes after birth and thrown onto a rubbish heap to starve for three days until he was found and rescued. If it weren't for his genetically advanced physical make up and the intervention of the Lilean spirit people, he'd have died. She made another mental note: take my time with this guy, don't push.

Here and there Vincent would make vague references to voices in dreams and she wondered if his experiences of them were similar to hers. Over the page he went into a little more detail about it and she read it with interest.

The voices and the dreams. Always the same every time. So much fear and rage. People dying, tombstones and a baby crying. The woman telling me something but I can't hear what she's saying. Am I going mad, am I crazy?

She understood a little of what she was reading of Vincent's experiences with the dreams, although the content of his was probably far worse than hers. Her heart went out to him. A couple of pages further on there were further entries regarding money.

Saw McGreedle handing over a pile of money to one of the SB Reps. Asked him what it was for. Was told you ain't seen nothing Domenico, get back on the job.

He made five entries in two days all about seeing money changing hands. The third of these entries again brought up the mysterious SB Rep.

Heard McGreedle talking to the SB Rep again today. Heard him say 'here's twenty five hundred more, there's no more till next month, tell the boss that's all we have.' That means in two days McGreedle has handed over more than 4000 to this guy. Why is the company handing over cash now, the SB Weapons contract is always done by auto transfer? Something's not right here. Gotta keep eyes and ears open now.

It was at this point that Vincent decided to use covert means to record what he was seeing and hearing and called in a couple of favours and got himself a tiny camera that looked like a shirt button and an audio recording device that clipped invisibly to his night sight goggles. The solar powered battery packs were quickly recharged with just 30 minutes of sun exposure, so he took to taking his breaks on the surface.

Called up a couple of guys who owe me. Got a cute little camera that looks exactly like a button from my uniform shirt and an audio pod the size of my thumb nail. Will fix to my UV goggles perfectly. Solar charge – 30 mins per 24 hours. Will take break topside once a day, maybe practice a little tapshots. Gotta sew this button on.

She didn't know what Tapshots was, but she made another mental note to find out. She was discovering that Vincent was both focussed and methodical once his interest got piqued.

She got up, showered and dressed and went looking for her new friends. She went to get some breakfast and found Byron there enjoying what looked like a bowl of red jelly. She looked at it and wondered why on earth anyone would want to eat red jelly for breakfast. He noticed her looking.

"It's called what can be roughly translated as food of life," he explained.

"Food of life?"

"Yeah, food of life. It's a highly enhanced and fortified extract of human blood. Blood is life, hence food of life." He looked into her eyes with a dead pan expression. "We still have the err, tools of the trade," he said as he opened his mouth displaying his fangs, "but it's no longer de rigueur to tear throats from living victims."

She was stunned at the matter of fact way he explained all this to her, like he was describing how to iron a shirt.

"Oh, I see, errm, okay." She hoped she didn't sound as taken aback as she was. She was just about to change the subject when he burst out laughing.

"Sorry I couldn't resist," he said between guffaws. "The look on your face, oh my god that's hilarious." He banged on the table as he laughed.

"You bastard," she yelled and went to smack him around the ear. He deftly avoided her strike and grabbed her wrist to avoid getting himself a black eye.

He was still laughing as he apologised. "Oh my god. I'm sorry, I'm sorry."

"I didn't know what to say." She was cross but saw the funny side and laughed with him. "How dare you, I'll get you back for that, just see if I don't."

He was still laughing but nodded. "Yeah I don't doubt that," he giggled. "You want some? It's just fruit extract and it's delicious, really."

After breakfast he told her that the data cube was finished being streamed and that a meeting was to be held to discuss its contents in thirty minutes. He also said he had a surprise in store for her, something that would be of great interest to her but he wouldn't be drawn as to what it was. They made their way to the obs room to find Lomas, Toma, Doctor Jam and a few others waiting for them.

"Good morning my dear," Lomas smiled. "I hope you are well rested and ready for another day. We're all waiting eagerly to see what Vincent has given us in this little cube." He smiled at her like a father.

"Yes thank you," she lied, deciding not to tell him about the nightmares just yet. "I'm ready for anything."

"Good good, okay Byron what do you have for us? The floor is yours." Byron went over to a low table upon which was a box about a foot square. He touched a few places and lights appeared all over it. From the top streamed an eerie white light which fanned out into a spray about three feet wide in the air above it. A few beeps and then they could clearly see people moving about and talking within this fan of white light. Farra was amazed.

"Wow that's incredible," she said aloud. Byron explained to her that what she was seeing was a holographic video stream. Effectively a 3D moving video of everything the tiny camera on Vincent's shirt button saw. It looked solid from any direction you looked at it. "My god," was all she could think of to say. The Drycenians looked at each other and smiled. They watched as a door opened and the camera entered a small room. A man was seated behind a desk and was talking to another who stood against the far wall. The talking stopped as the camera entered and the man behind the desk looked up.

"Three days from now, that was the agreement. Ahh Domenico, good, come in. Here are some new work order rotations for your team. Distribute them to your boys and work the new hours okay?" The camera gave a good shot of the whole interior of the room and everyone could plainly see everything that was going on. Another voice could be heard; one that did not sync with either of the two men in the shot.

"New rotations Sir? We've only just had new ones two days ago. We're up for our seventy two hour break tomorrow." That voice was like velvet, soft and slow and so deep Farra thought she could fall into it and drown.

"That must be Vincent talking," she said to her friends who all nodded in agreement.

"Never mind that," the man behind the desk barked. "Things have changed now. You and your team are to work these new rotations, no arguments. That'll be all Domenico." The man behind the desk turned to face his companion who hadn't spoken throughout this short exchange. He reached behind him for a small package. The other man came over to the desk and reached for it but as he took it, he looked at the camera suspiciously. The man behind the desk looked round and shouted at Vincent. "That will be all Domenico." The clip ended.

There were two hundred clips of film, all showing people meeting together, packages being handed over and after the first forty or so clips, stacks of money being packed up and handed over. One clip showed a group of five men studying a big chart on the wall which the camera showed to be a map of the mine complex. The men were concentrating on one area in particular and discussing storing something there.

"My god, that's where I was held. They must be discussing me or where they were planning to keep me," Toma exclaimed.

Throughout all the clips the friends watched so far, the same faces and names kept coming up. The man who sat behind the desk in that first clip turned out to be McGreedle. The quiet shady character who took that first package from him was identified in later clips as the SB Rep who was known as Bullet. This guy would often make references to someone whom he called The Boss, but this person was not yet identifiable. There then followed a clip showing what was obviously Vincent walking through the mine complex. No voices could be heard so the friends assumed he was alone. Along tunnels and down companionways he went until he came to a door in the wall that Farra recognised as part of what was called the bunkhouse by the workers. It was an area of the complex made into rooms where the workers lived during their five week rotational shift patterns. Three men shared a room. Each door had a two number code to identify it. This one was 4-27 which meant level 4 room 27. A hand reached out and knocked on the door, Vincent's hand. No answer. Another louder knock.

"Bobby. McGreedle wants you and the team up in the office right away," Vincent called out as he continued knocking. "Bobby. Bobby c'mon guys wake up." The hand reached down and opened the door, which swung open to reveal a scene of carnage. The three occupants of room 4-27 had been shot from point blank range and all three had holes in their chests that you could pass a fist through.

"Oh shit, shit," Vincent's voice, the shock clearly evident.

"My god," Farra and her companions all exclaimed together. They were sickened at the scene the camera was revealing to them but at the same time they were transfixed by it. Vincent walked over to the first body and reached out to touch something. What looked like an oily residue was crusted around the wound in his chest. The hand lifted up and the friends could hear sniffing.

"Trileneum?" they heard him announce with astonishment.

"Trileneum? Oh my," Farra said and looked at her friends.

Trileneum is a substance that is formed when a weapon called a Hellfire Pulse Laser Cannon is used against living flesh. It doesn't use physical bullets but uses a type of high energy pulse and creates that oily, crusty residue which smells very distinct. There's nothing else that smells like that and there's no other weapon that does that. The group of friends now knew without a doubt where that weapon came from.

"You know what this means don't you?" she said in shock.

Lomas looked sadly down at his hands before speaking. "Yes, the Transmortals," he said with a sigh.

She was confused now. This new development complicated matters and she wasn't sure what to make of it. Everything seemed simple up until now. She was to rescue Toma, find the book and data cube, find Donaldson, give him the package, get to Lilea and then, well then Leon would give her more instructions as to what she should do when she got there. Now this. A Transmortal weapon was now in the picture. How did this change things? She shook her head to clear the fuzz.

"So, what does this thing mean? Does it change anything and if so, how? I'm confused now," she said.

"It means that the Transmortals must've been involved right from the start," Lomas said, "and that the take over plot involved them, that Toma's abduction involved them, that Vincent's frame up involved them, the secret meetings, money changing hands, everything Vincent saw and which he's given to us in this little cube and the book. They must be at the bottom and the heart of it all," he explained.

"So," she continued, "it wasn't just a take over plot by a crazy man, it was something more than that? It was a plot involving the Transmortals somehow?"

"Yes," everyone chorused.

"And it would follow that the Transmortals are still involved, wouldn't it?"

"Yes," another chorus.

"But I thought the Transmortals were so powerful that they could just wade in and blow everything to hell as and when they liked. Why would they need to be so, so furtive about it?" she asked.

"Why indeed?" Lomas agreed.

"If they were involved it's no wonder they sent Vincent to Cryo Stasis," said Byron sadly. "They'd want to make absolutely sure he couldn't reveal anything. What I can't understand is why they didn't just kill him. Why put him in Cryo Stasis where there is always a slim chance he'd escape and reveal all?"

"He did escape," she said. "Leon told me he escaped and survived and still survives today."

"This means he's now in danger from them too then," Doctor Jam said. "Once they know he's up and around, they'll try to get to him and deal with him. It would be a shame to let that happen after what he's given us here, wouldn't it?" he looked around at his Drycenian companions who all nodded their agreement.

Lomas looked up, a decision having been made. "Then we will need to find him and keep him safe until this is dealt with, it's the least we can do." There were nods of agreement all around and Farra decided that now was an appropriate time to tell them more of what Leon told her.

"Leon told me that while I'm getting the book and cube to Donaldson, you must go and find Vincent as he needs to be present to get cleared of the crimes he didn't commit. Is that okay with you? Are you okay with being involved?" she asked them.

Lomas didn't think for long. "Yes it is and we are. When you find Donaldson and give him the book and this cube, tell him it not only involves the Transmortals and the take over plot he has so desperately wanted to deal with for years, but that it involves clearing the name of Vincent and removing the stain from his record."

The friends spent three more hours going through the rest of the data on the cube. Clips of meetings, conversations about money, references made to hide the package deep in the tunnel complex and scenes of men studying maps and charts. There were also still photographs of documents, work order rotations, accounts, charts and maps. Vincent became so trusted that he was able to access the little room on his own and took full advantage of those opportunities. These documents showed that McGreedle and his party planned to capture Toma and hide him deep inside the mine tunnels, that they changed the work order rotations so that only those they felt trustworthy would be around to see what was going on, that vast sums of money was changing hands and that the Moxal 3 Mining Corporation served as a kind of laundering centre for all of this stolen money. There were also forged galactic passports and personal documentation for McGreedle and five of his closest cohorts. There were many references to this Boss whoever he was but no mention of his real name or his whereabouts was ever forthcoming. At the end of the data string two last video clips remained to be seen. The first of these showed Vincent running along a tunnel with the sound of alarms ringing everywhere. When he rounded a corner he found himself in a blind ended tunnel with another two dead bodies at his feet. The same fist sized hole in the chest, the same oily, crusty residue, the same smell as before.

"Oh shit," Vincent could be heard exclaiming loudly to himself. Then more running along tunnels and up stairwells until he could be seen entering a room in the residential zone, number 1-8 clearly visible on the door. There was just time to see the door open and Vincent enter into a smallish room with just one bed before the camera shut off. In the last clip Vincent was obviously standing in a tunnel. A pair of hands came into view, Vincent's hands Farra supposed. Large hands, soft but precise fingers that held onto a small book that Farra recognised as his own notebook. A hand disappeared from view only to return a few seconds later with a small gadget. The other hand came up to the camera and suddenly everything started to shake wildly. Vincent had removed the camera button from his shirt and for a fraction of a second she saw him before the view changed.

"Oh my, Vincent, now I know you better," she murmured to herself as she fixed that image into her mind. The large expressive eyes that shone with insight and intelligence and even a tiny speck of fear bored into her mind. Help me, those eyes were saying to her. He was tall, well over six feet and very broad across. With massive shoulders and arms like tree trunks he was impressive sight to say the least. Then voices could be heard.

"It's all here," Vincent was saying. "The people, the meetings, the money, the documents, conversations and the bodies, all here. You're the man to understand it, here take it." There was a pause before another voice could be heard.

"Okay I'll take it Vincent, but there's not really anything that I can do about these claims of yours."

"Just watch the clips and read the notebook, it's all there. Something is going down in this place and I don't think I'm gonna be around long enough to get to the bottom of it, but you can. C'mon Donaldson you've always been fair to me, what's the problem here?" Vincent sounded irritated now. So he was talking to Donaldson, trying to get him to take the evidence and do something about it but he didn't seem too keen to be involved. Farra and her companions were all wondering how much he knew before Vincent's revelations came to him.

"You don't understand my position Vincent; you're not the only one who needs to take care here. Just because I'm in a position of some trust here doesn't mean I can fix everything that goes wrong. It's difficult and dangerous."

"For gods' sake Donaldson what the fuck is happening here? You're gonna sit on your ass while whatever is going down, just goes on all around you and you'll just close your eyes and carrying on with your filing? I'm the one they think murdered those guys. I'm being set up and you know it." Vincent was clearly angry now, that deep velvet voice had a distinct and unmistakable edge. Only the foolhardy would push much further.

Donaldson gave a resigned sigh. "Okay okay I'll take your evidence but I can't promise that I'll be able to do much. Here, give it to me. Now you never saw me, okay?" The sound clicked off and the data stream closed. For a few seconds nobody spoke.

Lomas voiced what they were all thinking. "That must've been just before he was taken into Cryo Stasis for the murders. We may be amongst the last to have seen him before that happened. He must've felt very alone. I don't know about anyone else but I'm going to make damn sure I do my best to clear his name." He looked around the room and everyone nodded in agreement.

Farra now felt as though she was really beginning to get to know Vincent Domenico. He was a hell of good looking man, damn was he fit! She thought of his eyes that so briefly looked into hers on the last video clip. My god she could fall right into his eyes and never be seen again, she thought to herself. She felt a surge of compassion as she thought of the position he found himself in and how he must have felt knowing that by trying to do right, he'd been set up as a murderer and would possibly pay with his life for something he didn't do. Parentless, friendless, homeless and rootless and still struggling with the voices in the dreams and thinking he was going crazy and now possibly going to be executed. She wanted to cry for him.

A voice cut into her meditations and brought her back to reality. It was Byron. "Remember I told you I had a surprise for you?"

CHAPTER SIX

He crept closer, eyes never leaving his quarry. He trod with care so as not to make a sound that would scare the creature away and lose him his meal. Over the past five years he became expert at this and he bided his time. There's no reason to rush things; take your time and wait for the right moment and you'll do it right first time. When he was sure he could get no closer without alerting the shy creature, he raised his blade. He closed one eye and made sure his aim was right on target and then with one swift practised movement the blade flew silently through the air and sank into the creature's heart. He walked over and crouched over the dying creature, looked down at it and placed a hand gently on its flank.

"Thank you for your life that gives me sustenance," Vincent said as he withdrew his blade from the now dead creature, scooped him up and carried him away. He always made sure he took only the old and weak when he hunted for his food. He enjoyed a special connection with animals and often felt more like one of them than he did a human being. He admired the simplicity of their existence; eat, sleep, keep warm. No fuss, no hate and no deceit. With animals you know where you stand. He always trusted them and they usually seemed to respond to him without fear.

The small cave entrance was well hidden in the cliff wall but as always, he stopped some distance off and took a little time to sit and watch, just in case. He took out his scope to check out the cave entrance and only when he felt sure there were no uninvited visitors lurking around, he got up and went in to prepare his meal. With expert precision he gutted, skinned and quartered the animal ready for cooking. He took the entrails out a little way away and left them for the wild creatures that roamed around these parts. He believed in sharing his good fortune with his animal brothers and sisters and they repaid him by alerting him if anything strange was around. He got to know their calls and cries and could now recognise a bark of fear or a growl of warning easily and never ignored them. Back at the cave he spread out the hide and started to scrape it clean. He could use the skin to make some new garments for himself; nothing was ever wasted. He was no tailor but he got by. When he escaped the Cryo Stasis facility he made a point of getting his belongings from the admin block. He wanted his own clothes and his blades back. Those coveralls they made him wear at the facility wouldn't last five minutes out here. He patched up his pants a few times over the seat and the knees and the elbows of his shirt but he was hoping to make himself a new one out of the hides of this particular creature whose leather was the softest he'd encountered since coming to this planet. With this latest piece, he reckoned he would have enough to make a new over shirt which would be more hard wearing and would be warmer in the winter months. If it was successful, he might even try to make a new pair of pants. But first things first, he was hungry and his thoughts turned to food.

A couple of hours later he ate a very acceptable meal of roasted meat and some edible roots he dug up. He knew what plant foods were safe to eat by studying the indigenous human life that lived on this planet. They knew nothing of his existence however but he got to know their ways very well over the time he'd been their secret neighbour. When he first came here and saw these humans he toyed with the idea of joining them and living amongst them but after a few weeks of secretly observing them he decided that would not be an ideal situation for him. They were very primitive humans and were a bit too unpredictable for his liking. They seemed peaceful enough most of the time but could suddenly become enraged for no obvious reason he could see. They were also very territorial and would have spats and fights with other groups of their own kind who strayed too near their boundaries. The winter before last, the one that Vincent always thought of as their leader passed away and there was much posturing and promenading from the other males who all thought they were the ideal candidate to take over his role.

He would never forget what happened next and would always thank his instincts for telling him to remain invisible. One afternoon everything came to a head and a fight broke out amongst the two leading contenders. It started with a bit of pushing and shoving but quickly escalated into a full blown wrestling match. The bigger of the two got his opponent on the ground and sat on him. He clenched both hands together into a club and raised his arms above him only to bring it crashing down onto the man's skull killing him quickly. Even though Vincent watched the proceedings from a safe distance through his scope he reckoned he could hear the thud and the squelch as the guy's head caved in. It wasn't so much the killing that shocked him, it was what happened afterwards that chilled him. The victor wrenched open his dead opponent's skull, reached in and scooped out some of the brain matter. Then he stood up and holding his prize high above his head he opened his mouth wide, displaying a fearsome pair of long fangs and roared so loud he really did hear it. Then he stuffed the steaming mush into his mouth and chewed. This sight sickened Vincent and he vomited all down his shirt front. He ran back to his cave stopping twice more on the way to bring up more of his insides.

"My god," he kept saying to himself. "My god he ate the guy's brains."

He kept well out of their way after that but still observed them enough to know what they were up to and to learn what he could eat and what he couldn't. He discovered for instance that there was a type of fish on this planet that was deadly poisonous. He saw a group of their kids playing by a small pond one day. They were playing at fishing and he supposed that such games helped them learn the survival skills they need when they grow up and need to provide for their group. They all lay down on their stomachs and sank their arms into the still water. Every so often one or another would suddenly turn on his back, his arms flying out of the water grasping a still flailing fish triumphantly in the air. They ate the fish raw right there by the pond and threw the inedible bits back into the water to feed whatever else lurked down there in the depths. One little kid caught a weird looking fish one day; one that Vincent had never seen before. It was big and brightly coloured with long dangling tail fins. All but one of them ate that fish and from the looks on their faces, thoroughly enjoyed it.

A day later he was out hunting when he heard cries off in the distance. It sounded like people wailing. He went towards the sound and used his scope to observe what the fuss was all about. He saw a group of the humans building a huge bonfire. A group of females were standing a little way off, wailing and beating their breasts with their own fists. One of the males turned and signalled to the others and from amongst the group he saw five of the males walk out towards the pile of wood, each carrying the body of a small child. The one small boy who had not eaten the fish the day before, stood there sombre hand in hand with his mother. The men stood over that fire all through the night, feeding the flames with more wood until the small bodies had been reduced to ash. A hole was dug and the entire remains of the fire was carefully scraped into it and covered over. When this was done, five women came over and placed small stones and rocks in the shape of five fishes as a kind of grave marker, each with long dangling tail fins. Vincent decided he never wanted to eat fish ever again.

The indigenous humans used spears for hunting. Some were small and thin and were used for throwing, others were longer and thicker and were used for jabbing at close quarters. Vincent found one of the small thin spears once at the base of a tree. The thrower had obviously missed his target and not been able to find it again. It was a rare find as they always retrieved these objects. He often wondered why, when they were easy enough to make. He'd seen them being made and each one only took an hour or so. It wasn't until he found this one he began to understand why they didn't like to lose them. The spear itself was about a metre long and made of strong but pliable wood from the tender branches of a tree that was plentiful everywhere he'd been on this planet. The wood was pale in colour and as smooth as glass but it was the sharpened tip that interested him. It was dark brown in colour and he could see from the way the light reflected off it, that it was covered in something sticky. He was careful not to touch the substance but he took a tentative sniff only to find that it was completely odourless. He guessed right away that it was a poison of some kind and he decided that it would be in his interest to find out where this poison came from, just in case.

It was a couple of weeks later that he found out the secret of the poison. There was another band of humans roaming nearby for a few days and the local group finally decided that enough was enough; it was time to go out and meet them with a show of force to send them away and he decided to tag along and watch the proceedings. The journey to meet the invading group of humans took them through a stand of big trees with long thick trunks several metres in circumference. The trunks of these trees had no branches at all until way up at the top where they spread out and intermingled with their neighbours to create a continuous green canopy overhead in which birds called and creatures lived. The men in the group looked up amongst the treetops as if they were looking for something in particular. A call from one of them and a pointing finger indicated they'd found it. One of the men, a small wiry man stepped forward and taking a long strap of thick hide that he'd been carrying over his shoulder, he deftly threw one end around the trunk of the tree and caught it as it came back around at him. He then knotted the two ends together and stepped into this loop. Resting his backside against this looped leather strap, he used it to shuffle his way up the tall straight tree trunk. By leaning out backwards with his feet at forty five degree angles he was able to climb the tree with seemingly little effort. Vincent was impressed and decided that one day he'd try it for himself. The man climbed two thirds of the way up the tree before stopping. From where Vincent was hiding he couldn't see what he was doing up there but through his scope it looked like the man was trying to cut something out of the tree trunk with a sliver of sharpened animal bone. After a few minutes of struggling, the man suddenly waved a hand down to his companions and dropped something down to them and then climbed down from the tree by the same method he used to climb up.

The group of men scouted around and got one biggish rock and one smaller one. They put the thing on the bigger rock and used the smaller one to crush it to a mush. Whilst this was happening, another man was making a fire nearby. Once the object had been crushed and pulped, they put it on a smooth stone that they carried with them. It had a small scoop in the centre, into which they carefully put the crushed up mush from the thing on the tree. One of the men then took another sharpened bone and made a small cut in his hand and held it up so that his blood dripped into and mixed with the mush. They put this rock onto the fire for what Vincent calculated to be around fifteen minutes or so before taking it off and using it to coat the tips of their spears. Vincent was amazed at what he was seeing and he made a decision that he would return and get some of those things from the trees for himself. It was always useful to have an assortment of weaponry at one's disposal in a hostile environment and there may come a time when an effective poison is just the right thing.

Later that same day when the group encountered their invading neighbours and decided to engage them the newly coated spears were used. Vincent was surprised to see that the spears didn't kill but just punctured the skin or cut it open. His local group didn't seem bothered and after the invading group were scared off, he decided to follow them instead of his usual neighbours. He wanted to see what happened next and why the poison didn't work. Over the next three days he camped out nearby and watched through his scope for hours at a time. The first thing he noticed was on the first day after the encounter he saw one man he recognised and he looked a bit under the weather and was sweating heavily. There was a slight oily sheen all over his body as if he'd been working out for hours. During the course of that first day he saw all the men he recognised and all displayed that same sweaty sheen on their bodies. Other than that they seemed ok and behaved normally. They interacted with each other, played with their kids, hugged their women and often had occasion to make physical contact with each other, sometimes just a slight brush as they passed one another by. On the second day all of the men from the fight looked decidedly ill, with pale grey complexions and a deep throaty cough. One young man was being comforted by his wife who wiped his brow with her hand, kissed him and kept physical contact with him for hours. The third day the young man was dead and the young wife displayed the oily sheen on her skin. After a week the whole group were dead and Vincent learned all he needed to know about the poison. It worked not by killing quickly as most poisons do, but slowly and by making its host poisonous so that everyone with whom they came into physical contact would also be poisoned. If he'd ever regretted not interacting with these humans before, he didn't any longer. He was yet to realise just how important a discovery this substance was to be.

It was getting late and the sun was setting over the distant mountains. Vincent loved to sit and watch the view on such evenings as this. Tonight though he felt a slight melancholy deep inside somewhere and sighed to himself; irritated by this feeling. He hated this; he knew what was to come and it depressed him. It made him feel like a weakling to be depressed. His mind suddenly filled with images he never saw in any waking moment of his life. As he looked through the cave entrance to the setting sun he suddenly saw a different landscape in his mind. This new landscape was filled with the same orange glow but it didn't come from a sunset but from fires that were destroying everything in their path. Buildings burned, people ran screaming from an unseen enemy and everywhere there were white trees that swayed sadly in the evening breeze. He felt the urge to run, but from what he didn't know. Then all at once there was silence save for the mournful sound of a woman crying into the night air. Terror gripped him as the images took over his consciousness and as he had learned, giving in to them made them end quicker. As the woman's cries became screams they were suddenly joined by that of a baby. The woman's cries stopped abruptly, a life ended bringing forth a new one. He walked towards the sounds feeling the need to hurry and as he came upon the scene that was now so familiar he saw her body.

She was beautiful and strangely familiar but he couldn't quite find the memory of how he knew her or where from. Her knees were drawn up and her garments soaked in blood, both her own and that of the birth that had just taken place. Between her thighs lay the screaming newborn, a large boy still connected to her by a pulsating cord. He looked at the baby and felt a strange sense of connection that he couldn't even begin to explain or understand. As he looked he became aware that he wasn't alone; a huge black mist was also drawn to the child. Vincent was stricken with terror as he watched the black mist approach but he was powerless to act or even run away into the night. The mist began to take a more solid form and he saw a huge man in a cape and cowl reach down and, taking hold of the child's ankles raised him aloft, slicing through the life giving cord which sprayed blood everywhere. The being held the child aloft while shouting something Vincent couldn't quite hear.

He screamed at the being to stop but his pleas were ignored. He tried to run at the man to rescue the child but he couldn't move. He was rooted to the spot, glued there by some invisible means that forced him to bear witness to this horrific scene. The being then put one large hand over the boy's face and smothered the life from him, then calmly threw the body into a midden and vanished into the night. Vincent screamed for the child and for his own inability to do anything to help and as always, he awoke from this nightmare sobbing for the child he didn't know but felt such a connection with. He curled up on the floor of his cave and wept at his loneliness as the sun set over the mountains.

He awoke in the middle of the night with a start and the sudden urgent knowledge that he wasn't alone. He leapt up from where he'd fallen asleep at the mouth of his cave in a foetal position after the waking nightmare of the evening before. His eyes felt swollen and his head ached but he shook himself awake and looked about him to find the source of this feeling of being observed. He melted into the wall and listened. He was proud of his sharp hearing and it served him well over the years. A slight noise from his right caught his attention and he strained all of his focus in that direction. The sound came again and this time he knew what it was; breathing. Someone or something was inside his cave and breathing at him in the dark. Oh how he wished he had his night goggles from Moxal 3 on right now.

Silently he reached down and slid the knife from its sheath at his hip and at that very moment something lunged at him. Instinctively he moved to the side and as he did so, the knife in his right hand entered the man's body and killed him, the poisoned spear in his hand falling to the floor. It all happened in such a rush, Vincent didn't mean to kill the man, he wouldn't have wanted to and now in the space of a couple of minutes he'd woken to find the home he'd made for himself invaded by a hostile with a poisoned spear that would definitely have killed him within three days. He suddenly felt very alone and far from home, but where was home? He had no idea but at that moment there was one thing he did know. Home wasn't here anymore. He'd have to move to another location and start over.

Within an hour he packed up all of his belongings and was on his way. He carried the body of the man up to the top of the cliff and dropped him over the edge so that if his fellows found him they'd assume he'd fallen and wouldn't realise that an alien human was among them and decide to come looking for him with those poisoned spears. As was his habit, he thanked the man for giving his life so that he could live before dropping the body over the cliff and he genuinely felt very sorry. He'd never killed anyone before except in the line of duty during his military service and it didn't feel good at all; after all he was the invader here and the guy was only defending what he saw as his own territory. If he moved briskly he should be able to make several miles before the sun came up so that if the group of humans did decide to follow, he'd have a good head start on them. He didn't think they would follow; he'd cover his tracks well enough but it was always best to be ready just in case.

He decided to move towards the mountains he'd spent the last five years watching at sunset and sunrise most days since his arrival on this planet. He made a remarkably accurate estimate that they were roughly a hundred miles away, give or take a few miles and he was confident he could reach the foothills in three days if no trouble befell him on the journey. He would do the walking in two shifts, from before dawn until mid morning, then from late afternoon until fully dark. That way he would avoid being out in the open during the greater part of the day when the local inhabitants were likely to be up and around. It also meant he could do the greater part of his sleeping during daylight hours and stay awake during darkness when there was the likelihood of more danger from predatory animals. During his time on the planet, he didn't encounter any predators that caused him any real worry for his safety. There was a type of wild dog like creature that roamed in packs of three or four, but they were timid creatures by nature and Vincent felt sure they'd not be brave enough to tackle anything as large as he was. He didn't allow himself to get complacent though and he was aware of the very real possibility that other, far more dangerous predators awaited him in other parts of the landscape.

As dawn broke on the third morning of his journey, Vincent noticed the change in the temperature. It was cooler here and he welcomed it. Where he'd set up home until just days ago, it was an almost tropical climate with hot sunshine and heavy downpours of rain. The winters were fairly cool but he'd never seen ice or snow here in all of his five year stay. He'd become so used to the heat that he now felt decidedly chilly. He'd reached the foothills of the mountains at last and found they weren't really mountains at all, more like very big hills and he felt sure he'd scale them easily in one days walk. He'd have to scale them too, he couldn't go around as they stretched off beyond the horizon in both directions and he was thankful that they turned out to be not as high as they seemed from all those miles back. He set up camp and decided to hunt for something to eat. He'd not eaten during his trek, deciding not to risk drawing attention to himself by lighting a fire to cook with so he went without and just drank from streams that snaked here and there all over the landscape. He learned that the only real way to tell if water was safe to drink was to see if other creatures drank there. If they did, then he'd have to trust that it was safe for him to do so. He had no other means to check for water safety so he had to take the risk. The water on this planet was a sort of earthy pink colour rather than the green or blue he'd seen on other planets and when he first arrived he thought maybe he was doomed to die of thirst or be poisoned by the water. As it turned out he found it tasted marvellous and never had any adverse effects on his health. He knew he'd been lucky and was aware that things could have turned out so much worse. He breakfasted on spit roasted meat that tasted like heaven after three days of fasting and relaxed him enough to make him decide to sleep for a few hours. He found the safest place he could and after sending out his thoughts for the nightmare to evade him, he settled down and was fast asleep within a few minutes.

"Vincent. Vincent." The voice came to him from far away as though carried on the morning mist from a time before the first dawn. "Vincent," louder now, closer. "Vincent, listen to me Vincent." A woman's voice; soft and friendly. He turned towards the sound and searched for its source but saw nothing but white mist. "I am with you Vincent. From the moment of your birth I have walked with you and will walk with you until you go to the land of the dead to join the ancestors." Such a soft voice, he felt as if someone were hugging him close and surrounding him with love. He reached for that voice with his mind; he wanted that enveloping love so much that it hurt. "Fear not brave one, you are not alone. I am with you as you meet your destiny; we are all with you, all the lost ones." The voice was so close it sounded like someone was right beside him, holding him close, safe. He'd never experienced feeling love before and this was overwhelming to him in its intensity.

"Who is it? Who are you? Where are you? I can't see you, please," he called out into the white mist, suddenly afraid of being alone again.

"Fear not brave one, the waiting is over now. The hand of destiny rests upon your shoulder. It is time to take up the sword and right the great wrong of our people."

"Destiny? what destiny? what people? what do I do? help me please," he pleaded.

"I am with you always Vincent, fear not. The fury of our nation will be your rock and your stay, as I promised at the moment of your rebirth. Trust Vincent, trust, trust." The voice faded with that one word repeating in his mind, trust, trust. He called out to the voice not to leave him but he was alone in the mist and he wept for the love he'd felt so briefly and lost. He awoke with the tears still fresh on his cheeks as the dream faded into the mist. He packed up, looked towards the mountains and set off towards whatever destiny awaited him.

The sun was getting low behind the mountain tops as he started upward. As he climbed he was aware for the first time of how beautiful this planet really was. Up until now his only concern was surviving and apart from the times he sat and watched the sunset and sunrise from the entrance to his cave, he never felt able to take the time to appreciate the planet's beauty on an emotional level. He looked back across the valley and could see the location that was his safe haven for the past five years. He stopped on the path and took a few minutes to look at it with real focus. He felt a little sad to be leaving the only place that offered him a home in order to run yet again. He wondered if he would have to run for the rest of his life. He hoped not but thought he probably would have to.

"Thank you," he said into the air. "Thank you for the safety, for the shelter." He turned away and continued to climb. The path he was walking took him up the side of the mountain in a gentle zig zag and as he climbed he was afforded the most wonderful view of this place that gave him refuge. He let his thoughts drift back to when he arrived here five years ago, scared and desperate, a runaway, an escaped convict innocent of the crimes he'd been accused of.

Vincent learned how to pilot during his time in the TCC. Tactical Combat personnel had no choice about it; they all learned to pilot and he loved it. He had a natural flair for it and gained his wings in record time. The dumpy little craft he managed to steal was just a tramper in its day to day life, but to Vincent it was a symbol of his liberty and freedom. After it landed on this planet and delivered him to relative safety, its engines died for the last time and he shed tears for it. He laid a hand on it and gave thanks before walking away. It took him four days walking to find the shelter of his cave and during that time he almost died of thirst and lost twenty pounds in weight due to not finding anything to eat. He had the misfortune to land in the middle of the only desert this planet offered and when he finally found the cave with abundant wildlife and plenty of water nearby, he thought he'd died and gone to heaven. From that moment on, the cave was the finest home he could wish for and he would never forget it. Now here he was five years later and he was on the move again. In one way he was sad. He found safety and was able to live reasonably well but being discovered by the inhabitants could only mean trouble for him and maybe even for them too. On the other hand being on the move again gave him something else to focus on, a new horizon to look for, new excitements perhaps. He didn't know but it felt good to have a new challenge again, he'd gotten soft.

"A new challenge will keep me sharp," he said as he strode purposefully forward.

CHAPTER SEVEN

"Come over here, look," Byron beckoned to Farra. She followed him over to a console. He flipped a switch and up popped what looked to her like a very high spec computer screen. To the left hand side was a small slot into which he slid a data chip. "Okay look at what I found," he announced with pride as he tapped out a couple of commands.

"Oh wow," she exclaimed as she found herself looking at Vincent's full work history, medical record, dismissal from duty report, crime report and sentencing decree. There was also a report on his escape from Cryo Stasis with a psyche evaluation chart. She was impressed. "My god, well done Byron, thank you," she clapped him on the shoulder and he smiled.

"No problem."

The earliest entry was an education report from a military training camp pre entry exam.

Subject – Vincent R Domenico. Gender – male. Age – 17 years 3 months. Race – Lilean.

Education history – home schooled. No official education records found.

Further relevant details – subject can only read/write the Lilean language. Entry exam translated into Lilean for this subject.

Results – Subject has an excellent grasp of mathematics and is able to perform mental calculations quickly. Shows an excellent aptitude for engineering skills and seems to possess a natural understanding of mechanics. Has an excellent memory and performed well in all memory tests. Seems to possess a natural in-built compass. During the survival testing, the subject seemed to know instinctively how to reach his intended destination. Officers attempted to get him lost to see how he would cope but they failed in every attempt to do so. Showed highly developed skills in the use of blades of all kinds and admitted to preferring them to other weaponry. He did however, show acceptable level of ability when tested with a range of other weaponry including handguns, TM 14's, laser launchers and other standard issue military hardware. Subject was quiet and observant, spoke only when addressed directly and followed orders promptly. The examination panel feels this subject would be acceptable for entry and recommends acceptance.

She scrolled to the next screen and found a medical examination report from the same military training body pre entry course.

Subject – Vincent R Domenico – Medical Report – Pre Entry.

Height – 6 feet 5 inches. Weight - 257 lbs. Race – Lilean. Eyes – black. Hair – black (subject shaves his head).

Known Medical History – subject reports no major health issues other than Lilean Flu at the age of six years.

Blood workup revealed the subject to be pure blooded Lilean with typical extra DNA segments that would be expected. Subject adopted at birth during the time of the Lilean tragedy and smuggled out to the Mexalon system planet 6 along with other Lilean survivors.

Distinguishing marks – subject has the expected Lilean star shaped scar over the sternum. As with all Lileans, wounds heal without scarring so no other scars are in evidence. Subject has the expected Lilean Form Hydroxylapatite/Supercollagen alloy bone structure. EEG shows subject has the typical Lilean thalamus, giving him a greater ability to withstand pain and although the subject denies it, he will probably also have the heightened states of consciousness typical of the advanced nature of the Lilean thalamus.

Strength test results – hand grip average – 75psi.

Femur loading capacity – magnographic analysis shows projected capability of 32,000psi.

Upper Body Strength – subject displayed average 1000 lbs capability during 20 minute upper body test.

Analysis – Subject is a typical healthy Lilean specimen with typically large upper body and associated strength and endurance capabilities.   As with all Lileans, this subject is suitable for endurance rather than speed.

Blood group – Lilean group 4 sub type B with normal Lilean blood iron levels.

Urinalysis Report – Healthy.

Recommendation – acceptance.

"Jeez this guy is built," she said as she scrolled to the next screen to find Vincent's military record. It consisted of the usual stuff, similar to what would probably be on her own record. Details of training, achievements, exercises, courses attended etc as well as several notifications for bravery and a report of his being awarded a medal for valour in the face of extreme hostility during a campaign on Regnor Prime. She was surprised to find there were several entries under the heading disciplinary actions. She didn't expect there to be any at all; he seemed like the perfect soldier so far. As she read on, it became clear that Vincent began to find the overbearing nature of his superior officers a little hard to handle. He was a model soldier until he reached his late twenties when he started questioning authority. One report told how, after being ordered to retreat to safety leaving three of his injured team mates to die in the field, he took it upon himself to return alone and rescue them. He got them back to safety but two were dead and he got a disciplinary for his trouble. He argued with his superior officers and she surmised that he probably lost all confidence in them after that. At the end of his third five year term, it was recommended that he retire from military service. She understood immediately what that meant. It means they told him either he leave quietly or he gets his ass kicked out the door dishonourably.

The next screen showed that after resigning the military, he signed up for cleaning duties with the Moxal 3 Mining Corporation. This time there were no medical tests or entry exams, he just signed up and got to work.

"Well that hasn't changed," she said to herself as she remembered her own very similar experience when she joined the company. There followed a list that verified what she saw in Vincent's little book; just a list of his changes in grade and assignment as he got himself promoted over time. She noticed there weren't any medical records nor any routine evaluations recorded. It was just the same list as in the little notebook. After working his way up he applied and was accepted to the Tactical Combat Centre, which is Moxal 3's extra training facility based on its moon. It is here that those cleaners wishing to become Rangers get the chance to show they possess the capabilities for the job. They get trained in advanced weaponry and solo combat skills so if the team they are responsible for gets killed by the Uvees leaving them alone, they are able to deal with them and get out to safety alive. Vincent's TCC record was as short and succinct as his Moxal 3 one was.

Moxal 3 Tactical Combat Centre – Training Record for Vincent R Domenico. Cleaner grade 4.

Weapon training – passed – 95% - issued with SB17.

Solo Engagement and Combat – passed – 98%.

Team Handling & Organisation – passed – 75%.

Flight Training - passed - 93%.

Passed – honours – promoted Head of Dept, Security Enforcement.

Assigned – Moxal 3 Mine.

Farra noted with some interest Vincent's percentage in his team handling was much lower than his other training grades.

"Not a people person then Vincent?" she mused. The next thing that came up was a document showing Vincent's new position as Head of Dept, Security Enforcement. It consisted of a simple statement of his new position, the salary and conditions and his signature and date. She scrolled again and the next screen showed another very basic report on his dismissal from employment.

Report of summary dismissal from employment – Moxal 3 Mining Corporation.

Employee Name – Vincent R Domenico, Security Enforcement Head of Dept.

Reason for action – conviction for murder & incarceration in Cryo Stasis.

The document was signed by McGreedle, dated and stamped with the company logo. Official and cold. No statement of what a good and honourable employee he was, no mention of his trustworthiness or loyalty, nothing.

"Phew," she said, "cold hearted bastards." She wondered how he felt at the time, being treated in such a cold and official way. The next document detailed his arrest, conviction and laid out his sentence. Again it was without preamble or sentiment. Simple and straight to the point.

Report of Arrest – Inter Galactic Law Enforcement – Agency 232a.

Prisoner name – Vincent Richard Domenico. Age – 37 years 8 months. Race – Lilean.

Reason for Arrest – multiple murders within confines of Moxal 3 Mining Corporation. Five victims (Robert Fleming, Davey Wexton, Brad Distenza, Grover Hartley, Stephanie Lyneman).

Witness details – Ranger Tomas Dolton, Facility Warden McGreedle.

Evidence processed – Hellfire Pulse Laser Canon. Accused's DNA was found on aforementioned weapon. 2 x witness statements detailing accused threatening 2 of aforementioned victims on multiple occasions. 2 x witness statements detailing seeing accused running from scenes of crimes in possession of aforementioned weapon.

"That's a crock of shit?" she yelled at the screen. "A gun with DNA on it and the say so of two other employees? For fucks' sake anyone can get your DNA. You have to give a sample when you take any job or travel anywhere off world. Jesus." She looked up to find Byron looking at her.

"You okay Farra?" he asked, concerned. "You want a drink or something?"

"Sorry, I'm fine. It's just so ridiculous. Anyone with half a brain can see the holes in that." She looked at him and felt impotent to do anything about it.

"I know, and we do know it was a frame up, a concoction. We know that, we just have to get it to Donaldson so that he can know it too."

"Yeah, let's hope he's more approachable this time than when Vincent went to him for help." She turned back to the screen and finished reading the document.

Trial summary – Witnesses took the stand & gave their evidence succinctly and without hesitation. Both displayed evidence of integrity and honesty. No cross examination was requested.

Jury reached unanimous verdict – Guilty on all counts. Accused retained in custody for sentencing.

Due to the nature of the accused and the very real possibility of his attempting to escape custody, sentencing to be brought forward by emergency review board. Sentencing will be heard in 24 hours.

"My god," Farra couldn't believe what she was reading. "Accused, judged and sentenced all in 24 hours." She looked at Byron.

"Yeah I know, I thought that part would interest you," he remarked. The document continued with the notification of sentence and it was as without warmth as the rest of it had been.

Emergency Review Board – Agency 232a – Sentencing Panel.

Accused – Vincent Richard Domenico.

Crime of which convicted – Multiple (5) Murder.

The Emergency Review Board, having been convened to pass sentence on the aforementioned accused, Vincent Richard Domenico, hereby decrees that he shall forthwith, be taken by the most appropriate means and be given over for incarceration in Cryo Stasis.

Sentence length – indefinite.

"Indefinite? Shit," Byron was looking over her shoulder. "I didn't read that far down earlier. My god, indefinite?" He was as amazed as Farra was and they both exchanged glances and exclamations. She scrolled to the next page.

Cryo Stasis Confinement Facility – Intake Report number 730257291-12/32D
Prisoner – 730257291-12/32D Vincent Richard Domenico.
Age at Intake – 37 years 8 months.
Race – Lilean.
Sentence – Indefinite Confinement.
Pre Confinement Psyche Evaluation Report.
Prisoner continuously asserts his innocence despite evidence and witness statements proving guilt. Refused to make eye contact throughout interview and was obstructive when questioned about his background/childhood/upbringing. Displayed a tendency to use distraction techniques to avoid answering direct questions and often replied in riddles. This prisoner has a tendency to use role reversal techniques during questioning in an attempt to gain dominance. Expertly switched roles during the interview on several occasions whereupon the Psychiatrist found himself the one being questioned. Continuously refuses to accept guilt. It is the opinion of the interviewing Psychiatrist that Prisoner 730257291-12/32D is suffering from delusional psychosis and paranoia. There are no apparent conditions that would deem cryo stasis unsuitable in this case.
Recommendation – Immediate confinement.
It was signed by a Doctor Robert James Mordlingham.
"Delusional Psychosis? What does that mean?" Farra asked.
"It means that the patient has delusions," Doctor Jam answered. "Strange beliefs that aren't true but which he believes in completely. The fact that Vincent kept asserting his innocence together with his err, slight lack of social and interpersonal skills made the diagnosis somewhat inevitable I'm afraid." He looked at her apologetically and she sighed sadly. She had to admit it; Vincent didn't do himself any favours that day.

The last document Byron found was an Inter Galactic Law Enforcement Memo concerning the Cryo Stasis Facility and Vincent's escape.

The Cryo Stasis Confinement Facility was based on an uninhabited moon of the Steran System. This location was chosen due to its lack of inhabited planets in the system itself. The Steran System has 2 suns so the facility used solar energy as its power source. A system of back up generators was put in place which was continuously topped up itself by solar energy so that when the moon entered its regular three yearly eclipses the system didn't grind to a halt and unfreeze all the inmates. Every six months a team was sent to check and test the whole system and it was during one such visit that a rookie technician made a fatal mistake and caused a small explosion which burned out the main back up system generators. Unfortunately for them, the technical team's only pilot was badly burned in the explosion and was unable to fly them out of the facility in order to obtain spare parts from the storage facility on Steran 7's second moon. One of the facility's own pilots was brought in as an emergency but he was unaccustomed to the controls on the technical team's ship and crashed it on take off, killing himself and two of the engineers. Another of the facility's employees was brought in to make the journey in one of the facility's own ships, which took off without trouble. During the three day round trip, the Steran system's primary sun gave off a gigantic solar flare that caused permanent and irreparable damage to the facility's solar energy cells, which stopped operating. Due to there being no back up system working at the time, a meltdown occurred.

The occupants of the facility were kept in underground bunkers, layered in 17 underground levels, each level holding 20,000 inmates in coffin sized cells. The cryo system worked from the deepest level up, so that in effect the cells at the lower levels got frozen first and the higher levels last. The whole system had to work harder to pump to the higher levels, than it did to the lower levels. When the system failed, it was the higher levels that thawed out first. As inmates began to regain consciousness and break out of their cryo cells, the facility staff became overwhelmed and unable to contain thousands of rapidly awakening murderers, violent psychotics and other assorted dangerous prisoners. The effects of Cryo Stasis take a while to wear off and for the first hour or so after thawing, most prisoners are very disorientated. This gave the facility staff a valuable window of opportunity in which to escape in their last remaining ship before their prisoners gained their senses and became dangerous. As they made their way to the hangar to abandon the facility and the moon, they found an escaping prisoner already boarding the craft and preparing to take off. They failed to get to the craft before the prisoner escaped and were stranded on the facility. In the ensuing riot, all the facility staff were murdered by the awakened inmates.

Once control was restored by an emergency team one month later, it was discovered that the Cryo Stasis procedure used by the facility was not as safe as it was thought to be. Many of the inmates were found dead in their cryo cells and forensic analysis showed they died during the cryo freezing procedure and had effectively been executed by freezing to death. Security film footage of the riot showed the escaping prisoner who was easily identified by the prisoner ID number printed across the back of his overalls. The identification was confirmed later by digital comparison of the video film footage and the prisoner's intake ID photograph. It was Vincent Richard Domenico. He became a wanted man across the whole galaxy and gained himself the legendary status of being the only man to escape the Cryo Stasis Facility.

At the bottom of the report were 2 photographs, one of which was Vincent's intake ID photo and the other was an image taken from the security footage. It was clearly him in both shots, no doubt. Farra looked at the photograph and tried to get a handle on the man. Those large black eyes that looked so defiant but at the same time seemed to shout "help me" bored into her soul. She had to admit, bald looked good on Vincent. She'd never given much thought to whether she liked baldness in a man or not, but she knew now that this guy suited bald completely. He had quite full lips that looked fairly feminine and were almost a perfect cupid's bow, if quite a large one. She was entranced by those lips. Wow, she thought to herself, those lips are just aching to kiss me.

"Byron, I don't suppose you have the security footage as well do you?" she smiled sweetly.

"Well, as a matter of fact I do, here." He tapped on the console and up came thirty seconds of grainy video footage showing the Cryo Stasis Facility hangar containing just the one ship. It was late afternoon and the shadows were long making it difficult to make out everything in the shot. It was a static camera but it gave a fairly wide field of view of ninety percent of the hangar area and part of the connecting passageway from the main facility administration block. This passageway was a simple covered walkway, just a roof held up by stone piers every thirty yards or so. After ten seconds of nothing, there appeared a running figure coming down the walkway. A very big man clothed in the standard issue inmates coveralls. He was bald headed and carried a holdall in his left hand. Once or twice he looked over his shoulder as he ran along the walkway, as if he was aware that someone was following him. As he got to the end of the walkway, he turned to his right, towards the camera and headed straight for the one remaining ship in the hangar. It was clearly Vincent, there was no doubt. One hundred and fifty yards or so of open space across which he ran like the wind and he was at the ship's nose. At this point more figures came into view along the walkway, five men in all. Three were dressed in white lab coats, obviously staff members and the other two also wore inmate's coveralls. One of the lab guys stumbled and fell and was set upon by the two inmates who could be plainly seen bashing him with their bare fists. Vincent looked back towards the walkway and hesitated for a moment. It was as if he was deciding whether to go and help or not. He glanced back at the ship, then back to the walkway where the remaining two lab guys were still trying to outrun the two inmates who were quickly gaining on them. Another glance back towards the walkway and then something extraordinary. Vincent dropped his holdall and took four or five steps back towards the walkway. He was going back to help! All at once the two inmates caught up with the remaining lab guys and set upon them. Vincent went back to the ship, picked up his holdall, climbed in and took off.

"Did you see that?" Farra looked at Byron, astonishment clear on her face. "He was going back to help them. Did you see that?"

"Yes I saw it, it's obvious that's what his intention was and this piece of footage will be added to the data cube you give to Donaldson. It will add a bit more weight to his case." He moved to the console and tapped a few more times. "We also found out about McGreedle, the Facility Warden at Moxal 3. See here? These documents are audits. Every year independent auditors would visit the Moxal 3 mine to check the books and all their records. It's standard practice in mining where valuable ore is being produced, to try to avoid fraud and racketeering. These documents show a steady decrease in the company's financial solvency over the past fifteen years. At the same time the amount of ore being brought out of the mine was remaining pretty constant so there is a big question mark over why the money was going down when the product wasn't. About two years ago the auditing body made a secret recommendation to the Mining Constabulary; the body that governs all mining operations, to have McGreedle pensioned off and replaced but nothing was ever done about it and he stayed there. There's even a document signed by a guy at the Mining Constabulary saying that no further action was needed as there was no evidence. And, get this, this was after Vincent would've tried to give Donaldson his evidence. Remember Vincent left there just over five years ago, and this happened two years ago. There was evidence but no one acted on it. This will be a valuable addition to the data cube evidence. Your friend Vincent is going to be cleared or I'll eat my hat," he smiled at her triumphantly as he delivered all this news to her. She was open mouthed.

"Jesus," was the only reply she could think of. "Have you found Donaldson?" she asked suddenly, aware that this was her next appointment. She hoped he was somewhere nice.

"Yes that was easy and very interesting. We discovered that he is stationed near to the Terramora system. We know that Terramora was at one time a victim of the Transmortals, nearly forty years ago and now they're rebuilding and are starting to get things going again and they're in the process of setting up governments, deciding who runs what and so on and so forth. Donaldson and the ANA are there in their official role as arbitrators to ensure fairness and make sure everything is done properly, cleanly and transparently.

"Okay so you say he's stationed near there? That means he's on a ship not on the planet?" She suddenly realised it wasn't going to be a case of simply walking up and ringing the doorbell.

"Yes, he's on one of the ANA Liners. It's basically a battle cruiser with its defence mechanisms hidden from sight so that it can be called a Liner. Because the ANA are supposed to be neutral, they need to be seen to be non confrontational, so no weaponry must be apparent. Believe me though, the ANA liners are no push over. They can defend themselves if needs be."

"So how do I get to him? Does he ever come down to the planet's surface?" She was already planning how to hijack a ship and possible methods of gaining covert entry to the ANA liner.

"The meetings they oversee are all done in public, in accordance with their policy of openness and transparency," he explained. "Anyone who wants to attend has to register their interest and wait to be called. Each person can attend only once per 3 months, so that the meetings aren't filled with the same people each time."

"So it could take months to get in," she was disappointed but decided she'd still investigate covert methods of getting to Donaldson if the proper way failed.

"Well it could, yes. There is another way though, I don't know how you'll feel about it."

"There's no way I'm fucking my way in, if that's what you're thinking," she said adamantly, glaring at Byron for even thinking of mentioning it.

"No no no, for heaven's sake. Part of the ANA strategy of being seen to be neutral and open, is that they always employ people from the local area as staff for the duration of their stay. Cleaning staff, cooks, waiters, porters, flight attendants, booking staff and even mechanics. All of these types of jobs are available to members of the public from the local area where the ANA is in operation. You could try to get a job aboard the liner if you don't get in the other way quickly."

"Oh, good idea, thanks Byron."

"There is also something else that gives you a great opportunity to get to him. He's agreed to go down to Terramora for three days for the celebrations to mark the twenty fifth year since rebuilding began. He's going to be doing visits, making speeches and baby kissing, the usual stuff so you may very well find plenty of opportunities but if you don't, you have the other two options," he smiled and she nodded. "Now let's get some lunch. Want some fruit extract?" he grinned as he ducked and expertly avoided the slap she aimed at his ear.

"By the way," she asked, "what is tapshots?"

"It's a game using two pairs of dice," he explained. "Why?"

"Vincent talks about it in his notebook. I just wondered what it was. Did the Doc find out where that leather came from?" she asked, suddenly remembering how soft it was. Byron nodded.

"Yes he did, let's ask him." They walked to Lomas' quarters where they'd been invited to spend their lunch time, chatting and joking with each other on the way. She was beginning to like Byron. He was clever and funny, a good combination in someone she'd love to have as a brother. She hoped he wasn't getting the wrong idea and misreading her friendliness as something more. As they passed along a long corridor she noticed photographs hanging on the walls. Landscapes interspersed with star maps. She stopped at one landscape that showed a mountain underneath a lilac coloured sky.

"Beautiful," she murmured. The next photograph was a star map with one of the stars on it was coloured red. She frowned, puzzled.

"The red dot is the location of the landscape you just admired," Byron explained. "Each pair of photographs is a landscape and a map of its location in the cosmos." She took more notice of the photographs as they walked along the corridor. There were mountains, oceans, deserts, snowscapes, volcanic eruptions, cities and jungles, each accompanied by its star map with its little red dot indicating its position in the heavens. The next photograph made her gasp. It was a country scene with a narrow lane and small dwellings on either side, with the shadow of a village in the background. What caught her attention though was that the lane was lined with trees. White trees that swayed in the evening breeze.

"My god, that's Lilea isn't it?" she gasped.

"Yes it is," he answered surprised, "how did you know?"

"I err, I dreamed of it," she lied.

"Those trees are only found on Lilea. Nowhere else has trees like that," he smiled. They're beautiful aren't they, so serene. They're called Whispering Trees because the Lileans believe that the sound they make as they sway back and forth in the wind is the tree spirits talking."

"Yes they're beautiful and I'm going to see them soon," she smiled as they walked. Just as they got to the end of the long corridor, she felt a throb in the centre of her chest and she stopped walking.

"What's up? Are you okay?" he asked, concerned. She closed her eyes and waited, she knew this was the signal from Leon that he wanted to speak to her.

"Yeah I'm fine, it's Leon," she assured him. As she allowed her mind to go inwards and leave the outside physical world behind, she heard Leon's familiar reassuring voice.

"Go back to the star maps. Go and look at the stars, please," he asked her gently. She turned and went back to the last star map, the one of Lilea. No response from Leon so she continued to the next, and the next and so on down the corridor until he told her to stop at one particular map. "Put a finger on the map and close your eyes child, trust me," he coaxed and she obeyed without hesitation. She put her right index finger on the map, closed her eyes and let her mind float. She noticed her arm begin to feel tingly from the elbow down to the tip of her finger. It wasn't distressing in any way, just strange. "That one, stop there," Leon suddenly announced and she opened her eyes to find her finger pointing at a system way off in the top right corner of the photograph. She closed her eyes again. "That is where my son is, where he has found save haven for the past five years. He is struggling with his past but Syra is with him and he is awakening. It is painful for him and he is so alone. He is moving towards fulfilling the prophecy given so many lifetimes ago. This is where your friends must go to find him. Tell them child."

"What is that planet called?" she asked Byron, who squinted to see the tiny dot high up in the photograph.

"Well let's have a look," he replied. "See these numbered markers around the borders of the photograph? They're a reference system so we know the location of all the dots in each photograph. Now let's see." He put one hand on the marker across the top of the photograph and the other hand on the marker down the side. "Fifty two by twenty seven, chart number 734501." He wrote the details down on the back of his hand. "Why?" he asked.

"Leon says that is where you will find Vincent."

During their lunch Byron used the console in King Lomas' quarters to call up the reference number he got from the star map in the corridor. After a minute or two of bleeps and clicks he looked up at them triumphantly.

"He's in the Vinbuk system."

"Vinbuk?" said Lomas. "Good choice of hideout if I may say so. There are only four planets in that system and only one is inhabited and then only by very primitive humanoids; rather like the stone age man of your Earth Farra. None of the other planets are of any interest to anyone; there are no precious ores to be gained from them. They're totally ignored as far as we know. Byron, how long will it take us to get there, find Vincent, get him aboard and get back?"

Byron scratched his chin and thought aloud. "About three days to get there. Say a day to look for him, locate him, persuade him to come with us and another three days to return to Terramora. Say a week to be safe Sir."

Lomas nodded and looked at Farra. "Okay so once you get to Terramora you have no more than one week to get the book and cube into Donaldson's hands. It's up to you how you achieve that and of course it goes without saying that we will equip you with everything we can think of that may aid and assist you in that task." He got up and went to the panel on the wall near the door, tapped a button and waited.

"Yes Your Majesty," a voice said.

"Lay in a course for Terramora, we must travel covertly."

"Yes Sir, right away."

"Oh and Perry?"

"Yes Sir?" the voice which Farra assumed must belong to Perry said.

"Show us the meaning of haste."

"Of course Your Majesty."

Lomas turned back to the little group and sighed. "Friends, we will soon be upon our task. Farra, you will be alone for your part in all this but we will do our best to ensure you have everything you need to provide you with safety, security and success in your endeavour. Never believe for a second that you are forgotten or lost."

Toma came up to her and hugged her. "I wish I could go with you but my position as the King's only heir forbids it. I will be with you in my thoughts."

"Okay young lady," Doctor Jam said. "There are things that I need your attention for. I have my own ways of helping you on your mission. Come with me please, we have little time and this is important."

"Okay Doc," she smiled as she allowed herself to be led out of the room. "By the way did you find out what creature that leather came from?"

"I did indeed and that's most interesting. It comes from the skin of a bird found only on Lilea. A giant bird called Malota. Lileans call them soaring angels because they fly so high and are so big," he informed her.

"That's nice," she smiled.

CHAPTER EIGHT

Vincent stopped to rest and drink some water. He took off the back pack he fashioned out of flexible saplings and leather strips and rummaged for his water carrier. He used the bladder of a creature he killed for a meal and after cleaning it out and tying up the urethra tightly, he wrapped a strip of leather thong around the top. It made a perfect water carrier and held enough to last him a whole day. He didn't bother making more than this one because small streams littered the landscape where he was camped and he never felt it necessary to make more. He slaked his thirst and then extravagantly poured some over his bald head to cool himself down. He ran a hand over his head and noticed it felt stubbly.

"Gonna need a shave," he said aloud. He looked up and then looked back the way he'd come and surmised that he was probably half way up the mountain. He guessed he'd been walking for around eight hours or so, give or take. He only stopped for short water breaks and once to sit and watch the sunset and walked throughout the night, making full use of the bright moonlight that lit the way for him. The sky was now just beginning to show signs of changing colour as dawn was approaching at last. He decided he would sit and watch the sunrise and then sleep for a few hours. The air on this planet was just a little too thin for him to function one hundred percent and he tired more quickly than he would elsewhere or if he had a breather unit on him. It wasn't too bad at ground level but as he climbed higher he noticed the effects.

As he got up to continue his climb he heard a noise from somewhere nearby. At once he was on full alert, blade in hand. He strained his ears but no sound came. He stood there for five minutes just listening but heard nothing. Slowly he started to walk again but kept his blade in his hand, just in case. After another couple of hundred yards of climbing that noise came again; an almost silent rustle. This time he could tell it was coming from his right a little higher up the mountainside and about fifty yards ahead. He scanned the area with his sharp eyesight but saw nothing but rocks and scree; no trees or plants, not even a blade of grass. He turned the blade in his hand to get it comfortable and so he could take action quickly if necessary. His nerves were on high alert and he was ready; he just wished he knew what for. As he came abreast of where he estimated the source of the sound came from he heard it again much louder this time. It was definitely a rustling, like the wind through the trees on a summer's evening but there was now an edge to it. Not quite a growl though, almost but not quite.

"Okay," he thought to himself. "Something is stalking me and thinks I'm its breakfast. Well sorry to disappoint you buddy." As he began to move past the area containing the source of the sound; his eyes never leaving that rock, he saw it and just had time to think, 'Oh shit,' before it launched itself at him. As the huge creature made contact with his upper body Vincent expertly let himself fall backwards onto his backside and then continued rolling backwards as he launched it back and over his head. As it stumbled and scrambled for purchase as it fell down the loose scree Vincent was back on his feet, backpack off and ready to receive it again. It looked basically cat like, about the size of a bear with greyish fur all over its body that gave it perfect camouflage against the rocks and scree of its mountain home. The source of the rustle came from its tail. The tail itself was fairly short and hairless but at the very end was a thatch of thick bristly spines that it vibrated to give the sound. Their eyes met and for a second Vincent felt he was being mentally scanned as though this creature possessed telepathic powers and was reading his mind. Another sound distracted them and at the same moment they both looked towards the source of this new sound. A small gurgling cry came from that same rock from which this huge creature launched itself at him just seconds ago. A tiny head appeared round the side of the rock and then another. Babies! This was a female nursing infants and Vincent was trespassing too close to her den.

This changed things; he couldn't kill her now not with infants to care for. Slowly and carefully he fumbled in his backpack for the left over meat from his dinner the night before. His hand rummaged in his pack for agonising seconds until he felt the lump of meat, grabbed it and pulled it out. He unwrapped it from its leather covering and threw it over to her while he slowly backed away. She raised her head and sniffed the air, intrigued by this new aroma. Vincent continued backing away while she sniffed and cautiously approached the lump of meat. As she reached it she sniffed it all over and the ground around it before raising her head high in the air, opening her jaws wide and giving vent to an almighty roar. She snatched it up and with a single bound was back with her infants who launched themselves onto the meat which was bigger than the both of them put together.

"Happy birthday kids," Vincent whispered as he continued backing away until he was at least two hundred yards further along the path. An hour later he was sitting on a rock watching the sunrise as he promised himself. It was even more beautiful out here on the mountain than it was framed by the mouth of his cave. He suddenly felt aware of how very alone he was and he shivered as the thought crept into his consciousness. He realised all of a sudden that it was nearly six years since he actually spoke to anyone, since he enjoyed a real conversation, an argument, a laugh. He let his thoughts drift back to the day he was taken to the Cryo Stasis Facility and how secretly scared he was at the thought of being frozen indefinitely for crimes he didn't commit. At the memory of those accusations his anger rose and he repeated the promise he made to himself on a regular basis.

"McGreedle, when we meet again I'm gonna slice you up and leave you for dog meat." This was one crime he wouldn't mind doing time for he decided. He remembered the Enforcement Agency guys coming for him and calling him off his shift and shackling him in front of his team so that he was embarrassed in front of the guys who were his buddies. That was bad manners he decided. To take someone in front of their buddies and make them look like a heap of shit in front of everyone like that, yep, that was bad manners and McGreedle owed him. On the journey to the Steran System and the Cryo Stasis Facility he was locked down next to a weirdo who sliced up his own kid and ate part of it for dinner. The guy kept looking at Vincent and grinning like a maniac.

"Whack job," he said aloud as he fumbled inside his backpack. He pulled out a small leather bundle and unsheathed his blade. Inside the bundle was a sharpening stick which he now used to make sure his favourite blade was razor sharp. Also in the bundle was a small piece of leather wrapped around a handful of soft animal fat that he'd rendered off from some of his meals. He took a scoopful of it in his hand and rubbed it onto his scalp before expertly drawing his now lethally sharp blade over his head and giving himself as good a shave as he could get anywhere else and have to pay for. After cleaning himself up he remembered that he gave the last of his meat to the creature for her infants and he was hungry. He'd have to hunt for something. Sighing, he got up and looked around; nothing but rocks and scree in all directions. There'd be no hunting here and even if he did catch something there was no wood around to light a fire with. He was used to roughing it but he wasn't prepared to eat his catch raw just yet!

He decided he'd be okay to wait. He enjoyed a good meal the night before and it wouldn't kill him to go a day without food. He'd done it before so he decided to sleep for a few hours; his legs ached and he was tired. This thin air up here was getting to him. He eased himself down into the lee of a large boulder; first making sure that nothing had made its home nearby and made himself as comfortable as he could. The big rock gave him shade so the sun wouldn't roast him as he slept and within a few minutes he was asleep. Almost immediately a voice woke him.

"Vincent. Vincent, wake up. Vincent." He leapt up from under the rock, stood on the path and looked both ways to try to find who the voice belonged to. He was surprised to see that instead of the usual bright sunny morning he was used to on this planet everywhere around him was thick fog and he couldn't see more than a couple of feet in any direction.

"Who's there?" he called but got no reply. "I know someone is there. I'm armed, come out."

"Vincent, do not fear, I mean you no harm." It was a woman's voice. As he looked she came into view through the fog. She was beautiful and looked like a warrior princess. He was aware that she seemed familiar in some vague way but he couldn't quite put his finger on where or how he knew her. "I am Syra, I am your friend Vincent. I have always been your friend." She continued approaching him, only stopping when she was a couple of feet in front of him. She almost matched him in height and had the same large black eyes as his and long black curly hair tied up on top and the same star shaped scar in the middle of her chest. "I was with you at your death and brought you back to your rebirth. I stayed by your side for three days and nights as you cried into the night amongst the filth and I have stayed by your side every moment since. You are never alone Vincent, know this and remember." At this she reached for his hand and memories flooded in; a tidal wave of despairing, horrific images. The same ones he saw in his dreams only this time the reality of them was overpowering.

He was back in the burned out landscape where fires burnt brightly. He looked around at the scene and it all felt so familiar, as if as if he knew this place but from when or where he didn't know. A woman's cries caught his attention; cries of agony and pleading for help. He sprang into action and raced towards the sound which came from the ruins of a building nearby. As he picked his way into the ruined home her cries were suddenly joined by those of a baby. Loud lusty cries and as they grew in intensity her own cries faded away to silence. He found them in what was the front room of the house. She was lying on the floor, her legs apart, clothes in disarray and sodden with blood; both her own and that from the birth. The newborn boy lay between her thighs, a big child whose birth must have caused her much agony. The boy screamed into the night, attached to his now lifeless mother by the still pulsating cord.

"No," he cried out. "Someone help, please." He started towards the baby but before he reached him, he realised he was not alone. He turned and saw a huge man watching the scene seemingly oblivious of his presence near the child. He was dressed in shiny black armour of some material that looked hard but it didn't clink as he moved around. A long black cape billowed from his shoulders to the floor and covered his head in a huge cowl. It was billowing in the breeze giving the impression of a big black cloud. Suddenly he remembered the black mist from his nightmares. This was what it was he saw in those dreams that upset him so. The man started towards the screaming baby and showed no awareness of Vincent's presence. He scooped up the child by his ankles, slicing through the cord as he hoisted him high into the air letting him dangle there, the cord spraying blood everywhere. Vincent screamed but couldn't make himself heard. He tried to run at the man but he couldn't move from the spot. Then a familiar voice, the woman distracted him.

"You are here just to observe Vincent. These are but shades of things now past. Memories of a moment long ago, forgotten and buried in the depths of a troubled mind struggling to find a purpose. Watch Vincent, watch and remember. Allow those buried moments to come forward now; it is time for you to awaken to the past so that you can move to the future. Do not fear, I am with you, watch." The man in black held the newborn boy high aloft and screamed, his voice spitting with venom.

"You will not be the one foretold to me Lilean child. You cannot kill me. You will not bring me down. You will not see me out. No prophecy of yours will end my days. You and your people will be forgotten before I am replaced." With those last words the man tucked an arm under the baby's body and with his other hand, smothered the life from him. When the child's screams stopped, he threw the tiny body into a midden and walked out of the ruins. Vincent was beside himself. Anger and pain coursed through him as tears poured down his cheeks. He tried to pull away from Syra to run to the child where he lay in the filthy midden but she held fast.

"Look Vincent," she smiled at him before pointing towards the place where the child lay. As he looked, he saw a group of misty spirits form out of thin air and group around the tiny body. They extended their hands and chanted words he couldn't understand.

Suddenly from amongst the ghostly throng Syra walked forward to the child. Vincent turned to her; she was still here with him holding his hand but at the same time he was watching her over there. He was puzzled.

"Remember Vincent. Let the memories come now." She indicated for him to watch the scene. As the spirits chanted Syra bent over the child's body and spoke to him gently. Although they must have been twenty feet away Vincent could hear every word she said even above the chanting of the spirits. "It is not time for you to journey to the land of the dead, child. Come back now little one, rejoin the land of the living and fulfil your destiny as was prophesied so long ago. I will walk beside you always brave warrior and the fury of the lost ones will be your rock and your stay. Come back now child, follow my voice and return to us." Suddenly a loud cry rang out into the night. The boy lived and lay there screaming amongst the filth. All at once the ghostly throng disappeared, all but Syra who remained. She turned and spoke as if talking to someone off to the side but Vincent could see no one else around. "I am Syra and I will be with him always. I will guide him and help him discover his destiny. He will have a life of many trials and sacrifices and often will have no one on whom to depend or lean for support. But fear not, I will be with him. He will not be alone and he will grow into a fine man, a warrior who will right this great wrong. The fury of the Lilean race will be his rock and his stay. Now give him his name." As Syra stood looking, Vincent heard another voice but could see no source that explained who it came from.

"I name him Vincent Richard." Vincent was shocked beyond belief. This scene of horror of which he had no memory, that haunted his dreams and gave him nightmares was his own birth? He didn't know how or what to feel in those first moments after hearing that voice giving him his name. Who did that voice belong to and why couldn't he see him? So many questions. Syra read his thoughts and tried to soothe him.

"It is time for you to awaken to the past Vincent. To allow these memories to come forward so that you can be whole again.

You are a man now, the brave warrior foretold to the ancestors so long ago. It is time for you to right the great wrong, to end the tide of evil that destroyed your home and those of countless others on other worlds. Wake up now Vincent. Wake up." The scene began to fade and Vincent found himself back on the path in the fog, Syra's last words still ringing in his ears. "Wake up now Vincent. Wake up. Wake up."

Vincent started awake and for a moment he didn't know where he was. He leapt to his feet and looked all around. The sun was up and he could see for miles in all directions. Where was the fog and where was Syra? He sat back down in the lee of the rock and hugged his knees as he remembered the events that were unfolded to him. He tried to think about what he always thought were his childhood memories but it was all so patchy and many bits were missing. As a little kid he always had a phobia about being left alone but his adoptive parents were always quite laid back about it and didn't make a fuss with him and he grew out of it. His first really solid memory was when he must've been around four or five years old and his brother was teasing him as usual. It was around the time he found out he was adopted by the family. Wesley was a year older and always bullied and teased him. He couldn't remember one single incident when Wesley was kind to him. It started with one of those moments all parents know will happen but are never quite prepared for. It started with a question. Kids are known for asking embarrassing questions at the most inopportune moments like waiting until you're in a large crowd before asking where babies come from. It was a moment like that which signalled the end of innocence for Vincent and he so often regretted asking it during the intervening years. He got to that age where he began to notice things, especially things that weren't as they should be or things that didn't quite explain themselves clearly and he asked Wesley the question he would always regret asking.

"Wes, why is my name different to yours?" Vincent was only four or five but he realised that all the other kids he knew all had the same last name as their brothers and sisters, except him and Wesley and naturally it bothered him and he wanted to know why.

He learned early that he was Vincent Richard Domenico but his parents and his brother weren't Domenico, they were called Sylvana. His parents took some time with him and explained that his real parents had gone to somewhere called the land of the dead and that they were the lucky ones to be looking after him until he grew into a man. They told him he was special because most parents don't get to choose their kid, they have to take what comes and that because they chose him meant he was special. They told him that he was called Domenico because that was his real parents name and that they used to live nearby, were really nice people and how they felt so lucky to have him live with them. They even showed him a photograph of his parents and the Sylvana's taken some years before and Vincent agreed they looked like really nice people. They gave him that photograph to keep and he put it by his bedside and said goodnight to them every night before he went to sleep.

One day, a few months later when Vincent was beginning to relax with the knowledge of his being adopted and his real parents having died Wesley was being a bully as usual. He was making a fuss because Vincent's bedroom was bigger than his own and as he was older, he should have the bigger room. Vincent told Wesley he thought both rooms looked the same size to him but Wesley wouldn't have it. He marched into Vincent's room and started wrecking it. He pulled the bedcovers onto the floor and stomped on them, he threw Vincent's toys, tore his favourite story book and then he caught sight of the photograph by the side of the bed. He ran over and snatched it up. Vincent was horrified and pleaded with him to give it back.

"No Wes, give it back. It's mine, it's mine. Give it back," but Wesley wouldn't listen. Vincent was begging and pleading but Wesley just stared at him and grinned. Then, holding the photograph high in the air so Vincent couldn't reach it no matter how hard he jumped, he tore it into shreds and let the pieces drift down over his head. Then he laughed. He laughed so hard that his eyes screwed up and he hugged his sides. Vincent stopped yelling and just stood there ashen faced, eyes wide as though in a trance.

Something was changing inside him; he could feel it happening but didn't know what it was or why. Something died inside Vincent that day and something else was born in its place. As he stood there amidst the remnants of that photograph he felt himself go cold right through to the bone. His vision blurred and for a second he thought he felt something being cut away inside him. He realised he hadn't taken a breath for several long seconds and even though he tried to breathe, he couldn't. It was as if there was a huge hand over his mouth, stifling him. His head felt funny and he thought he would like to just drift away somewhere like an autumn leaf on the wind. It felt so wonderfully calm now, and he knew he wanted to just drift away.

"Come back," he heard a woman's voice on the same breeze that was beckoning him to go. "Come back now child, follow my voice and return to us." Her voice was beginning to be distracting now and Vincent did so want to float off on the breeze with the leaves. "I will walk beside you always." He found that no matter how hard he tried he couldn't ignore that voice and all the leaves blew on their way without him.

"Vincent. Vincent!" his mother screamed as she held the little boy in her arms. By this time he was turning blue around the lips. She didn't know how long he'd been like this but it must be several minutes. She was frantic, terrified and panicking as she tried to get him to breathe. She shook him hard, slapped his face and tried to open his mouth but his teeth were clamped tight. Her husband rushed in at that moment wondering what the commotion was about. He saw the scene before him and went white for a moment. He grabbed the boy from his wife and gently blew into his nostrils, forcing air into the tiny lungs. Vincent at once coughed and spluttered and vomited and most importantly, he breathed. Then he sobbed his little heart out for hours on end, right into the night long past the time he should have been sleeping, he was sobbing. He cried for his loneliness, for the loss of the only photo of his real parents, he cried because his brother was so horrid to him and he cried because he wanted so much to float off with the beautiful autumn leaves on the wind but the woman's voice distracted him and the leaves flew off without him.

Vincent's relationship with his brother Wesley never recovered completely from that day onwards. Something was permanently changed and even at such a young age, he was aware of it even though he didn't know what it was. He was too young to realise that he built his first wall that day, a wall that he continued to build around his heart over the intervening years until he entombed himself within an impenetrable fortress through which no one was allowed to pass. Everyone who knew him saw the change in him. The neighbours and friends of the Sylvana's would comment on how distant he was lately, how aloof he was with them and how he never smiled much anymore and they remarked how long it was since they heard him laugh. He remained polite with everyone, he was never rude and always did as his parents asked and was always to be seen doing chores around the home which he did without needing to be persuaded, but there was a part of him missing. Joy, that's what it was, the joy was gone.

As he sat hugging his knees in the lee of the rock, all of these memories came flooding back in a tidal wave that overwhelmed him. He sat there shaking from the intensity of the emotions as he realised that even at such a young age he had a flashback of his birth experience. Somehow during the intervening years he hardened his heart so much that he blocked it out completely. Life was something Vincent always had to cope with, rather than enjoy. He couldn't even remember what joy felt like and as the tears fell and splashed off the stony path, he realised just how lonely and unloved he always felt. He lay down on his side and immersed himself in the feelings and realisations as they washed over him in a painful yet cleansing tidal wave.

As the rawness of the pain from the emotional dam bursting began to settle, he sat up and tried to take stock of what he just experienced. He remembered things he forgot long ago. He had a flashback of his birth on that day with Wesley and the torn photograph. He remembered that huge black caped figure smothering him. He remembered dying and wanting to leave this life behind and he remembered the woman calling him back. It all fitted with the images he saw when she took him back there in the fog. He remembered how the torn pieces of the precious photograph lay around his feet and how he thought they looked like white petals. This made him think of the white trees he saw in his image with Syra, how beautiful they were. He remembered her telling him that he must remember what was forgotten and now he was and it hurt, no wonder he blocked it all those years ago. He suddenly thought of his adoptive parents, Rayna and Marcus Sylvana and how hurt they must have been as he grew older but more distant from them. They were good to him, saved him from death and took him in and told him he was special and Rayna screamed for him when she thought he died in her arms. They loved him as much as any natural parents would and he slowly but surely froze them out along with everyone else as he got older. He realised he couldn't remember if he ever actually told them he loved them and that made him feel unutterably guilty and sad.

"I'm sorry Mom, Dad," he said aloud, "I love you." A sudden pain in his chest made him take a sharp breath in. Instinctively he put a hand to his chest. The pain was right on his scar, the little star that all his people carried. It began to throb and as it did so, he thought he heard a voice deep in his mind, very far away.

"Vincent." It was the woman Syra, of that he was sure but the voice was so far away. He knew it was inside his head, but at the same time it sounded like it was a long way off. His chest throbbed again. "Vincent. Hear me Vincent." Louder this time but still so faint. Another throb. "Time to move on now, must hurry Vincent. Hear me. I am always with you." He could hear her fairly well if he made an effort to block out everything else. That was hard for him to do, as he had to live by his wits for so long and his quick reactions and heightened awareness saved his life so many times, it wasn't easy for him to let his 'radar' down. It was the only way to hear Syra though, so he made the effort and found it made a real difference to the clarity with which he could hear her. Another painful throb. "Must move Vincent, hurry." She sounded urgent. He got up and brushed himself off and took a moment to use some of his water to wash the tear stains from his face before packing up and rejoining the path up the last leg of the mountain.

For the next four hours as he laboriously climbed Vincent learned to let Syra in and after so many years of walking silently beside him she felt the joy of seeing him finally realise he wasn't alone. She was immensely proud and moved at his courage and strength and felt privileged to be chosen to walk beside the prophesied one. By the time Vincent finally reached the top of the mountain, the little scar on his chest no longer stung painfully when Syra wanted to speak. All he noticed now was a much more tolerable throb, which he took as a signal for him to let his mind drift sideways a little. He'd get the hang of it before too long, of that he was confident. When he set his mind to something he didn't let go until he was happy he'd succeeded. As he took the last few steps up the path, the now familiar throb came again. He stopped walking and turned his mind inwards and waited.

"Vincent. It is time to meet your destiny now. Not since the day of your birth have you set eyes on what you're about to see and now it is time to look upon that face once again. Not since he drove the life from your body has he seen your face. Today he will meet the child that is now a man, he will realise the innocent child he slaughtered so many to reach and kill has become a fine warrior and he will look upon your face as his life ends and the dark days pass forever." His head swam as he brought his mind back to his physical surroundings. So this was the plan was it? He was going to get to meet that black caped figure in person and pay him back once and for all? He learned during those last few hours of climbing that those black caped beings wiped out most of the people on the planet that was his and his people's real home, that they killed his real parents as he was being born, and that they spread their evil over many planets, brainwashing countless numbers and killing those that refused to bow down to them. Well that was fine with him, he was happy to pay the guy a visit. Very happy indeed.

Purposefully he took the last few strides to the crest of the mountain and looked down at the vista. He looked down and saw it, the huge dome growing out of the planet's surface like a boil. Set amidst the lushest vegetation he ever saw. The dome looked totally out of place here on this planet inhabited by the most primitive of humans; little more than grunting savages who ate each other when they got annoyed!

"What the fuck?" he said aloud as he scanned the area noticing several other identical domes, the farthest one being probably a mile away as the crow flies. "My god what the fuck are these?" he asked.

CHAPTER NINE

Pzolgon rose from his throne to address the multitude gathered in the vast Atrium. This day dawned with a very grave matter to be addressed; one that was foretold an immeasurably long time ago and was now to come to pass. He looked down at the countless silent throng gathered here and knew what must happen. His expression was dark as he addressed his people.

"Adherents of the Transmortal truth. I stand before you this day to bring you grave news. It has been brought to our consciousness from the Great Immortal that the time foretold to us so long ago is soon to come to pass. The one who has been prophesied will soon draw his first breath. The one who wishes to keep us from The Veil." The crowd of adherents all drew in a breath, shocked at the news they were hearing. Pzolgon continued. "Ever since the first Pzolgon journeyed to The Veil and returned blessed with the gift of Transmortal Truth has this time been foretold. Over thousands of lifetimes we have known and prepared for the coming of this evil one. Ever since that first Pzolgon began to pass on the gift of Transformation to the unfortunate mortals, we have waited for this dread moment. This morning our Visionary saw the moment the evil seed was sown into the fertile soil of the uninitiated. Now that seed lives and grows in the filth of its mother's mortal womb and plots against the great Transmortal Truth." Shocked murmurs began to wend their way around the Atrium as the Adherents heard what Pzolgon was telling them. "Adherents, we have devoted our lives to bringing the gift of Transformation to those unfortunate uninitiated; to offering them the greatest gift the Great Immortal has to offer, to bringing them The Veil. Are we to stand by and let this evil doer keep countless millions from receiving this greatest of gifts?"

The crowd of Adherents roared into life. "No, no, no." Pzolgon looked around the Atrium at the multitude and smiled.

"How do we proceed?" he challenged them.

"Kill the evil one," they all replied as one.

"It will be done," Pzolgon assured them. "We cannot allow one evil doer to prevent the coming of The Veil. It will be done." He turned and strode out of the Atrium, the Adherents' roars ringing in his ears.

"So where is he, this evil one?" he asked his Visionary who was deep in a trance like state communing with The Great Truth.

The Visionary was at the Windows of Time looking for the evil one's whereabouts. This device is what the Transmortal Visionaries use to see through time, both past and future. The device consists of two ice blue coloured crystal spheres each four inches in diameter onto which the Visionary holds. As he opens his vast mind the power of these magical crystals enhances his mind's energy field to such a degree that he can see vast distances through space and time. It takes many years of training for the Acolytes before they are able to use the Windows of Time without damaging their minds permanently.

"Well, where is he?" Pzolgon was getting impatient with the Visionary.

"He's in sector eleven, a system called Lilea. He is due to take his first breath in one month." The Visionary saw the look of satisfaction on Pzolgon's face at this knowledge.

"Good, that gives us plenty of time to get there." He strode out of the Visionary's temple and went to speak to his commanders. "Sector eleven, the Lilean system. We must travel invisibly and get there quickly; the evil one will draw his first breath in one month."

"At once," the Commanders responded together, thumping their right fists against their chests in the customary salute to their Pzolgon. They returned to their positions and steered the enormous silent Transmortal ship on its way to the Lilean system to keep this most important date with destiny and kill the evil one.

The vast hulk of the Transmortal ship is at all times a mobile battle ship, home to the Pzolgon, Visionary and the Adherents, and place of the Oracle of Transmortal Truth. The Oracle is at the very heart of the ship and is the place where all new initiates are brought for their transformational procedure. The Transmortals have one sole aim, to bring every human life to the Oracle to receive the Transmortal Truth. Only when this is done; when every human life and mind receives the Truth, can The Veil come into being and take them all into the presence of the Great Immortal for eternity. While there is even one human mind that does not receive the Truth, The Veil cannot be manifest. Those that choose transformation willingly have a pain free and untroubled experience within the Oracle, but those who resist and must be forced to receive the Truth find the experience most distressing. Many die during the transformation process and all the deaths are celebrated. It is the Transmortal belief that those who die during transformation are the lucky ones for they are believed to be taken directly to The Veil by the Great Immortal. The process of transformation has many effects upon the one receiving the Truth. It extends their life span by hundreds of years and gives them immense psychic awareness and telepathic abilities.

The very first Pzolgon stumbled his way upon the Transmortal Truth by accident. He was a young man at the time, just twenty six years old and in the prime of his life. He became ill due to an infection he received from an insect bite and he went to the very brink of death and hovered there for many weeks. As he traversed his way between life and death, he grew accustomed to his new state and eventually his soul lost all connection with the imperfect physical life, where there is no truth. When his body returned to life the soul within it was changed forever. He had received the Transmortal Truth, glimpsed The Veil and once he returned he knew what his great quest was to be. He knew he must give others the gift of the Truth, taking them to the edge of death and using his vast telepathic mind to hold them there until their souls forgot their connection with physical life and returned changed forever.

Some of the early experiments with transforming the uninitiated resulted in a disaster whose effects are still evident today. The ones chosen to receive the gift were very primitive humanoids, taken from their own primitive home world to the

Transmortals new base for transformation, but the process changed them in a way that was unexpected. They did not return true the way of the Transmortals, but broke away and went their own way. The first few Pzolgons spent thousands of years perfecting the process of transforming the uninitiated, but those early subjects eluded all attempts to make them true Adherents of the Transmortal Truth. They returned the changed ones to their original home world and forgot them. They chose new subjects and over thousands of years their numbers grew and they spread to neighbouring planets, bringing the Transmortal Truth with them wherever they went. They saw themselves as the bringer of the greatest of gifts; the opportunity to enter The Veil and be in the presence of the Great Immortal. Those early transformation test subjects did not simply vanish into the vastness of the universe though. After all, they were transformed forever, just not in the way that was anticipated. They grew and flourished at a rate unheard of in normal evolution and they soon became a powerful, mighty race. All of the subsequent Pzolgons knew of these early initiates, it was Transmortal history that every Adherent knew and studied. Those early initiates were transformed, and so they believed that they would not stand in the way of the coming of the Veil, as only those who have not been through transformation were to be feared.

The Veil is a place beyond physical death, beyond what might be called heaven or the spirit world or land of the dead. It is beyond everything that is known or unknown. It is a world of pure psychic energy where souls abide without desire for physical life. The Veil cannot exist where there is want for physical life. Those that receive the Truth within the Oracle emerge with no want or desire for physical life; they wait only for the coming of The Veil and they know in order for it to come into being, every human soul must be transformed. As the Transmortals grew in number, now and then one would come who was able to develop their psychic and telepathic powers to an immense level. These became Transmortal Visionaries, scanning through time itself and advising their Pzolgon. It was one such Visionary who first glimpsed the evil one. He was scanning through time looking for anything noteworthy to report to his Pzolgon, when he saw it, one single man bringing an end to the Transmortal Truth forever. He was horrified and reported it immediately to his Pzolgon, and the prophecy was born. Over the intervening millennia Visionaries came and went but always the evil one in the future was observed and, as his time grew close, the Transmortals decided it was time to face the prophecy, and they drew their plans against him.

Pzolgon was in the throne room when the announcement came through. "Mighty Pzolgon, we're approaching the Lilean System now Sir." He looked up and smiled to himself; at last his date with destiny was here and he would show the Great Immortal that no prophecy was going to prevent the coming of The Veil. This would surely please the Great Immortal, who might even grant him increased powers and dominion over many more of the unfortunates who were still without the Transmortal Truth. He rose and called to his aides.

"It is time, prepare me for battle," he ordered as they rushed around him, fussing with his armour, cloak and cowl.

The Lileans didn't know what hit them when the Transmortals descended onto their planet. They cloaked themselves so they could arrive invisibly before the evil one's people could save him. The multitude of Adherents swarmed over Lilea, killing everyone they saw and showing no mercy. They razed the great cities to the ground, burned homes and all who dwelt there and when they came upon pregnant women, they tore the new lives from their wombs and snuffed them out, celebrating each death that took a new soul directly to The Veil. These Lileans, the people of the evil one would themselves swell the ranks of the Transmortal multitude and receive the Truth. Those who refused would die. Pzolgon didn't normally take a personal part in the gathering of souls but he knew this day was different. This was the day that was prophesied and he was the one destined to meet and kill the evil one. So he strode across Lilea amongst the multitude, looking for newborns or those of the women who were obviously near to giving birth and he took great delight in his task for he knew that the Great Immortal was watching and would be pleased.

He was watching the fires burning the Lilean civilisation to ashes when he heard a woman's cries nearby. As he walked towards the sound, another cry joined hers; the cries of a newborn. Suddenly his mind was filled with images of death; his own death and the falling of the Transmortal Empire. He probed with his psychic mind towards that cry and knew without a doubt that this child who was just taking his first breaths, was the evil one. He strode onwards to meet his moment of greatness and saw before him the woman, dead upon the ground. The newborn was lying between her thighs still attached to her by the cord. He knew that this child was the evil one, he even killed his own mother being born from her body! He stood there in the Lilean night, the winds catching his cloak and cowl, making them billow out in all directions. As he watched, his fury grew until he could contain it no longer. He would snuff out this evil doer right here and now. He strode purposefully over to the child, took hold of his ankles and deftly sliced through the life giving cord as he hoisted him high into the air. How could a mere newborn snuff him out? This weakling child who was without the Truth would never prevent the coming of The Veil. He screamed his anger at the boy, spitting with rage into the Lilean night.

"You will not be the one foretold to me Lilean child. You cannot kill me. You will not bring me down. You will not see me out. No prophecy of yours will end my days. You and your people will be forgotten before I am replaced." Roughly he cradled the boy, put his other hand over his face and smothered him until he breathed no more. The evil one was dead. He, the Mighty Pzolgon was the one to outwit the prophecy and ensure the coming of The Veil. He felt sure the Great Immortal would smile on him and his people now. He tossed the child's body into a midden. "Filth is as filth does," he murmured to himself and strode away to announce the success to the multitude. As the Transmortal Army left the Lilean System, they celebrated their victory over the evil one, over the prophecy that hung over their heads for many thousands of years and they felt sure the Great Immortal was happy with them.

Pzolgon snapped himself out of his reverie. He often let his thoughts drift back to that glorious day when he destroyed the evil one. It was his defining moment and one of which he was immensely proud. The intercom interrupted his thoughts.

"Mighty Pzolgon the Visionary requests your presence; there is an urgent matter he wishes to bring to your attention." He got up and sighed to himself and made his way to the Oracle to see his Visionary. What could he want now? When he entered the Oracle the Visionary looked at him gravely, his worried expression evident. What he discovered would wipe the smile from the Pzolgon's face forever.

"Mighty Pzolgon, a grave matter indeed has come to my attention." The Visionary was pacing up and down, wringing his hands.

"Well what is it, dammit man, out with it." Pzolgon had little patience today.

"I was scanning the time stream as normal and I err, I found something that isn't supposed to be there." He looked genuinely frightened now and his fear began to percolate to Pzolgon himself.

"What have you found? Tell me Visionary or do I have to tear it out of your mind myself?" he threatened.

The Visionary looked terrified at the thought and continued, if rather falteringly. "It seems that err, that is, it seems as though umm, that he still umm, lives," he backed away from Pzolgon once he got the words out, terrified of what his leader might do to him in his anger. Pzolgon didn't at first understand what the Visionary was on about, but slowly realisation crept through his mind and as it did so, he became enraged.

"He lives? How can this be? I killed him myself at the moment of his birth. Tell me this is not true Visionary," Pzolgon roared, anger, fear and loathing fuelling his rising temper.

"I cannot Mighty Pzolgon for it is true, he still lives and breathes. He is still the one prophesied." The Visionary backed himself right into the corner of the Oracle chamber; there was nowhere else to go.

"Where is he? Where is he? Tell me where he is now." Pzolgon was beside himself with rage and it took all of his willpower not to crush this messenger of doom right here and now.

"He is at the site of the first Oracle from the very first Pzolgon all those lifetimes ago. The place where our first mighty ruler began to transform the uninitiated and the place where the early initiates turned their backs on the Transmortal Truth. He is on the planet Vinbuk Sire." Pzolgon thought this was interesting and ironic that the evil one should find himself at the very place where their own first leader began to perfect the transformation process and where those early subjects turned their backs on the Truth. Maybe this was the Great Immortal's way of granting him the privilege of righting the great mistake made by that first Pzolgon. Maybe in killing the evil one in that place, the stain left by those early mistakes can be erased and allow them into The Veil untainted by the errors of the past. He marched out of the Oracle and ordered his Commanders to travel invisibly to the Vinbuk System with all haste.

Vincent looked down at the domes and even from the top of the mountain where he stood, they looked huge. He squatted and rummaged in his backpack for his scope and scanned the whole area below. No signs of anyone around, in fact they looked as if they'd been deserted for hundreds of years. In places there were cracks and holes in the domes and the vegetation encroached so far that they were almost completely covered over. Syra told him he was to meet his moment of destiny here so he guessed whatever it entailed was down there in those domes. He put away his scope and started down the mountain. It took him considerably less time to descend than to climb and after six hours he was standing at the edge of the greenest oasis he ever saw. He decided that first things first, he'd been without food long enough and whatever was going to happen to him and whatever his destiny was, he was going to do it with food in his belly. Being hungry can keep you sharp, but being too hungry can be a distraction that can cost you dear. Within an hour he caught his meal, skinned and cleaned it and was roasting it over a fire and it was smelling wonderful. His mouth watered and his belly grumbled in anticipation.

With his hunger satisfied he set off towards the domes and whatever awaited him there. The vegetation enveloped him and he felt the cool moistness of the air on his skin. After his climb in the unrelenting sun this was a very welcome change and it revived his mood so much that he could almost say he was enjoying the walk. Most of the plants and trees were ones he didn't recongise; where he lived in the cave the vegetation consisted of low scrub and brush with the occasional stand of those tall trees that gave the poison. Here the vegetation was thick but not so dense that he needed to hack his way through. He could stroll easily and take time to look at his surroundings, get the feel of it. He noticed a group of trees he recognised up ahead and he moved towards them, an idea suddenly springing into his mind along with the now familiar throb in his chest, just below his scar. He guessed Syra thought it was a good idea too.

There were half a dozen of what he now called 'poison trees' and he decided that now was the time to see if he'd watched the other humans closely enough to be able to climb them as easily as they did. He selected one from the group and took off his backpack. He picked it apart so that he was left with a long length of strong hide and, taking a couple of practice swings first, he swung one end around the tree trunk and grabbed it as it came back around at him. So far so good. He knotted the ends together forming a loop and stepped into it. He leaned back, testing his balance and the strength of the strap. When he felt happy, he placed one foot on the tree at knee height, leaned back letting the strap take his weight and lifted his other foot up. He was leaning too far back and toppled over onto his backside hard. He got up and tried again, this time taking the strap much higher up. He got both feet up and took a few seconds to gain his balance before shunting the strap further up the tree and gingerly taking another step up. In a rather ungainly and inelegant fashion, he made progress up the tree. It took him almost an hour to climb up, find the hard little poison capsule growing out of the trunk, dig it out with his blade and climb down again. He was exhausted and decided the indigenous humans deserved a bit more of his respect than he'd given them. He sat down and breathed hard. His arms ached, his legs ached and his back was stiff but he made it and he was proud of himself. He built a small fire and looked around for a couple of rocks to crush the poison capsule, which he found was the home of an insect that obviously burrowed into the bark to make its home. Once crushed into a rather horrible looking yellow mush, he took out the blade he used for shaving and cut himself on the arm. He allowed several large drops to fall onto the mushed up poison capsule before rubbing the wound vigorously. Immediately it stopped bleeding, the rubbing causing the blood to clot in seconds and he knew that within a day there would be no trace of a scar. He picked up a small stick and stirred the blood into the mush and put the rock on the fire. When it turned a glossy brown, he took it off and put it aside to cool.

He used the time to relax and really look at his surroundings and the beauty of it made him wonder about his home and his people. Growing up with the Sylvana family was relatively good all in all, apart from the ever present Wesley of course. They taught him at home rather than sending him to school and he learned the basics quickly. He could read and write and do basic maths before he was eight and had a good basic all round education by the time he left home at seventeen to join the military. He remembered how optimistic he was when he left Mexalon to seek his future, how he finally felt like a man and thought life was going to be good to him if he grabbed it with both hands. He was brought up to be polite and courteous and to obey authority without question and that's what he tried his hardest to do. In those early years he did okay too but as he grew in experience and understanding of people, the disillusionment started to creep in and slowly he began to realise that not everything they told him to do was necessarily the best idea.

As he sat there amongst the trees he realised for the first time how naïve he was back then and how it hurt to realise that life and especially the people he met, were not as altruistic as he was. That was when he started to withdraw from them and they noticed. People began to comment that he seemed distant and kept asking him if everything was okay. It didn't take him long to realise that he was never going to meet anyone who could be truly real and so he gave up looking. He went inwards and became his own ally, his own confidante and his own best friend. He learned that when you rely on other people for anything, where there's even a small chance of them letting you down, they would. People disappointed him greatly back then and it took him a few years to realise he would just have to give up the struggle with them. It was too emotionally traumatic being in the never ending cycle of hoping to find someone real, working at the friendship and then coping with the disappointment when they let him down yet again. He became a loner.

He picked at a small twig, stuck it in his mouth and chewed as he thought back to the times when he had the dreams and how frightened they made him. The images were frightening in themselves but it was the thought that he was crazy that was most frightening. When the voice joined the dreams he really worried for his sanity, so much so that during one particularly active dreaming phase, he tried to go without sleeping at all just so he wouldn't have to face them again. He managed three days before he finally passed out and ended up in the medical centre. Instead of preventing the dreams he actually made it worse for himself, as he slept for twenty four hours straight and it seemed to him as if he spent that entire time within the dream imagery. He awoke convinced he was crazy and it began to affect him in his job as a soldier. Pretty soon after that he was summoned to his commanding officers who told him in no uncertain terms that they thought it best he retire honourably from military service with fifteen years untainted service and a medal for valour. He took the hint. Vincent is many things but stupid isn't one of them.

He leaned over and reached for the small rock that held the cooling poison gloop. He decided it was cool enough so he spat out his twig, got up and carefully wrapped the rock in a thick layer of leather and tied it up securely so it wouldn't leak. He rebuilt his backpack and set off through the verdant forest. It was beautiful here, he decided and in different circumstances he'd be happy to settle here. It offered him everything he needed; plentiful food, water and shelter and no people to bother him. He was allowing himself to daydream and was so far inside of himself that he almost didn't hear it. The smallest of sounds came to his sharp ears and he was instantly alert, the daydream vanished away. He stopped mid stride, hand going instinctively towards the blade on his hip and strained his ears and his awareness. The forest was full of sounds; birds sang, the trees rustled in the breeze and creatures called in the distance, but that sound didn't belong somehow. It made a blip on his internal radar and he learned long ago never to ignore it so he wasn't going to start now. His sense of not being alone was triggered very gently and although it was so subtle it almost wasn't there, it was there. He stood for long minutes listening, looking and expanding his awareness but the sound didn't come again. He moved on, feeling no immediate danger but still having that inner awareness that he wasn't alone.

Three hours later he emerged from the forest and found himself at the base of the first of the huge domes. It loomed up and away above him and as he looked at it, he realised it was very old indeed. The surface itself was made of a patchwork of hexagonal sections of some material that obviously used to be very shiny, like glass but now it was weathered and the surface was pitted; in places there were giant cracks and holes. It hadn't been cared for in hundreds of years and Vincent decided it must be long abandoned. Maybe whatever civilisation lived here died out or left to find shelter elsewhere. It seemed odd to him that the only other humanoids he saw here were so primitive yet here was something only a very advanced race could manufacture. How could such an advanced race and such a primitive one evolve together on the same planet? He was musing on this question when that sound came again, still far away and so quiet it almost wasn't there, but he heard it. He spun around, unsheathed his blade and scanned the forest in front of him for whatever was stalking him but saw nothing. No creature leapt at his throat, no savages with poison arrows ran at him, all was quiet and peaceful. It was beginning to freak him out now; he wasn't used to being the prey. He saw plenty of action during his military career and as a Ranger in the mines on Moxal 3 he dealt with plenty of the fearsome Uvees and was even wounded by them a few times. He'd never been in a situation like this before though. It was as though whoever or whatever it was that was following behind, was just enjoying playing with his mind, trying to psyche him out and frighten him into making a fatal mistake. Well he had news for them, no one fucked with his mind and got away with it for long! He shook the feelings away, determined to keep control and retain the upper hand. He hadn't endured so much in life just to end up as dog meat on some rock out in the middle of shit knows where. They could take all the time they want, he would wait and be ready to show them once and for all that they really didn't know who they were fucking with this time.

After a quick look around, he found a door in the side of the dome and gently tried the handle. It shook in its frame but held. He realised that his only choice was to force his way in which wasn't his first choice of action in such circumstances. He'd much rather go in quietly when he didn't know what he was going to find inside and keep the element of surprise on his side. Shit, there was nothing for it; he was going to have to make a noise! He stepped back a pace and with one firm kick, the door broke into pieces. He moved into the doorway, alert for whatever might be waiting for him inside.

Vincent entered the ancient dome and took another step towards fulfilling the prophecy given to his ancestors many lifetimes ago. Syra, ever vigilant for her charge's safety, was unseen by his side as always and a mile back in the forest, unnoticed by Vincent, they crept forward silently, knowing that their bellies would be full before too long.

CHAPTER TEN

The Drycenian battle cruiser settled into orbit around Terramora Prime ready to plant Farra into the community so that she could deliver the evidence package to Michael Donaldson. The ship remained covert in order to avoid any unnecessary complications arising from the Terramoran authorities or the ANA wondering what they were doing there. They couldn't allow anything to risk the success of the operation Farra was about to embark upon so secrecy was paramount. Farra, Lomas, Doctor Jam, Byron, Toma and few others were deep in conference, discussing the operation as they had done constantly throughout the trip from the Moxal System.

She was fitted with a highly enhanced Biomed Implant by the doctor so that her health could be kept at optimum while they were out of range and unable to get to her aid. This device is one of the very latest Drycenian medical advances. It consists of a tiny implant into the brachial artery of the arm which constantly monitors the blood as it passes through it. Sensors within it detect any toxins or harmful impurities. If something harmful is detected, the sensors signal to an extraction valve which filters the bloodstream of the foreign contaminant until the sensors signal it to stop. These impurities are treated by a Pulse Wave Energy implant that renders them inert and turns them into harmless pale creamy coloured pellets that can be removed and discarded with ease. All that is visible on the skin's surface is a shiny silver metallic kidney shaped plate about 3 inches long. The surface of the plate contains minute solar cells which power the system and the whole thing is covered with Drycenian symbols and decoration to disguise the solar cells and make it more aesthetically pleasing. All Drycenians have these devices and Farra felt honoured to be fitted with one. It made her feel as though she was really one of the family. All she must do is make sure the surface of the plate gets at least one hour of sunlight per week of continuous use to ensure the system works at optimum. Just going about her normal daily business would be enough; it's easy to get one hour of sun on your arm in every week even if you only emerge for a few minutes each day.

The only thing that might be a problem is that these devices mark you out as Drycenian right away. Anyone fitted with such a device must be either a Drycenian or a friend of them and people might very well question her about it. Because the Drycenians are a secretive race who tend not to involve themselves closely with other races, people are curious about them and are bound to question anyone with any knowledge or experience with them. Farra knew that she should endeavour to keep it covered at all times when in the company of others and to make sure that she was alone for a few minutes a day in order to keep the solar cells charged without people's curiosity getting in the way.

The doctor also implanted a minute tracking device in place of the temporary one she had when she went into the Moxal 3 mines to retrieve the evidence package. This new tracking implant works permanently and is attached as an add on to the Biomed Implant device and is powered by the same solar cells. It contains a signal booster that enables the tracking signal to carry over vast distances via Pulse Wave Energy beam. This has the dual advantage of being able to resist contamination from other wave signals enabling it to travel unhindered at above light speed and it is as yet undetectable by any tracking device other than those of the Drycenians. This part of the Biomed Implant sends out an automatic signal every six hours that can be picked up by a long range signal scanner within the Drycenian battle cruisers. The signal consists of a tracking code for location purposes, as well as data from the Biomed sensors. All the time that the sensors are working within Farra's bloodstream, they will send out this signal letting the Drycenians know that she is still alive and at least relatively healthy. If she were to die or if the blood filters stop working for some other reason the sensors would send out an emergency signal to the Drycenians. This way they would know that she is in trouble or has died and could retrieve her body. If they get to her body within seventy two hours of death and get her into the tank, they can revive her. Any longer than that and there's no chance but at least they would be able to ensure her remains were treated with the honour and dignity deserved by one who has saved their race, as she did by rescuing Toma and ensuring the King has a healthy living heir.

They also kitted her out with a Magnopik; the automatic lock picker she was so amazed by back in the Moxal 3 mines, a large tub of Tutsie – a Drycenian word meaning beautiful blue which is the blue wound compound Toma gave her and a Unicom transmitter fitted into a standard inter galactic cell phone headset. This device is a super powered one way cell phone type of device that she can use to transmit voice messages back to them, much like calling them up on a cell phone. It's just a one way device though, they can't answer her but if she needs help she can call for it and if there are any necessary last minute changes of plan, she can warn them. Being fitted into a standard intergalactic cell phone headset means she can use it anywhere without drawing attention to herself. So long as she makes sure she looks likes she's hearing the other side of the conversation, no one will be suspicious. As with all Drycenian devices, the carrier wave is undetectable and only receivable by Drycenian technology.

Lomas bestowed upon her a magnificent gift of a Drycenian Royal Dragon Dagger. This blade is beautiful and she was visibly moved when he gave it to her. The hilt is fashioned in the shape of a fearsome winged dragon and she found when she hefted it that it automatically adjusts itself in the users hand to be the perfect weight for its user. The blade itself is just shy of nine inches long and has four sharpened recurved barbs carved out of the top edge. The blade is made of tempered Drycenian Minneva which never rusts and its edge, once sharpened will never dull. At the touch of a secret button in the hilt the blade retracts and the wings fold in so that it can be safely stored within its ornately carved scabbard. When worn on the hip, it looks like a rather intricately carved oblong metallic carrying case, ten inches by two inches by one inch. When placed within the scabbard it locks itself in place and can only be retrieved by the thumb print of its owner being pressed to a special one centimetre square plate on the top leading edge of the scabbard itself. All she has to do to call it into service is to take it from the scabbard, making sure her thumb touches the little plate and as it emerges from the scabbard, the blade shoots out and the wings unfurl. This magnificent instrument is ceremonial for the Drycenians and only given to those who deserve the highest of honours but that doesn't mean it isn't usable. It's beautiful to look at, safe from being taken and used against its owner and deadly in service.

"Farra," said Lomas emotionally. "I give you this gift to be your guardian in times of unrest. He will always be at your side ready to defend your life and purpose. Whenever your life or safety are in peril, know that he is with you. Call on him and he will be forever, your friend. We cannot be there to give you aid and you must face the trials and dangers of the coming days alone. Never for a moment doubt that wherever we are, we are working tirelessly to assist you to bring light into these darkest of days. We will not rest until we have returned Vincent to safety and freedom and the loving embrace of his people and together, all of us, walk with him as he fulfils his destiny. Know with all of your heart that we are thinking of you and loving you every moment whilst we are away from your side." He took a pace back, placed a hand on his own ceremonial dagger and bowed his head. "My sword and my life." She stood to attention, placed her hand on the magnificent dragon dagger that now graced her hip and bowed her head in response.

After much hugging and well wishing, tears from Toma and Doctor Jam who dabbed a handkerchief under his eyes constantly, she boarded the same little ship that rescued them from Moxal 3 for the covert trip down the to the surface of Terramora Prime. During the flight she had time to reflect upon everything that happened during the past few weeks and months. In just over seven months she'd come from being just another Earth gal who loved the military, to being a Lilean chosen one given the task of saving the only Lilean left who could fulfil a centuries old prophecy and save their race and countless other worlds and the lives that lived upon them, to saving the only living heir of the King of the legendary and secretive Drycenian Nation and here she was on her way to deliver a package that contained the only things that could save Vincent and therefore, the Lilean race, to a man who few got anywhere near. She felt incredibly proud, immensely humble, a little scared and very very alone. She wiped away a tear from her cheek and sent a thought out to her father.

"Pop, I hope you're proud of me." A throb from her little scar and Leon's voice inside her mind. "He is child, he is."

She bade a warm farewell to the Troopers who delivered her safely and covertly to the surface of Terramora Prime before setting off in the direction of the city. The Drycenians kitted her out with suitable clothing so that she would blend in without calling attention to herself although Terramora Prime is known as a cosmopolitan planet where people from all over can come and mix together and be welcomed. The area she found herself in was a little way out from the city and still showed signs of the Transmortals having been there. This must once have been a magnificent forest but what were once majestic trees reaching gracefully to the heavens were now blackened stumps and the once rich brown soil was now grey with ash. She was pleased to see that everywhere she looked amongst the sad black wrecks of the ancient forest, seedlings and saplings were growing by the thousand. Green and full of life, they reached for the sun, refusing to desert this planet that was their home. Some of the oldest of these saplings were twenty feet high or more and home to birds and creatures who all scurried and flew and crawled and crept about their daily lives, a living reminder to all with eyes to see that mother nature will not be controlled and where she chooses to lay her hand, life will not be lost for long. Farra saw and it gladdened her heart and gave her hope that Lilea was also enjoying a similar rejuvenation.

As she approached the city she could see how much rebuilding was taking place. Everywhere she looked people were working; building new homes, making existing ones safe, clearing rubble from as yet untouched plots and there was a tangible sense of optimism and hope. Scaffolding loomed and men ran up and down ladders singing and whistling whilst children played kick the can on newly cleared plots of land that had been made safe for them. People of all different cultures, races and colours worked together rebuilding this world for no other reason than it was the right thing to do for those in need. They smiled as they worked, they sang and they whistled while they laboured, they made jokes and laughed together as they shifted, cleared and hauled. Farra thought that she would enjoy being here amongst these hopeful happy people. She smiled warmly to a man who waved to her as she passed by the building he was reglazing. As she rounded a corner she came upon a scene that wiped the smile from her face. A crowd was gathered around the remains of a building that wasn't yet cleared. A man was standing apart from the crowd and seemed to be addressing them. As she moved closer she was able to hear what he was saying.

"No longer will your humble servant know the pain and agonies that he once endured. Universal God, in your great wisdom you took this child to be at your side and while we weep for him having gone from us, we celebrate his awakening into your glorious sight. Take his hand oh Lord and walk by his side into the garden of heaven, too long has he waited here in darkness and we humbly beg forgiveness on the troubled souls of those who took him from us. We commit the soul of this perfect unstained child unto you oh Lord, forever into paradise, Amen." Those gathered around whispered whatever Amen was appropriate and right for their beliefs, all united in one moment to pray, no matter what the faith or creed of the hands that beseeched. Moist eyes were dabbed with handkerchiefs and the crowd backed away reverently allowing Farra to see what it was.

Amongst the ruins that they were just starting to clear for rebuilding, they'd found a tiny skeleton of a baby. A doctor and three funeral administrators examined it and identified it as a male of less than three months; the statutory age for DNA printing that would give his name and family details so that he could be reunited with them. As she stood looking at the tiny remains, she was reminded of the story Leon told her of Vincent's birth and the Lilean massacre by the Transmortals. How easily those fragile bones could be Vincent's she thought to herself as she watched the funeral administrators cover and remove them into a waiting cart. As the animals clopped away the crowd of men who had been praying just seconds ago, picked up their shovels and picks and continued laboriously clearing the ruins of the building. As she continued walking she noticed a signboard propped up against what must have once been the doorway. She cocked her head to the side so that she could read it. The tears came and she didn't try to stop them as she read "Happy Hat Day Nursery, all under fives welcome."

Her Drycenian friends equipped her with all manner of maps and documents so that she could fall right into society here without raising any suspicions, so she handed over her identification document with a smile as she registered for a room in the city's biggest hotel, The Metropol. The desk clerk was a small thin man who didn't seem to know how to smile. He looked flustered and irritated so she gave him her warmest smile.

"Hard day?" she asked. He looked at her and for a moment she thought he was just going to ignore her attempt at a friendly gesture. Then he gave a heavy sigh.

"Yes actually, sorry Miss err, Duncan but it has been a trifle stressful today with the new turnaround happening tomorrow. Always so much work to do and not enough time. Still I shouldn't complain really, so many people all wanting to help and make sure everything is done right. I should be glad." Then he managed a weak smile. Farra and the Drycenians had studied the Terramoran system of administration during their journey here and she knew the desk clerk was talking about the register of those wanting to attend the ANA meetings on board the liner. She felt a bit guilty adding to the guy's workload but this was important for a lot of people.

She smiled even wider. "Ahh so am I too late to register? I was a bit delayed. I meant to be here yesterday to get it done but err, circumstances overtook me." The clerk looked at her and for a moment his face remained expressionless. Then he smiled and shook his head.

"Oh no it's okay. Here, give me your documentation and I'll sort it for you. By the time you've freshened up and had a drink and some lunch, I'll have your poll card ready for you. But err, promise me one thing?" He lowered his eyes and looked conspiratorially at her.

"What?" she whispered back.

"That you won't tell anyone I hurried it through for you? There'd be a riot if it got out to the masses," he laughed.

She laughed with him and hoped it looked genuine. "My lips are sealed," she promised, and she would keep that promise, she decided.

The room was basic but clean and would serve her well enough. There was a bed, a night stand, a chair and a closet. A tiny bathroom contained just shower, basin and toilet. Everything was the most basic possible but perfectly clean and although it wasn't a palace, she couldn't find anything she could complain about. She was hot and tired and would take a little while to acclimatise to the weather on Terramora, which was hot and dry and after the perfectly controlled environment on the Drycenian ship, was a bit of a shock. She chided herself for having gone soft and stripped off her clothes to take a shower. The water was deliciously cool as she stepped in and stood there letting it cascade over her head and all down her body. She caught her reflection in the mirrored shower walls and smiled. She still wasn't used to seeing herself with a golden tan and wrinkle free complexion. Once her tan developed she decided to get Doctor Jam to re colour her tattoo to make it stand out more. She had the big dragon tattoo done on her back while on leave from the DSTU's about five years ago and her male colleagues teased her for ages about it, calling her the old dragon for weeks. She never regretted having it done and she found that most of the men who saw it when she wore skimpy tops in hot climates, thought it was cool. She never got bad comments from men about it but did get a few from women. She chose to assume they were just being catty and jealous and she paid them no mind.

She looked at her little scar, the Lilean star on her breast bone and smiled. She was proud of that too and hoped that the Lilean people would accept her when she went there. She was aware of a growing feeling of wanting to be connected with Lilea on a deeper level, as though she wanted it to be home somehow. She wondered what Vincent was going through at this moment as she washed her hair and freshened herself up. Was he suffering, was he hurt? She felt a bit guilty standing here in relative luxury when he was probably living very roughly and having a hard time. She suddenly wished very much to let him know she was fighting for him, that he wasn't alone and that she was working towards freeing him. Then she thought of that tiny skeleton in the ruins of that day nursery and then of the images Leon gave her of the day of his birth. Suddenly she felt very far away from him and wished so desperately to let him know she was his friend. All of the recent trials and dangers she'd gone through, the changes to her life and destiny came tumbling upon her and she gave in to them and sobbed as the cool water cascaded down over her.

She lay down on the bed in her room, clean and cool and refreshed from her shower and from letting all the pent up emotions go. She was suddenly very tired and allowed herself to drift off to sleep. Leon was waiting for her in the hinterland between sleeping and waking. He smiled and took her hand gently. "Look," he said, pointing behind her into the mist. She strained her eyes but even with her state of the art eyesight she couldn't see anything in the fog. "Look, there," he said again and as she looked a vague shape formed out of the dense mist. She couldn't make it out at first but as it gained solidity she saw it was a man asleep. It was Vincent, she was sure of it. The bald head and massive arms and those lips, it had to be.

"Vincent?" she looked enquiringly at Leon, who just smiled and nodded.

"Yes child. He is sleeping now, in this same moment of time many worlds away. You are both in the hinterland together. I've awoken you in this moment but his guide Syra is keeping him asleep. Go to him." He indicated with his hand. She looked up at him questioningly but he just smiled. "He will not wake, nor will he respond, but he will hear you and somewhere inside, he will remember and your words will stay with him. Go to him child."

She realised now, Leon heard her thoughts when she was in the shower and he knew of her distress. She walked over to where Vincent lay; a shimmering shade but himself nonetheless. She knelt down and just looked at him for long moments, getting to know him as best she could. She felt a bit intrusive doing this while he slept but she might not get another chance. She gently put a hand on his face and traced her fingers down his cheek and over those lips. She leaned down and whispered into his ear, suddenly needing this conversation to be private between them.

"Vincent. Don't worry. I am fighting for you. You are not forgotten. I am working to free you and bring you home. Don't be sad Vincent, don't think you have no one to care. I care. I care very much. Sleep well and wake refreshed my friend. Be safe, and remember, I care. Remember that Vincent, I care and I'm fighting for you." She kissed those lips and he vanished. She looked at Leon. "Where did he go?" she asked and he laughed quietly.

"He woke up my dear; your kiss woke him up." He put his arm around her shoulder and pretended not to notice that she was blushing. "Now Farra," he said gravely. "Tomorrow you will be informed that you have not been allocated a ticket for the next meeting. Don't worry, all is not lost. As you already know, Donaldson has agreed to make a visit to Terramora to a celebration for the twenty fifth anniversary of the beginning of the rebuilding programme. He will be staying in this very hotel. The top five floors have been set aside for him and his aides. Security will be very tight but you will have better opportunities to get to him than you would at a meeting on the ANA liner. I will be with you and I will guide you every step of the way. You will need to trust me and do what I tell you without fear. Can you do that?"

"Of course, whatever it takes. Just say the word and I'm there," she promised. Leon smiled and didn't doubt her word for a second. "Thank you so much for letting me speak to Vincent," she said, her eyes welling up again. "It means a lot to me, and I hope to him too."

"He will remember your words. They will be there within him and they will make a difference," he promised her. "Now sleep child."

She awoke refreshed and thought she should go and get something to eat, so she dressed in what she thought would be coolest and most comfortable and went down to the dining room of the hotel. She found herself a table on the veranda and sat looking out across the garden to the city beyond. It was a hot climate on Terramora but at least she was sitting in the shade, for which she was grateful. The city was undergoing a continuous programme of renewal from the centre outwards and people came from many planets to get jobs and help out. Everyone knew of the ever present threat of the Transmortals and they knew that it could one day be them needing this help on their own worlds. This kind of thing was making people put their differences aside and pull together and she was sad that it took such a tragedy to achieve a harmonious united front. Each building first had to be demolished if it couldn't be repaired; the rubble cleared and searched for remains, which then had to be dealt with in the proper manner, then a new building could be put in its place. It was painfully slow but the people worked patiently and diligently, with smiles on their faces and songs on their lips. Everywhere one went in the city there were builders, labourers, glaziers, painters, carpenters, power companies, water companies; everything had to done again from each humble brick to state of the art technology and it was happening in every city on Terramora and, supposed Farra, on Lilea too. Everywhere there was a tangible sense of hope for a brighter tomorrow, it was infectious and she began to relax.

"Excuse me, Miss Duncan?" A voice beside her made her jump. It was the desk clerk.

"Oh, hello there," she smiled warmly.

"I have your errm, documents ready for you Miss," he said looking around to make sure no one was listening in. He handed her an envelope with a smile. Suddenly she got an idea and when she felt a throb in the centre of her chest she knew it was a good one.

She looked up at the clerk and smiled her warmest smile. "Thank you very much, I really appreciate the help. Would you like to join me for a drink of something?" she offered. The man looked about to refuse but then changed his mind.

"Oh, well I err, that is, I'd be happy to, thank you." He sat down next to her and called a waitress over. "Have you settled into your room okay? Is everything to your satisfaction?" he enquired, confident that it would be.

"Oh yes thank you, the room is immaculate. My compliments to your cleaning staff, they do a wonderful job," she said and meant every word.

"Good, good, If there is anything you need, you have only to ask." He was really beginning to come out of himself. She wondered how often people extended the hand of friendship to him and thought that it was probably not that often. The job of a hotel desk clerk involves being seen as the receptacle for complaints and having to be polite to everyone all of the time. She was sure she wouldn't last a day in such a job and she decided she was going to make an effort to be nice to this guy for however long or short her stay would turn out to be.

As she walked through the city she pondered on what the desk clerk divulged to her about the impending visit by Michael Donaldson and his ANA cronies. He was due to arrive the following afternoon and stay for three nights. The entire top five floors of the hotel were sealed off and reserved for them with Michael Donaldson staying in the Penthouse suite at the very top. On the first evening he would attend a dinner for all of the city bigwigs to celebrate the twenty five year mark since rebuilding began. On the second morning he would attend a memorial service for all the souls lost during the Transmortal attack which would involve laying the foundation stone for a memorial garden fountain in their memory. The same afternoon he would go on a tour of the city to see the rebuilding in full swing and would return and spend the evening at a concert put on in his honour. On the second morning he would go on a tour of the still undeveloped and unrepaired areas outlying the city, to include a visit to the rapidly regrowing forest that Farra saw on her walk into the city.

She learned that Terramora is famous for its ancient forests which are held in very high regard. Trees on Terramora are seen as visible manifestations of God, due to their long life and their gift to humanity of the very air that we breathe. To lose those ancient forests was seen as almost a worse tragedy than the loss of the people. It was to the Terramorans, as if God himself had been killed. Now that they were happily re growing, no state visit would be complete without an official visit there. Donaldson was to make a speech to the people at the forest, before returning to the hotel for a brief lunch, followed by a visit to three state of the art care facilities where injured survivors of the Transmortal attack still lived and were looked after. That second evening he would spend in his hotel room, preparing for his return to his space ship the next morning. So Farra now knew his schedule, all she needed to know was when to strike, where to strike and how.

She was beginning to feel as if she were about to melt in this heat. Having to keep her arms covered so as not to divulge the existence of the Drycenian Biomed Implant on her arm didn't help matters. She longed to remove her jacket but she didn't dare; she didn't want to mess things up now that she'd come this far. She crossed over the street and saw a row of newly opened shops so thought she would take the opportunity to get out of the sun and go in and browse. To her complete and utter delight she found a shop selling women's clothes and spent almost an hour rummaging and trying things on before emerging with her new purchases. The fabrics were the softest and lightest she'd seen since the Drycenian skin mesh she worn when she was tanked.

She managed to outfit herself with a new pair of trousers and a roomy over shirt with long sleeves and a hood to keep the sun from her head. Both were made of a woven fabric that was as light as chiffon but resisted the heat of the sun so the skin beneath could stay at a reasonable temperature. The hood was strange and she didn't understand what it was for until the sales girl explained. The hood was so large that it would go not only over the head but right down over the face as well. There was a slit cut out for the wearer to see where they were going and when worn, the whole head and face would be completely covered. The sales girl told her that many people who came to Terramora lived on planets that didn't have such a fierce climate and so these hooded shirts were designed so they could keep cool and comfortable and not damage their skin. They proved so popular that even the Terramorans themselves now wore them during the most fierce heat of the day in mid summer whenever they went outside in the sun. She also indulged in a pair of light shoes that would be wonderfully cool on her feet. She always wore sturdy boots and although safe and protective, they didn't exactly help keep the feet cool and sometimes she longed to go barefoot. There would be times when these would come in handy, she was sure and anyway, she is a gal and gals love shoes.

CHAPTER ELEVEN

Farra followed the crowds of eager onlookers as they all made their way to the outskirts of the city. Their destination was the ancient forest and Michael Donaldson's speech. As she walked amongst the people of Terramora, she was again struck by a tangible feeling of optimism and hope. These people were amazing, she thought as she allowed herself to soak up the energy of hope as it poured from every one of them. As they walked, the city became less and less new and more ruins were visible. Mounds of rubble were regular sights and here and there amongst the debris could be seen personal items that once belonged to more of these happy, hopeful people. A shoe, a hairbrush, a child's toy all stark reminders of the true cost of the Transmortal attack. Now and then someone nearby would remark that they used to frequent this or that store, restaurant, place of worship or whatever the ruin they were passing used to be. Not once did she hear a single person say anything about wanting vengeance, nor even express anger at what happened here. She supposed that during the past decades since the attack, time healed the survivors' hearts enough for them to leave their anger behind and move forward to their future. Whatever, she was impressed by their optimism and compassion.

As they approached the edge of the forest, she moved off to one side and stood amongst a stand of tall bushes. The evening before as she lay in bed Leon appeared and they went over the events of the day to come. He seemed a little evasive she remembered, but he always saw her right and she could find no reason to doubt him now. He told her during that first day when he let her speak to Vincent, that she would need to trust him without question so she was going to do so. There was a raised platform on which a lectern had been erected for Donaldson to make his speech to the people of Terramora. A knee high rope surrounded the platform indicating without being invasive, that this was the boundary beyond which no one must go and instinctively she noted how easy it would be to jump over if need be.

Behind the platform, stretching into the distance was the forest. The fresh new green amongst the blackened stumps of the old making a powerful backdrop. At the back of the platform, she could see Donaldson's security aides. Some in suits talking into headsets while others dressed in combats scanned the crowd and readied their weapons. Leon told her this would be her moment of destiny for it was during this speech that somehow she was to pass the package over to Donaldson and get away again without being arrested or shot. She wasn't sure how it was to happen though and it was this detail that Leon seemed a bit vague about.

"You will know when the right moment presents itself," he told her. "Act quickly and without hesitation for you will have just seconds to pass over the package and say what needs to be said."

"I guess I'll just have to wait and keep my eyes and ears open," she mused to herself as she waited for Donaldson to start his speech. A throb from the centre of her chest told her Leon was nearby and wanted her attention. She closed her eyes and allowed her mind to go inwards and waited.

"Watch and listen child. Use your eyes and ears to their fullest potential, they will show you the moment for action." She frowned, what did he mean, use them to their fullest potential? She now had better eyesight and hearing than anyone she ever knew; even without stretching them she could hear and see stuff others had no hope of noticing. Almost silently the realisation crept to the front of her mind and she knew what he meant. She was to use her eyes and ears at their fullest capability, which meant that she must listen and look for something from far away.

"Oh I see, well you could've just told me that," she sent the thought to Leon with a light hearted tut.

As Donaldson climbed up to the lectern and received his applause, Farra opened her ears to hear the tiniest of noises and she zoomed her eyesight in to the maximum and scanned the horizon. At first the noise almost overwhelmed her but the Drycenians taught her a technique of blocking out unwanted noise so she could concentrate on hearing the tiny noises. Everything settled into a tolerable murmur and she could clearly hear the trees swishing in the breeze, birds calling and creatures snuffling about. As she scanned the horizon the far tree line leapt forward to greet her and she was able to alter her focus to scan at various distances as quickly as she would with her normal eyesight.

Fifteen minutes into the speech and she heard it. A tiny cracking sound that just didn't belong. Like someone stepping on a twig in the forest. The forest! She scanned the horizon and all distances in between in the direction that sound came from but saw nothing out of the ordinary. She was about to start panicking when something glinted off to the left of her visual field. She immediately focussed in on it and saw to her horror that it was a man hiding in the far tree line. That glint was the hot Terramoran sun glinting off the shiny metal body of the lethal looking laser weapon he was aiming at Donaldson's back as he gave his speech.

Shit, she thought to herself. He's going to be assassinated right here in front of me. She raced into action, pulling her hood up over her head and down over her face so she wouldn't be recognised and get herself arrested or shot at for lunging at Donaldson. She raced from the cover of the bushes, leapt the rope barrier and jumped up the steps of the platform in one bound. She launched herself at Donaldson's chest, knocking him backwards off his feet, the momentum of her weight carrying them both back down the rear of the platform and sending them both sprawling to the ground. As they were in mid flight, the shots rang out. Two of Donaldson's security men were killed instantly and another was badly injured and unable to move. The soldiers were at that moment returning fire into the distance and running through the forest towards the assailant. As Farra and Donaldson landed in an ungainly heap on the ground, she knew there was just seconds to get the package over and say the most important words of her life. She reached inside her shirt and removed the package and offered it to him. Her face was covered by her hood but he was aware of a pair of startlingly green eyes looking back at him.

"Who are you? What do you want from me?" he asked as he tried to regain his breath and his composure.

"Never mind. Take this package please. Remember Moxal 3?" she asked him and he nodded. "This package contains Vincent's book and data cube; the one he tried to give you years ago. He is innocent of the crimes he was convicted of and the data that this package contains proves it. It will also help you deal with the Moxal Revolutionaries once and for all. Vincent is innocent. You must clear his name for at this very moment he is bringing to an end the evil that once walked here on this very spot. He has suffered so much for crimes he didn't commit, use this and clear him. Please." She leapt up and turned to run away before the remaining security forces could catch her as an accessory to attempted murder. Donaldson didn't know who this was but he knew it was definitely a woman and as she turned to run, he just had time to catch sight of a beautiful dragon through a tear in her over shirt before she disappeared into the crowd and was gone.

Farra ran like she'd never run before, cutting into alleyways and side streets and back tracking on herself to outwit anyone that might be following. After forty minutes she found herself in an as yet completely undeveloped part of the city where all was still in ruins. Windowless walls loomed all around, their sightless eyes looking down at her as she stopped running to catch her breath. For a moment she thought these monoliths were mocking her as she stooped, hands on her knees heaving to get her breathing back to normal. She was sweating like a bull on heat and badly needed a cool drink. She wandered into one of the empty wrecks that was once a grocery store and made her way to the rear, climbing over rubble and packets and bottles whose labels had long since faded to nothing. She found a dark corner and stripped off her hooded over shirt and was dismayed to see a tear down the back. No wonder the heat got to her! She rummaged in her bag for the clean shirt she stowed there and put it on; no one would recognise her now in a different shirt. She crumpled up the torn one and set light to it and stayed with it to make sure it all burned away.

She trod the ash into the rubble with her boot, got up and nonchalantly made her way back into the city to get a cool drink. As she was walking, she saw security patrols racing through the streets, sirens sounding and horns blaring. People leapt out of the way to avoid being run over as the ANA thundered passed and everywhere people were gossiping about what just happened. She decided that the best way to appear blameless was to pretend she had no idea what was going on, so she stopped by a small group of women who were talking and asked them what happened.

"My dear didn't you see? Michael Donaldson was almost killed out at the forest about an hour ago," an elderly woman informed her. She tried to look shocked.

"Oh my god, that's awful. Is he ok?" She hoped she was being convincing and by the way the woman responded she guessed she was doing a fine acting job.

"Well, it seems that someone took a shot at him while he was making his speech. Killed two of his men too and another got shot in the leg. Donaldson wasn't hit though, thank heavens. Can you imagine what the repercussions would be if he'd been killed?" The woman was in her element being the one with the news and she was revelling in having this crowd hanging on her every word. Here and there the other women would gasp and utter a "gosh" or an "oh my god" with a hand to the throat in genuine shock. Farra joined in with them and listened intently as the old woman continued. "Apparently someone from the crowd ran at Donaldson and knocked him down before he could get shot by the killer. The security service reckons that it must have been someone who was in on the plot but got cold feet at the last minute and decided to save him instead of help to kill him." The women continued with their "oh gosh's" and "oh heavens" as Farra feigned a missed appointment and excused herself.

So she was right to run away. It was inevitable to her that the security service would automatically think she was involved if she stuck around or got herself caught. She decided it was time to send a message to the Drycenians to bring them up to speed. She got out her Unicom Transmitter, pressed the activation button and waited for a few seconds before she started talking so that anyone watching would assume she was waiting for the other end to pick up. She tried to sound as if she was actually talking to someone, but she found it difficult and just hoped that no one was close enough to hear her.

"Hey guys it's me, how ya doing? I'm fine thanks. It's very hot here but it's a nice place. The package has been delivered safely but there's been a development. Someone tried to assassinate him. I got to him just in time and prevented a disaster and got the package over. We just have to hope he does the right thing with it; it's all down to him now. This is one bit of the plan over which none of us have any control. Thing is though, I had to make a quick getaway after saving the old guy and now they're looking for me. They think I must've been involved in the assassination plot but got cold feet at the last minute. I was disguised so they shouldn't know it was me, but you never know. Anyway, just wanted to bring you up to speed. Whatever happens, you must get Vincent, he is your first and only priority right now okay? Hope everything is going well your end and I wish you success at finding Vincent quickly. Farra out." She pressed the transmit button and waited for the three beeps to let her know her message was on its way. Within a few minutes her Drycenian friends would receive the message, even though they were three days away at the battle cruiser's top speed. She was impressed beyond belief at their technology. "Now I gotta get a drink." She strode into the first café she came across and ordered herself a bottle of the local beer. She thought she'd never tasted beer as good.

He watched her from across the street, his anger rising with each passing minute. How dare she come here and ruin everything he took years planning for. He first got suspicious of her when he saw her at the forest. She made a point of standing amongst some bushes, rather than amongst the crowd and she obviously wasn't paying attention to the idiot's speech as she kept her eyes on the far tree line. It was as if the bitch knew that Jackson was there. He couldn't believe it when she suddenly launched herself at the old guy moments before Jackson opened fire and saved the old bastard. The worst thing was when he listened in on her cell phone call and heard her mention Vincent. His equipment couldn't hear the other side of the call though, only hers and he supposed it could be a coincidence. There must be thousands of Vincents in the galaxy, but supposing, just supposing! He was incensed and felt like tearing her head off right here and now. Well the bitch was going to pay, and pay dear.

As Farra enjoyed her beer she began to relax. She was sure no one would recognise her as she'd been wearing the hood of her over shirt right down so only her eyes showed. She would make sure she continued to be careful though, and she wouldn't wear the local over shirts any more, just in case it triggered anyone's suspicions. She was about to order herself a second beer when she felt a rather sharper than normal throb from her chest. She closed her eyes and allowed her mind to drift slightly. Leon's voice was there loud and urgent.

"Farra my child, something is going to happen very soon that will frighten you. I beg of you with all my heart, do not fear. I am with you always, you must believe this now more than ever before." He sounded worried, and this worried her.

"What on earth is the matter? What's going to happen?" she asked, already frightened.

"Before this day is finished, you are going to be assaulted by someone who is also very important to this whole journey that we are all embarked upon. He will find you and assault you and take you captive. I beg of you child, don't fight him please. Be submissive and allow him control of the situation for now. I will be at your side every moment, I promise."

"What? You're kidding right? For fucks's sake Leon tell me you're kidding." She shouted her thoughts at him, incredulity and shock flooding her mind.

"Please Farra my dear," Leon responded. His voice now had an edge. She noticed and was instantly cowed.

"Sorry, it's just a bit of a shock y'know. What do you want me to do then?" she asked, taking a sharp breath in and forcing herself back into operation mode.

"Allow him to abduct you, don't escape him. His mind is highly unstable but if he feels he has complete control he will do what needs to be done, you will come to no harm and he will have helped you a bit further along on your quest. If you get feisty with him, he might lose it and just kill you. Promise me child."

"Shit, okay I promise." She ordered another beer and a shot to go with it.

She tried her hardest to look as if she hadn't a care in the world as she strolled nonchalantly through the streets of the city on her way back to the hotel for dinner. Try as she might she just couldn't do it. What the hell was Leon thinking of, telling her to let herself be assaulted and taken captive? For fucks' sake whatever next? After all she'd been through during the past weeks and months and all of it for the good of others. She put her life on the line for a guy she'd never met, nearly been eaten by the Uvees, shot at by Rangers and nearly got her head blown off by some lunatic just a couple of hours ago, and now she was to happily let herself be kidnapped? Good god is this guy Vincent really worth all of this? As she asked herself the question she already knew what her answer would be and that just made her more frightened than she already was. She thought of her Drycenian friends, racing across the galaxy at this very minute to Vincent's aid, just because she persuaded them to help her help him. She thought of the Lilean people she saw in the visions Leon showed her, of their suffering at the hands of the Transmortals and how Vincent was at this moment trying single handedly to bring their evil to an end for the good of the whole galaxy. And then she thought of Vincent being murdered while taking his very first breaths all those years ago as his mother died giving birth to him. She thought of him trying to understand what was going on back on Moxal 3 and wondering why no one would help him. She thought of him being taken away and accused of terrible crimes he didn't commit and how scared he must've been as he was led away to be frozen indefinitely at the Cryo Stasis Facility. She thought of him alone on some rock somewhere with no one to talk to or lean on for moral support and she thought of him wondering if he'd even live through the next days, let alone if he'd ever be a free man again. She finally thought of him as he laid there asleep when she kissed him and she realised how very important he was becoming to her, above and beyond the mission they were all on. She didn't want to feel like this; she didn't need this complicating matters that were already complicated enough on their own. She had relationships in the past; she hadn't lived like a nun but she'd never really been in love before. She almost got engaged once but then the guy ran off with a female soldier he was on an exercise with on Layton 7 Moon Base. That broke her heart and her pride too, but then five months later he got himself killed in action and she felt vindicated. That helped her a lot; it would've taken her ages to get over that betrayal if he wasn't killed. She was experienced enough to understand where her feelings were wanting to go but she was sure she was strong enough to prevent them from having their way. She snapped out of her daydreams and realised she'd gotten herself lost.

"Dammit," she cursed out loud, realising she should have been paying attention to where she was going. She decided to go into the next store she came to and ask the way back to the hotel rather than walk around for ages hoping to accidentally get back to somewhere she recognised. She rounded a corner and found a café so she went in and asked the man at the counter for directions. "Excuse me, how do I get to the Hotel Metropol from here? I've got a little lost." She shrugged her shoulders hoping he'd take pity on her and give her good directions.

"Afternoon ma'am, your quickest way is out of here, turn left up the alleyway, then left again at the end. Down to the end of that road, cross the street and then take the first right. It's about fifteen minutes walk." He smiled patiently, obviously a bit put out that she wasn't even planning to buy a coffee.

"Thank you so much," she smiled as sweetly as she could before leaving the café and trying to remember the directions. She looked to the left and saw a narrow alleyway. It was just a gap between the café and another building rather than a proper thoroughfare and she supposed that only the locals really knew about it and used it much. It was rather picturesque; kind of old fashioned like in a painting. She was so busy admiring the old worldliness of the place that she didn't notice the presence of the man who hid in the doorway of the warehouse next door.

Before she had time to gather her thoughts and realise what was happening, she found herself suddenly flung bodily against the wall so hard it knocked the wind from her lungs. She panicked, instinctively going to reach for her blade as a distinct throb came from her chest. She was being pinned against the wall from behind by a big man with incredible strength and as she fought for breath she tried hard to reach the blade that sat on her hip. She felt the throb in her chest but in her panic it didn't register into her consciousness. There wasn't time to prepare herself for this and make sure she didn't fight, she was just acting on instinct like the good soldier she was. Another throb, this time much more painful and she felt it and recognised it. She cried out with the pain of it as she struggled with the man and it made her lose her focus so he over powered her with ease and restrained her hands behind her back. He snapped some kind of handcuffs on her and then she felt a blade at her throat and hot panting breath in her ear.

"You fuckin bitch," he spat at her between panting breaths. "You're gonna fuckin pay for this mess." He dug the edge of his blade into the skin of her throat, making her tilt her head even farther back which hurt her neck terribly.

"What do you want you moron," she gasped as she tried to force herself into a submissive stance that just wasn't natural for her. The man said nothing, but forced her to walk up the alleyway to the end. After checking both ways to make sure no one was coming he marched her forcefully across the street and threw her into the back of an ex military armoured shunter buggy. She rode in these vehicles many times during her military service and she knew without trying that there was no way she was going to escape. They are basically an armoured box on either wheels, tracks or hover mode that the military use to carry soldiers across terrain safely where there is a significant threat from hostiles. It can also be used as a very effective mobile prison. It can be solar powered in sunny climes or magno batteries in other regions and is impervious to everything but the most powerful laser bombs and pulse weaponry. She knew that now he got her in one of these, she was going where he wanted her to go.

They bumped along for what seemed like hours before rumbling to a stop and all the time she was laid in the back in the dark still handcuffed and scared. The little star shaped scar on her chest was now throbbing quietly but constantly to let her know Leon was with her and it helped, sort of. The restraints on her wrists were cutting painfully into her skin and the arm she was lying on had gone completely numb. She kept rolling over onto her stomach to let the blood get back which meant she bumped her head, nose and chin so many times during the trip that she didn't know what bit of her hurt the most. The shunter buggy isn't designed for comfort and she knew she'd be black and blue when she got out of there. Suddenly the door opened and she was temporarily blinded as the bright Terramoran sun exploded into the inside of the dark vehicle. The man grabbed her roughly by the ankles and pulled her out backwards into the fresh air. She couldn't stand at first and he had to hold her up to stop her from collapsing onto the ground in a heap.

"Stand up," he yelled at her and shook her from behind. She tried to keep still and make her numb knees work. She took a quick look at her surroundings and noticed that they were in an area of forest a long way outside of the city. There was no way she'd be able to escape even if it were a good idea; there was nowhere to hide amongst the young saplings and seedlings. The sound of an engine approaching from far away caught her powerful hearing and she looked towards the sound. Focussing her eyes, the scene jumped towards her and she saw a man riding a hover cycle coming this way. A shove from behind made her lose her concentration and she turned to see herself looking at a small space ship. It was small, just a planet hopper really and nothing at all special. There were no identifying marks so she could tell where it came from or who owned and operated it. As she looked at the ship her captor became aware of the hover cycle approaching. He grabbed her by the restraints and pushed her forward to meet the cycle and its rider. The rider dropped the bike and ran towards them, yanking off his goggles and throwing them to the ground. Fear was written all over his face as he approached them.

"For fucks' sake Boss, you didn't tell me I'd have to be shot at and chased all over the fuckin planet by the security forces. What the fuck did you get me into here?" he yelled pointing angrily at her captor.

She was stunned. he'd called her captor Boss. She wondered if he was the mysterious unnamed Boss from the Moxal 3 saga but he wasn't going to be pushed around and he reacted accordingly.

"So what, you think I'm stupid huh Jackson? You think I don't know you and this bitch here got an alternate plan to take what's mine huh?" He jabbed her hard in the back when he said the word bitch and she felt drops of spittle on her neck as he continued ranting at Jackson who she now realised must be the assassin whose plan she foiled when she saved Donaldson. Oops, no wonder they're annoyed, she thought to herself. "There's no way I'm gonna let a stupid fuck like you ruin everything I've worked for all these years, Jackson. You and this bitch ain't gonna take away what's mine, not now not ever." A shot thundered in her ear so loud she cried out in surprise and pain as her eardrums almost exploded. Jackson's chest imploded, leaving a large hole big enough to put a fist through. His eyes were wide in surprise as he fell backwards onto the Terramoran forest floor. She had seen that type of wound before, on Vincent's data cube. It was the calling card of the Transmortal Hellfire Pulse Laser Canon. She was suddenly convinced there was a link between what occurred back on Moxal 3 all those years ago, and what she witnessed here today.

The Boss shoved Farra roughly towards the little planet hopper ship so hard that she lost her balance and fell. He grabbed her and yanked her up to her feet and as he did so, she came around to face him and found herself looking at something she recognised but had never seen on anyone else but herself before. It was hot on Terramora, the sun relentless and her captor had opened the first few buttons of his shirt, revealing a small star shaped scar in the centre of his chest, right on the sternum. This guy's Lilean, she thought to herself, shocked at the discovery. He saw her gaping at it.

"What the fuck you looking at?" he demanded angrily, "you gotta problem?"

She didn't quite know how to answer him. "I err, no, no problem," she lied as he pushed her roughly towards the planet hopper's rear hatch.

The little planet hopper was fairly spacious inside and she found herself seated in a fairly comfortable seat at the rear. The Boss restrained each of her arms to bulkheads so although she was at last sitting relatively comfortably, her arms were stuck out sideways at ninety degrees from her body, held there by the restraints. As he tightened the restraint holding her left arm, her Drycenian plate became uncovered and he noticed it. There was a tense moment of silence as he looked at it, and then at her face questioningly.

"What the fuck is that?" He jabbed at it with a finger. When she didn't answer immediately he looked her straight in the eyes challengingly. His question gave away the fact that he didn't know what it was or where it was from, so she risked a complete lie and hoped he bought it.

"I broke my arm a few years ago on some shit pile of a planet out in the middle of god knows where. The army medics were gonna amputate but the locals said they could save it if we treated em easy. This is the result. They saved the arm but I have to have that thing on it all the time to hold it all together or something." She silently prayed.

"Rather you than me," he replied and immediately lost interest. She sighed deeply and thanked god. A throb from her chest in reply told her Leon was close. The Boss put an additional restraint around her middle and the seat and more around each ankle, she wasn't going anywhere in a hurry.

"Where are you taking me?" she asked him, trying not to sound too confident.

"To your death, now shut the fuck up," he snarled as he took the pilot's seat and began tapping switches and buttons. The engines roared into life and with a shudder that became a rumble that became a bone shattering vibration, the little planet hopper leapt from the surface of Terramora Prime for the last time.

CHAPTER TWELVE

Michael Donaldson was tired. It was too hot for him here on Terramora Prime. He was sweating heavily and he could feel a headache starting. He was now regretting agreeing to come and stay on the planet but he knew the importance of the occasion and the good impression his presence would give. It was so important for everyone to be seen to be moving forwards away from the Transmortal attacks and anything he could do to help was okay. If only it weren't so damn hot! A hand on his shoulder made him spin around.

"It's time sir," an aide whispered into his ear. Thank goodness. Once he got this speech out of the way he could maybe get into somewhere a bit cooler. He nodded to his aide, climbed the steps to the podium and rested his hands on the lectern as he accepted the applause graciously. There were hundreds of people here and he was gratified to see so many came to this ceremony. Trees were thought of almost as deities here and that made this speech important which is why he'd been up till the early hours writing and rehearsing it. Less than ten years ago his life was so different and if anyone told him then that in a few years time he'd be the guest of honour giving such an important speech on Terramora Prime, he'd have told them they were crazy. He was a good man and he knew it and was proud of his morals.

He always knew he wasn't the type to thrive in the military and he wasn't built for combat. He never had the personality for it either; he always lacked that edge that those in combat need to survive. He never believed that the whole answer could be found in simply cleaning up situations. He always felt a need to know why things happened and why people did what they did and he always believed that discussion and understanding could build bridges that the military approach couldn't. As a teenager his buddies called him a pacifist and he was bullied some over it. When he was younger it seemed like the only way to be thought of as a real man was to join the military and go kick some ass. He always secretly thought that idea was a bit like de-evolving but he kept the opinion to himself to avoid more bullying than he was already experiencing.

While his buddies were working out and joining the junior military corps, he was sat in debating class discussing the topical issues of the day with others like himself. He was in his element in those classes and graduated knowing that whatever he did with his life, it must be something that involved encouraging openness and honesty amongst people. He hated secrecy and cliques and all of the underhanded double dealing he knew went on in most organisations and companies. The institutionalised bullying tactics used to keep the workers out of touch and obedient that he came across time after time annoyed and dismayed him beyond belief. As he stood there waiting to deliver his speech, he was proud of having kept to his morals and wished that those bullies from his childhood could be here now.

"Ladies and gentlemen, friends. We are here today to give thanks not only for our own survival, but to give thanks to God for honouring this world with a new forest. As these precious new saplings grow and thrive to once again grace this earth with their beauty and reverence, we are reminded every day that he is with us, that he watches over us, that he smiles upon us and that he loves us. Twenty five years ago those first survivors took their first brave steps towards renewal. As they stooped to gather up those fallen stones and began to rebuild this magnificent world, their vision and hope for the future of all, reached his eyes and he was pleased. Those who have carried on this work throughout all of the intervening years had that same vision and those who still carry on the work today and into the future have that vision. Your vision, your hope, your certainty of renewal has become a living reality in these precious new trees that grow alongside you. Their strength, their determination and their will to survive and regenerate is a consequence of your own belief and a symbol of that vision. As you bury those lost during those tragic days, these living manifestations of God's love grow ever more beautiful. As you set each new stone in its rightful place, this forest spreads its grace a little further across your world and into your hearts. Friends, please join me in a prayer of thanks." The crowd bowed their heads as one. "Almighty God, on this new day as we stand here amongst these living symbols of your love we offer our thanks that they have returned to grace our world. We give thanks for the life giving air that is their gift to us as we strive to rebuild this world to be a place of friendship and welcome to all your children, wherever they may be from and however they choose to know and honour you in their turn. We stand in awe at the strength and courage displayed here every day since those terrible days so long ago. Almighty Father, as we stand here today, we humbly beg forgiveness on those who once walked on this world with darkness in their hearts and separated us from those we love. As these new trees grow, we ask that their grace find its way into the hearts of those dark souls who need it most, so that they find the courage to reach out their hands and find you. Amen." As Donaldson looked up he saw many heads nodding in agreement, a few eyes being dabbed and one or two openly sobbing and being comforted by those around them. He'd done a good job and he was glad he spent so much time working on the speech last night; he wanted to make a lasting impression that would help to spur things along as the rebuilding continued. It was time for summing up and a gracious goodbye. He looked back down at his notes.

He just had time to register the fact that someone was leaping over the rope barrier that kept the crowd at a respectful distance from the podium, before he felt a body crash into him and send them both sprawling down the back of the podium to the ground below. He heard shots ringing out over his head as they flew through the air and shouts and panic from all around as he lay on the ground with the body on top of him. He was winded and clutched at his chest as he struggled for air. The body on top of him moved and allowed him to sit up and he looked at it. Whoever it was had covered their head with a hooded shirt; one of those new fashion ones designed to keep the sun from the face and although he was unable to see the face he was aware of a pair of startlingly green eyes looking at him from under the hood. It was a woman, of that he was in no doubt. Only women wore these new over shirts and those eyes were feminine, soft and he just knew they meant him no harm. She reached inside the shirt and for a moment he wondered if he'd got it wrong and she was about to shoot him. She brought out a small package just a little bigger than a pack of cigarettes and held it out to him.

"Who are you? What do you want from me? he asked her. Then, as if to confirm his intuitive feeling that she meant no harm, she spoke.

"Never mind. Take this package please. Remember Moxal 3?" Moxal 3? Why the hell would she be mentioning that place? He nodded and she continued. "This package contains Vincent's book and data cube, the one he tried to give you years ago. He is innocent of the crimes he was convicted of and the data that this package contains proves it. It will also help you deal with the Moxal Revolutionaries once and for all. Vincent is innocent. You must clear his name for at this very moment he is bringing to an end the evil that once walked here on this very spot. He has suffered so much for crimes he didn't commit, use this and clear him. Please." She leapt up from him and ran off but as she turned to run away, he noticed her shirt had a small tear at the back and through it he could see a beautiful dragon. She disappeared into the crowd within seconds and as Donaldson looked about him at the chaotic scene, he wondered how Moxal 3 could be connected with the shooting here today, or if it even was connected, or why.

"Sir, Sir are you hurt?" a voice shouted at him from his left. He turned to look and found one of his aides lying on the ground with his leg all bloody.

"No I'm okay, what the hell is going on here?" he asked before realising the absurdity of the question.

"Don't know Sir. Shots came from somewhere back in the far tree line. The security forces are tracking its source." The man lying down cried out in agony as he clutched at his leg.

Donaldson shouted for his aides. "Morley, Johnson, get over here and help Wickley, he's been shot." A man ran over to them and crouched by Donaldson. It was Morley.

"Johnson is dead Sir, as is Norman, are you hurt?"

Donaldson shook his head. "No I'm okay. Help Wickley please; his leg is shot to pieces."

Morley leapt up and ran over to Wickley who lay there moaning in pain. "It's okay buddy, try to relax. Help is on the way."

The next two hours passed in a chaotic rush. The crowd rushed away in all directions, screaming as they ran to find cover as the security forces rushed towards the far tree line in search of the gunman. Medical aid rushed to the scene and the two dead aides were taken away by the ANA. Wickley was treated at the scene before being returned to the ANA liner for treatment in its on board medical centre. Donaldson was fussed over by Morley who urged him to return to the liner himself for safety.

"Please Sir, your safety is paramount. I must urge you to return to the liner immediately. If you get killed here the ANA and all it stands for will be in jeopardy."

Donaldson listened politely but his mind was made up. He was staying. "If I run away at the first sign of trouble, what impression does that give people of what the ANA stands for? I'm staying here and that's final. Thank you for your concern Morley. You do your job well and I appreciate your candour but I'm staying."

"Yes Sir," Morley replied obediently. Donaldson knew that he was probably cursing him under his breath and he understood why.

"Let's get back to the hotel now eh?" Donaldson clapped Morley on the back and smiled as he gently patted the package hidden beneath his shirt.

Back at the hotel, he retrieved the package the woman gave him and examined it more closely. It was wrapped in soft leather and contained an old style data cube and a little notebook.

"My god, it is the same one," he exclaimed as he handled the book and let his thoughts drift back to that day on Moxal 3 when the big Lilean met him in the tunnel and tried to get him to listen. The guy was aware that something wasn't right with the Moxal 3 Mining Corporation and came to him with evidence he took the trouble to gather secretly. Donaldson joined the fledgling ANA because its aims and objectives matched everything he wanted his life to stand for. Back in those days he was just a new recruit; he had no real authority of his own to wield when faced with corruption and double dealing within companies and organisations. He was sent on his first position in the field and ended up at the Moxal 3 Mining Corporation as a representative of the ANA. Officially he was supposed to ensure that the company practised their business in a legal and safe manner by observing the day to day running of the place and by being a listening ear for the employees who may want to discuss the way the company operated and treated them to someone outside of the company who was neutral and objective. He tried to do exactly that but McGreedle had no intention of opening up to him. He guessed straight away that there was something wrong and he didn't trust the Facility Warden one little bit.

When the big Lilean guy gave him the book and data cube he thought all his luck was in and in his innocence, told McGreedle that he was going to get the authorities onto him, that he now possessed evidence of everything that had been going on. All that brought him was the pleasure of being beaten black and blue and having his quarters ransacked by McGreedle's lackeys. They found the evidence and took it, leaving Donaldson with nothing with which to back up any claims he might make against the company. He was hog tied by his own stupidity and Vincent suffered as a result. After the guy was arrested and sent to Cryo Stasis for his trouble, Donaldson almost gave up the ANA in disgust. He took a leave of absence and talked the whole thing over with his supervising officer and after being given a thorough telling off for being so stupid, was given a transfer away from Moxal 3. Now here he was all these years later and head of the ANA with all the clout he could ever want. How often he wished to be able to fix the Moxal 3 situation and make it up to the big

Lilean guy who showed trust in him, but without the evidence he could do nothing. Now Vincent was back and giving him another chance to listen and help and do the right thing and he decided that he'd not rest until he'd made sure it was fixed right this time.

"I am so sorry Vincent, for everything. I give you my word here and now that I won't let you down again," Donaldson vowed as he opened Vincent's book and began to read. As he leafed through the pages it all came flooding back to him. The secret meetings, the suspicious looking weapons company man who scared the shit out of him just by looking at him a certain way, the dwindling money and the murders. One of the victims was a woman who always made an effort to smile and say hello to him and he even wondered if he should ask her out but never had the nerve. All of these memories and many more came back to him as he sat in his hotel room in just his underwear because it was too hot for him on Terramora Prime. He punched his cell phone and waited for Morley to answer.

"Morley, I need a digital streamer as soon as you can. Oh, and make sure it's capable of reading a series Seven Oxicon cube will ya? Quick as you can buddy." He got dressed in the lightest and coolest clothes he possessed and poured himself yet another glass of water. When Morley finally turned up with a streamer capable of reading the Oxicon cube, Donaldson was pacing the room.

"Sorry it took so long Sir, those cubes are way out of date now. What the heck do you want one of those for?" Morley asked. Donaldson took a moment to think about his closest aide. Morley was one of those men who had a devotion to duty that was so strong it bordered on obsession. Sometimes it blinkered him, hampered his ability to be flexible. He always did his job properly and Donaldson never had cause to doubt his loyalty either to himself or the ANA aims and objectives.

"Morley, you have always been my most trusted aide, no, my friend. I have never doubted your loyalty to the ANA cause or myself and I trust that you hold openness, truth and right as the greatest priority. I need to trust you now more than ever before with something so important, both to me personally and to the very future of many other worlds in the galaxy. I need to know I have your unflinching loyalty and total confidence for what needs to happen in the immediate future. Please tell me that my affection for you as my friend has not clouded my judgement of you."

Donaldson looked Morley right in the eyes and for a moment they stared at each other. The slightly overweight but still fit and handsome black man looked back at Donaldson for no more than a moment before replying. "You have my word, my loyalty and if necessary, my life Sir." Donaldson smiled, relieved that he was still a good judge of character.

"Okay, shut and lock the door and help me upload this cube." For long hours into the night Donaldson and Morley studied the contents of the data cube and notebook. They both felt confident that not only would Vincent easily get his freedom, but also that they could finally deal with the Moxal 3 revolutionaries. As dawn broke over Terramora Prime, they had the skeleton of a plan.

"We both know that in order for Vincent to get his freedom, he must attend the hearing in person right?" Morley said and Donaldson nodded in agreement, it was standard ANA procedure. "We also know that he escaped from Cryo Stasis and could by now be hell knows where. How in gods name do we find him and get him here?"

"Look," said Donaldson suddenly. "This page here, it says he escaped in the one remaining Cryo Stasis ship." Morley nodded as he re read the document. "Well the first thing we do is to work out how far that ship could travel fully fuelled, and all habitable planets in that area can then be searched."

"But that could be hundreds Sir, it could take years to find him," Morley replied.

"Well it's better than just sticking a pin in a map or doing it alphabetically ain't it?" Donaldson argued. "What other way is there? We have to start somewhere."

"Yeah I guess you're right Sir. I'll do the math and work out how much ground we have to cover and pray there aren't too many planets in that area?"

"Great, and meanwhile I want all resources put onto the Moxal 3 Mining Corporation right away. I want the full force of the ANA to go in unannounced and sweep the place clean. I want every piece of paper, data chip, journal, log books, hell I even want what's been scratched onto the toilet walls, everything."

"Yes Sir, I'll get that underway now." Morley dialled the secure line on his cell phone and called for an emergency meeting in four hours. By the time the men got a couple of hours sleep, showered, dressed and sat down for lunch, the full weight of the ANA was speeding its way into a lockdown for the Moxal 3 Mining Corporation.

Back on board the ANA liner Donaldson took another look at the data cube. There were a few documents added at the end of the data stream that seemed different to him, but he wasn't a real techie and didn't know why. He called Morley who came over and took a look. Donaldson pointed out what he was looking at. "Look, here at the start of this bit of the data stream. It's different from the rest but I'm not technologically minded. I'm a paper pusher. You know more about this than me, tell me what this is and what it means."

Morley took a close look and looked thoughtful for a few moments. "I see what you mean Sir. That part of the code tells us when this document was added to the stream. Look, if you look back at these earlier documents you can see those same areas of code right?" Donaldson looked and nodded. Morley continued, trying to keep it simple. "Notice how the numbers are going in chronological order?" Donaldson nodded again. "That shows us that the documents were added a few days apart, a week or so with some of them, but most are no more than a day apart, some just a few hours. Then we come to these last few, and the numbers suddenly jump way up." He looked up at Donaldson.

"Which tells us what?" Donaldson asked, hoping Morley knew the answer.

"It means that these documents were added years after the first ones, very recently in fact. Hang on a minute, let me convert this code and I'll get an exact time frame." He tapped a few buttons and then looked back at Donaldson. "My god," he said in shock.

"What? What is it?" Donaldson demanded.

"Sir, these last few documents were added just days ago, a couple of weeks." Both men stared at each other, then at the screen and then back at each other.

Donaldson broke the shocked silence first. "So, what does this mean? Who added them?"

"This other bit of code here will tell us that Sir, give me a minute." Morley tapped again and Donaldson waited as patiently as he could. "What the hell? But that can't be, it's just impossible." Morley clapped a hand over his head and just stared at the screen, unable to articulate what he was seeing.

Donaldson erupted. "Well?"

"Sorry Sir, it's just a shock. You'll never guess who put these documents on the stream."

"No I won't. Why don't you just tell me." Donaldson was trying not to shout, he was really trying.

Morley apologised again. "Sorry Sir, it's the Drycenian Nation. They put these last few documents into the stream for us to find."

Donaldson's jaw dropped in complete shock. "Are you sure?"

"Yes Sir, no question. I checked twice. The Drycenian Nation is responsible for these added documents."

"My god, how are they involved in this, and why?" Donaldson asked aloud, knowing Morley wouldn't know the answer.

Suddenly Morley had an epiphany. "Sir, we all know the Drycenian Nation has technology the rest of us can't even dream about. The fact that they added these documents, all pertaining to Vincent I hasten to add, shows that they are at least a little concerned that the truth comes out and he gets his freedom. They must also have had some input into getting this evidence to you, via the mysterious woman." Donaldson was nodding at regular intervals. "So, they have enough intelligence to work out that no one knows where Vincent is. They also must know that he needs to be here in person to be able to be granted his freedom." Donaldson listened intently and now the penny was beginning to drop. "It would then be fair to assume that they are also taking pains to try to discover his whereabouts, right?" He looked at Donaldson who agreed.

"Yes it would. They aren't going to give us all of this and help us so much, only to then leave us to do the hard part ourselves, knowing we've a nearly impossible chance of finding him. Are they?" Morley didn't think so. Donaldson made a decision. "Okay this is what we'll do next. I want McGreedle, Ranger Thomas Dolton and the SB Weapons Rep guy arrested. I also want anyone else found to be involved in the revolutionary plot arrested. Bring them all here under the highest level restraint for crimes relating to fraud, embezzlement, flouting health and safety legislation and multiple murder. Once we have them secured, we will announce publicly that we have them for crimes relating to a political plot aimed at gaining control of a large sector of the galaxy. We don't at any time mention Vincent. We must also let it be known that they are accused of multiple murders on Moxal 3 several years ago. Once that goes out across the airwaves, the Drycenians will pick it up and know we are onto things. That might encourage them to come forward and announce their involvement to us."

Morley got up and headed for the door. "I'll put it into action right away Sir," he said as he left the room.

Donaldson banged the gavel on the table and called the meeting to order.

"Okay people what do we have?"

"Sir, it seems that Moxal 3 suffered something of a meltdown a couple of weeks ago."

"What kind of meltdown?" Donaldson asked.

"Well, a few of the survivors have told us that on the night it happened the emergency shut down procedure was put into action. There was panic everywhere but nobody knew what had gone wrong or what had caused the emergency. Several surviving employees told us that it had something to do with what they termed The Animal," he said as he looked at Donaldson.

"The Animal? What animal?"

"Well Sir, it would seem that the Moxal Mining Corporation Rangers had somehow got hold of a prisoner whom they kept down in the deeper layers of the tunnel complex. Employees who wanted to see this prisoner were charged five packs of cigarettes each." Donaldson was confused at this. "What? What prisoner? And why hold anyone down there? What had he done? And why would people want to pay in cigarettes to see him?"

"Well, it seems that none of the employees had ever seen one before, they all willingly paid up to get their first look."

"Their first look at what? What hadn't they seen before? Come on man educate me for pity's sake before I have a heart attack here." Donaldson was trying and failing to remain patient and calm.

"A Drycenian Sir. They had captured a Drycenian and were holding him there in the tunnels. One can only assume it was some kind of blackmail kidnapping." Murmurs went around the room at the mention of the Drycenians and Donaldson and Morley looked at each other knowingly. They both now knew why the Drycenians got themselves involved in this.

"Oh shit," Donaldson said out loud as he put his head into his hands and sighed. He looked up and continued. "Okay what else do we know? Anyone?"

"Yes Sir, after the emergency services from Moxal 3's Tactical Combat Centre on its moon were deployed, they found the Facility Warden Mr McGreedle's body in the aircraft hangar. It was evident from the body that he'd been killed with a Hellfire Pulse Laser Canon. A Transmortal weapon Sir." More murmurs of shock went around the room and this time Donaldson and Morley were among them.

"The Transmortals are involved in this? Jeez whatever next?" Donaldson didn't know what to think. "Anything else? What about the SB Weapons guy, do we have him? And the Ranger, what's his name?"

"Excuse me Sir, no we don't have the SB Weapons man, he is called umm, let me just check, oh yes here it is, he is a Mr Andrew Midship, commonly known as bullet, but we do have the Ranger, err a Mr Dolton his name is. We also have five witnesses willing to appear to testify that they personally saw the Drycenian prisoner and two who are willing to testify that they saw large sums of cash being handed over to Mr Midship on more than one occasion. They will be here within a week or so."

"Okay I want it put out that Mr Andrew Midship is wanted for arrest but I want it for official ears only. I don't want every merc and bounty hunter in the galaxy getting in the way and getting themselves killed. Where is Midship from?"

The delegate checked his report. "Err one moment, let me check. Oh yes, he's Lilean." Donaldson and Morley looked at each other again, what the heck was going one here?

"Okay covertly check the comings and goings from Lilea over the past six months and see if Mr Midship has been around."

"It's been done Sir; he left Lilea seven years ago and hasn't returned. We are keeping a covert check on things in case he surfaces there, but we're not hopeful." Donaldson had to agree it was a little unlikely that the guy would just turn up at home as if nothing had happened after the meltdown at the mine. He began to doubt he'd ever be seeing Mr Midship and that irked him no end.

"Do we yet know who committed those murders on Moxal 3?" He looked around the room expectantly. "Anyone?"

"Sir, I thought they'd been solved years ago. Didn't someone get convicted of those murders?" A few of the delegates were nodding in agreement. This was a tense moment and Donaldson had to make a quick decision. He took a deep breath before speaking.

"It has come to my attention that the person convicted of those crimes is almost certainly innocent and that the real killer is, and has always been, still at large. If we can right that miscarriage of justice along with dealing with this irksome revolutionary thing, we can all sleep a little more soundly in our beds. Now, when the witnesses are questioned, I want those murders solved. Am I making myself clear?"

"Yes Sir," all the delegates replied as one.

The meeting dragged on and on. Plans were made, decisions taken, tasks were delegated and Donaldson began to feel as if there was a real chance of righting his biggest mistake. He carried the shame since the day it happened and if he could look Vincent in the eyes and shake his hand and ask for his forgiveness, he could look at his reflection in the mirror with a little less shame as he shaved his face every morning.

"Has there been any luck in tracing the woman who saved me from getting killed?" he asked. All the delegates shook their heads. It was a young delegate who spoke.

"No Sir, we have put out an arrest warrant for her but without a description there isn't much hope unless someone inside the assassination plot comes forward."

Donaldson hadn't mentioned about the dragon tattoo he saw on the woman's back through her torn shirt. He didn't want her killed as a suspect for he firmly believed she was innocent of any involvement. He did want to meet her though to thank her for saving his life and giving him the opportunity to secure Vincent's freedom. "Okay, keep looking and making enquiries but I want everyone to be sure, she is to be treated well if she is found. I don't believe for a minute that she was involved in the plot to kill me. I believe she wanted only to save my life and I wish to give her the thanks she deserves for such a selfless act. Under no circumstances must a contract for her capture be put out to the general public. If I find out that someone has leaked this and some merc gets hold of her and kills her for a payday, heads will roll. Do you all understand me?" Everyone nodded and Donaldson hoped they'd got the point.

CHAPTER THIRTEEN

Inside the dome all was in darkness and it took a few seconds for Vincent's eyes to adjust to the gloom. He felt vulnerable there in the doorway with the light behind him but he didn't dare move in case there was just a sheer drop down to certain death below. No one rushed at him though and a few seconds later he was able to take his first good look around the place. It was immense and he noticed the area of dome that was visible above ground was only part of it; as he looked down the stairwell he saw to his right he noticed it went down several storeys, maybe a hundred feet or more into the ground. He was standing on the top floor with the curve of the dome rising above him, and what looked like a sort of reception area stretched out in front of him. There were the tattered and weathered remains of seating areas and low tables strewn with dead leaves and broken pieces of whatever it was the dome was made of. A bar went halfway around the circumference of the room and he could still see bottles stacked up on shelves behind it. The labels were still readable on most of them, although he found he couldn't read the writing on them for it was in some weird language he'd never seen before let alone learned. He wondered if he should try one, after all a beer is a beer. He selected what looked most like a bottle of beer and examined the cap. It wasn't immediately obvious how to open it but after a bit of fumbling and then resorting to brute strength, he was soon enjoying a remarkably good beer, given that it was his first for nearly six years.

He scouted the room, looked into cupboards and drawers but found nothing of interest so he decided to check out the floor below. He gingerly tried the steps in case they were rotten from years of being open to the weather but they felt as firm as if they were brand new so he slowly descended, blade in hand. It was pretty dark down here and he didn't have a flashlight so he looked for any obvious signs of lights.

"Where the fuck are the lights in this place?" he asked himself in a whisper as he looked around the walls. He found an almost invisible plate on the wall at shoulder height, so he went over to examine it. As he approached and stood in front of it, the lights suddenly went on of their own accord. He jumped back in alarm, but realised that the plate was probably a motion sensor activated light switch. He looked around and found himself in what looked like offices. Being under the ground, the lower floors of the building weren't restricted to being set into a circular pattern so the rooms he found himself looking at here were arranged in an ordinary looking corridor. He tried all the doors and found the same set up in all of them, desks and chairs and all manner of weird looking technology. They were obviously some sort of computer devices but he couldn't remember ever seeing anything like them before, and he'd been around. It felt so weird; this place was obviously abandoned hundreds and maybe even thousands of years ago but this technology seemed modern, so modern in fact that he wouldn't mind betting it was state of the art even now. "What the fuck have I stumbled onto here?" he asked aloud. After finding that all of the rooms were identical, he went down another floor and found himself in another identical corridor as the one above.

The rooms down here were more recognisable as living quarters. Each room was again laid out the same as all the others and contained a bed, a closet, a shelf, another weird looking type of computer monitor thing and a weird looking shower cubicle and toilet. As with the floor above, the corridor had an almost invisible plate on the wall which activated the lights when he approached. He searched each of the rooms but found nothing of any interest to him in any of the closets or shelves, in fact there was nothing at all in any of them; they were completely bare, as though whoever stayed here took everything when they left. Not even a piece of paper was to be found anywhere. He sat down on one of the beds to think about this new discovery and found himself realising how supremely comfortable it seemed after five years of sleeping on a pile of animal hides and brush on the floor of a cave. Almost without thinking he allowed himself to lie back full length and as his body settled, he felt like he was floating on a cloud. Without even realising it, he fell asleep almost immediately.

Syra approached the sleeping Vincent as he lay there on the bed. She looked down at him and smiled and felt so proud of how far he'd come in so short a time. He was so troubled and suffered such pain and turmoil in his life but still here he was putting his life on the line again for others while still believing no one cared whether he lived or died. She was very happy that he was now accepting her presence and listening to her guidance; that he was beginning to understand her role in his life was so very important and there were times when she wondered if she would ever be able to awaken him fully.

She reached into his mind with her own. "Sleep Vincent. Stay sleeping and listen. Listen carefully brave one; remember the words you will hear. Sleep and remember." She stepped back as she saw the image of the girl approach her sleeping charge. She was beautiful and strong, a true warrior and she cared so deeply. Syra knew this girl was the right choice; the ancient ones had been right in their choosing of her. Leon had approached Syra and told her of what transpired and they both felt it would be right for them both to allow this moment between them. Vincent felt so alone for so long and his awareness of his solitude was troubling for him even though he carried the burden well; it would help heal his heart to experience this now. This was the right moment. The girl too, she was beginning to be aware of the strength of the connection that was taking place between them and the need to pass on some comfort to Vincent was becoming distracting in its strength. Her survival and courage to do what is right depends upon her being able to act without emotional burdens right now. Syra held Vincent's mind with hers, keeping him asleep so the moment could happen between them and she would make sure he remembered.

Vincent descended into sleep without even being aware of being awake just a moment ago. He was so tired, so very tired and it felt so good to be lying on a soft bed again. He heard a familiar voice from far away; Syra was talking to him but it was such a struggle to hear her. He was beginning to understand now that she was there to help him and he wasn't crazy so he listened for her. He strained his ears but couldn't hear her voice. Somehow he just knew he must listen so he focussed on listening and waited to hear. Suddenly a woman's voice; a voice he didn't recognise was there. Who was this, where was Syra? He listened to the voice, it sounded friendly and he realised he wanted very much to hear what she had to say.

"Vincent, don't worry. I am fighting for you. You are not forgotten. I am working to free you and bring you home. Don't be sad Vincent; don't think you have no one to care. I care. I care very much. Sleep well and wake refreshed my friend. Be safe, and remember I care. Remember that Vincent. I care and I'm fighting for you." The voice was full of emotion and he knew that the person speaking meant every word, but who is she? Where is she? He didn't know the answers but as he listened to her soft voice and heard the words he felt his heart expanding. He felt her energy nearby but he couldn't see her. He looked around but all he could see was the white mist of the hinterland surrounding him.

Her energy felt so warm, like she was wrapping him up in a soft blanket and holding him close. Suddenly her energy became over powering in its intensity and flooded over him in a sudden rush. He felt as though the woman and her emotions were all over him, inside him and taking hold of his heart in her hands. He realised as he lay there bathed in the mystery woman's energy and words of comfort that she was giving him love so unconditionally he thought his heart would explode. He felt so much all at the same time, shock at the intensity of her feelings and the effect it was having on his own, a longing for it never to end and despair at his own loneliness. Someone was loving him and he wanted so much to feel that love, to be surrounded by it, to return it. He felt the woman's energy come so close that his whole being was absorbed by it and for a moment it almost felt as if he'd been kissed. He awoke with a start and sat up to find himself still in the room inside the dome. He looked around the room to get his bearings and sighed as he remembered the dream of the woman's voice. He realised he was still alone after all; it was just a dream.

It was so real though, that voice was really there as much as Syra's was when she spoke.

"Was it real? Was it real? Please, was it real?" he cried aloud and when he felt the throb in his chest in response, he sighed deeply, fighting to control his emotions.

The next floor down was occupied by three large rooms behind clear doors that opened with a swish as he approached. He entered the first room slowly. He looked for the plate that operated the lights, touched it and watched the room snap into view in front of him. It looked like a clinic of some kind or a hospital operating theatre with a shiny silver table in the centre and all sorts of machines everywhere. He walked around the room and looked at the machines but couldn't discover what they were or how they might be used. A silver tray lay on a shelf and when he examined it he found what looked like surgical instruments. He'd never been in a hospital and never had any kind of operation so this stuff was completely outside of his experience. He'd taken his military colleagues to hospitals when they were injured but he'd never seen the inside of an operating theatre in his life. From what he was seeing here though, he'd lay money on this being some kind of hospital or clinic. He left and went into the second of the three rooms, to find an identical set up as the previous one. The only difference here was a digital chart readout that he guessed must be from the room's last patient. As with the beer bottles, he couldn't read it due to the strange language and symbols it contained. He put it down and went to check the last of the three rooms, expecting it to be exactly the same.

The third room was the same as the other two but this one looked as if it was left in a hurry. So much of a hurry in fact that the doctors must have left in the middle of the procedure, because there was the remains of a body still on the table. It was no more than a skeleton now but still he approached cautiously. He saw that the top of the skull was removed and there was even a small surgical instrument lying within the empty cavity. The bones looked human, if a little small and he guessed this person must've been either fairly young and not full grown or a rather short adult, maybe even a short race of people. That's when the penny dropped and he realised what he was looking at. This skeleton belonged to one of the indigenous humans he was surrounded by back at the cave. A look at the mouth and jaw gave him his final evidence of this; those large fangs were identical to the ones he saw on his neighbours as they ate their enemies!

"My god, what the fuck?" he said aloud as the realisation of what he was seeing hit home. From his five years at the cave he never once saw any of his neighbours do anything that made him think they had access to this type of medical care and he was never aware of any other humans visiting the planet. "But this place has obviously been abandoned for centuries," he said aloud as he tried to put the pieces of the puzzle together, and failed. The place was beginning to give him the creeps!

He descended to what turned out to be the lowest level and found one large door in front of him. It was solid and ornately carved and covered in strange designs and symbols he couldn't understand except for what looked like stylised depictions of planets and solar systems. There was a sign over the door which again he couldn't read, but he guessed it told him what the room was or was used for. He knew the only way to find out was to go in, so he gave the door a shove. The huge room looked like it could hold several hundred people all at the same time and he was just about to wonder how it seemed so much bigger than the ones above, when he remembered that he was deep underground and this room was obviously cut out of the bedrock much bigger on purpose. At one end was a raised area with two steps leading up to a large ornately carved chair that looked like a throne. His boot steps echoed softly as he walked around the perimeter of the room examining the intricate paintings on the walls depicting what looked to him like triumphant battle scenes, bodies scattered on the ground and large black cloaked figures standing over them. As he looked at the black figures with their cloaks billowing in the wind, he remembered the imagery of the day he was born and that evil black figure who killed him and his people. He was stunned by this realisation and started to back away from the paintings in shock.

"Vincent." A voice from behind made him turn and spring into defensive mode, blade in hand. Syra was standing across the room from him and it was the first time she'd appeared in solid form to him while he was fully awake. "Vincent. The cycle of time is almost complete. All moments have led to this one in which we now stand. The waiting is almost over and the time of your destiny approaches fast. The ones who you see on these walls are the ones who sent our people to the land of the dead, who sent you to the land of the dead moments after your birth that had been prophesied to the ancients so long ago. Many worlds mourn those lost at the hands of these evil ones you see on these walls. You have suffered so much Vincent but you have become a fine man and a brave warrior and we are so proud of you. All of the lost ones love you so much and are with you always." She approached and reached for his hands.

"There is only me. How can I fix this? I'm just one man," he asked her.

"You are the only one to bring this evil to an end Vincent. There is no other in the land of the living to whom destiny has given this burden. Only you have been deemed worthy of this mighty task that has brought you so much pain." Her eyes never left his as she spoke.

"But what do I do? How can I?" He was desperate for answers.

"The evil ones are coming Vincent, they are coming for you. I have kept your presence from their sight until now, until the moment prophesied arrived. They see you now and they come for you. You are not fighting alone dear one, others have your back. Know this and believe it. The answer lies in the trees Vincent, the answer lies in the trees." As she faded away Vincent knew immediately what she meant. The answer lies in the trees and in the poison he worked so hard to acquire from them.

Over the next few hours he explored the other domes and found that with the exception of one, the others were all identical to the first. The odd one was very interesting and gave him the answer to the question he'd been so desperate for Syra to answer. The last dome was given over completely to the production, care and distribution of a water supply to the other domes. The whole of the depth of this dome was filled with one vast tank and the walls were lined with machinery, digital monitoring devices and quality control consoles. He was able to work out what it all was due to seeing similar stuff during his military career. When he was sent to worlds that were pretty inhospitable, the army had to provide basic facilities such as water and they had a mobile water collection and treatment facility that they would set up for the soldiers to use. From what he could see here this one worked in pretty much a similar way and this was the obvious choice for him to use to attack the enemy when they arrived. If he could find one of the uptake valves that led into the tank, he would be able to put the poison into the whole supply so that all who drank or washed themselves in it would be affected. Then it would just be a case of surviving for a couple of days until it did its job.

He filled his own empty water carrier that he made out of the bladder of an animal he'd killed for a meal and tied the top securely. If he was frugal with it, it would last him a couple of days, long enough to maybe get away into the forest to find more anyway. It was all he had so he'd just have to be careful with it and hope luck smiled on him. Once he secured his own supply, he focussed on finding an uptake valve through which he could upload his deadly cargo. It took an hour of following pipe work until he found it tucked away in a dusty corner amid a maze of pipes and tubes. There was a bank of valves, twenty four of them in total in two rows of twelve and he knew by the configuration of the connectors which ones were uptake and which were outlets. He checked the row of valves one last time to make sure all of them led to the same main intake pipe and when he was satisfied, he gently unscrewed one of the valve connectors. He rummaged in his backpack and gingerly removed the precious bundle wrapped in leather. He didn't want to rush and end up killing himself at the eleventh hour so he forced himself to slow down and take care. He carefully unwrapped the bundle and poured the glossy brown liquid into the valve before securely replacing the connector. For a moment nothing happened and he was about to curse out loud when all of a sudden the poison rushed out of the valve with a whoosh and into the main supply. Before long Vincent knew that the whole supply would be contaminated, he just hoped there was enough poison in the water to work properly. He'd just have to hope so, it was all he had and he knew there wasn't time to go and get some more, not with it probably taking him over an hour just to get up the tree and down again. He picked up his backpack and started the long climb back up to ground level.

As he reached ground level he became aware of a vibration coming to him through the floor he was standing on. It was gentle at first but soon became so distinct he couldn't ignore it and he paused in the doorway of the dome as the vibration became a rumble and then a roar as dust and debris from the forest began to swirl madly around in the air. A sudden sharp pain in the centre of his chest confirmed what he was already starting to suspect; that rumbling could only be caused by one thing, a space ship was landing nearby. For a moment he was not sure what he should do. Should he hide somewhere in the dome or should he run into the forest? If he hid inside the dome he would be trapped, possibly with no way out and a dwindling water supply but if he was outside, in an environment he felt surer of, he'd have more chance of remaining unseen. The choice was made. He took a deep breath and bolted out of the door as fast as his legs would carry him. A big man built for endurance rather than speed but his powerful body propelled itself toward the tree line very fast and within a couple of agonisingly long minutes he was deep in the cover of the trees and vegetation. He ran for five minutes before finding some deep brush to hide in to regain his breath and his bearings. He hoped that he hadn't been seen as he ran from the dome but then he remembered that he had to force his way into the place and the sight of the totally destroyed doors would let the enemy know that someone had been snooping around.

He allowed himself a minute to regain his breath before rummaging in his backpack for his scope. He had to move a couple of hundred yards to the right before he could get a decent view of the dome complex, but when he could see what was happening he was shocked. The most enormous space ship he ever saw sat several miles away, crushing and destroying the forest and vegetation under it and for several hundred yards all around. Within the few minutes it had been since landing, there were already hundreds of black clad enemies emerging from the large exit on one side. Like a tide of ants they began to slowly swarm through the forest and Vincent realised that they'd be on top of him within twenty minutes or so.

"Shit," he thought to himself as he realised how overwhelmed he was by their sheer numbers. He had to think quickly and he forced his mind to focus. He knew he must buy himself some distance and time, so he carried on running. He knew he couldn't just go back up the mountain though; he'd stick out like a sore thumb on that barren rocky scree. No, he'd have to move sideways and put some distance between himself and them that way. He settled into his natural easy rhythm as he ran through the forest and he knew that with a twenty minute head start and his capability for endurance, he could put a healthy distance between them. As he rounded a stand of large brush, he suddenly stopped dead in his tracks as a very strong and uncomfortable feeling pervaded his mind. He was being observed. By what or by whom, he didn't know but the feeling was so strong he could almost feel himself being scanned. He felt surrounded and he felt vulnerable for the first time in a long while and he remembered feeling certain that something was following him as he made his way through this forest earlier. Another sharp pain in his chest brought his awareness back and he carried on running. With enemies behind and something unknown around him, he felt like he was stuck between a rock and a hard place but it was Hobson's choice, so he chose the forest and its unknowns rather than face the black clad evils that had murdered him the day he was born.

He ran and kept as straight a course as he could parallel with the mountain range and into a seemingly unending forest. He ran for two hours at a comfortable pace before stopping for a drink and to get his breath back and to try to relax his muscles and think. He swallowed several large mouthfuls of the water before sitting down behind a tree to think and rest his legs. As he was starting to devise a plan of action for himself, he became aware of a noise that didn't belong in the forest. It sounded like a high pitched whine, like an insect but far too loud and as he listened, it got louder. All at once something came down out of the tree tops at him and he found himself staring into what looked like a glittering, glowing sphere of icy blue light. For long seconds he stared at it, knowing neither what it was nor what he should do. Then another sharp pain from his chest spurred him into action and he rose from where he'd been sitting, all the while expecting it to start shooting at him or something. It didn't shoot at him; it simply sat there in mid air three feet away. He allowed his right hand to very slowly and subtly fumble for the blade on his hip before suddenly bringing it up and around in an alarmingly fast sideways arc and striking the ball dead centre. The light went out and it fell at his feet in two pieces and he could see that it was a ball of some kind of crystal. There were no moving parts from which it could get its power of flight or manoeuvre; it was just a solid lump of crystal. He was more than a little intrigued and picked a piece of it up to examine it further but before he could do so he felt the barrel of a weapon press itself against his temple.

Instantly he ducked as an ear splitting explosion roared over his head. Within a fraction of a second he brought his right arm, still holding his blade, across his body to his left before swinging it back with all his Lilean strength and as he regained his full height, the blade sank into the man's heart so far that his body would have a bruise in the shape of Vincent's fist around the entry point. The man made a curious gurgling noise before sinking slowly to the ground. Vincent bent and picked up the man's weapon before checking all around for more of these invaders. He donned his backpack ready to set off running but before he could take his first step, he heard the sound of a twig snapping behind him. He may not be the fastest runner in the galaxy but his reactions were always razor sharp and he spun around to find himself staring at another black cloaked figure like the one he just killed. Within a second he raised the weapon he took from the dead man and fired. Nothing happened, not even a click. The black cloaked figure grinned.

"It will only work for its owner, evil one. Now you are our prisoner and must face the Pzolgon. Come." Vincent's captor nodded his head in the direction of the domes, indicating that he expected him to just obey and march back to whatever peril awaited him there. Who or what was a Pzolgon he had no idea but he was damn sure he didn't intend to find out until he was good and ready. He took a step forward as if to acquiesce but what his captor didn't notice was the lightening fast way he flipped his blade around in his hand so that he was now holding it by the blade tip. The captor again indicated for him to walk and as he began to make his way around behind him, Vincent spun around to his left. Bringing his right arm up and back he let the blade fly at just the right moment and watched it sink into the man's throat. The captor dropped his weapon and frantically grasped at his throat as he tried to breathe. As the black gloved arms turned red from his own blood, he slumped to the ground at Vincent's feet.

He went to retrieve his blade and pulled it out of his would be captor's throat with a sickening squish. After wiping it clean on the man's cloak, he started running. He came upon a grove of tall trees with yellow leaves that carpeted the ground below and as he ran through them, from behind a tree stepped another black cloaked figure just in time to catch him squarely on the temple with the butt end of his weapon. Vincent was aware only of a sudden dull ache in his head and the realisation that all of a sudden his legs were like jelly and his feet seemed to weigh a ton apiece. As he sprawled onto his face in the leaves he discovered that he was finding it very hard to focus his eyes and ears and everything seemed to be going inwards. Time began to slow for him as he heaved himself onto his side before rolling over onto his back, the pack on his back acting as a pillow. As he forced his eyes to focus, he saw another black cloaked figure approach and crouch by his side before helping himself to the blade on his hip. As the figure readied his weapon and aimed it at him, Vincent saw it.

The creature suddenly launched itself at Vincent's would be killer sending him sprawling fifteen feet away across the little woodland glade. As the man screamed and tried to shield his face with his arms, the creature looked over at Vincent. It was basically cat like, about the size of a bear with grey fur and a tail with bristles that vibrated and made a unique sound all its own. As both creature and Vincent looked at each other, a moment passed between them. Recognition passed across the creature's face as it gave Vincent a slow blink, before raising its head and giving vent to an almighty roar and sinking its teeth into the man's face. As Vincent descended into darkness he knew it was the same female to whom he'd given his last portion of food for her infants. Before his eyes closed completely, her message rang loud and clear through his mind.

"Thank you brother."

CHAPTER FOURTEEN

King Lomas paced around the obs deck, hands behind his back. He was a patient man but this business was so important that every second of time wasted could cost so much. He was pleased beyond belief that Farra had safely delivered the evidence package to Donaldson but worried about how events on Terramora Prime took an unexpected turn. Questions raced back and forth in his mind but he found answers to none of them but they raced anyway and as he paced, he fretted. Who tried to assassinate Donaldson and most of all, why? Farra saved him from the assassin's gun but the man himself was still at large according to the message she sent them. Was she in danger? He wanted most of all for her to be safe but she made a specific point in her message of saying they must focus on getting Vincent to safety first and he knew in his heart that he couldn't let her down. If they failed to find him and secure his return to Terramora he could never be granted his freedom and the stain would never be removed from his record. He knew Farra would never forgive him if he caused that to happen so they raced across the galaxy as fast as the battle cruiser would carry them heading for the Vinbuk System to rescue Vincent. They were almost there and Lomas paced with rising agitation as he waited for his officers to report their arrival.

"Your Majesty, we are arriving at Vinbuk 3 now Sir." The intercom buzzed and Lomas raced to the bridge of his vessel without bothering to reply. At last, at long last they were here and if luck would smile on them today, they would secure Vincent and be away within hours.

"Thank heavens, I thought we'd never get here," he puffed as he entered the bridge. "Scan for bio signals immediately." As he watched his faithful crew obeying his commands without hesitation he suddenly felt very proud of them all and how throughout all of what transpired during the past weeks, not one of them questioned him. One of his officers then announced something that dismayed them all.

"Your Majesty, the Transmortals are on the planet's surface."

"What? Oh no, please no don't let us be too late to save Vincent." Lomas was horror stricken at this news and thought that Vincent would be bound to be dead by now and all would be lost. How in heaven's name would Farra receive this news?

His officer interrupted his despairing thoughts again and what he said lifted his spirits a little. "Sir, something's odd down there," the officer frowned as he studied his instrument panel. "If I'm interpreting this correctly, it would seem the Transmortals are dying in their thousands. My bio scans are picking up the expected Transmortal bio energy signals by the hundreds of thousands, but as we speak the numbers are falling. The bio signals are just, well Sir they're just going out, disappearing." The officer looked at Lomas, puzzled. He was equally puzzled and went to the instrument panel to check for himself. Sure enough the numbers of living Transmortal bio signals were falling rapidly, many thousands a minute at a rough estimate.

"How very odd. I wonder what is happening to them down there," Lomas said. "Any other bio signals apparent?"

"Yes Sir there are. There are a great number of animal bio signals in the same locality as the dying Transmortal signals and a number of humanoid bio signals one hundred and eleven miles east of this locality," he reported.

Lomas was almost too afraid to ask the next question but he knew it had to be asked. He took a deep breath. "Is there a Lilean bio signal evident anywhere at all?" He closed his eyes and prayed as he waited for the officer to re adjust his scanner to the known Lilean bio energy frequency and re scan the planet.

"Yes Sir, just the one, and it's a living signal. He's alive your Majesty, we're not too late." The officer risked a smile at his King, who let out an anguished gasp of relief and almost burst into tears. He sent up a silent word of thanks and sighed deeply.

Immediately he focussed on the task ahead of them. "Where is he," he asked.

The officer took a second or two to scan for a precise location of the Lilean bio energy signal before looking up at the King with a frown evident once again on his face. "Right in amongst the dying Transmortals Sir. It would seem as if they have him in their custody. Either that or he's managed to hide out right in the middle of them without being detected, which as we know is quite impossible with their psychic and telepathic powers. If you were to ask me to theorise, I'd say they have him prisoner and we have an extraction mission on our hands. We can't get to him without either waiting to see if they all die, or going in now, which will inevitably mean engaging them." Lomas was faced with a terrible choice, either waste valuable time waiting for all the Transmortals to die of whatever it is that's killing them before going in to get Vincent, and possibly finding that whatever killed them kills him too while they're waiting, or go in now and use force. He didn't like either of the choices; he didn't like them at all.

The Drycenians are not a fighting race. Over the millennia they learned to leave the more volatile emotions in the past and have lived as silent, invisible and legendary observers of humanity. With their vastly superior technology they were able to observe the other races in the galaxy as they grew and evolved and began to stretch their wings into space, which meant they were usually able to be the first alien race these new neighbours encountered. The Drycenians believe that as a peaceful friendly race, that first tentative and important meeting was more assured of reaping friendly relations into the future and more times than not, they were proved right. Being a little on the secretive side, due to their awareness of the importance not to interfere with any of their neighbours natural evolutionary cycles by inadvertently passing on advancements in technology or the like, they became the stuff of legends and fireside stories. This does not mean they cannot defend themselves or take a pro active stance, far from it. They are more than capable of being amongst the most fearsome of aggressors, but it goes against their nature and they gain no joy in taking such action. Lomas weighed up the pros and cons in his mind and knew there was only one choice. They would have to go in and engage the Transmortals. The decision made he wasted no more time.

"Battle stance at once, we will engage the Transmortals to secure Vincent's safety." He turned and left the bridge and headed for the armoury.

The enormous Drycenian Battle Cruiser landed at the edge of the forest, twenty miles to the east of the Transmortal ship. Within ten minutes thousands of Drycenian Troopers riding battle boards with their King and Prince Toma at their head were racing through the forest towards the dome complex. At three miles out, they stopped and dismounted from their battle boards. Powered by Pulse Wave Energy, these machines allow the Drycenians to travel extremely quickly over great distances at three or four feet off the ground. They are essentially just a flat oval board on which a man can stand and are operated by a relatively simple joystick. They take some practice to use efficiently but once mastered, they are valuable in situations where fast travel and stealth are necessary. Lomas decided they would walk the last three miles and set off at the head of his ever faithful army of Troopers, his son and heir at his side.

He argued with Toma when he announced he was accompanying them. Toma was his only heir and without a King, the Drycenian Nation would lose its continuity and the people could become unsettled. Toma however was not to be dissuaded and Lomas was secretly proud of his son for making such a decision. As a proud young man it was necessary for him to regain some of the dignity he lost by being held prisoner on Moxal 3 and having to be rescued by a female, even one they now loved as much as Farra. As the silent army entered an area of low scrub, where the trees gave way and let a little more light in, they saw the first of the bodies. They approached cautiously and noticed that the corpse seemed to have had its face and throat torn off, as if it had been attacked by some even deadlier enemy than itself. As they continued making their way carefully through the scrub, more bodies lay everywhere and all with the same injuries. Lomas remembered the bio scan that revealed the presence of non human animals in the area and he wondered if they were the cause of the injuries they were seeing here. His next thought was to wonder if they were in danger themselves from these unknown killers. As they climbed over a small rise and looked down at the dome complex a mile below, he got his answer.

"My god, look at them all," Toma exclaimed as his eyes took in the scene that his brain refused to believe. Lomas and all the other Drycenians were having the same difficulty believing what they were seeing. All around them and down to the domes themselves lay dead and dying Transmortals, thousands upon thousands of them. Amongst them, going from corpse to corpse were the creatures. They were basically cat like, about the size of a bear with grey furry bodies and hairless tails that sported a tuft of bristly spines at the end that vibrated as they gorged themselves on the sudden and fabulous repast. The Drycenians stood there on the crest of the rise and watched the gory scene below and were so riveted on what they were seeing that they didn't at first notice the creatures wending their way between them.

"Oh god look," a Trooper cried from Lomas' left and they all looked. One of the creatures had come up from behind and joined them on the crest of the rise to look down at the scene below. As they looked at it, another joined them between Lomas and Toma and others, a hundred or more of the creatures stood shoulder to shoulder with the Drycenian army looking down at the hellish scene below. Not once did any of the creatures show aggression to them, they simply stood there with them and watched. The creature at Lomas' side suddenly looked up at him and their eyes met. He got the distinct feeling that this creature and he were communicating at some deep unknown inner level and if he was pressed on the matter hard enough, he'd have to admit he felt there was intelligence there too, intelligence and understanding way beyond their physical evolution. The creature gave Lomas a slow blink and the spell was broken and as one, the creatures took off down the slope to join their fellows and fill their hungry bellies.

"Let's go, remain alert." Lomas gave the order and the Drycenian army started down the slope towards the domes. As they reached the bottom and began to tread their way through the carnage the creatures accepted their presence without a single sign of aggression, intent only on feeding. Here and there amongst the adults youngsters could be seen learning from their parents and feasting on the free food. The first of the vast domes loomed in front of them and Lomas gave the order for them to investigate the perimeter with extreme caution and to fire at will if necessary. Four Troopers approached the dome and began to make their way around the circumference whilst Lomas and the others watched for any sign of Transmortal attack. After a few minutes one of the Troopers hailed Lomas through his communication implant.

"Your majesty, you need to see this Sir. We're at five o clock from your position, awaiting your arrival." Lomas set off at a run with the rest of his army following behind. As he approached the position of his Troopers he found them waiting outside an open doorway. The door had been forced and lay in pieces on the ground. This was of little interest to him; what alerted the Troopers and was now shocking the rest who saw it, was the sign above this entranceway.

"Community 1," the sign read in clear Drycenian script.

"What the fuck?" Toma exclaimed aloud as everyone looked at each other, the shock evident on their faces.

"Drycenian script? We've never had an outpost here have we?" Lomas asked.

"No Sir, never," a Trooper replied.

"No one else in the known galaxy speaks our tongue do they?" Toma said.

"No Sir, no one," was the emphatic reply.

"But these bodies are not Drycenians. Look at them, they're clearly Transmortals. What the hell has been going on here?" Toma asked, knowing that his fellows didn't have the answer.

"Let's hope we find out inside, come on," Lomas ordered and cautiously they entered the dome.

They found themselves inside what looked like a reception lounge. There were seating areas and tables upon which books and papers were strewn as though the readers just got up and left. There was a bar whose shelves were still filled with bottles of many sizes and colours. Byron walked over and examined some.

"Sir, look at this. All the bottle labels are written in Drycenian script, just like the sign. Look here's a bottle called Canto, and there's one called Silma over there." Lomas went and examined the bottles with a frown.

"Sir, these books here, and the papers, they're all in Drycenian too," a Trooper called from the other side of the large room and Lomas went to look. He examined a few of the papers and found them to be discussing the pros and cons of some kind of medical technique.

"This is getting weirder by the minute," he remarked to the Trooper, who nodded in agreement. "Get these papers to Doctor Jam, he might be able to understand them more, I'm not a medical man." The Trooper gathered up the papers and tucked them inside his jacket. They descended to the next floor down, alert for the slightest noise that might signal a Transmortal waiting to ambush them. They found themselves looking along a corridor lined with doors, some of which where standing open. On the floor were several dead Transmortals. As they traversed the corridor examining the rooms they found them to be offices of some sort. Again they noted the presence of many dead Transmortals and the abundance of computer hardware and data chips.

Down on the next floor they found what were obviously living quarters. Each room was obviously occupied as there were belongings strewn about and the beds were unmade. More books and other documents were found and all were written in Drycenian.

"Father, look at this," Toma called and Lomas went over to find him reading a sheaf of papers describing what looked like some time back in Transmortal history.

"Hang onto it Toma," Lomas ordered and his son tucked it away safely inside his jacket. In one room the bed was occupied by a not quite dead Transmortal. He was close to death but still just conscious and his laboured breathing and unearthly colour told the Drycenians that his time would come soon. He was no threat to them so they went over to him and as they approached the bed, he opened his eyes and reached out a hand in a beseeching gesture. He strained to speak but could only utter a couple of words before exhaustion took over.

"Water," he gasped at them imploringly in Drycenian.

Toma looked at his father who nodded slowly. He went to the night stand and poured a glass of water and took it to the dying man. When he opened his eyes again and saw the glass being offered to him, his eyes went wide with terror and he shied away from Toma's hand as it held the glass out to him.

"Water," he said again and Toma moved the glass closer.

"This is water. Here, drink it," he offered the dying man the glass once more but he turned his face away, the fear obvious.

"Death, water," he gasped again, "water, death."

His eyes glazed and as the life left him the Drycenians looked at each other and then at the glass held in Toma's hand. Lomas immediately communicated with his officers and told them that in no circumstances was anyone to drink the water here. Once he received assurances that the order would be followed by all, he signalled a Trooper to take a sample and have it scanned immediately. The Trooper obeyed without hesitation. Lomas then ordered some Troopers to remove the body back to their ship for analysis so they could work out if the water had killed him or if something else was to blame. They made their way down to the next floor and found three rooms that were recognisable as medical bays. In one room there was even a skeleton still on the table. As the Drycenian group approached the table and took in what they were seeing, they all looked at each other, unable to speak for the shock they were all feeling. Toma expressed what they all felt.

"Shit. Oh my god. Oh shit look at it. It's a Drycenian. It's one of us father. What the fuck was going on here?"

Lomas was nonplussed and couldn't answer right away. He searched his mind for understanding but found nothing more than a few threads. "I haven't the faintest idea my son but I aim to find out." He looked around the room and saw something that gave him some hope. "Look at that," he indicated a shelf on the opposite side of the room. Below it was a data scanner that they recognised. "That's a scanner, an old type for sure, but I recognise it, and those chips up on the shelf, look there must be fifty or more of them. If they all have information on them we might get some answers to our questions. Gather up all data chips you find, all of them mind, don't leave one behind. I want answers and I mean to have them," he ordered.

"Yes Sir," came the reply immediately.

"Now let's see what's down on the next floor," he said as he strode purposefully towards the stairs. On the lower floor they found one large room that looked like a gathering place. There was a large seat at one end which one accessed by climbing a couple of steps. All around the walls were paintings depicting battle scenes with the Transmortals always triumphant.

"Look at this here," a Trooper called and they all went to look. "This must be a depiction of the Lilean attack; these dead bodies all have the Lilean star on their chests."

"So Vincent must be here in this painting somewhere," Lomas said and searched until he saw a depiction of a Transmortal holding a baby aloft by its feet. All around were hundreds of Lileans beseeching the triumphant Transmortal to spare the life of the child, their hands raised towards it, despair etched on their faces. "Here, here he is, look," he pointed out the scene to the group who all gathered around to look. "I want all of these paintings photographed, don't miss a single detail out. Now let's check the next dome." They made their way back up to the surface and went through the same procedure with the next dome and the one after that.

It was during their search of the fourth dome that they found Vincent. As they descended to the bottom floor to find themselves in yet another large gathering area with painted walls they were stunned to find two examination tables in the centre of the room, both tilted at forty five degrees so that the bodies upon them were almost in a standing position. One was clearly a Transmortal and the other was Vincent.

"It's Vincent, he's here," Toma ran over to him and saw the Lilean star on his chest. He laid a hand on his chest and closed his eyes. After a few seconds the faint heartbeat could just be detected. "He's alive, quick get the Doctor down here now," he screamed at the Troopers who ran from the room shouting into their communication implants. Lomas went over to the Transmortal body and checked it for signs of life. There were none and he breathed a sigh of relief. He noticed something glinting on the body and reached over to look. It was a large medallion in the shape of a sun and had clearly recognisable symbols on it.

He was stunned, amazed, delighted and humbled all at the same time and as he spoke to his crew, they noticed he had tears in his eyes. "He did it, Vincent did it. He's fulfilled the prophecy and ended the Transmortal threat forever. He's killed their leader, look," he held up the medallion for all to see and there was a stunned silence as they looked at the King's Crest that lay around the dead Transmortals throat. The very same King's Crest that their own beloved King Lomas wore around his own throat at all times. It was his badge of office, the sign of his Kingship and symbol of the continuity of the Drycenian Nation as it was handed down from King to King through the generations. He ripped it from the Transmortals body and went over to where Vincent's body lay. Laying a hand upon his brow he leaned down to him and whispered into his ear. "Vincent, you are safe now. We are your friends and we are going to help you. You have triumphed in your great task here. Now we will care for you and return you to full health. Fear not."

Doctor Jam arrived panting and sweating and ran to Vincent's side. "Oh my dear friend what have they done to you?" he said as he took a mobile body scanning device from his pocket and ran it up and down all over Vincent's body. The little device bleeped and blinked and for a full five minutes no one uttered a sound. When it was finished he put the device away and scratched his head.

"Hmmm," he muttered to himself out loud. Lomas and the others were more than a little impatient for news.

"Well?" Lomas yelled a little too harshly and was instantly sorry. "I'm sorry Doctor Jam, forgive me for my impatience."

"Of course Your Majesty," the doctor replied, "I understand completely. This will be a little difficult; it's not just a case of lifting his body from this table and getting him into a tank back on the ship," he explained in as clear a language as he could.

"Why not? What's the problem?" Toma enquired for all of them.

"Look here, at this," he said as he indicated something at the very back of Vincent's head as it lay on the table. Everyone gathered closer to see what the doctor was showing them and from what they could see, there was some kind of device attached to the back of Vincent's head that was also attached to the table itself. The doctor continued explaining. "He has something implanted into his brain and this device is receiving commands from somewhere; my guess would be that dead Transmortal on the next table." He looked at Lomas as he explained all this to him.

Lomas looked puzzled. "But how can it be receiving commands from a dead body, a dead brain?" he asked, hoping the doctor would know the answer.

"What we know of Transmortal dogma tells us that they become the way they are by going to the very edge of death itself and holding there until all soul memory is wiped clean. When they are then returned to waking life they are effectively a blank canvas ready to be uploaded with a new identity, a new set of beliefs and new soul memory." The doctor looked around the group to see that they were all still following him. Nods all around told him they were and he continued. "This Transmortal was somewhere within that process with Vincent when he died, leaving the process unfinished." He looked at Lomas, hoping he understood what the ramifications were without him having to take more time spelling it out for him. The King's vacant look told him to continue explaining. "Which means that he is therefore unable to return him to waking life. Vincent is now permanently stuck somewhere between waking life and the very edge of death."

"Oh no, that can't be," Lomas declared as if by commanding that it be so, it would be so. "There must be a way around it, there has to be." He looked at Jam imploringly.

The doctor scratched his chin and thought for a few moments before looking up at Lomas. "In theory it's simple; we just reverse the process he's already gone through."

"And how do we do that?" Lomas asked.

"As I say, in theory it's simple. We alter the device so that it undoes everything it's done so far. We put it into reverse if you like. But we can talk this through on board the ship; the first thing is to get Vincent on board and at the moment where Vincent goes, the table must go also." The group jumped into action. With the use of several of the Troopers battle boards and with much heaving and shoving, several banged elbows and trapped fingers; they got Vincent and table back up to ground level. After several minutes rest to get their wind, stretch sore backs and massage painful fingers, they connected a bank of battle boards together and managed to fly the table with Vincent still on it, back to the ship where he was immediately installed within the medical bay. Back in his own space with his own equipment at his disposal, the doctor felt much more at ease and in control of the situation and sat down to think.

As the doctor sat in the medical bay pouring over ideas and theories for hour after hour, Lomas and the Troopers stripped the dome complex of every data chip, book and document they could find. Then they took the body of the Transmortal leader up to the surface and laid it upon the ground. A fire was burning fiercely nearby and every single Drycenian except the doctor, stood to attention row on row. Lomas approached the body.

"I speak now for all those lost at your hands in all the worlds upon which your stain has remained. Too long has the universe given you shelter while you spread your evil. I stand over you now representing those nations still weeping and those of whom none remain to weep at the desecration you brought to their lands. We are a peaceful nation who finds no joy at the extinction of a race. We travel the galaxy extending the hand of friendship to all with whom we come into contact in the hope of forging unbreakable bonds of compassion and unity. As I stand over you now in your hour of extinction I let it be known across the universe that we will weep with those who lost so much at your hands, we will weep with all who mourn for those you took from them. As I stand over you now I let it be known across the universe that we will not weep for you, we will not mourn at your passing and as your memory fades into the grey mists of the past so shall all that you stood for be forgotten forever." He took a step back, removed the fabulously ornate dagger that hung from his hip and raising it high into the air cried. "The prophecy is fulfilled and the prophesied one has triumphed." With one single powerful blow, he brought his dagger down and took the Transmortal Pzolgons head cleanly off his body. Stooping down he lifted it high into the air as the crowd cheered and whooped and wept with happiness. Stepping over to the now blazing fire, he thrust it into the flames.

As the Drycenian battle cruiser raced across the galaxy on its way back to Terramora Prime Lomas addressed his crew.

"Friends, we made a solemn vow when our blessed friend Farra saved my son. We vowed to give her every aid in her quest to ensure Vincent's name is cleared of the stain it has never deserved. As our good doctor still works to find a way to bring him back to us, we affirm our vow. Vincent will be there to have his name cleared and gain the freedom that is rightfully his. If he walks into the hearing himself or if we have to carry him there ourselves on that table, he will be there and he will have his freedom. Does anyone disagree?" He allowed several long seconds of silence to go by before continuing. "Now we all need to help the doctor find a cure. Search through the data chips and papers we took from the planet. Anything that may give us a clue as to how to reverse that device, the slightest little thing. No matter how small an idea, flag it up to the doctor. Now let's get at it."

As the hours passed and the data chips, papers and journals were scanned and their information digested, the Drycenians found a truth so utterly surprising that they didn't know how to react to it. In the earliest years when the Transmortals were perfecting their transformation technique, they found a planet inhabited by very primitive and savage humanoids. They took them all to an uninhabited planet they set up as their new base and used them in their first mass transformation experiments. They took care to bring along trees and plants that these primitive savages would recognise and feel at home with. It didn't go to plan though and after five thousand years, the Transmortals gave up trying to transform these humanoids. The ones they experimented on were returned to their original planet and left there. These changed humanoids flourished and evolved at an alarming rate, so much so that they had technology vastly superior to any to be found anywhere else. They were peaceful and friendly and kept themselves to themselves. They became the stuff of legends. They became the Drycenian Nation. They were so shocked at this discovery that they didn't know how to even begin to discuss it. Four hours later they were still pouring over data streams and pieces of paper littered the floor on the obs deck. Lomas was almost asleep when the intercom buzzed.

"Your Majesty," Doctor Jam sounded excited. "Come to the medical facility quickly please." Everyone looked up and exchanged glances, then as one the group lunged for the door. As they burst in through the door of the medical facility they were met with Doctor Jam who was wearing the biggest smile they had ever seen. "Welcome your Majesty, please come in. May I present Vincent Richard Domenico." As the doctor moved aside Lomas saw the familiar tank. He approached cautiously and peered inside through the liquid that was gently cradling him in its healing depths. He moved around to the rear of the tank to try to see the back of his head. The device was gone. Lomas looked up at the doctor in complete surprise as his jaw dropped and his eyebrows shot upwards.

The doctor smiled broadly and explained how he found the answer. "It came to me all of a sudden. I was pouring over medical texts and theories until my brain was numb and I was about to despair. As I began to sink into a fit of anger and depression at my own impotence I let my thoughts wander to Vincent and his life. I remembered all that we've learned about him from Farra, his life and his experiences and I thought of his birth. It was then that it hit me and I almost fell off my seat. You see, we know that the Transmortal process involves taking the victim to the edge of death and holding them there don't we?" Everyone nodded. "And we also know that the process only works once, the Transmortal process doesn't work on anyone who has already been to the edge of death, to the place they call The Veil. With me so far?" More nods. "Vincent was murdered just after birth. He will have gone not only to the edge of death but a way over it before being brought back by the Lilean spirit people." As the doctor looked at his friends he noticed mouths begin to open and eyes begin to widen as understanding began to take hold. "This means that the device attached to his head wasn't able to do its job at all. There was no process that needs reversing because that process cannot happen to him. He is immune to the Transmortal process. All I had to do was surgically remove it and repair the damaged neural pathways. A few days in the tank and he'll be as good as new. Why your Majesty are you all right Sir?" the doctor asked.

"Yes Doctor," Lomas sobbed. "Yes indeed I'm okay.

CHAPTER FIFTEEN

"Mighty Pzolgon, we have secured the evil one as you desired. He is under guard in the atrium."

Pzolgon looked up at his officer and let out a shriek of triumph. "At last my moment has come. Take me to him." The officer escorted Pzolgon down to the lowest level of the dome and stood aside to let him enter the atrium first. Inside the giant chamber, in front of the Pzolgon's throne, lay the unconscious body of Vincent. He approached cautiously; afraid he might wake suddenly and kill him after all. "Are you sure he is secured?" he asked the officers.

"Yes mighty Pzolgon," came the unified reply.

He went and looked down at the body. He was confused. "But how can this be? He is just a man. He has not even any armour and his only defence is a primitive blade. Are you sure this is the evil one? There has been no mistake?"

"There is no mistake mighty Pzolgon," the voice belonged to the visionary who had just entered the atrium. "This is the evil one foretold to us so long ago, the evil one that you will now destroy and in doing so, secure the coming of The Veil for all."

Pzolgon looked at the visionary and smiled at the thought of destroying forever this evil one who would keep them from their destiny. He crouched down by Vincent's side and looked closely at him. "He is a fine specimen for an uninitiated. Strong and powerful and determined. He has led us quite a dance has he not? We are a just and fair race and we will honour him as a fine opponent. Prepare the multitude for viewing. Everyone must be given the opportunity to look upon his face and meet the one who tried so courageously and failed to outwit the Transmortal Truth." The officer left the room to carry out the orders.

Pzolgon ordered the atrium guards to remain on full alert in case Vincent awoke unexpectedly and caused a problem for them before the given moment when he would destroy him forever.

Until that moment arrived there would be celebrations to honour the Pzolgon who helped secure the coming of The Veil. "This is a sacred site where the very first of the Pzolgons began to bring the gift of Transformation to the uninitiated. Those first early experiments may have failed but with our vastly superior knowledge and capabilities we have endured and become the mightiest of all races. I want this sacred site cleaned up and returned to its former glory to stand as an eternal testament to this day when we overcame the evil one. He will remain here forever and Transmortals of the future will make pilgrimage here to look upon his face and pay homage to the one who destroyed him. Give the orders."

"Yes mighty Pzolgon." The officer ran from the room and gave orders for the dome complex to be cleaned and repaired, for the vegetation to be cleared back for a mile in all directions and gave orders for new paintings to be added to the atrium walls depicting this most momentous of occasions. The Adherants worked tirelessly for twenty four hours, cleaning, repairing, clearing vegetation and restocking the complex. The power supply was checked and overhauled, the armoury restocked and the water supply was switched on supplying the life giving liquid to all parts of the complex. Vinbuk 3 has a hot climate and the extra workload made the working Transmortals very thirsty. They were very grateful to have such a large ready water supply of their own. There was no necessity for rationing the water, everyone could use as much as they wanted; the filtering and cleaning system meant that they would never run out of water. So they drank, and they drank, and they drank.

It took two days for the first of the Transmortals to start to feel the effects of the poison. After four days the first deaths occurred and sixty five percent of the Transmortal population showed symptoms. Panic set in and the scientists were working round the clock to find the cause of the sickness that was depleting their numbers by the hour. Pzolgon was furious as the death toll rose and by the time his visionary died, he was uncontrolled with rage.

He spent hour after hour down in the atrium with the still unconscious Vincent, pacing up and down raving in his madness.

"You will not kill me Lilean; I told you on the day of your birth you would not see my downfall. It is you who lie here unconscious at my feet and yet still your infection spreads. I will not allow you to stand in the way of Transmortal Truth and thwart the coming of The Veil. You will not keep me from my destiny." He raced up to the medical centre and spoke to the doctors. "Prepare the evil one for initiation at once," he ordered.

The doctors looked at him in surprise. "Initiation mighty Pzolgon? You aren't going to destroy him?"

"This is a sign from the Great Immortal; he wants the evil one to receive the great wisdom that he has denied all of his life. In his ultimate wisdom the Great Immortal wants the evil one to receive the Truth. A far greater victory lies in transforming the evil one to the right path than in simply wiping him out. Prepare him; I will take him through the transformation myself."

"Yes mighty Pzolgon," they obeyed as he turned and swept out of the room. The doctors brought the device down to the atrium. Vincent was laid upon a transformation table, and another empty one stood by the side ready to receive the Pzolgon. Once attached to the back of Vincent's skull, the device would attach itself to the neural pathways deep inside his brain. The Pzolgon would then take himself into a deep trance state and link telepathically to the psychic sensors in the device. He would then transport Vincent to the very edge of The Veil and hold him there until his soul memory was wiped clean. Once his soul became an empty vessel, Pzolgon would channel the Transmortal Truth into his brain, before escorting him back to waking consciousness as a new Transmortal which would complete the transformation process.

"Attach the device to the evil one," he ordered and his doctors obeyed. In twenty four hours the device would make the necessary neural pathway connections and the process could begin. During the course of those next twenty four hours more of the Transmortals died and ninety eight percent now displayed symptoms. Pzolgon was entirely convinced that this was caused by

Vincent somehow and nothing any of his officers said would deter him from what he saw as his holy mission. It was also during those twenty four hours that the last surviving doctor finally found the cause of the sickness. By the time he discovered that the water was poisoned, all but the Pzolgon and he were dead and he himself had but hours to live. He dragged himself to his room and after making a last plea to the Great Immortal; he climbed into bed and waited to travel across to The Veil.

When the device finally indicated that the time for the transformation process to begin was upon them, Pzolgon himself finally showed symptoms. He climbed up onto the transformation table and took himself down into deep trance and reached for Vincent with his mind. Try as he might he could not find him, it was as if Vincent was not there waiting for him. For three days he searched the hinterland frantically for the evil one in order to escort him to the edge of The Veil, but he never found him. It was only as he found himself crossing over into The Veil for good that he saw Vincent for the last time and try as he might, he could not reach him with his mind, for he himself was now crossing into The Veil and Vincent was not. Vincent was back across the edge, watching him go.

The doctor awoke to find strangers in his room, gazing at him. He didn't recognise them as Adherants and he reached out beseechingly to them. They didn't look sick yet, so he tried to tell them about the water in the hope that they would remain healthy and continue serving the Pzolgon . He could hardly speak.

"Water," he rasped. One of them brought him a glass of water and offered it to him obviously unaware of the poison. He used the last of his strength to try to warn them once more. "Death, water," he gasped one last time, "water, death," and as he found himself floating towards the edge of The Veil, he was surprised to find his own mighty Pzolgon already there.

"Vincent? Vincent. Wake up Vincent." The voice drifted through the darkness and Vincent reached for its comforting familiarity. "Wake up brave warrior." Much as he felt he wanted to just drift through the darkness, he found himself reaching for that voice instinctively and as he got nearer and nearer to its source, the need for it became stronger and stronger and the desire to leave this darkness grew. Awareness finally reached him and the darkness began to lift until he found himself in the white fog of the hinterland between waking and, somewhere else.

"What happened? I was running, there were figures chasing me, the creature came." Memories came to him little by little and he worked to piece them together in his mind. He looked up and saw Syra standing before him.

She reached out a hand to him. "Come Vincent, I have much to show you." He stood and took her proffered hand and as he did so, he thought he felt electric sparks travel through him. The fog of the hinterland cleared and a new scene appeared to him. A beautiful panorama surrounded them and as he looked all around, he knew he didn't recognise this place.

"Where are we?" he asked.

"We are at the place where the evil began so long ago. Look, here he comes." She pointed and he looked. The young man ran through the trees, his dog at his heels. He was singing at the top of his voice and Vincent didn't think he ever saw anyone so carefree and happy. The man dropped down and lay on the grass to look at the sky. His dog lay down beside him, panting.

"Oh Luzca, isn't this the most beautiful day ever? I don't ever want to leave this place. It's the most perfect place ever. Don't you agree old boy?" He reached over and scratched the dog's ears. Vincent looked at Syra, he didn't see anything evil here.

She caught his thoughts and answered before he could ask. "This is what was to become the evil you fought so bravely today. The same evil that wiped out so many races across the galaxy and almost wiped out ours. This happy, good man is soon to become the very first Transmortal. Watch, over there." He looked and saw something hovering over the man's face. He batted at it lazily with a hand but it returned and bit him and he jumped up in pain.

"Ouch, damn you bug," he slapped it to the ground and stepped on it. "How dare you taint this beautiful day. Come

Luzca, let's go home to eat, race you." The man and the dog raced off back the way they'd come.

Vincent looked at Syra, confused. "So he was bitten by a bug, so what?" She took his hand and they both turned around through one hundred and eighty degrees. As they turned, the scene changed again and he found himself inside a small room. There was a bed at one end and a window but nothing else. He went over to the bed and saw the same young man he'd just seen happy and carefree running through the trees. Now he looked entirely different though. His neck was swollen and black, he was sweating profusely and his eyes darted to and fro beneath his eyelids. His head thrashed from side to side and now and again he made unintelligible noises. Suddenly Vincent heard voices approaching and two people entered the room. A woman rushed over to the bed and sat and tried to soothe the young man's turmoil. The other, a man put a hand on her shoulder and just looked at the young man as he thrashed.

"My dear you must realise there is little hope now. A month he has lain here like this with no sign of his fever breaking. He is hovering at the edge of death and all we can do is wait and pray. It is up to him now, him and God." The woman burst into tears, huge racking sobs that made her whole body shudder. Suddenly the young man in the bed stopped thrashing and his eyes stopped darting beneath the lids. His mouth opened very slightly and Vincent heard him sigh deeply. He was gone. The woman screamed and flung herself down on the bed, shaking at the young man's shoulders. She begged him to return, she screamed at God for taking him and little dog howled. Vincent felt Syra take his hand and as they once again turned through one hundred and eighty degrees, they found themselves in the same room, with the same bed and the same young man dead within it. It was night time and the stars twinkled in the sky. He was just about to enquire of Syra as to why they were here when he heard a gasp from the bed. He turned and looked and saw the young man again begin to thrash and gasp for air. His eyes opened wide and he thrust away the bed cover. As his breathing returned to normal Vincent noticed something different about him. He was now surrounded by a grey cloud.

"What is that cloud?" he asked.

"It is his energy field, his aura," she replied. He also noticed the young man's eyes were now very different from before. They no longer showed that spark of joy but had a lifeless quality about them. They say the eyes are the windows to the soul and it seemed to Vincent that if this were true, then this man had no soul. The young man got up out of the bed and stumbled from the room. Vincent heard shrieks from below and guessed the other residents of this home had just got the shock of their lives.

Once again Syra changed the scene and this time he found himself in what looked like a courthouse. The young man stood in one corner, the same dead eyes looking at the crowd that filled the room. A man spoke and everyone listened.

"From this day forward you are hereby banished from our sight. We cannot let you continue with your blasphemy and your evil ways. You are never to return to this kingdom." Vincent looked at Syra questioningly and she took his hand and the scene changed. This time they were in a dingy basement room full of cobwebs and dust. It was very dark with only candles lighting the room and as Vincent strained to see, a scream rang out. He rushed towards the sound and saw the young man standing over a young boy. He held him firmly by the head, his fingers pressed against the boy's temples. His eyes were closed and his mouth was moving but no sound came. The young boy screamed and struggled and then suddenly went limp. The young man laid the body down and continued pressing his fingers to the boy's temples and speaking words that Vincent couldn't hear.

"What is he doing to him?" he asked.

"He is transforming him. Already he has the madness that became his new truth. He is compelled to change others to be like he is and in his mind he feels he is giving them a great gift. These very early attempts were clumsy and many died at his hands. That's why he was banished from his home world and came here. He returned changed as you saw. The process extended his life by many times its original allotted span and it gave him great psychic and telepathic powers, which he used to change others and in so doing, began to create the Transmortal army. The process also changed his brain in many other ways and because of this, those who were transformed made huge leaps forward in technology, many hundreds and thousands of years before they would normally have done. They all felt that it was their duty to spread their gift to all worlds and all peoples as it is only when every human life has been transformed that their own heaven can come into being. A place they call The Veil."

"But that's crazy, you can't just force your own beliefs onto someone," he replied and she nodded.

"Yes Vincent it was madness and many suffered and died because of his madness. Look." The scene changed again and he recognised where they were. They were back on the planet where Vincent found refuge and as they both watched, they saw the young man and a number of followers capturing the primitive indigenous humanoids. It was dangerous as Vincent knew these humanoids had vicious fangs and were in the habit of eating those they didn't like.

He looked at Syra. "They came here and changed these humans too?" he asked and she nodded.

"Yes Vincent, they came here too and used the very same technique on these primitive, savage humanoids. They found them on a distant planet and brought them here to their base along with the trees and plants that were familiar to them and used them in early experiments with transformation. This was their first big mistake and one that helped you in your great task today. Once they had been captured they put them through the same transformation but when they returned they had changed in a very different way to the others. Look." She pointed as the scene changed and Vincent found himself looking at a group of indigenous humans who had been transformed. Whereas before the procedure they were savage and aggressive, now they were passive and gentle.

He was amazed. "But how come?"

Syra smiled at Vincent as she explained. "You see Vincent, transformation means change. You take something as it already is and change it to something else; something which it was not before. The Transmortals we all know were savage and evil and forced their ways upon others whether they wanted it or not. Before they were changed, they were peaceful, good people. These humanoids however, started out savage and aggressive bullies who forced anyone who they came into contact with to adhere to their rules or die. Once changed, they could not be the same as they were before. A transformation had to occur and so it did and they returned from the procedure transformed from savages into peace loving, gentle people with great knowledge and insight who yearned to explore and meet new races and forge new relations with their neighbours."

"How did the Transmortals deal with that?" Vincent asked, guessing it probably pissed them off mightily.

"They were very angry and tried to repeat the procedure to change them again but one cannot be transformed more than once. So they banished them back to where they found them and forgot them without realising that these new beings would become not only one of the mightiest of races but also the most friendly and insightful of neighbours to all who would encounter them. As with all Transmortals their life spans were dramatically enhanced, as were their brains and so they too made technological advances at an alarmingly fast rate. But always, everything they do is done for good and they are your friends now Vincent and today they will save your life and bring you back to waking consciousness. You know of them as the Drycenian Nation." She smiled as he listened to all she told him.

"The Drycenians? They're Transmortals? So the Transmortals are my friends now?" he asked, incredulous.

"They are at this moment, also discovering that their race was created inadvertently by those early Transmortals. Until now they knew only that there was a gap in their history that they had never been able to fill. As they rush to your aid today, they will also find this missing piece of themselves. They are your greatest allies Vincent, trust them always. You will not survive without the help they rush to bring you as we speak." Her tone was gentle as always but Vincent detected a tone he dare not ignore. She continued as the scene changed again. "Look, you made another friend who feels compelled to give you assistance." He looked and saw something he remembered from the moment before he blacked out. He could see himself lying on the ground, a Transmortal standing over him aiming a weapon at his chest. From his right he saw her rush to his aid. The creature leapt at the Transmortal and together they rolled over and over for fifteen feet or more until finally coming to rest against a tree. The creature looked back at the prone figure of Vincent and long moments passed as their eyes met and understanding was passed. As the prone figure of Vincent lost consciousness, the creature sank her teeth into the Transmortal.

Vincent was awe struck. "I remember that happening before I blacked out. My god I wasn't dreaming," he exclaimed.

Syra smiled and shook her head. "No Vincent you weren't dreaming, look." She indicated behind and as they turned the scene changed and he found himself standing on the ridge above the dome complex. Most of the Transmortals were dead and dying from the poison and many more were stumbling around with advanced symptoms. Suddenly from all around him, creatures like the one who he encountered leapt from the trees and descended towards the domes. The Transmortals didn't stand a chance against them with the sickness and many of them were alive as the creatures began eating them.

Vincent gaped. "My god look at them all," he gasped and Syra smiled.

"Look, here are your new friends now." She indicated and he looked up to see hundreds of men reach the ridge where he was standing. As they stood there more of the creatures joined them on the ridge and one in particular caught his eye. A female was standing beside one of the men on the ridge and as he watched, they both looked into each others eyes and a similar moment passed between them. A moment Vincent shared with one of the creatures himself, maybe even that same female. He was humbled beyond belief at the realisation that so many were willing and ready to help him, humans and animals alike. These men knew nothing about him yet here they were coming to save his life. And these creatures whose world he shared repaid the simplest of kindnesses on his part by helping him defeat this huge evil. He was greatly moved as Syra took his hand and once again the scene changed. He was in what looked like a rather sparsely furnished hotel room. Discarded clothes on the bed revealed that the room was occupied by a woman. The sound of water came to his ears and he automatically looked towards the open door to his left. He went to look and saw a small bathroom. A woman was in the shower and he automatically looked away, not wanting to intrude on her nakedness. Syra held his hand firmly and urged him.

"Do not fear Vincent, go on in." He looked at Syra, who nodded encouragingly and he entered slowly, feeling like a voyeur as he saw the young woman standing in the shower. She was beautiful with long dark curly hair and a dragon tattoo on her back. As she turned around to face him he was shocked to see the Lilean star on her chest and he gaped at Syra, who smiled gently. "She carries the star Vincent, but she is not Lilean. It was given to her as a gift from the ancient ones who made a choosing at the same time as the prophecy came to them. They chose her to be the one to aid you in your great task and she accepted their gift willingly and proudly. She has suffered greatly Vincent and is still suffering due to giving you aid. Look." As he watched he noticed the woman was weeping. Her gentle tears turned to huge sobs that shook her body as she slumped down in the shower. He crouched down and Syra put a hand on his shoulder. "She weeps for you Vincent. She weeps for your suffering but not her own and her only thought is of your safety and happiness. Come, let me show you."

She bade him stand and took his hand and the scene changed again and he found himself back in the hinterland. He could see nothing at first but then a form began to take shape. A man lying down. As the shape became solid he recognised it as himself asleep on the bed in the dome. For a moment nothing happened but then another shape took form out of the mist and he saw the woman come up to his prone sleeping body. He saw her touch his face and whisper in his ear. He remembered the dream of the voice telling him someone was fighting for him and not to fear, that he wasn't alone and that she cared. Then the woman bent forward and kissed him and all at once the prone figure of himself vanished. He remembered having woken with a start after that strange feeling of the woman's energy enveloping him. He looked at Syra, surprised.

"It wasn't a dream? That was her, the woman in the shower?" Syra nodded. "But how?" He shook his head; he couldn't work out how she could have met him in the hinterland.

"The same way you are here now Vincent." She allowed him the time to work it out for himself.

"But I'm here because you brought me here," he looked puzzled but then the penny dropped. "So her guide brought her? She has a guide too?" he asked.

"Of course Vincent, all Lileans have an ancient one who walks with them, that is why we all carry the star."

"But she isn't Lilean, you said she isn't Lilean."

"She is a chosen one; she was given the star and a guide to walk with her. A very special guide." Syra saw Vincent's look but before he could ask, she changed the scene again. He found himself in a tunnel in complete darkness. Syra held his hand and all at once the darkness faded and he recognised the Moxal 3 mine.

"What the?" he began but Syra shushed him.

"Watch Vincent." As he watched he saw the woman again. She was accompanied by one of the Rangers, a guy he didn't recognise. He took five packs of cigarettes from her and showed her into a room. Inside the room was a young man Vincent recognised from the dome complex. He was with the people standing on the ridge. What was he doing here? The woman was speaking, saying hello and telling him to be ready. Then she left and immediately the scene changed. Vincent found himself outside of this same room once again. The woman approached silently and expertly downed the guard. She opened the door and called to the young man and together they set off through the tunnels.

"But how will she survive down there, she doesn't have any goggles?" he asked.

"Her guide is with her leading the way."

"Where is he? Why can't I see him?" This was the question Syra hoped he wasn't going to ask just yet.

"You will, soon. Be patient Vincent." He watched as the pair made their way through the tunnels to freedom and he watched as they ran off away from the mine. Syra took his hand again. "There is one more scene I want to show you before you return." As the scene changed he found himself on a planet he didn't recognise. They were standing at the edge of a large crowd who were all looking at a man making a speech in front of them. Vincent was amazed to recognise the speaker.

"Donaldson? My god is that really Donaldson?" he asked and Syra nodded.

"Yes Vincent, it is."

"That son of a bitch refused to help me all those years ago and helped get me locked in Cryo. I hope to god I meet him again."

Syra put a hand on his shoulder. "Vincent, he has carried the shame of that event with him every moment of his life since and never a day has gone by when he hasn't wished to go back and change things. That event changed him and changed his life and today something is going to happen that will allow him to do what he has so often wished to do. Watch." As he watched he noticed someone in a hood suddenly dash from the bushes and leap at Donaldson, hitting him with the full force of their body and sending them both sprawling to the ground. Gunshots rang out and people panicked and screamed. The hooded figure took a package out from under their shirt and handed it to Donaldson.

"Shit. Oh my god, that's my notebook. The one I gave Donaldson back in the mine that day," he exclaimed and Syra nodded.

"Yes Vincent. She put her life danger to bring this to Donaldson once again in the hope that he would now do what he couldn't do all those years ago. Listen to her," Syra urged and he squatted down to catch the last of her words.

"Vincent is innocent. You must clear his name for at this very moment he is bringing to an end the evil that once walked here on this very spot. He has suffered so much for crimes he didn't commit, use this and clear him. Please." Vincent stood and watched her run and disappear. He was shocked and humbled all at the same time and didn't know how to react.

As the scene faded and the mist returned once again, he turned to Syra. "What do I do now? Is it all over? Where is the woman? Is she okay?"

Syra smiled at so many questions. "Vincent, your task is far from over. You have fulfilled the prophecy given to the ancient ones so long ago and all of Lilea will honour your memory forever. Your new friends are at this minute saving your life. Go with them Vincent, for they race to bring you to freedom. Donaldson is also fighting for your freedom and waits for you. Be brave and trust them, don't let her efforts be in vain because of your fears. Trust Vincent, trust them, trust her." As Syra vanished into the mist Vincent felt himself being pulled violently backwards. As the white mist of the hinterland faded into blackness once again, he grew frightened. He held on to Syra's last words and searched for the light. When he saw the dim light streaming towards him, he relaxed into it and waited for consciousness to embrace him once again.

CHAPTER SIXTEEN

Vincent fought his way back towards the white light and as waking consciousness enveloped him he became aware that he felt strange. It felt as if he were floating and he was cold. He started to shiver and then he heard shouts; someone giving orders and then calling his name. He struggled to hold onto the voice but it kept drifting and he was so cold, so very cold. The voice came again.

"Vincent. Vincent can you hear me? Vincent. Move your fingers if you can hear me." He concentrated his mind and tried to connect with his fingers but they felt so very far away and numb with cold. He turned his head towards the sound in an effort to hear better and the voice came again. "Hold on to my voice Vincent, now try to move your fingers if you can hear me, try really hard." He tried again but it was no use, he couldn't reach his fingers, they were just too far away and too cold. "You will soon be warm Vincent, don't worry." He cried out with his mind, begging for warmth as the voice continued to talk to him. "You are safe now Vincent. All of the enemies are dead and you are safe here. We are here to help you get better." At last he began to feel the temperature rise and as the warmth pervaded his body he felt his connections with his extremities return. He moved a finger and the voice sounded pleased. "Well done. Now I'm going to talk and you move your finger when you want to say yes, can you do that for me?" Vincent moved his finger and the voice continued. "Wonderful, now are you warm enough?" He indicated yes.

By this slow and painstaking process Doctor Jam learned that Vincent returned with all of his mental faculties intact and would make a full recovery. He learned that he felt no pain but he needed the tank four degrees warmer than normal, which was about average for a Lilean patient. The only two things that were worrying the doctor were how he was going to react when he awoke fully to find himself breathing liquid and how he would react to the change back to air. With his Lilean physique he could be quite a challenging patient if he decided to thrash and panic and he decided to have a supply of tranquiliser handy just in case. He thought it may be a good idea to begin getting Vincent used to the reality of his liquid environment gently, rather than waiting and letting him find out all of a sudden when he wakes fully. He took a deep breath.

"Vincent, can you still hear me?" The finger moved. "Good. Now I want you to listen very carefully. Do you feel as if you're floating?" Yes. "Good. Now that is because you are in a very special place right now, a place that you will never have seen before. It is so special that it is the only place that can make you better right now, do you understand?" Yes. "Okay. Now you are floating because there is a very special and magical liquid all around you. This liquid is healing all of your injuries and making you well again. Do you understand?" Yes. "Great. This liquid is so special that it is even breathing for you." Vincent's body twitched frighteningly and for a second the doctor thought he was going to panic. What he wanted to avoid more than anything was having a huge panicking Lilean on his hands. He continued his soothing words. "Don't worry Vincent; the liquid is doing everything your body needs right now, even breathing. You are getting all the things your body needs to repair itself from this liquid. Your lungs are having a well deserved rest and this liquid is making them stronger and more efficient than they've ever been before."

Vincent's chest heaved and the doctor's heart sank as he thought, oh fuck. He knew right away Vincent was trying to breathe normally and would be panicking and thrashing within seconds if he didn't get him calmed down. If he damaged the tank he could set his own recovery back and even cause himself more damage, not to mention hurting his medical staff in the process. He had to force him to calm down so he tried to get an authoritative edge to his voice and sound commanding.

"Vincent listen to me. Listen to me now. You must stop moving, you must remain still and you must stop trying to breathe normally. The liquid is breathing for you, let it do its job. Now calm down please." He shouted in command and instantly felt sorry but it seemed to do the trick. By now Vincent's hands where on the inside walls of the tank and Doctor Jam knew within seconds he would be thumping and trying to escape. As he watched him forcing himself to calm down he was amazed. This poor man who never saw a tank before, let alone had to breathe liquid quartz emulsion, was now bravely fighting the most natural of urges because he trusted him.

Vincent's eyes flicked open as the man shouted at him. He told him he wasn't breathing and sure enough, when he tried to, he found he couldn't and started to panic. As the man shouted at him to calm down and let the liquid do its job he remembered Syra's words, trust them. So he forced himself to calm down and as his eyes strained to make sense of what he was seeing he heard the voice again.

"Hello there Vincent, welcome back." The voice was coming from his right so he turned to look for it and saw a face looking at him through the liquid. The face smiled and he raised a hand in response. "Are you in pain?" He moved his head side to side. "Good, that's wonderful. Are you warm enough?" He nodded. "My name is Doctor Jam and I have been looking after you since we got you away from the Transmortals. You will be able to come out of the liquid in a day or so, once your brain is completely healed." At the mention of his brain Vincent frowned. The doctor noticed and explained what the Transmortals did to him. "The Transmortals put a device into your brain that they wanted to use to make you into one of them. I removed it and now we need to let things heal completely before getting you out of there. Now, do you see that button there, by your right hip?" He looked and nodded. "If you need anything at all or if you're worried or just need someone to be here, just press that okay?" He nodded.

Lomas entered the medical bay like an excited kid with a new toy. He couldn't wait to meet Vincent alive and well. The doctor was there to meet him.

"Your Majesty, welcome. Come and meet Vincent." The doctor stood aside and there was Vincent in the tank. He approached slowly and looked into the liquid. The man was huge, a fine Lilean if ever he saw one, no wonder he was the prophesied one. As he met Vincent's gaze he smiled.

"Vincent. My name is Lomas and I am the King of the Drycenian Nation. We are so very proud to have you as our guest and it is an honour to meet you at last. When we found you deep in the bowels of the dome, we feared you lost. Welcome to my ship; treat it as your home for the duration of your stay. We are at this moment racing with all haste to Terramora Prime to make sure that you are given your freedom from the false claims made against you back on Moxal 3. Michael Donaldson is working to free you as we speak but you have to be there in person and we intend to get you there. There is no ship in the galaxy as fast as ours; you can rest assured you will make the appointment and you will get your freedom." Lomas smiled as Vincent raised a hand in response. "We made a solemn vow to do all in our power to help you to get the stain wiped from your record and bring those responsible to justice and we always keep our promises." Vincent nodded slowly. "Concentrate first on making a full recovery; you are receiving the very best of care I can assure you. We will talk properly when you're out of there."

Doctor Jam took a few moments to have a final run through with the Troopers. "Now gentlemen one more time. Mallon, you will be on Vincent's right, and Belmore, you will be on his left. Stix and Wemlo, you take either side of his legs, around about the knee area would be best. Have you tested your equipment fully?"

"Yes Sir, all functioning perfectly." The Troopers were instructed to wear Casmet Brachial Armour to give them the necessary extra strength that they might very well need in the next few minutes. These devices are worn on the arms like elbow length metal gloves and when the wearer needs extra strength that his physical body doesn't possess, the devices give him that extra power. The doctor was worried about this coming procedure so he decided to bring the Troopers in for safety's sake.

"Now, the tank will empty and the sides will descend, leaving Vincent on the table. I suspect he will thrash and panic and because of his physique, the damage he could do to himself, the equipment and me, would be considerable. You are to restrain him only enough to prevent him causing damage, do you understand? He's not a prisoner." He gave the Troopers a grave look as they nodded.

"Yes Sir, we understand. We will be careful Sir."

He walked over to Vincent, who was watching the conversation intently through the liquid in the tank. "Vincent I need you to listen to me very carefully now okay?" Vincent raised a hand. "Okay. Now, it is time to bring you out of there but this can be an uncomfortable experience for those who aren't used to it. Do you remember when you first woke up and nearly panicked?" Vincent nodded. "And you remember how I told you how important it was for you not to panic and thrash about?" Another nod. "Good. Well we have to have that conversation again now okay?" Vincent rolled his eyes and the doctor suppressed a grin. "I know I know but it will all be over in a minute or so. The liquid that surrounds you will flush away and the sides of the tank will descend, leaving you lying on the table." A nod from Vincent. "Once your lungs have no more liquid filtering through them, you will naturally start to cough and vomit." Vincent's eyes widened. "Don't worry about it, just allow your body to expel the last of the fluid from your lungs, the more you relax into it, the quicker it will all be over. If you panic and thrash about, it will take much longer."

Vincent looked at the troopers and then back at the doctor, his eyes widening accusingly. The doctor looked sheepish as he explained. "Vincent, you are an immensely strong man, much more so than we are. If you should panic you could damage yourself, the equipment and errm, us. These men are only here to prevent you from hurting yourself or wrecking the place, okay?" Vincent stared at the doctor, and the doctor stared back. "Okay?

Shall we start now or would you rather think about it for a while?" Vincent got the point and raised a hand and nodded. The doctor indicated for the Troopers to take their positions. He counted down from three and pressed the switch. Immediately the liquid flushed away and the sides of the tank dropped through the floor and Vincent was up in a flash, sitting on the table coughing and vomiting the remaining fluid from his lungs. At first he behaved himself and the doctor was delighted, but then when he tried to take a breath in and started a fresh coughing fit, he panicked.

"Gentlemen," the doctor shouted at the Troopers, who all took hold of Vincent as he instructed them. As Vincent struggled, the Troopers Casmet's did their job and kept him from causing mayhem in the medical bay. The doctor stood behind him to keep him in a sitting position. "Vincent please stop struggling. Please, it will end sooner if you stop fighting it. Please trust me on this." As Vincent panicked and began to struggle for air, he felt himself being restrained and no matter how much he wriggled and fought, they were stronger. He heard the doctor shouting and it was only when he caught the words, trust me, that he found the strength to stop fighting. His body heaved as he coughed and vomited and choked up the remaining fluid in his lungs. God how his lungs burned, he felt they were going to explode through his chest if he didn't get air soon. As soon as he allowed his body to get on with the job, it was all over very quickly and with one last heave, his lungs were finally free to breathe and man, did that feel wonderful. The doctor indicated for the Troopers to step away.

"Thank you gentlemen, good job," he smiled as they left the room. He busied himself removing the various wires and tubes from the garment Vincent was wearing and waited for him to relax into breathing normally again. "Well done Vincent, feels good to breathe normally doesn't it?" Vincent nodded and looked down at himself. He touched the silver garment he was wearing. It felt just like his own skin. "The garment forms a bond with your own skin and makes it porous so that the fluid in the tank can get directly through into the cells of your body and do its job quicker. In a couple of minutes the garment will begin to disintegrate as your skin returns to its normal non porous state again. Now, how does your head feel?" he asked as he checked Vincent's eyelids and pupils, probed his ears with an instrument that beeped and felt the glands in his neck.

"Fine, great actually," Vincent said as he shook his head and rolled his neck around.

"Good, good. Now let's get you into a shower to clean up shall we? Come on; let me help you off the table." He helped him into the next room to shower.

"Did I hurt anyone?" Vincent asked.

"No, no damage done."

"How long was I out?"

"Just a day here with us but it must've been five or six in total with the time you spent down in the dome. Here we are, now step up there, that's it."

Once showered and dressed, Vincent felt better than he felt in years. He went back into the medical bay to find the doctor talking with another man he thought he recognised.

"Ahh Vincent hello again, how are you feeling?" The man came toward him and offered his hand, which Vincent shook whilst still trying to remember where he'd seen him before.

"I feel great, thank you for everything. I owe ya one I guess." He remembered how much these people had done for him and didn't want to forget to at least say thank you even though it sounded a bit inadequate.

"You don't owe us anything my friend. After what you've done for the whole galaxy, you owe no one anything. I am King Lomas VII. We spoke a couple of days ago while you were still in the tank. Do you remember?"

So that was it. "Ahh, I knew I recognised your face, yeah I remember you. Umm, how should I address you. Is Sir okay?" He suddenly felt awkward; he'd never met royalty before but Lomas put him at ease.

"Officially it's Your Majesty the first time and Sir after that, but unless it's a state occasion, then Lomas will suffice. Let me show you around, come." He gave Vincent the tour and then showed him his quarters. "Come and go as you please. There is no where off limits to you. You are not a prisoner here, you're an honoured guest. Now, let's go to the obs deck, we have much to discuss." He led Vincent to the obs deck and introduced him to Byron, Toma and the others. Vincent looked at Toma and remembered where he'd seen him before.

"You were the one held in the mine," he said and Toma looked surprised.

"Yes, you know about that? But that happened after you left, how did you know?" Vincent suddenly realised what he'd done. He wondered how they would take the information that he spoke to a spirit woman. Lomas saw he looked a bit awkward and saved the day.

"Ahh of course, we keep forgetting. Your spirit friend will have told you, yes?"

He looked up at Lomas in surprise. "You know about that? How?"

"We are Drycenians Vincent; there isn't much we don't know." He raised his eyebrows and everyone laughed. "We've never personally encountered one before, but we got used to knowing they're around from Farra."

Vincent hadn't heard that name before. "Farra? Who or what is Farra?"he asked.

Lomas indicated for him to sit. "She is a woman who is also fighting to bring you your freedom."

He realised this must be the woman he saw in the hotel room. "Oh, you mean the dragon woman? Is that her name? Farra?"

Lomas looked at the others. "Dragon woman?" he asked.

"Yes, that's her," Jam smiled "Your Majesty, she has a large dragon tattooed on her back. When she had the melanin implant put in, she got me to re colour it for her so it would stand out more. It's quite fine I must say, a beautiful work of art."

Lomas' eyebrows went right up to the top of his head. "Good lord."

Suddenly a Trooper came in and gave something to Byron, who took it over to a machine and pressed a switch.

"Here's the data from all those chips we took from the domes Your Majesty. We hope they will fill in all the missing pieces."

Vincent remembered what Syra told him. "You haven't figured that out yet?" he asked them and they all looked at him.

"Well we've discovered most of it yes, but not the finer details," Lomas replied.

Vincent didn't know whether to tell them or not. He sent out a question with his mind, should he tell them? A throb from his chest told him yes, he should. "While I was out, my err, guide showed me stuff. Stuff from way back in time and stuff from now. She showed me how the Transmortals began. When they first started trying to umm, change people, they went to a planet someplace that had primitive, savage humanoids who were cannibals and they brought them to the planet we just came from and set them there so they could breed and be nearby for their experiments. They brought their trees and plants too to make em feel at home I guess and they did their thing on them. Trouble was it changed them the wrong way from what the Transmortals wanted. The process makes a person into the opposite of what they already are and these humanoids were already savage and violent so when they changed they became passive and friendly. They tried to do them again but it only works once. When they realised their mistake they took the ones they'd changed back to their own planet and left them there. Those became you people." He looked at all the stunned faces that stared back at him and didn't know what to say. "Sorry, but it's true. No use letting you spend however long trying to figure it out when I already know."

Lomas got up and walked to the observation window. "So it is true and we are Transmortals. My god I don't know how to feel about this. It never crossed my mind that this may be why our language was everywhere down there."

"Seems to me it doesn't matter what you call yourself or where you're from, it's what you do that matters," Vincent replied to the silent group.

Suddenly the intercom buzzed with a message for the doctor. He went to see what it was and returned excited. "That poison you put into the water supply Vincent, it's from something called the Polea Beetle," he explained.

Lomas and the others looked up in surprise. "Polea? Are you sure? But that's a Drycenian poison," Lomas exclaimed in surprise.

"Yes sir, I had it checked twice. It's Polea. Remember what we got from the data chips from the domes, and what Vincent has just repeated to us? They not only took the humanoids from the planet, which we can assume is Drycenia 4, but they also took the trees and plants? It stands to reason that the trees would've brought along their own parasites and other minute inhabitants, doesn't it?"

"Yes, it does doesn't it?" Lomas could hardly take it all in. "How will everyone take this news I wonder," he pondered aloud.

"Well I won't tell em if you don't," Vincent offered, trying to sound light hearted.

Lomas took a deep breath and turned around. "Of course, what possible good could come from telling the whole galaxy? They don't need to know just yet. Maybe in a few thousand years or so. Now, sit down and let's discuss what will happen when we get to Terramora Prime."

"I'd like to know about this Farra too," Vincent asked and Lomas nodded.

"Of course, ask anything you want to know."

On Terramora Prime, Donaldson was reading the riot act to his delegates and making sure that they understood that the mystery woman who saved him should not be harmed and was not to be held as a prisoner. Now that the Moxal 3 business was in hand, all they must do now is find Vincent. He hoped with all his heart that his instincts were going to pay off and that the Drycenian Nation had the problem in hand. Surely they wouldn't leave the hardest part of the job to those least likely to succeed, would they? He was pondering this thought when the door burst open. An admin clerk rushed in.

"I'm terribly sorry gentlemen for intruding but there is an emergency call for you Mr Donaldson on the secure inter galactic channel. I know you said you weren't to be disturbed but I think you'll want to take this call Sir." Donaldson wondered who could be calling him on the secure channel; there was no one in the field at the moment that would need to do so. He was intrigued so he nodded and the admin clerk handed him his communication headset.

"Michael Donaldson here, who is this?"

"Mr Donaldson thank you for taking this call. My name is King Lomas VII of the Drycenian Nation and I offer you warmest greetings. I am calling to inform you that I have Mr Vincent Richard Domenico here with me on board my vessel and to let you know that we will be with you within 2 days. Let me also take this opportunity to thank you from the whole Drycenian Nation for believing in us and for having the insight and courage to let right be done. I also have the greatest of pleasure in informing you that Mr Domenico has single handedly defeated the Transmortal threat permanently and that their race is now extinct. Until we meet soon Mr Donaldson." Donaldson struggled to find the words as the tears started down his cheeks. The delegates looked on, puzzled,

"God speed Your Majesty."

Byron rushed into the obs deck to find Lomas and Vincent and the others already there.

Lomas saw the worried look on his face. "Byron, something's bothering you, what is it?"

"Yes Your Majesty I am worried. You see, we haven't heard from Farra since her last message about the shooting."

"But there is nothing for her to report so why would she?" Lomas asked.

"I suppose so Sir." Byron reluctantly had to agree that Farra wasn't going to just call them up to say hi when they couldn't reply to her. "It just doesn't seem like her to just wait patiently, I'd have thought she'd have been calling to say where the fuck are you or something like that."

Lomas turned to the doctor. "Is her implant still working?"

The doctor nodded. "Yes Sir, perfectly."

That pleased Lomas, who turned back to Byron. "So long as her implant is working, we know she's alive and healthy. Don't worry just yet Byron."

"No Sir, sorry Sir."

Two days later they arrived at Terramora Prime and the circus began. Donaldson was taken to meet Vincent in the privacy of the Drycenian vessel.

"Vincent, I'm so pleased to be able to meet you again to right the wrong that was done to you. I offer you my sincerest apologies for the part I played in the terrible things that happened to you and I want you to know that I fully intend to put that right today." Vincent took his proffered hand and shook it, squeezing just a tiny bit too hard.

"Thank you Donaldson, better late than never," Vincent smiled as Donaldson worked his fingers to get the blood flow going again. Lomas stifled a giggle as Donaldson continued.

"Now. We managed to get Ranger Dolton here and we have five witnesses testifying that Prince Toma was held prisoner in the mine and we have another two who will testify that they saw large sums of money being handed over to Mr Midship."

"Midship? Who the fuck is Midship?" Vincent asked.

"He was the rep for SB Weapons. Oh sorry you'll have known him as Bullet," Donaldson explained.

"Oh him, so that's his name huh? What about McGreedle, you got him too? Vincent asked.

"No I'm afraid not. He's dead."

Vincent looked surprised. "Dead? Really?"

"Not only that, but he was killed with the same weapon used in the other five murders, a Hellfire Pulse Laser Canon. A Transmortal weapon as you know. Did you ever see or handle such a weapon on Moxal 3?"

"No, never. I know what they are. We saw them in the military from time to time and we learned how to recognise the signs but I never handled one and I never even saw one on Moxal 3."

"Then we will put pressure on Ranger Dolton. He is our only apparent witness to you having committed the murders. Now that McGreedle is dead he may feel safe enough to tell the truth."

"Mr Donaldson may I comment here," Lomas asked.

"Of course Your Majesty, please."

"As you may be aware, we are lucky enough to have some pretty nifty gadgets at our disposal, and we do have something that might help uncover the truth."

Donaldson was intrigued. "I'm all ears Sir."

For three days the trial concentrated on the Moxal 3 fraud, the money going missing, Toma being held prisoner and employees paying in cigarettes to go and see him. McGreedle was found guilty of fraud and false imprisonment posthumously and sentenced to have his remains interred permanently within the confines of the Laxmay Penitentiary. Midship was found guilty of kidnap and fraud and assisting an unauthorised political revolution and was sentenced in his absence to life in a maximum security prison facility and a warrant was issued galaxy wide for his arrest.

Donaldson addressed the court. "We now turn our attentions to the five murders that took place on Moxal 3. Murders that Mr Vincent Richard Domenico has previously been convicted of." Murmurs travelled around the court. Donaldson continued. "I call Ranger Dolton, previously employed at the Moxal 3 Mining Corporation." The Ranger was brought in and questioned about the murders. At first he stuck to his story that he saw Vincent threatening two of the victims and saw him running from the scene in possession of the Hellfire Pulse Laser Canon. Donaldson approached him. "Mr Dolton you are sure that your statements regarding Mr Domenico are accurate?"

"Uh yes Sir, yep, all true," Dolton grinned at the court.

Donaldson then played his ace. "In that case Mr Dolton you won't mind submitting to a turn in a Magneto Pulse Wave Scanner?"

"Huh? A what?" Dolton looked at Donaldson without the first clue what he was on about.

"You've heard of the Drycenian truth machine I take it?" Donaldson asked and Dolton nodded.

"Oh yeah I've heard of it, who hasn't. No one but them Drycenians have that kinda stuff. You ain't got access to their shit, nobody does."

"No, but if we did, would you submit to a test?" Donaldson prayed he'd take the bait.

"Hell yeah, of course I would. I'm telling the truth as a good citizen. But I don't see any Drycenians nor their machines here, so y'all gonna have to believe me when I tell ya I'm telling the truth." He sat back and grinned at the court as Donaldson turned around and addressed them.

"I call His Majesty King Lomas VII of the Drycenian Nation."

An audible roar of shock went around the courtroom and when Donaldson turned to face Dolton again, he was delighted to notice that the Ranger had turned quite white. The court hushed as the doors opened and in strode Lomas in all his best royal garb. He went to town on his appearance for this and the crowd were suitably awe struck. He took the stand and Donaldson approached him.

"Your Majesty, if I may be allowed to ask you some questions?"

"By all means Mr Donaldson, I'm happy to answer any questions you may have."

"Thank you Sir. Do you have a Magneto Pulse Wave Scanner?"

"We do indeed."

"Has its use been proven in a court of law?" Donaldson asked and when Lomas listed the famous cases where it was successfully used with one hundred percent accuracy, he asked if they might use it here today.

"Of course we'll be happy to assist you in any way we can."

Donaldson turned back to Ranger Dolton and smiled broadly. "There Mr Dolton, all settled. Will 4pm be suitable?" The crowd giggled and Donaldson turned to walk away.

Dolton leapt up. "Okay okay okay I'll tell y'all." He knew that if the machine found him to be lying, his sentence would be much worse than if he told the truth by choice.

"We're all ears Mr Dolton."

"It was the Boss's idea all along. He wanted Domenico put away for good and he meant to make it happen. He hated him for some reason. No one knew why and no one was shit stupid enough to ask. He had the Hellfire Canon. Said he got it from his home planet where them Transmortals had been and he found it amongst the rubble and bodies and shit. He said everything was going to plan until Domenico arrived at the mine and him just being there put him on edge so bad we all felt it. Once Domenico arrived the Boss went nuts about fixing him and getting rid of him. Someone asked him why don't he just shoot him and be done with it, but y'know what? The guy said he didn't want him to just die, he wanted him to suffer for years and years first. The boss was mad crazy and everyone, and I mean everyone, was so scared of him they'd sell their own mammas if he told em to."

"And you are willing to submit to the truth machine with this new statement?" Donaldson asked.

"Yes, absolutely, it's the truth. Domenico never killed no one. Everyone liked the guy. He was a bit of a loner. Kept himself to himself but he was fair and the guys liked him. Shit, even I liked him."

"What is the name of this character you call, Boss?" Donaldson asked.

"No one ever knew his name. Everyone called him Boss. All we knew is he made the rules, when he said jump you said how high and we all guessed he had some history maybe with Domenico, them being the same an all."

This last statement caught Donaldson's attention. "The same? In what way, the same?"

"They both got that thing," Dolton said, waggling his finger towards his own chest. "That scar thing. They're from the same planet and they both got the same mark, the Lilean Star I think it's called."

Donaldson hadn't been prepared for this at all. "The Boss is a Lilean too?"

"Yeah."

"Dolton, do you happen to know how Mr Domenico's DNA was put onto the Hellfire Canon?"

"Yeah the Boss said he had a sample of Domenico's DNA and he put it on the Canon himself, personally."

"Is there anything else you wish to tell us Mr Dolton?" Donaldson asked.

"Yeah, he also killed McGreedle. And I did see that happen and yes I'll do the machine thing and tell y'all the same thing."

The jury reached their verdict in just one hour and filed back into the court room. Donaldson rose and addressed the packed court.

"I call Mr Vincent Richard Domenico into the court." The crowd fell silent as Vincent walked into the court and took the stand. There were sighs and murmurs of "wow" and "gosh look at him" from the ladies amongst the crowd. Donaldson addressed the jury. "Will your spokesperson please stand."

The man at the end of the row stood. "I am the jury spokesperson Sir and I inform you that we have reached a unanimous verdict."

"Please inform the court of the jury's decision," said Donaldson as he closed his eyes and prayed like he'd never prayed before.

"We the jury in the case of Vincent Richard Domenico do hereby find him not guilty of the crimes for which he was previously and wrongly convicted." He sat down and Donaldson fought to keep his composure. He turned to face Vincent and for the first time he really felt as if he could look him in the eyes.

"Mr Domenico, I am proud and happy to declare here today to all persons on all worlds throughout the galaxy that you are and always have been, innocent of any wrongdoing. It shames me to know that you were treated so harshly and suffered so greatly due to a miscarriage of justice and I am proud to be able to right that wrong today. You are a free man and there is from this moment on, no stain whatsoever upon your character or your record." He then turned and addressed the court. "I also have pleasure in announcing to this court and to everyone throughout the galaxy who cares to listen, that Mr Domenico did just 7 days ago, single handedly defeat and kill the Transmortal army. His Majesty King Lomas VII of the Drycenian Nation was there and saw for himself the dead body of the Transmortal leader and has personally confirmed that the Transmortal race is now extinct. What Mr Domenico has done for us, whilst still being regarded as a fugitive and a criminal of the worst kind, goes beyond all my experience of compassion and humbles us all." Donaldson stood, turned to Vincent and started to applaud. Within seconds every single person in the packed courtroom was applauding and there wasn't a dry eye in the house.

CHAPTER SEVENTEEN

It took seven days of hopping from planet to planet and system to system, stopping to refuel and re supply the little ship before the Boss and Farra finally took off on the last leg of their journey. Farra was quite pleased for the regular stops as her captor allowed her to get up and go outside, under heavy restraints of course. This meant she could get some sun on the solar cells in her Biomed implant so the Drycenians would be able to track her and come to her rescue if need be. These regular little sojourns also meant she could stretch her legs and take a pee. She was very angry that he stripped her of the Unicom Transmitter that would have allowed her to call them and inform them of what happened. Not that she knew exactly where she was of course, but at least she would be able to tell them she had been kidnapped. With her Biomed still signalling, they wouldn't be any the wiser until they returned to Terramora with Vincent and found she wasn't there to meet them. There were any number of opportunities for her to get away from her captivity but Leon told her not to, so she reluctantly allowed them to pass her by. He hadn't actually hurt her though, she reminded herself for the umpteenth time. He was full of bullshit and swore at her and called her a bitch all the time but she viewed that as just bravado and posturing and didn't allow it to get to her. As they landed yet again for what she assumed would be just another rest and refuelling stop, he turned around and grinned at her.

"Hey honey we're home," he said and guffawed loudly. He left her restrained in the little ship and she wondered if he was going to leave her there for the duration. The seat she was strapped into wasn't that comfortable any more and her backside was completely numb. She desperately wanted to walk around and hoped she was to be moved to somewhere else. It was night time on this planet and through the open doorway she could see only the dark shapes of trees and a building about two hundred yards away.

Her night sight wouldn't work whilst she was in the lighted environment of the ship so she was unable to see much. She wondered where they were. A throb in her chest told her Leon was with her, so she closed her eyes and let her mind go inwards a little so that she would hear his telepathic voice.

"We are home Farra," he told her.

"Home?" We're on earth?" she asked him.

"No child, we're on Lilea. My home and Vincent's home. And your home too if you wish it to be."

She smiled and felt quite emotional knowing that she had finally reached Vincent's home world. "Lilea? Oh, oh wow, Lilea." She craned her neck to try to see more from the open doorway but it was too light inside the ship to see out into the dark. She remembered the photograph she saw on the Drycenian ship and wondered if it was all as beautiful as that.

"Yes my dear, it is all beautiful and now it will be beautiful forever. I have something to tell you, wonderful news. Vincent has fulfilled the prophecy, the Transmortals are now extinct. The ancient ones sing with such joy in the land of the dead."

Farra was silenced by this news. Shocked and delighted all at the same time. "He did it? That's fantastic," she cried through tears of relief and happiness. "Is he okay? What about the retrial?"

"He is well and is with the Drycenians and is at this moment receiving his freedom." She couldn't speak, she burst into tears. "I am so happy I cannot begin to tell you Farra. All of us in the land of the dead are bursting with happiness and joy that Lileans can now grow and be fruitful as we were before. I am so proud of my brave son; he has shouldered his burdens with such dignity and strength. How I wish I could be there to hold him, I never got to do that. I passed before he was born."

She could tell Leon was becoming emotional and this made her worse. "Oh Leon, I'm so sorry, I wish I could help."

"Do not be sorry child. He and I will meet again when he joins me in the land of the dead as we all must do one day and then we will have all of time to be together as father and son at last. Now, it is important that you do not tell anyone of the news I've just given you, especially your captor. He is not to know of Vincent being cleared. Do not tell him about the Transmortals either no matter how tempted you may become. Promise me." She promised.

The Boss returned to the little ship and finally allowed her out of the chair and into the Lilean night air. As she stepped down from the ship, she allowed her night sight to kick in and looked all around at the landscape. She saw ancient forest trees looming all around and one large building and she wished she could have got here under better circumstances but it sure felt good to be here at last. A rough shove from behind almost made her fall over.

"Get moving bitch, I ain't got all night," he snarled and led her at gunpoint towards the building she could see taking form out of the darkness. Once inside, she saw it consisted of just two rooms, one of which contained a barred cell just eight foot square and no window. He installed her inside the cell and finally took off her handcuffs. There was just a bed with no blankets and a pail for a toilet. "Make yourself at home honey," he said and whistled a tune as he turned and left the room, leaving her alone. She looked at her surroundings, saw the pail, sat down on the bed and dropped her head into her hands. She heard thumps and bangs from the next room and wondered what he was up to.

Leon appeared and tried to encourage her not to let her spirits sink. "Farra, do not despair child, all will be well. You only have to endure for a few more days, then the sun will shine for you, I promise. You have been so strong and brave and I am so proud of you, I think of you like a daughter." He approached the bed and sat next to her.

She looked up at him. "You do? Thank you Leon that's a lovely thing to say. I feel so alone right now and I feel guilty for feeling depressed about it knowing all that Vincent had to endure for all those years and how bravely he coped."

"Farra, Vincent is a full blooded Lilean, a perfect example of our race. We are warriors at heart, defiant and focussed and with a capacity to endure pain and hardship way beyond many other races. You are from Earth. Most Earth people are still learning to put aside their political differences. They are aggressive but they aren't natural warriors. They let their emotions make their decisions and they don't endure well when hardships abound. Earth people like you Farra are very rare, that is why you were chosen for this task because although you are from Earth, you have a Lilean spirit inside." He smiled gently and wiped away her tears.

"I'm so happy for Vincent," she said. "I'm so happy he's got his freedom. How he must be feeling right now I just can't imagine. And I was a part of making that happen, I'm real proud of that Leon, real proud," she sniffed and wiped her eyes.

"You are more than a part of it Farra, you are half of it," he replied. "If you hadn't rescued Toma, or found Vincent's book; if you hadn't got it to Donaldson and saved his life too, Vincent would still be a fugitive. Do not ever think that Vincent doesn't know what you have done for him, don't ever think that, not ever okay?" Farra nodded as she sniffed. Leon stood up suddenly. "He's coming back, wipe your eyes quickly child, don't let him see you upset." He disappeared just as the door opened and the Boss came striding in with a plate in his hands.

"Hey honey, I cooked dinner for ya. Ain't I the perfect man huh?" He stooped and shoved the plate under the bars towards her. She looked down at it. It looked disgusting and she felt like kicking it back at him. She didn't think Leon would be pleased with that though, so she stooped and picked it up.

"Thank you," she said politely, trying not to puke. He seemed happy with that and with a grin, he turned and left the room. She looked down at the plate and tried to figure what it contained. It was dark brown and gloopy with orange lumps and there was a hunk of bread the size of her fist by the side. "Must I?" she asked.

"Yes my dear, you must," came the reply.

"Do I even want to know what it is?"

"No child, you don't. Just swallow without chewing and it'll go down quicker."

The next morning, after spending a very chilly night on the bed with no blanket or pillow, Farra was wakened by her captor banging on the bars of the cell. She leapt up at the sudden noise and then cried out in pain as she realised she had a painful crick in her neck. She was cold and stiff all over and thought if she has to spend too many nights on that bed she'll end up an invalid.

"Wakey wakey darlin, rise and shine." She was beginning to get seriously irritated with his pseudo redneck act. He shoved a cup of liquid under the bars at her, which she took and sniffed. She was amazed to find that it smelled wonderful. She took a tentative taste and was even more surprised to find that it tasted as good as it smelled.

"Thank you," she said and meant it this time. "What is it? It's good." She tried some non confrontational conversation and thought that if she stroked his ego a bit, he might be lenient with her. He smiled at her compliment, too thick to realise she was playing him.

"Well thank ya kindly ma'am, it's called Parsch. It's dried leaves of the Parsch plant steeped in boiled water," he informed her.

"Oh, like tea," she said and made a vow to remember this brew.

"Tea?" he asked. "What's tea?"

"It's basically the same as this, but a different plant."

"Oh, right, yeah, tea. Now, what the hell do you think you were up to back there. You've really fucked things up for me y'know and I'm real annoyed about that." He dropped the smile and turned aggressive in a second and Farra was caught unawares.

She didn't know how to respond effectively. "Well I err, didn't want the guy to get killed. He's a good guy. Isn't he?" she asked, trying to appear stupid. Her captor wasn't appeased though.

"Yes he's a good guy, that's the fuckin reason I wanted him done you stupid bitch and now you've gone and fucked it all up, damn you. Damn you," he snapped and started beating on the bars of the cell like a crazed animal, yelling abuse at her and calling her all the names he could think of. The tirade went on for two minutes before, with a final kick, he turned and walked out of the room and slammed the door behind him.

"Jesus," she exclaimed. She realised suddenly that she needed to pee. She turned and looked at the pail and her heart sank. "I can't, I just can't," she said aloud.

"Yes you can child, trust me," Leon's voice in her head. This went on for day after day. She forced down his revolting food, drank his wonderful tea and listened to his crazed rantings. At no time did he touch her or threaten to hurt her. He just seemed to need someone to rant at, and rant he did. He ranted about everything. He ranted about her saving Donaldson. He ranted about Johnson not killing him. He ranted about being a nobody all his life. He ranted about his buddies not doing what he told them to do, but most of all he ranted about his kid brother. He was loved more. He was more special. He got more toys as a kid. He was stronger and bigger. He did well in the military blah blah blah. Farra was bored sick of hearing about it all and often had to physically bite her tongue to stop herself from yelling at him to shut the fuck up. When, on the seventh morning the routine started again, she put her head in her hands and thought that if this went on much longer she would commit murder and happily go to jail. After an hour she managed to pretend to be listening while allowing her mind to drift a little and was dreaming of what Lilea looked like at dawn when he said something that snapped her back to reality in an instant.

"And why did they have to pick that kid huh? Why him? Why Vincent? Why couldn't they have found a girl or a different boy, why Vincent huh?" Farra snapped her head round at the mention of Vincent. She was now all ears and wished she'd been listening more intently. When he finished his daily rant and stormed out of the room, she sat down to think. He mentioned Vincent but was it the same Vincent?

"Yes Farra it is Vincent that he is talking about. His name is Wesley Sylvana and Vincent is his younger brother." Farra gaped as Leon gave her this news. "Remember I told you that Vincent was found by a group of my neighbours, one of whom was still nursing her own child so she took Vincent to her own breast?" Farra nodded as she remembered. "Wesley was that nursing child and from the day Vincent was brought into the family, Wesley hated him."

Farra stood up, shaking her head. "So he tried to kill Donaldson to prevent him from freeing Vincent? But how did he know anyone was trying to get him cleared? I don't understand."

"Everything has been Wesley's doing Farra. You have already begun to wonder whether he is the mysterious Boss from the Moxal 3 plot haven't you." She nodded. "You're right child, Wesley is that mysterious unnamed Boss."

Her jaw dropped. "But why? Did he want to take over the sector or something?"

"No, he used that as a lure to get McGreedle and the Rangers involved. All he was trying to do was ruin Vincent's life. He'd been siphoning off money from the mine for some time in the hope of bribing Vincent's military colleagues to get him killed but when Vincent left of his own free will and took the job at the mine, Wesley saw it as a gift from heaven and a sign that what he was doing was the right thing."

"So the murders were deliberately pinned on Vincent to get him jailed." She was beginning to understand.

"Yes. Wesley fixed the trial and bribed all those that needed a push in the right direction. That's why it all happened within twenty four hours; everyone was being paid by Wesley to send Vincent to Cryo Stasis, the one place he felt sure Vincent would never get out of."

"I bet he was mad as hell when he found out he escaped," she grinned. "I'd love to have seen his face that day."

"He was worried that Donaldson, who by now was head of the ANA would be incapable of being bribed if Vincent were ever to get a retrial so he thought it best to kill him to make sure it never happened," Leon told her.

"So that's how this whole thing fits together. But why kidnap Toma, what was that all about?" she asked.

"That was Wesley's fine idea. He thought that if he could get that tagged onto Vincent too, the Drycenians would never allow him to ever be free again. Little did he know how close he came to starting an inter galactic war. If Toma had been killed, the Drycenians would have shown everyone just how capable they are of being aggressive. I shudder at the very thought and am so glad it's been avoided."

"So this is why you got me to allow myself to be kidnapped. So I can uncover the mysterious Boss man and get the final piece of the puzzle sorted?" She now thought she had it all straight in her mind.

"Yes, mostly that. But I wanted to make it up to Vincent for having a rough childhood at Wesley's hands and also for not being there for him. Oh the Sylvana's were good people and treated him well. They loved him, but Wesley is their child too. Their hearts were torn between the two and he suffered at Wesley's hands. As a child Vincent was an emotional boy and Wesley's tauntings and cruelties hurt him greatly. He still has that hurt inside and this is a way of allowing him to let that go."

Farra realised how impotent Leon must have felt having to watch Vincent suffer so much and not be able to help. Her heart broke for him.

"Thank you my dear," he said, having picked up her thoughts.

That evening, Farra was pacing her cell, trying to figure everything out in her head, to get it all to fit so that she could understand and really feel it. It was getting dark and she realised that Wesley hadn't brought her anything to eat.

"Why hasn't he brought me any food, he's late today?" she pondered aloud.

"Farra, all hell is going to break loose in a few minutes. Your moment has come, be ready. Oh, and err, keep sharp." Leon sounded agitated so she didn't feel like smiling at his use of her dad's phrase.

"Why, what's up?" she asked but there was no time for him to answer as her attention was drawn to thumps and bangs and shouting from the next room. It sounded like Wesley had lost it completely, but over what? Suddenly the door burst open and he stood in the doorway, his face like thunder. She took one look and realised she was scared for the first time in ages. She wasn't scared because he was getting aggressive, she could handle that just fine and had done on numerous occasions during her military service. She was scared because Wesley was crazy and here he was going nuts on her, with her locked in a cell and nothing with which to defend herself. He was carrying her plate of food. For a moment he just stood in the doorway like a statue, then with a speed that frightened her he suddenly launched the plate at the cell, where it hit with a clatter and scattered the brown gloop everywhere. She jumped back, startled out of her wits and nearly fell as she bumped into the edge of the bed.

"You've ruined everything and I am gonna slice you up and hang you up on the wall." Wesley slowly walked towards the cell and Farra noticed a huge curved blade in his right hand. She wished he hadn't taken her waist belt from her. If she had her dragon dagger she would be able to take him on with no trouble at all whereas unarmed, she was probably toast. Just when she remembered that the Drycenians had given her bone structure extra strength, she also remembered that Wesley was Lilean and that meant he was still naturally stronger than her enhanced strength allowed her to be. "You know what I just heard?" he teased. She guessed but shook her head innocently. "He's gone and done it; he's actually gone and done it."

"Who? Done what?" she asked, trying to sound inquisitive.

"Darling Vincent has defeated the Transmortals and is a national hero. And do you know what else is good today, bitch?" She shook her head, knowing what was coming. "He's had a retrial and Donaldson gave him his freedom. They know he didn't do those murders and now he's a free man and probably on his way home to a hero's welcome and all because of your interference. This is all your fault," he screamed at her. "You are so gonna fuckin die." He stepped back from the bars and fumbled in his pocket for something. He drew out a key and walked towards the cell door. As he was about to unlock the cell, something beeped in the other room. It sounded like an inter galactic communicator. He went to answer it. "What?" he yelled into the device. A pause.

"Yeah I just heard about it too, the worst news ever but y'know what? All is not lost. So he comes home a hero right? Well we give him a few months to settle in and then people start dying and then when they find his DNA on the bodies, his hero status will make him an even bigger figure of hatred than before." Wesley giggled into the communicator and listened as the person on the other end replied. After a minute or two he continued. "Yeah I got it all here, the data chips, accounts, journals and logs from the mine and the canon too. I'll deal with the stuff don't worry, it's history already and then I'll deal with the bitch too. Then we just go back to our normal lives for a few months till I give you the nod okay?" He put down the communicator and went into action, Farra temporarily forgotten, much to her relief. He rummaged through drawers and cupboards and boxes and collected up together what she guessed was evidence that placed him firmly at the helm of everything that had happened and probably more she didn't know about. Finally he reached into the back of a cupboard and drew out the Hellfire Pulse Laser Canon.

She had seen this weapon only once before, during her military service. It was standard procedure for all personnel to be familiar with it and its effects upon the body so that they could recognise any signs of a Transmortal presence. It wasn't a huge weapon but it was an impressive size nonetheless. It was said to be easily operated with one hand so she guessed it didn't weigh that much. It had a seven inch long barrel about three inches in diameter. At the base of the barrel it bulged out and she could see tiny holes or vents that she remembered being told during her military service were to allow air to get in and cool the laser so it didn't over heat and explode. It was jet black and had symbols carved all over it. At the end of the handle was a clutch of wiring that hung down in a mess that looked totally out of place on this sleek uncluttered weapon. It was as if it had been tampered with or enhanced in some way by someone who hadn't the artistry of the original inventor. She guessed that must mean Wesley had been fiddling with it. He saw her looking at it and held it up.

"Beautiful isn't she? A piece of art this weapon is. I picked her up about a mile away from here when I was exploring the outskirts of the city that hadn't been cleared yet for rebuilding. Buried under a heap of rubble still attached to its Transmortal owner. Y'know each one only works for its owner? Took me a year to reconfigure it and make it work. Artistry in action, that's what she is, beautiful and deadly." He aimed it at her and touched a small button with his thumb. The three inch diameter barrel started to glow with an eerie light that was blue black in the middle and ice blue around the outside. It was mesmerising and yes, beautiful. It was well named, Farra thought as she looked at it.

He switched it off and laughed. "Don't think you're getting off that easy, I'm gonna do you slow and easy like, real slow and easy. Oh yeah." He put down the canon and walked towards the cell, letting his eyes travel up and down her body deliberately. She was sickened and scared. A throb from her chest told her Leon was nearby but she couldn't detach her mind enough to hear him telepathically. Another throb, more painful this time and she turned away from Wesley, hoping that without seeing him, she'd be able to concentrate on listening for Leon. Suddenly his voice came through, far away but she heard him.

"Don't kill him, just stun him. Get the evidence and your comm device and run like you've never run before."

She heard the cell door creak open behind her. She remained still, her back to the advancing Wesley. For what seemed like years he remained too far behind for her to act effectively so she stood still. It was a battle of wills, who would break first? She waited for something to happen and as time seemed to slow to a crawl, she felt herself wanting to scream at him to get it over with. She also realised that this was a deliberate tactic to psyche her out, to scare her and she hated to admit it, but it was working. She decided not to act until she was outside of the cell. Once out of the confines of her prison she knew she stood a better chance of getting away but if she tried to take him on in here and he got the better of her with his Lilean physique, she would be back to square one. Outside the cell she could take time to get the feel of his power without the possibility of him locking her in again. Suddenly and without warning she was shoved against the wall of her cell so hard it knocked the breath from her lungs. Jesus he was strong and so quick!

As she struggled for breath, Wesley took the opportunity to press himself against her body from behind. She could feel him getting aroused as he squirmed against her backside whilst still holding her arms in an iron grip that would have probably broken some bones if she hadn't had Doctor Jam's help. Wesley was getting very aroused and Farra couldn't help but realise that he was probably intent on raping her first and, she figured that if what she could feel was accurate, he'd hurt her badly if he wasn't careful with it. She didn't think he was too worried about being careful with her though. She had to rethink her plan quickly. She couldn't afford to wait until she was outside of the cell if he meant to rape her in here first. There was no way she was going to submit to that, no matter what Leon might say.

Wesley leaned forward and whispered in her ear. "Oh yeah baby, you want it so bad don't ya? I'm gonna enjoy you before I kill you." He pulled both of her arms behind her and held them firmly with one hand. She then heard the unmistakable sound of a zipper being undone and she got scared. Her chest throbbed in response to her fear and she tried to control herself. Wesley started to moan and she guessed what was going on behind her back and it sickened her. He suddenly whipped her around to face him and then made the most stupid mistake of his life. He let her arms go as he pushed his body against hers and started to wriggle his hips against her. She could feel him, enormous against her lower belly and she almost cried out in terror. An agonising throb from her chest and she forced herself back into control of her emotions. She put her arms around his neck in a feigned embrace which only served to make him even more aroused.

"Yeah baby I knew you'd enjoy it. Can't resist me can ya. You want me to fuck you before you die don't ya?" He moaned again and with one final thrust against her, his body shuddered and Farra fought to keep from being sick and crying out. With her arms around his neck and Wesley still emptying himself down her front, she deftly brought her hands up to his ears before suddenly and expertly using all of her enhanced strength, pressed hard into the nerve points just underneath them. Within seconds he fell to the floor unconscious and she left him there with his trousers around his ankles, his huge erection still pumping.

She gaped at it, she couldn't help herself. "My god," she murmured and then, "ouch," as another painful throb seared through her chest.

Leon appeared and gestured to her. "The evidence, quickly child. Put it in that sack, all of it. Don't leave any of it behind." She did as she was told. "Good girl, now your comm device, in that box under there." She retrieved it and realised its solar cells were almost empty. There was just enough juice left to make one call.

She pressed the button and waited for the beep. "Guys, it's me, Farra. I'm on Lilea. It's Wesley, it's Wesley, he's behind everything. Warn Vincent, it's been Wesley all along, he's the boss man."

The device clicked off as the last of its power died. That reminded her of her Biomed implant and she hastily pulled up her sleeve to find it was not working at all. She realised she'd been in the windowless cell more than seven days and it was out of power.

"Shit, it's dead. Now the guys won't be able to find me Leon," she panicked.

"Fear not child, trust. Now retrieve your blades and run. Wesley won't be out for long and although Lileans aren't built for excessive speed, we can keep going forever. Run like the wind, your only hope is to get some distance between you so you can hide."

She opened the door and ran towards the trees as fast as her legs would carry her. As she ran, she cried. She cried because she was scared that she almost got herself raped. She cried because she was on a strange planet with no friends around her. She cried because she felt more alone than ever before. She cried because she wished her dad was here to comfort her and she cried because she wanted Vincent to come and rescue her but even if he did, he wouldn't know where she was and she didn't even know if he'd want to anyway.

CHAPTER EIGHTEEN

Lomas escorted Vincent from the still applauding courtroom. Once outside they were greeted by a very agitated Byron. "Congratulations Vincent, I'm delighted that right has been done at last," he offered his hand which Vincent shook. He then turned to Lomas and his smile vanished. "Your Majesty, forgive me for dampening the happiness of this wonderful day but something very grave has happened," he was clearly very worried and both Lomas and Vincent looked at each other.

"Whatever is the matter?" Lomas asked.

Byron was almost in tears as he continued. "It's Farra Sir, I just knew something was wrong, I just knew it. It's her Biomed, it's stopped." The smile fell from Lomas' face. He turned to Vincent and took both his hands in his own.

"Vincent, it has been an honour to know you and a privilege to give you aid. If you should ever need our help you have only to call and we will be at your side. We must help Farra. Without her none of this could have ever come to pass and she needs our aid now and we cannot forsake her. Forgive me for rushing away like this, please." He squeezed Vincent's hands and went to turn away but Vincent held on.

"Sir, do you really believe I'm just going to take all this help and walk away? She put her life on the line for me and that means something. I intend to go with you."

Lomas let out a breath of relief and squeezed Vincent's hands again. "Come on everyone, back to the ship."

"Doctor, when did Farra's Biomed stop working? When was her last signal?" Lomas asked.

"Fourteen hours ago Your Majesty." Doctor Jam turned to Vincent and explained how the Biomed worked. "It sends us a signal every six hours. If two signals are missed then our computer flags up an emergency warning to us, which happened two hours ago."

"And what did the last signal show us of her condition?" Lomas continued.

"Very high activity in the sympathetic nervous system, accelerated levels of adrenaline and noradrenalin Sir," he explained without preamble.

Vincent looked at him. "Meaning?"

"Oh, sorry," he replied. "It's a clear sign that her body was experiencing what is colloquially termed the fight or flight response. She was either fighting for her life or she was terrified for it. Either one is not good, not good at all."

Lomas put his head in his hands. "Oh no, please God no."

The doctor then produced a light at the end of what seemed a very dark tunnel. "We did also get a very precise location of her last signal. We can at least go and look for her. Even if we can't rescue her we can at least umm, retrieve her."

Lomas looked up at him. "Where did the signal come from?" he asked.

"Well that is odd Sir. You see her signals for the last seven whole days originate from the same place, the very same spot to be exact. She seems to have spent her last seven days in the exact same spot and up until the Biomed's solar cells ran down, she was alive. Twelve hours ago she was alive. And she is on Lilea Sir." Vincent and Lomas looked up in surprise, and then looked at each other.

"Lilea? She's on Lilea? But why?" Lomas asked. She was supposed to wait for us here."

"We have to go there, now," Vincent urged.

Lomas looked up at Byron. "Set course for Lilea, we must travel with all haste."

"How long will it take to get there?" Vincent asked.

"At full speed, nine hours seventeen minutes," Byron called over this shoulder. Both Vincent and Lomas knew that the next nine hours and seventeen minutes would be amongst the longest of their lives.

Vincent got up, rubbing his backside.

"It's all in the balance. Don't lean too far, just go with it," the Trooper explained patiently to Vincent as he fell from the battle board for the umpteenth time. He got up and tried again. He was determined to get the hang of this thing. "It's because of your size Vincent," the Trooper explained. "The boards aren't technically designed for someone of Lilean proportions so you will have to find the right balance by trial and error."

Vincent looked at the trooper. "Thanks buddy, that's real helpful."

Three hours later Vincent could be found racing the Troopers around the cargo bay and winning sometimes too. They weren't having fun with him but were teaching him to fine tune his control of the board so that he could do more than just go in a straight line. He would need to be able to weave and slalom with lightening fast reaction times. They set up a course of poles and watched him weave in and out. He was getting good at it and even though the situation was grave, he was rather enjoying this gadget.

The Trooper called him over. "Hey Vincent, take a break buddy, have something to eat. Come back in an hour and see if your body remembers huh?"

Vincent jumped off and clapped the Trooper on the shoulder. "You're just sore cos I'm faster than you," he smiled as he walked off.

The Trooper laughed and called after him. "We'll see about that buddy. Gonna get some egg on that face of yours."

Vincent turned and laughed heartily for the first time in ages. "Horse shit." He turned and ran out of the room and went to get some food. He found Lomas, Toma, Byron and the doctor already there.

"Ahh Vincent, how's it going? Nothing broken I hope," Doctor Jam enquired.

Vincent shook his head. "No Doc, nothing broken, except Trooper Caman's pride that is cos he can't catch me." He sat down and helped himself to some food from the fabulous choice that was laid out before him on the table. Lomas and the others watched as he piled his plate high before placing it on the table before him and smiling. He was just about to sample some when he caught the others looking at him. "What?" he asked the laughing Drycenians.

Byron was the first to stop laughing enough to answer. "That would feed one of us for a whole day," he gasped between guffaws.

Vincent shook his head sadly at them. He then stood up, took off his shirt and raised his arms to the sides and braced all of the muscles in his arms and chest and showed them the most magnificent eight pack they'd ever seen.

"My god," Byron's jaw dropped in awe.

Lomas looked up and smiled. "Byron, close your mouth my friend," and everyone laughed as he got up and helped himself to more food.

Over the meal they discussed what they knew of the situation, which was painfully little and explored several possible scenarios that might account for what happened.

"Maybe she got the chance of a lift to Lilea and took it on impulse," suggested Toma. "She did seem to have a kind of," he looked at Vincent briefly, "some kind of growing connection with the idea of going there." Vincent caught the look and didn't know quite how to respond. He felt a little awkward and didn't want to admit that he understood because he was feeling it too.

Lomas shook his head. "No, she wouldn't have done that. She knew we were going to be arriving on Terramora with Vincent for the re trial and she'd not have missed it willingly." Everyone thought about that and had to agree that it was true; she wouldn't have wanted to miss meeting Vincent at the earliest opportunity.

Doctor Jam was deep in thought, but now he spoke up. "We all agree that she wouldn't have willingly missed meeting us on Terramora. She would have wanted to meet Vincent and she wouldn't just go swanning off to Lilea to see the countryside and miss meeting us, yes?" Everyone nodded. "So we have to assume that she went, err, unwillingly then, don't we?" he looked around at the others.

"Yes," Lomas agreed sadly, "unfortunately I think we do."

"It has to be connected to the shooting. The attempt on Donaldson, it just has to be. It's the only plausible explanation for it," Byron said. "Whoever tried to shoot Donaldson must've got to Farra and taken her against her will." Everyone nodded.

"But why take her to Lilea?" Toma asked out loud. "Why kidnap someone and take them there?"

Vincent remained silent during this discourse but now he looked up. "When I was in the military I did a lot of rescue missions and without exception, every single time, the kidnappers take their victims to where they feel comfortable, where they know the land and the resources well. Where they feel at home."

Lomas looked up at him, eyes wide. "You mean her kidnapper's home is Lilea? Her kidnapper is a Lilean?"

Vincent shrugged. "I'm not saying definitely anything, just that it's always been that way every time I've seen it. My money's on the kidnapper being a Lilean."

"And that would also infer that her kidnap has something to do with you Vincent," Doctor Jam said. "After all, Lilea is not a centre of any political disharmony at the moment. In fact the only reason it's in the news at all right now is because of you."

Lomas heard all this and was puzzled. "If we can assume that it had some connection with the attempt to kill Donaldson, then we can also assume that it was an attempt to get at you. Someone wanted to sabotage your re trial and prevent you from being cleared and gaining your freedom."

Byron was nodding but then frowned. "Yes but why? Why would someone want to stop Vincent getting proper justice?" he asked.

"Well just think about it," Doctor Jam said. "He single handedly defeats the Transmortals, becoming an inter galactic hero over night and ensuring that he never has to pay for another drink as long as he lives. Someone's jealous. The oldest sin in the book and the worst."

"No no no," Byron said, "it can't be. The attempt on Donaldson happened before word of the Transmortal defeat got out. That took planning, it wasn't some spontaneous impulse thing, it was cold and calculated and planned."

Lomas thumped the table in frustration. "So we're no nearer," he began but an alarm sounded and everyone jumped. He leapt up and went to the intercom. "Yes, what is it?"

"A Unicom transmission Your Majesty, it must be from Farra," a voice reported.

"Play it, play it," Lomas ordered. Everyone fell silent and waited. Beeps and clicks and then static. Then suddenly a voice Vincent recognised from his journey through time with Syra. It was Farra.

"Guys, it's me, Farra. I'm on Lilea. It's Wesley, it's Wesley, he's behind everything. Warn Vincent, it's been Wesley all along, he's the boss man." Static returned and the message ended. Vincent was shocked, his eyes wide with disbelief and horror.

"Wesley? Who the hell is Wesley?" Lomas asked, looking around at his companions.

"Wesley?" Vincent said aloud. "My god, Wesley?" He closed his eyes, the emotional pain visible on his face as he took in what he just heard. He remembered how his older brother taunted him throughout their childhood, how he bullied him and how he tore up his real parents' photograph. At the memory of the photograph he couldn't stop a tear from falling, which he angrily wiped away.

Lomas saw his new friend's obvious pain. "Tell us Vincent, tell us," he urged as he sat down and waited for Vincent to speak.

"Wesley is my older brother," Vincent said and waited for the group to finish expressing their shock. "I don't know how much you know about me, but the Transmortals, when they came to Lilea they killed most of the Lileans and err, me too." He looked at the group expecting to see disbelief on their faces and was surprised when he didn't find it.

"We know," Lomas said. "We know you were killed at birth and revived by the Lilean ancient spirits to fulfil the prophecy and we know your father died too and your mother died giving birth to you. That's about it in a nutshell."

"Well err, I was found by a group of survivors, some neighbours of my parents and they adopted me and brought me up as their own. They already had a son, Wesley. He hated me. He tormented me throughout my childhood and made his parents' lives hell because of it. And mine too. That's why I left to join the military as soon as I could. I'm actually not surprised that he's behind all this. It all makes sense now." He sighed deeply and hung his head.

"I can sort of understand his position," Doctor Jam said, "from a strictly professional point of view you understand," he added hastily as everyone glared at him in surprise, "Until Vincent came along, he was his parent's sole focus of attention, and then suddenly he found himself with not only a sibling, but one who by virtue of the strange circumstances surrounding his arrival into the family was unique. He must've felt terrible jealousy and didn't know how to handle those feelings appropriately so he turned them towards the obvious, the source of those feelings. Vincent. If you add into that mix the defiant nature of the average Lilean, the habit of not letting go once they get their teeth into something and the almost warrior like mentality, it was a foregone conclusion that he wasn't going to get over it very quickly." The group nodded in understanding.

Lomas began to wonder if this would affect the way Vincent could help them deal with this situation now that they knew it was a personal vendetta. He hoped not but he knew he had to ask. "Vincent, this news not only brings clarity and understanding of all that has gone on, but it also has the potential to make any further choices in bringing this matter to a satisfactory close, difficult. You must think and decide how you wish to proceed with regards to Wesley. We will be at your side in whatever decision you make but one thing will not be compromised, we are going to retrieve Farra. Is that going to be difficult for you?" He looked into Vincent's eyes and waited for him to answer. He didn't have to wait long.

"Your Majesty, it doesn't make my decisions difficult. In fact it helps me finally to realise that there can be no bridge building with Wesley. There have been times when I've wondered whether it was time to try to get along with him, but now at least I don't have to waste my time on something that's doomed to failure. I just want the right thing to be done now so everything that happened, everything that I remember can be put away. Wesley did his best to make me hate my life and took every opportunity to fuck me up and he almost got what he wanted. You know he once tore up the only photograph I had of my real parents? Right in front of my eyes he stood there and tore it into little pieces. That nearly killed me that day and I've never forgotten how that made me feel and he is not getting away with any of this now. Yeah this is personal, it's always been personal, but there's others involved now. Others who put themselves on the line for me even without knowing anything about me and made me feel like I deserved to be heard and have a life worth living. Others like you people and Farra. That means more." The look in his eyes told Lomas that he need not worry about his loyalties being torn. He wished he could make things less emotionally difficult but he knew that all he could do would be to give Vincent better memories for the future and he fully intended to do just that.

Byron took a quick look around to make sure nobody was coming, before slipping inside Vincent's quarters. He laid what he was carrying on the bed and slipped out and returned to his post and hoped no one questioned him as to why he spent four hours on the streamer looking up Lilean history. Lomas was standing at the navigation post with Vincent, discussing tactics. They would be arriving at Lilea any moment now and had pinpointed the position of Farra's last Biomed signal. The scanner showed a largely forested area where a couple of small rescue vessels could land without drawing attention.

"There are a few buildings around but they are scattered fairly widely so we shouldn't have any problems," the Navigation Officer assured them both. "Farra's last signal came from inside one particular building, here's a digital chart showing the layout." He flipped a switch and a digital diagram flashed up showing a building surrounded by forest. "The nearest other building is three miles away Sir," he informed them.

Lomas was pleased that at least there was one problem they wouldn't have to deal with. "Good, that's a relief. I see that forested area is pretty thick. How are you coming along with the battle board Vincent? Will you be able to cope in such a thickly forested area do you think?" he looked at him hopefully.

Vincent nodded without hesitation. "No problem at all. Now when do we get there?"

"Right about now," the Navigation Officer reported. "Switching to a holding orbit. The landing site is right below us Your Majesty."

Lomas wasted no time. "It's time gentlemen. Let us be on our way and pray we find our friend safe."

Vincent returned to his quarters to collect what he needed for the rescue mission. He saw the tiny package on his bed and wandered over to see what it was. A small box about the size of a pack of cigarettes with a card attached.

"Vincent, it has been a privilege serving with you. I am proud to call you friend."

He was stunned and wondered what on earth this was all about. Inside he found a small photograph of a man and a woman standing side by side, arm in arm. The woman was obviously pregnant and both were beaming with pride as the man laid a hand lovingly on the woman's swollen belly. At the bottom of the photograph were some words that Vincent found hard to read through his tears.

Leon Domenico, sector 184 governor. Cecily Domenico & unborn son Vincent Richard.

He was overwhelmed at the gift and sat down on the bed and just looked at it for long moments as the realisation of how much he missed them came flooding back. He knew that his spirits lived on in the land of the dead; the Sylvanas instilled in him the Lilean belief system right from day one but he missed having their physical presence and guidance and he often wondered how his life would be different if they lived. Something caught his eye in the corner of his vision and he turned to see Syra standing beside him.

"Your mother lives in the land of the dead Vincent. You know this. She was strong and determined to remain long enough to bring you into the world and she remained by your side until you were found and nurtured safely. She loves you with all of her being."

Vincent cried out as he heard the truth that he'd waited so long to hear. "And my father?" he asked through his tears.

Syra smiled. "He walks beside someone, as I walk beside you. He is both guide and friend to a soul making their own special journey to their destiny. He sees you on your own journey and is so proud to call you son."

"Why doesn't he walk with me?" Vincent asked, a stab of jealousy streaking through his mind. He was instantly sorry. "I'm sorry for my words Syra, forgive me."

She moved closer and put a hand on his shoulder. "Do not ask for forgiveness when what is said comes from love. He cannot walk beside you because of that very love that you both have for each other. That bond would prevent him from allowing you to receive the gifts of pain, loss, sorrow and trial. His love would prevent you from growing fully."

"Pain is a gift? If that's so then I've been blessed all my life," he said bitterly.

"Yes you have indeed been blessed Vincent, for that pain has given you strength. That loss taught you to strive. That sorrow taught you to love and those trials taught you to endure. Without those qualities you would not be who you are now and could not be who you will be in the future."

Vincent understood her wisdom and nodded through his tears. "I know what you say is right Syra, it's just that I'm so alone?"

She took both his hands in her own. "You are not alone brave one. You have never been alone. I have been with you every step of your journey and will be for every step still to be taken. Now you have others who already recognise and acknowledge a growing bond of love for you. All they wait for is for you to open your heart and receive it." She pointed to the photograph.

"Why did someone do that for me? I can't believe it, I'm a stranger to them."

"Because they love you Vincent," she smiled.

As the little craft made its way silently down to the surface of Lilea, Vincent thought about what Syra said. Logically he knew it must be true but emotionally he found it incredible that someone could show such love to someone who is almost a perfect stranger. Then he remembered the creature on Vinbuk who saved his life by killing the Transmortal. All he did was give her some meat for her infants. It didn't immediately occur to him that perhaps that meat saved them from starving to death but when it did, he began to realise for the first time that there are far more connections that we make with others than anger and naked survival. Love was never too big a part of his life. Throughout his childhood Wesley tried to ensure he knew that he wasn't loved and although the Sylvanas were completely fair with them both, he always knew that he was the one who didn't actually belong. He realised that they felt torn between him and Wesley and so he left to join the military at seventeen and hadn't seen them since. They didn't part in anger and there wasn't any definite estrangement between himself and the Sylvanas, but he felt as if going back to visit would be awkward for them. He also knew that if he went to visit and found them distant with him, he would find that difficult to cope with emotionally. He suddenly regretted not keeping in touch with them and for the first time he realised what it meant that they took him in when he needed someone the most. He realised for the first time what prompted them to do it.

As he sat in the little ship on his way home to Lilea, he recognised love for the first time and his heart opened a little wider. He looked at his companions, all strangers until a short time ago but in that time they'd travelled around the galaxy to help him, putting their lives on the line and were still doing it now, and someone had cared enough about his feelings to give him a photograph of his real parents, just because they knew it meant the world to him. For the first time he felt like he was part of a family. He then acknowledged why they were here. Not just to bring Wesley to justice, but to find Farra. A woman he'd never met but who put her own safety on the line more than once for him. He realised he cared very much that they find her safe.

Dawn was breaking as the little craft landed almost silently near the building. As the group stepped out onto Lilean soil they noticed another craft nearby, a little planet hopper partially covered by brush as though someone wanted to hide its presence. After checking it and find it empty, they crept towards the building.

Lomas called Byron over. "Any bio signals?"

Byron took out the little scanner and pressed his thumb to the screen. "None Sir."

"Come on then." Lomas strode purposefully forward towards the building. A door was standing open on one side and they entered to find themselves in an entrance way with a door on either side of them. They took the left hand one and found a messy room that was obviously an office, bedroom and kitchen all in the one space. Empty boxes were strewn everywhere and dirty cooking utensils were piled high. Off in one corner was a filthy toilet and basin. Some dirty clothes lay in a heap on the end of the bed and Vincent went to examine them. In the pocket of a jacket he found a folded piece of paper. He opened it carefully to find a dishonourable discharge notification from a military academy. Wesley's name was stamped across the top and under reasons for discharge it said simply, pre intake psyche evaluation found subject suffering from possible psychotic disorder. He showed it to the others.

Lomas sighed deeply. "This is a terrible business. Well we now know for sure that what Farra told us was true and that they were both here. Let's see what's next door." The next room was much larger, easily three times the size of the previous one and contained a cell at one end, the door of which stood open. A shelving system went along one wall and everywhere there were boxes and cartons strewn about, as if someone was looking for something in a hurry. The cell contained a bed and a pail that stank very strongly.

Lomas closed his eyes and sighed deeply, covering his eyes with a hand as he fought to control his emotions. "Oh my poor dear child, what have you had to endure?"

"Your Majesty," Byron called suddenly and everyone looked round.

"What is it?" Lomas replied hopefully.

Byron looked upset. "It's DNA sir, Lilean DNA."

"Well we know Wesley has been here, it's no surprise that there'll be his DNA here. There's probably Farra's too," he said as he looked round at the pail in the corner of the cell.

"I know that Sir, but this," he faltered.

"What, Byron? Come on out with it," Lomas said firmly.

"It's semen Sir," he informed them as he failed to prevent a tear from rolling down his cheek. The group fell silent in horror until Lomas expressed how they were all feeling.

"Oh my god no, not that please. Not Farra." A crash made them all jump and turn around to see Vincent tearing the shelves from the wall. He hurled dusty boxes and broken machinery parts around and finally collapsed against the wall screaming with rage. No one told him to be quiet or to calm himself; everyone felt the same and waited for him to expel his anger.

Finally he called to Byron, who ran over. "Look for blood, her blood."

"Blood, why?" Byron asked.

"Because if he, if he raped her, there'll be blood, lots of it. If there's no blood, he didn't. Now go look, please." Byron went to search the room and everyone stood quietly.

"I don't entirely understand, educate me please," Lomas said

"Well Your Majesty," Doctor Jam began. "Farra is from earth, Wesley is Lilean."

"Yes we're all well aware of that doctor, get to the point please," Lomas was getting impatient.

"Well it's like this, Lilean men are, they are, well you saw Vincent in the tank."

"Yes I did, so what?" Lomas still didn't understand.

"Well umm, he's a fine figure of a man wouldn't you agree Your Majesty?" Jam blushed and Lomas got the point.

"Oh I see, yes I get your point. Oh poor Farra, how she must have suffered." He was stricken with worry. Ten minutes later and Byron reported to a very relieved group that there wasn't a drop of her blood to be found anywhere.

"Oh thank heavens," gasped Lomas and everyone nodded.

"It doesn't mean he didn't try though," Vincent reminded them, "just that he didn't succeed."

"We need to concentrate on tracking them," Byron said. "If Farra was running from Wesley, which we can just about guarantee was exactly what happened, then there will probably be evidence of her flight. She may have left a pretty clear trail."

"We can hope for that," Lomas said before turning to Vincent. "Can't your spirit friend help us find her? Could you ask?"

Vincent thought about it. "I'll try but everyone will have to be quiet and give me time." He looked at the group and everyone nodded. "Okay." He got up and went into the cell and lay down on the bed. He closed his eyes and mentally called to Syra for help. He waited for what seemed like several long minutes, calling to Syra constantly to come to him. Just as he was about to give up, he heard her voice. It sounded a long way off but it was there. He fixed his attention on it and let his awareness of his physical surroundings drift into the background and as he did so, her voice became nearer and stronger.

"I am here Vincent, I am with you and I hear your plea. Go to where the angels soar atop the skull. There you will find them both."

Byron tapped his comm device. A voice from the battle cruiser orbiting above them came back instantly. "Yes Sir."

"Look up anything you can find on Lilean landscape around our current location, specifically anything connected with angels soaring and anything called the skull. And please be quick."

"Yes Sir, immediately," the voice replied and everyone waited. Minutes ticked by in silence, everyone deep in their own thoughts, all of Farra.

Suddenly Byron's comm device beeped. "Sir, there's a place called Skull Mountain five miles from your location. Local folklore says that it's the place where angels soar because it's home to a giant Lilean bird called the Malota. I'm sending you a location tracker now." The comm device beeped again and Byron nodded.

"I have the signal, thank you. Ok gentlemen, mount up." The group ran out of the building, climbed onto their battle boards and raced off towards the forest.

CHAPTER NINETEEN

Farra ran like the wind towards the tree line. She knew in her heart at this moment she was running for her life and she might not survive the next few hours. As she ran, she cried for her Dad, for Leon and the Lileans, for her Drycenian friends and for Vincent. The Lilean forest swallowed her up and she found herself in the thickest forest she had ever seen. Her night sight kicked in and the place leapt into life before her. It was more beautiful than she could ever imagine and as she ran and wondered whether she was going to die, she decided that she didn't mind dying in this beautiful place and that even if her remains were never found, her spirit would be at peace in this paradise. As she ran she prayed. She prayed that her Drycenian friends would continue to live peacefully and spread their goodness far and wide and to as many new worlds as possible. She prayed that the Lilean ancient spirits would now be at peace in the land of the dead knowing that the prophecy was fulfilled and that justice was done and the evil was now gone. She prayed that Leon would be proud of her, that her dad would be proud of her and she prayed that Vincent would find peace and happiness as a free man at last. Then she gave thanks for being allowed to be a part of it all.

She wondered what creatures might be lurking in the shadows and from time to time she heard cries and calls, squawks and rustles as she ran through the trees and vegetation. She suddenly found herself at a fork in the path and stopped, unsure of which way to go. "Which way, which way Leon, please," she begged and as she looked both ways she heard a cry from her left. She turned to find a large bird standing twenty yards down the left path. It looked right at her, let out another cry and took off. She set off after it, deciding that was as good an answer as any. Since Leon awakened her she became vastly more open to these subtle communications and she learned to take notice of them and go with them. The path wound its way around and gently upwards before ending up on the outskirts of a village. She stopped and looked around her while catching her breath and noticed that she was not alone. Leon was standing on the opposite side of the dirt road that skirted the tree line. She ran to him.

"Leon, thank god, I thought you'd gone. I called but you didn't answer," she said.

"You saw the bird didn't you?"

She looked at him in surprise and nodded. "Yes, but I," she started but Leon interrupted her.

"I told you I would always be with you. You weren't in the right state of mind to be able to communicate when you were running through the forest. Your mind was too fixed on your immediate survival needs to make the necessary adjustment. You know already that you need to let your mind go inwards a little and let the physical world retreat a bit in order to hear me clearly."

"Yes I know," she replied.

"It wasn't appropriate or possible for you to do that whilst running for your life and feeling emotional turmoil. I was answering but you couldn't hear me. So I asked the bird to do it for me. A solid physical answer was what you needed and you followed without questioning it. Well done child, I'm proud of you." He kissed the top of her head.

"I'm sorry," she replied, contrite.

Leon shook his head. "No child, no. Now come, I want you to do something very important. This ancient village was my home. As you can see it is still in ruins. These outlying areas haven't been looked at for the rebuilding programme yet, so it is now as it was then. Walk with me?" They walked along the dirt road and entered amongst the ruined buildings. It looked like a ghost town to Farra and she was more than a little scared. Broken walls loomed up on either side. Empty windows and doors yawned at her menacingly as the wind whipped and howled through them. They passed by the ruins of a church, the Lilean star carved on its remaining walls still visible.

"Cecily and I attended that church and Vincent was to be renewed there," he smiled, lost in his memories.

"Renewed?" she asked.

"Oh it's when newborns are welcomed into the physical life at the beginning of their physical journey and they are given their name," he smiled sadly at the memory of what was to be but never came to pass.

"Oh I see, like christening," she said and he nodded.

"Yes, sort of like that." They walked on and found themselves in a village square. Ruined buildings lined all sides. Some were recognisably shops and businesses, others not recognisable as anything and a couple were much larger than the others and looked like public buildings. Leon confirmed this.

"That was the school where Vincent was to attend. That there was the library where I spent many happy hours learning about all sorts of things. They even had some actual old books there from the time before digital streaming and data chips and holographic viewers. Amazing. That building there was where I worked as Sector Governor. That's the town council chamber where a lot of us stuffy old men spent our days." He smiled and she laughed at the notion of him being a stuffy old man. They crossed the square and went up a narrow street between two ruined buildings that loomed as they passed by. Farra shivered and held tight to Leon's hand. On their right was what looked like an area of waste ground surrounded by railings.

"This was the public garden where we would have community gatherings and celebrations, music events and where weddings took place. Cecily and I married in there amongst the most beautiful plants and flowers you ever saw. Oh what an occasion that was." He stopped at the entrance to the garden and noticed the large ornate gate was gone. With a sigh, he shook away the memories and spun them both round on their heels to face the ruins of a small building. "Farra, this was my home," he said without preamble and she looked at him in shock. Before she could say anything he continued. "This is where Cecily and I lived and where Vincent was conceived one beautiful summer evening. It is where Cecily and I died and where Vincent was killed by the Transmortals and brought back from the land of the dead by the ancient ones, where he lay dying for three days until some neighbours found him and took him in. This is the place Farra of those images I've shown you and of which you've dreamed so often." He looked down at her and smiled. "Come," he urged and walked towards the ruins.

As they entered the grounds between the stone pillars, Leon pulled her over to one side. Reaching his hand into the tangle of branches that now grew all over, he pushed them aside and bade her look. A simple sign fixed to the stone announced, Domenico. The roof as well as the entire upper storey was gone and only a few pieces of the lower walls still stood. He guided her up the stone steps towards what used to be the front door and urged her inside.

"This will be upsetting Farra but it is more important than you know that this final task be done. Not just for me, but for Vincent and his future happiness." He turned her slightly to the left and she saw it. The bones of what was clearly a hand were poking out slightly from under a piece of wood that entirely covered the rest of the bones.

"Oh no, Leon," Farra cried as she realised what she was looking at.

He urged her on. "Go on, please." She approached the corner and gently lifted the piece of wood aside. The skeleton lay on its back, one arm across its belly and both legs splayed open. The remains of a garment lay beneath the bones and she saw a string of beads around its neck. As she looked upon the bones of Vincent's mother, she was stricken with grief.

Leon called to her gently. "There child, to your right, under the rubble." She turned to see a pile of rubble and debris. She squatted and began to remove the lumps of stone and rubble gently. After a few minutes a skull appeared and then more bones. As she uncovered the second skeleton she noticed a large hole in the centre of the chest, large enough to pass a fist through. "It was impossible for my body to survive that weapon. I didn't want to go but I had no choice," Leon explained.

She placed a hand gently upon the bones of the hand and wept for Leon and his wife. "Oh Leon," was all she could say.

"Farra, look, on the hand," he urged and she looked. She brushed away a pile of dust and saw a large gold ring upon the bones of the middle finger. There was a design of some kind on it but she couldn't see what it was. "That is the Domenico seal," Leon explained. "Every Lilean male passes his ring down to his first born son. It is an important symbol of the continuity of Lilean life and connections with family and all those in the land of the dead who wore the same ring before us. Every Lilean who has his family seal upon his finger is making a tangible connection with all of his kin who went before. It is about connections Farra, connections, roots and belonging. With the ring, he not only knows those connections and roots exist, he feels them. Vincent has never had that in his life. Wesley wears the Sylvana seal and Vincent is all too aware that he has never felt he belonged anywhere, to anyone. Bring him here Farra. Bring him here and let him find me and his mother so that he can grieve for us in the proper manner and make those connections anew. Bring him here so that he can find this ring, my ring, his ring, our ring. Please," Leon begged. Farra promised through her tears.

"Whatever it takes, I promise I will get Vincent here, I promise," she sniffed and he sighed, relieved. Then he looked up, worried.

"Cover us back up, leave no sign. Quickly child." She raced around recovering the skeletons so that they were completely invisible. By the time she was finished, Leon was pacing. "Quickly my dear, Wesley has almost caught us up. Run child. Out through the back and up the lane, hurry child. Keep going uphill." She didn't need telling twice. She was off like the wind; her determination renewed now that she had another goal to reach that involved Vincent's happiness.

She ran through the back of the little ruined home and out through what remained of the garden. Leaping the low wall that still marked the boundary, she set off up the lane. The little road twisted around and up and then came to another fork. Which way? She remembered Leon's instructions to keep going uphill so she set off to the right. As the incline levelled out a little, she rounded a bend and saw them. She gasped at the sight of the beautiful white trees that lined the lane and swayed gently in the breeze and she could hear the whispering they made as they swayed. This was from her dream, it must be the same place. The little homes either side of the lane and those trees were exactly as she dreamed them. The sight took her breath away and without knowing what she was doing, she approached one of the trees to hear its whispering. As she did so, she remembered how in her dream, the branches became arms that grabbed at her cruelly and she stopped in her tracks, afraid. Before she could back off and run, she was grabbed from behind and held in an iron embrace. She screamed and fought but couldn't free herself from those arms.

The now familiar voice whispered in her ear. "Gotcha bitch. Thought you could escape me did ya? Didn't think I was gonna forget about you did ya? After our romantic moment, how could I leave you?" Wesley snarled as she screamed and fought and kicked, to no avail. He held on tightly as he fixed restraints on her wrists then steered her forwards. "Move," he ordered as he shoved her roughly. "You're gonna get what you deserve for what you did to me and I'm gonna enjoying givin it to ya. And then I'm gonna kill ya," he guffawed loudly at his own joke as he steered her up the hill.

With Byron leading the way with his tracker beacon beeping, Vincent and the Drycenians sped through the forest on their battle boards. Vincent was true to his word and never fell off once. The forest seemed to go on forever but Byron's tracker kept beeping and they knew they were headed in the right direction. Vincent couldn't get the thought of Wesley trying to rape Farra out of his mind. He knew the damage that would be done if a Lilean male were to force themselves onto an Earth female without her being accepting and ready. He remembered a Lilean colleague in the military who married an Earth woman and he told Vincent how careful he had to be to make sure she was ready for him, otherwise it would hurt her terribly. The guy told him of a Lilean soldier he heard about who raped an earth woman while on a mission to sort out an uprising on some moon somewhere. He thought she was from the enemy side and forced himself on her as a kind of war trophy and she bled to death very quickly. He went to prison for a long time for that but only survived three months before getting himself killed by other inmates who regarded rapists as little better than child murderers. Vincent knew that if they found Wesley had forced himself on Farra, he would kill him. He didn't tell his Drycenian friends this of course, he knew they would not let him accompany them if he did. If Wesley raped Farra, she was dead and so he decided he'd happily do time for her.

As they made their way through the forest, Vincent looked at his surroundings and realised that it actually felt like home. He never got the chance to come back to Lilea but it still felt right to be here. If everything turned out right this morning, he decided to remain here and make a life for himself, and even perhaps? Suddenly Byron stopped and Vincent brought his mind back to the task in hand. They came out of the forest and found themselves in a ruined town.

Lomas called to Byron. "How much further?"

"Just over a mile Sir," Byron replied. Lomas made the decision to dismount from their battle boards and walk the rest of the way.

A sharp throb from Vincent's chest made him stop walking. "Stop," he called to the Drycenians, who all did exactly that and turned to look at him. "Syra is here, please wait a moment," he asked. Lomas nodded and everyone stood silently, allowing Vincent to let his mind drift inwards a little to meet Syra's voice.

"Vincent, brave warrior. You are here to save a life, not take one. Do not despair, trust. Now go quickly, uphill to the place of the skull where the angels soar." He told his friends that Syra said they were to go uphill. He left out her admonishment of his angry thoughts though. They moved on, making sure they went uphill at all times and soon found themselves walking along a lane behind the ruins of some small homes. As they walked on, a scream suddenly rang out into the dawn. It sounded a way away but it was clearly a woman. The group stopped and looked at each other, then all started to run towards that sound. They continued up the lane as it wound its way upwards until they came to a fork. The left went away downhill while the right continued climbing, so they went to the right. As they reached the top they found the incline starting to level out a little and the going became a little easier. The lane turned to the left and they found themselves in what remained of a residential street. Ruined homes still stood on either side and beautiful Lilean Whispering Trees lined both sides of the lane. All of the group including Vincent stopped and gasped in awe at the sight.

Lomas voiced what they were all thinking. "Oh my, of what more beautiful a sight I cannot even dream." Everyone nodded in agreement and then another scream rang out, nearer this time. Byron used his tracker device and found the scream came from the same direction that they were to be going. They ran towards the sound. As they turned at the bottom of the lane of trees they found themselves in a gorge whose walls loomed up on either side.

As they walked, Byron suddenly called out. "Look, up there," he pointed and everyone looked. At first no one could understand what he was pointing at but then as their eyes adjusted they saw the rock face at one side of the gorge looked just like a skull. "That must be the place of the skull don't you think?" he asked. Everyone nodded and they started towards it. They came to a path cut into the side of the rock that led straight up to the skull. They started to climb, Vincent in strong leaps, the Drycenians a little slower. At the top of the path a few scrubby trees and brush obscured their view. Once they pushed through these, they found themselves looking towards a rock ledge over looking the skull. At the very edge of the two hundred foot drop, Wesley held the still screaming Farra.

Wesley dragged and shoved Farra all the way up to the top of a large rocky outcrop that over looked the village and forest below and a beautiful sight it would have been in happier circumstances. She was terrified and screamed at the top of her lungs and begged him to pull her back from the edge. She heard a cry from above and looking up, saw the huge birds soaring in the sky. It was the same scene from her nightmare; this was the place where she sat and looked at the birds. Now she understood why the dream turned into a nightmare as the birds tried to make her fall.

Wesley enjoyed her fear and laughed at her. "Scream all you like, there's no one around to hear ya. Ya know what, all that yelling and screaming is making me very excited. God how it turns me on." He manoeuvred himself behind her, deciding to keep well away from those fingers this time even if her hands were restrained. He didn't want to fall to his death. She cried and her knees buckled under her, sending them both to the ground two feet from the edge. Wesley reached around and grabbed her breasts, squeezing them painfully. She cried out in pain. "Yeah I know ya want it too," he rasped into her ear as he pawed at her.

She was both frightened and disgusted and tried to wriggle out of his embrace but he was way stronger than she, even with her enhanced strength she couldn't free herself. He slid one hand down her body towards her crotch, before pushing her face down in the dirt. He put one knee into the small of her back, preventing her from moving or getting away and she heard the sound of metal as he unsheathed a knife from his belt. Her back hurt like hell with all of his weight on one knee pinning her to the ground and she was finding it hard to breathe. Suddenly she felt him fumbling with her belt before cold metal touched her skin. She realised he slipped his knife inside her belt and with one strong movement, he sliced through it.

"Tell me how much you want it," he sneered. "Tell me you want me, I know ya do," he said as he put one hand onto her backside and squeezed.

From the cover of the brush, Vincent and the Drycenians watched in horror as Wesley battled with Farra at the edge of the cliff.

"No, no," Vincent called out in a whisper. "Oh god we have to save her quickly."

"Let me by, "Byron whispered at his side and crept past silently.

"What are you doing?" Vincent hissed at him.

"Look down here, the cliff curves and it's further out here by us than it is where they are. If I can get right to the edge here, I can get a shot and he'll fall that way rather than off the edge," he explained.

Vincent nodded and looked up, suddenly having an idea. "You get into position, then I'll go around behind and distract him. With his back to you, you can get an easier shot." Byron thought about it and nodded. He crept away towards the edge of the cliff, careful to be as silent as he could. When Vincent saw him look up and nod, he began to creep in the other direction, making his way around to the rear of Wesley's position. As he passed by a couple of Troopers, one of them put a hand on his arm.

"Sir, you might need this," he said offering Vincent what looked like a short stout stick with a nozzle at one end and a button at the other. "It's an omni whip. It's very simple to operate. Aim, press the button and hold. A cord will fire out the other end and wrap itself around the first thing it comes into contact with. It will hold itself in that position all the time you have your hand on the trigger. Once you press the trigger, a guard will flip out from around the button and clamp your finger there, keeping it pressing on the trigger. In order to let go and let the whip unwind, use the other hand to twist this section here, got it? If she goes over, you can save her from up to fifty feet away, but no further."

Vincent took the device and put a hand on the Trooper's shoulder. He didn't even know his name but he was giving all he could to help. "Thank you," he said and continued around and into position. One in position he stood up and sauntered in Wesley's direction. "Hey there bro," he called and enjoyed the look of shock he saw as Wesley looked up and saw him standing there. "I wouldn't do that if I were you." He looked Wesley right in the eyes and waited for him to react.

"So, little brother not only refused to lie down and die but he has to return a fuckin hero. You and this bitch here ruined everything for me. My whole fuckin life has been a worthless heap of shit because of you," he screamed at him, Farra temporarily forgotten.

"Wesley, your life was what you made it, not me. If it turned out to be a worthless heap of shit, that's because you made it that way. What did I ever do to you Wesley? How did I ever hurt you?" He hoped that by baiting Wesley, he'd come for him and leave Farra safe so that the Drycenians could get to her.

"How? You really have to ask? Just by being there you stupid fuck. By always being so damn special. The special little governor's boy saved from the Transmortals," Wesley spat.

"You think I had it easy being part of your family?" Vincent retorted angrily. "You took every opportunity to make me feel like an outsider. Weren't you just glad when I left and never came back? Wasn't that enough?"

"No, it wasn't enough, it will never be enough," Wesley snapped back. He suddenly turned around and grabbed Farra by the arms and shoved her towards the edge of the cliff.

She screamed for Vincent "Vincent. Vincent please help me."

As he raised the omni whip and took aim, Wesley suddenly fell forward onto his face.

"No," Vincent screamed as he fired the omni whip in Farra's direction. As she found herself falling she thought of Vincent and was glad that she finally got to meet him before she died.

"Oh Vincent," she sobbed as she fell.

Vincent fired the omni whip and held on. For an agonising couple of seconds nothing happened and then all at once he felt a weight and leaned back. He pulled and held on as the Drycenians raced to grab her and pull her to safety. When she was safe, he released the omni whip and ran to her.

"Farra," he took her face in his hands. She burst into fresh tears of relief and fell into his arms. He held on and cried with her as their Drycenians friends secured Wesley in restraints. Lomas, Toma and the others let them have a few moments together. After everything they'd both been through in the past weeks, this moment of bonding was the most important of both their lives.

Doctor Jam looked at Byron and then at Lomas, both of whom had tears in their eyes. He smiled and shook his head at them for being so easily moved, before dabbing at his own eyes with his handkerchief.

Donaldson brought the packed courtroom to order and waited for the spokesperson of the jury to deliver the verdict.

"I am the jury spokesperson. In the case of Wesley Sylvana, we unanimously find him guilty on all counts of Fraud, attempted murder, multiple murder, kidnap and attempted rape and we recommend permanent incarceration in Precklerdale Ultra Secure Psychiatric Facility Sir." He sat down and Donaldson addressed Wesley.

"You have been found guilty by a competent and trustworthy jury. I agree with their recommendations and declare that you shall be immediately removed to Precklerdale Facility, where you shall remain for the rest of your life. Upon your death, your remains may be repatriated to Lilean soil if those of your kin should request it. This court is now concluded."

"Vincent, I have something I need to show you, the last two pieces of the puzzle. Please take me to that village near Skull Mountain," Farra asked.

Vincent looked puzzled. "What do you want to go there for?" he asked.

"Trust me please, just one more time. All will become clear when we get there," she cajoled him and he finally agreed. When they arrived in the village, she took his hand and showed him around as Leon did with her. "This village was your parent's home Vincent, they lived here," she smiled as he looked at her questioningly. "That church there was where they attended and where they planned to do your renewal ceremony. You want to go in and look around?" she offered and he nodded. She showed him the town council building where Leon worked and the library where he studied. Then she took him along the lane between the two high looming walls, to the public garden. "This was where your parents were married on a summer's day amongst the most beautiful plants and flowers, surrounded by their friends and loved ones." She showed him around the garden and noticed many of the plants were regenerating themselves and were growing strongly. It reminded her of Terramora and the forest.

"How do you know all this?" he asked her and as she felt a throb from her chest she looked over Vincent's shoulder. Leon nodded to her.

"Because your father told me, and he showed me as I'm showing you now." She watched as the shock on his face turned to understanding.

"He walks with you? It's you that Syra meant when she said he walks with someone special?" he asked and she nodded.

"Come with me." She took his hand and led him towards the ruins of a small dwelling opposite the public garden. At the entrance she stopped and gestured to him to look. "Here, look," she said as she pulled away the overgrown vegetation to reveal the little sign.

"Domenico," Vincent read aloud. He looked at her in shock. "They lived here?"

She nodded gently. "Yes Vincent, they lived here. Come inside, please." She led him gently up the stairs and through what remained of the doorway. She led him to the corner and took a deep breath. "Vincent, you remember those images you told me about the day of your birth?" He nodded and she indicated the piece of wood. He stooped and lifted it up. As he looked upon the bones of his mother he cried out and she held him. All of the years of isolation, of his rootless existence and of his loneliness came flooding back and he cried out, determined to expunge the pain from his soul finally. For a long time he sat there sobbing over his mother's bones. He placed a hand on the ground between her splayed legs.

"Thank you for giving me life Mother," he sobbed as he straightened out her legs and took off his jacket and laid it over her. He took the necklace from around her neck and slipped it into his pocket.

Farra was silently holding onto him as he grieved but now she whispered gently to him. "Here Vincent." She indicated the pile of rubble to her left as she moved out of the way, allowing him to move over and begin to remove the stones. He removed them gently, one by one until the skeleton was completely uncovered. She indicated the ring. "He wanted me to make sure you found the ring Vincent, the Domenico seal. It's yours by birthright and he wants you to have it." Vincent took the ring from his father's bones and put it on his own hand where it fitted perfectly.

They stayed in the ruins of the little Domenico home for many hours. Day turned to evening and all the while, Farra sat and held Vincent as he grieved and cried out his pain. Finally, as the sun set and exhaustion took over, they both fell asleep between the bones of his parents. Farra awoke suddenly and it took a few seconds to realise where she was. The white fog of the hinterland between sleeping and waking surrounded her and Leon was there waiting for her.

"Thank you so much Farra, I cannot express in words how much you have done for us, for my family. You were the right choice and it is an honour to walk beside you." He squeezed both of her hands in his and then drew her close and hugged her like a father.

"Does this mean I'll never see you again?" she asked.

Leon looked shocked. "Goodness me child no, whatever next. There is much to do before your time to join us in the land of the dead arrives. I told you I will walk beside you always and I will."

Suddenly another voice could be heard. A woman's voice that Farra didn't recognise. "Husband, must you keep her all to yourself? Stand aside now and let me meet her." Leon stepped aside and Farra saw a beautiful woman come and join them. She took Farra's hand and smiled. "I am Cecily Domenico. Leon's wife and Vincent's mother. I cannot thank you adequately for all you have done for us and for Vincent, save to tell you that we regard you as a much loved and welcome part of our family." Farra was deeply touched and couldn't reply.

As they embraced a third voice approached. Another woman who Farra didn't recognise. "May we interrupt this happy family gathering to make it complete at last?" They all looked and saw a beautiful young Lilean woman who looked like a warrior princess approach them with Vincent. "I am Syra and I walk with Vincent. Come Farra, walk with me a while," she held out a hand to Farra, who took it and together they walked and talked about Lilea and the whispering trees, giving Vincent time to meet his parents and complete his healing journey.

Farra awoke to find the sun just beginning to rise. Vincent lay, his head cradled in her lap. She laid a hand on his shoulder gently and he stirred. As they rose and stretched themselves he suddenly grabbed her hand.

"Come with me," he said and led her out of the house and across to the public garden. They sat and he pointed to the sunrise. "Those five years I spent on Vinbuk, I used to watch the sunrise every morning and the sunset every night and wonder if I'd ever be doing it on Lilea. Watch this one with me?" He put his arm around her shoulders and together they watched the sun come up. As the sun rose high into the sky he reached out and turned her face to his. "Will you help me bury my parents?" he asked her.

"Of course I will, if you want me to," she said.

He traced his finger down her cheek. "And will you help me rebuild the Domenico home and this whole Village?" he asked as he ran a finger gently under her chin.

"I'd love to help you Vincent," she smiled up at him.

"And will you live here with me?" he asked as he ran a finger across her lips.

"Yes Vincent, I will."

He bent and kissed her, softly at first, then as she responded to him, more urgently.

"I will never hurt you, ever," he promised as she put her arms around his neck and pulled him to her. As the sun rose high into the Lilean sky, Vincent loved her. Softly, gently, slowly at first, then passionately and as they lay together naked under the Lilean sunrise, they both knew they were home at last.

THE END

COMING SOON

THE LILEAN CHRONICLES: BOOK TWO ~ THE SLEEPING

Just as Vincent and Farra begin to relax after their battle with the Transmortal Army, a new terror befalls Lilea. As they look forward to their pledging ceremony the first signs of something wrong become apparent. They cannot understand why their spirit guides left them and it isn't until the Lilean people begin to succumb to a mysterious affliction that they realise a new evil is among them. Plunged into a terrible nightmare, Vincent battles to find reality amongst the make believe as he struggles to come to terms with loss and betrayal.

Many days away across the gulf of space their Drycenian friends suddenly find themselves hosts to some uninvited guests who beg them for their help. Whilst racing to Lilea they must find a way to communicate with their new guests in order for them to know how to aid their friends. It is up to one man to venture into the darkness alone and put his own soul at risk to save Vincent, so they can try to end this new evil and save Lilea from the terror of The Sleeping.